A CALL TO ARMS

A Prophecy

Geoffrey Morgan

iUniverse, Inc.
New York   Bloomington

iUniverse books may be ordered through booksellers or by contacting:

iUniverse
1663 Liberty Drive
Bloomington, IN 47403
www.iuniverse.com
1-800-Authors (1-800-288-4677)

ISBN: 978-1-4502-0648-8 (sc)
ISBN: 978-1-4502-0650-1 (hc)
ISBN: 978-1-4502-0649-5 (ebook)

Lbrary of Congress Control number: 2010900810

Printed in the United States of America

iUniverse rev. date: 02/02/2010

To Gordon

(If only dreams came true.)

Preface

The British parliament consists of the House of Commons and the House of Lords, the equivalent of the U.S. House of Representatives and the Senate, respectively. The members of the House of Commons sit for a term of five years maximum. However, if the opposition parties can gather enough votes beteen them, they can force an election at any time during the term. The House of Lords cannot reject legislation passed to it from the Commons but it can delay its enaction. The next election must be held before the end of June 2010

The winning party's leader becomes Prime Minister, and Tony Blair held the office until 2008 when he was forced to resign by his arch enemy in the party, Gordon Brown. The two have been at loggerheads since 1996, when both men agreed to a pact whereby Blair would rule for two elections, and then hand over the post to Brown. However, after winning the third lection in 2005, Blair reneged on his promise, and refused to step down. This led to open warfare within the party. Brown won the day, and Blair was ignominiously forced to resign in 2008.

A ruthless Gordon Brown (journalists call him the Brown Terror) claimed the prize, and was elected party leader by Labor's National Committee. The post should have been open to all Labor party members, but Brown closed out all prospective candidates, and elected himself to the post. So the UK is now ruled by an unelected

Prime Minister sponsored by thirty-three party hacks. Even President Karzai of Afghanistan has more legitimacy.

There are 646 members of the House of Commons. They are paid good salaries and expenses and set their own rates, which are far above the mean salaries for members of the public. There are also 72 MEPs (members of the European Union) living high off the hog in Brussels. The EU now passes 80 percent of the laws of the Union, which means that the 646 British MPs, 724 Peers, and 72 MEPs are now obliged to rubber stamp these laws, and pick the bones out of the remaining 20 percent. I believe the total number of legislators in the U.S. Congress is 535, serving a population of 304 million—one legislator for every 568,000 citizens. The UK, with a population of 60 million, has 1,370 legislators. This figure equates to approximately one legislator for every 44,000 citizens doing only 20 percent of the work load. Nice work if you can get it. They also take seventeen weeks of holiday in the year.

Britain is now the most spied on nation on earth, a fitting label for the nation that produced George Orwell, the author of *1984*. We have over 4 million CCTV cameras, one for every fourteen citizens. Depending where they live, on any one day a person can be captured on camera three hundred times. Refuse bins (four of them) are each emptied once every two weeks. If they are in the wrong place, the lid is not closed, or they are placed more than thirty centimeters from the curb, they will not be collected. If they are put out on the wrong day you are liable to a fine of $1,600. The same fine applies if you put the wrong refuse in the wrong bin. How do the authorities know? They sneak up in the early hours of the morning, and put a spy camera hidden inside a tin of baked beans in the bin.

A General Election is due in June 2010, and under normal circumstances, the Conservative party should walk it. However, they have a mountain to climb due to adverse demographics. The north of the country is solid Labor as are most of the cities. On top of this Tony Blair created an obedient voter client state by opening up our borders to all comers, and bribing 6 million civil servants with top wages and gold plated pension pots, which are denied to workers in the private sector. However, no matter who is elected to parliament, our affairs are in the hands of the European Union, a monolithic entity that is run by twenty-seven Commissioners with a figure-head President, elected by these same commissioners behind closed doors. All documentation has to be translated into more than twenty different languages

This is the state of affairs that has prompted me to write this novel. A cry in the dark if you like. I remember the days in the eighties and nineies when our country was in the safe hands of Margaret Thatcher and the Conservatives, and honesty, integrity, and social cohesion were the order of the day. Years of balanced budgets, full employment, and, more importantly, a nation at peace with itself.

Today, thanks to the New Labor project elected in 1997, we are bankrupt, and it is only a matter of time before the International Monetary Fund is called apon to sort out the mess; as they did before in 1976, when Labor last ruined the economy. We now have a situation where the main political parties no longer care about the health of the nation, for they are too busy fighting each other for the right to govern in 2010. Parliament is totally discredited and such is the contempt voters hold them in, pollsters are forecasting that it will be a miracle if more than 30 percent of the electorate vote in the General Election. The nation is now one seething mass of discontentment that will bring rioting to the streets when the IMF eventually put their demands on the table and the government is forced to come clean.

Now, if I was younger, I would be tempted to join the many leaving this broken nation at the first opportunity. Americans beware. Do not let your rulers take you down this road. The decline of the UK is an example you should avoid at all costs.

The SAS (Special Air Services) is the pride of the British army. Its elite reputation has been established by the fearless nature, and love of country of its adventurous members. Their exploits are legendary, but many remain unreported due to the necessity of keeping their identities and modus operandi secret. This is why I have chosen this unit as the spearhead of a task force that will drive out the politicians who have bankrupted our nation, and return to its shell-shocked citizens the hard fought freedoms they once took for granted.

Chapter 1

Luke Dryden was only six years old when his father was killed in the Battle of Goose Green in the Falklands War, so the tragedy did not have too great a bearing on his life until his later years. The loss was softened, to a great extent, by the arrival in his Shropshire village of his grandparents, who were determined to do what they could to help their daughter-in-law, Molly, and their two grandchildren, Luke and Jenny, in their hour of need. General John Dryden had served with distinction in the Parachute Regiment during and after the Second World War, and he immediately set about giving Luke all the love and attention his father would have lavished on him, had he lived.

Luke's mother never remarried, and consequently his upbringing was to be greatly influenced by his grandfather, whom he came to address as "General." It was only natural that his early life would be dominated by all things military, for that was the General's great passion and also, it seemed, that of all his friends who came to visit them. It was also easy to see why his father had enlisted in the army at the age of eighteen and reached the rank of major in the Paratroop Regiment before he was killed in action.

Luke took to the new regime like a duck to water, spending long hours after school in the war room the General had constructed in the attic of his bungalow. Indoor war games became a way of life, and as Luke grew older, these were complemented with physical training exercises in the nearby woods, long route marches, and camping under the stars.

The General would read to him for hours on end on subjects that were barely touched upon in school, such as ancient history, the Greeks and Romans, Alexander the Great, Napoleon, the American Revolution and that country's ascension. And more especially the British Empire, its wars and campaigns, and its armies and their leaders. As he assimilated all this martial knowledge, Luke began to acquire a taste for the things the General detested above all: politics and its consequences for international military actions. He was only fifteen years old when he made the big decision that would shape his future. He would become a soldier-statesman like Wellington and Winston Churchill.

The General could hardly believe his ears when Luke first broached the subject as they slept side by side in their sleeping bags on a hillside that overlooked the sleepy village of Clun.

"Luke," he protested, "there is no such thing as a soldier-statesman. You have to be a politician to be a statesman, and to a soldier, a politician is six meters lower than a snake's belly. The two never can go together. A soldier is honorable, courageous, and patriotic, whereas a politician is inherently dishonorable, cowardly, and about as patriotic as Lord Haw-Haw, Pierre Laval, and Quisling all rolled into one. They hate the military except when they need them to mend their fences for them, for they begrudge the money they have to spend to keep a standing army at the ready. These scallywags are responsible for the death of every British sailor, soldier, or airman killed in action in modern times. They require us to put our lives on the line while they wine and dine in their ivory towers and deny us the arms and equipment with which to fight the enemy on equal terms. They praise us when we are fighting their wars and denigrate us after we win them. In peacetime, they throw thousands of soldiers onto the scrap heap at the whim of an incompetent chancellor who has squandered the wealth of the nation on useless, mad-cap follies.

"Take the Falklands War, for example. Your father would be alive today if it were not for the fact that the chancellor at that time was strapped for cash. So one of the economies he made was to scrap our sole warship patrolling the South Atlantic, thus sending a message to the Argentinean junta that if they wanted the island, it was theirs for the taking, along with the company of troops defending them. But it's not just the chancellor. The foreign office is packed to the rafters with slimy anti-colonialists and republicans who will not rest until every British overseas colony or possession of whatever size is surrendered, whether the inhabitants want independence or not."

The General paused for a moment as he took a couple of puffs of his briar pipe.

"Now look at Suez. Our forces did everything they were asked to do under the most difficult circumstances imaginable. We were given hardly any time to prepare for it, and everything had to be organized in the greatest secrecy, for political reasons. We took all our objectives, and there is no question but that if we had been allowed to follow up, the Egyptians would have laid down their arms and Nasser would have been forced into exile. But no. The Laborites and pacifists in Parliament saw a way they could bring down the government, and instead of backing our soldiers, who were dying for them every day in the Canal Zone, they stabbed them in the back by calling for an end to the fighting. Their craven actions brought in the Americans who, as usual, saw another opportunity to twist the lion's tail and enhance their own ambitions in the Middle East. Once again, they sold us down the river and turned the politics of the Middle East upside down. We lost a lot of good men in that war, and their sacrifice has never been properly acknowledged by our scurvy politicians to this very day. You see, they all want to bury it, as the debacle reflects badly on them, and if the many instances of heroic actions that took place are publicized, people will ask why our forces were asked to shed so much blood for a cause that was doomed to failure in the first place."

Luke was impressed though unconvinced. "But General," he would argue, "the Duke of Wellington and Winston Churchill were soldier-statesmen, and look what they accomplished. Both of them saved our country from tyranny."

The reply would always be the same. "That's true, my boy, that's true. But what you must understand is that the Iron Duke was a much better soldier than he was a statesman, and Winston was a much better statesman than he was a soldier. The two don't go together, never have, never will. Cromwell was the first Englishman to admit the fact four hundred years ago."

Luke was about to reply but had second thoughts. How could he argue any further with a man who enjoyed forty years of military service?

He looked keenly at the old soldier. *If I could achieve half as much in my life as he has, I would be satisfied,* he thought. The shoulders were not so straight now and the hair was almost white, but the jaw was just as firm and the eyes as blue and keen as fellow officers half his age. He remembered how proud he had been when he attended his first Armistice Day ceremony and saw him leading the contingent of Paras past the Cenotaph, head erect, his chest covered with medals, and his silver-topped cane keeping time with the beat of the Grenadier Guards band leading the march down Whitehall. The man's strength of character, his wisdom, and his love of country had persuaded him long ago that he would follow in his footsteps and those of his father. Now, as sleep drew him deeper into his sleeping bag, he asked his final question for the night:

"General, you've told me all about the great times you had in the army but you've never once mentioned any bad times. Surely, there must have been disappointments."

There was a long silence, and Luke suspected that his companion had fallen asleep.

"Just one of any importance, my boy," came the answer. "I was with the Paras in Libya in '42 and I volunteered for duty with Colonel David Stirling's Long Range Desert Group, later renamed as the SAS, as you know. It was in the lull before El Alamein, and we were going mad with the inaction. Rumor had it that the group was a pet creation of Churchill, took orders only from him, and was given priority in the supply of arms and equipment. They chose their own targets, and when replacements were needed, the first call of port was the Paras. I was bitterly disappointed when I applied for service with them and was turned down, without any explanation for their decision. To cap it all, two other officers from the battalion were accepted. As it happened, three weeks later, El Alamein blew up and we were kept busy all the way to Tripoli and then D Day. Sad to say, the two officers who were accepted were both killed on the group's attack on Rommel's desert headquarters."

The general waited for further questions but none came. He smiled contentedly and looked up at the countless stars in a faraway sky. "Look after Luke," he murmured. "One day he'll surely be a credit to us all."

Luke was a natural for the army. He was tall, rugged, and courageous, and he affected a devil-may-care attitude that concealed a shrewd brain for military matters. Those who knew his family swore that he was the image of his father: jet black hair, high cheekbones, and deep blue eyes that had the ladies fainting at his presence. He excelled at very nearly everything he did at Shrewsbury College, and when he left, he immediately joined the army and graduated from Sandhurst with honors. A year later, he was in the Paras, and six months after that, he experienced his first tour of duty in Northern Ireland.

It was a baptism that was to form a lasting impression of the bravery and fortitude shown by British troops as they fought a satanic enemy with one hand tied behind their back. They were restrained by devious governments that gave secretive comfort and aid to the terrorists as they changed the rules of engagement time after time in their favor and put the lives of the soldiers at even greater risk with every cowardly concession they made to the terrorists.

At the end of his first tour, Luke formed the opinion that the government would sell its soul to accommodate the incessant demands made by Adams and McGuinness, of Sinn Fein and the IRA. By the end of his second tour, he was convinced that not only would they do that but they would also pull the army out of Ulster altogether, leaving the unhappy province to the tender mercy of the murderous Provos. Nothing else could explain the treasonable way the Blair government wined and dined the pathological killers, gave them financial aid, implored them to sit in Parliament, and took their side in every major dispute with the Unionists.

Nor would he ever forget the eagerness with which both the Northern Ireland office and the ministry of defense would investigate even the slightest infraction of the rules of engagement and prosecute British troops on the flimsiest of evidence from Republicans. To his horror, he began to notice how the army high command was gradually being politicized by the government and were forced to agree to tear down watch towers and reduce troop numbers to dangerous operational levels.

Sickened by the appeasement of the enemy and the ever-increasing restrictions placed on the army, Luke applied for leave and went home to his roots and the love and comfort of his family.

The General listened gravely to his grandson's outpourings as they retraced their bygone steps in the countryside around their village. It was obvious that he was fully aware of the horrendous burdens placed upon the army in Ulster by the duplicitous Labor government for he would curse mightily as the names of the ruling ministers were mentioned and become positively apoplectic when Adams and McGuinness were mentioned. Only when they were sitting in the study late at night would the old soldier speak calmly and rationally. Even then, the anger within was sometimes betrayed by the smoke emitted from his favorite briar pipe: a lazy plume at times but more often than not angry puffs fired at the ceiling above.

It was on the last evening of his leave that the general gave out his measured opinion. "Luke," he said candidly, "there is only one place for you to go in this man's army, and that is the SAS. You've got all the requirements necessary. Jock Wingate is the only ranking soldier in the British army who will stand up to the politicians and say, 'this far and no further.' They are frightened to death of him. When that fool Coward, the defense secretary, signaled he was going to visit the base, Jock sent a message back saying, 'You may enter but I cannot guarantee your return.' I'm told that Jock's desperate for new recruits but only if they're good enough to pass selection. How about it, Luke? A British soldier could ask for no greater ambition."

"You wouldn't be thinking of asking Jock to make things a little easier for me just for old time's sake, would you?" Luke asked jokingly.

A shocked look appeared on the General's face. "Good God, Luke, if I did that, you wouldn't get past the guardhouse even. Not only that, but I would lose the great man's friendship for evermore."

Luke had no illusions about the task facing him when he entered the gates of the fabled Regiment in Credenhill, Herefordshire. He had witnessed the return of many a crestfallen Para, including his own CO and a junior lieutenant, some of whom had failed the induction course at the first fence and others who had survived to the last day of the ordeal only to be rejected with no explanation whatsoever for the fatal decision. The tales they told about the hardships and indignities they had experienced were listened to with awe by their comrades in arms, particularly those with similar intentions to try for the Regiment. Some of the claims were greeted with derision, but Luke knew for a fact that they were rarely exaggerated. He spent countless hours boning up on the history of the Regiment and the induction course that had been set up by its originators and refined over many years, until it finally became the most comprehensive and demanding examination of a soldier's ability to fight, survive, and triumph over any adversity devised by man. He knew too that the high rejection rate was the best recruiting sergeant the Regiment possessed. For it acted as an effective deterrent to gung-ho pretenders and offered a magical incentive to those who instinctively knew they were able to attain the highest standards demanded and thereafter be prepared to lay down their life for their comrades, their queen, and their country.

His service in the Paras plus his extensive knowledge of military tactics stood him in good stead, and he was awarded his badge after nearly two years of intense physical abuse and mental torment, which he swore he would never undergo again even if his life depended on it. But it was well worth it, and in the end, Luke knew he had attained a vital part of his boyhood dream at last. Action, adventure, individual accomplishment, and comradeship without equal in any army in the world. What more could a British soldier ask for?

Chapter 2

Captain Luke Dryden hardly had time to sew on his badge before he and his troop were posted to the White Mountains in Afghanistan. Their task was to relieve 3Troop, who had been operating in the area continuously for nearly three years, supporting the Americans in their relentless pursuit of Bin Laden, his deputies, and their Taliban sympathizers. The search had been going on for years, and the Americans had expended billions of dollars on a mission they deemed far more important than events in the rest of a war-torn country that was clinging onto a semblance of government in Kabul while the nation was being divided up between the Taliban and the feudal warlords.

Captain Steve Chambers, the leader of the troop they were relieving, filled Luke in on the situation in the mountains and the immediate area along the Pakistan border. "It's like nothing I've ever seen before and hope I never see again," he said grimly. "It's all grunt and grind, false intelligence, chasing shadows, and bombing the shit out of anything that moves, including us. I've lost four troopers with another six injured to the bomb-happy Yanks in three years, so watch your step."

"Friendly fire?" asked Luke.

"If you want to call it that." The voice was bitter. "They're on drugs again, just like in Vietnam, only this time it's heroin. The stuff is dirt cheap. The locals don't just sell it by the gram, they serve it out with a ladle."

"We had a patrol come in one night to a forward outpost. They radioed they were coming and gave the right password but the dope-heads opened up with everything they had. Tommy Briggs was killed outright and Chippy Woods died in hospital the next day. The Yanks are shit-scared of being captured. Not surprising, really. The locals don't just take prisoners, they chop off their heads and stick them on posts along the road."

"And Andrews and Howard?"

"I was leading the patrol, two either side of a mountain. Bill radioed to say him and John had found a cave and were going in. Half an hour later, along comes a B2 and drops two bunker-busters on his position. Me and Bruce Palmer got showered by shit coming down on our side but we escaped with a few cuts and bruises. We went round the mountain and saw half of it was missing, and Bill and Johnny were buried under the rubble. That was nearly a year ago, and they are still under it. There's no chance of ever recovering their bodies."

"How did the Yanks know where to drop their bombs?"

"Bill must have radioed the coordinates in to HQ before they went into the cave. Why, I don't know. Anyway, that was no reason for the Yanks to let loose. They should have waited until they got the all-clear from me. That was when the boss came over and gave the Marines OC the bollocking of his life. He was replaced a few months later; you must have heard about it."

Luke nodded. That was when relations between the SAS and Blair's government started to go pear-shaped.

"What is it with the Yanks?" growled Chambers. "Everybody knows Bin Laden and his boys aren't in the mountains any more, they're across the border living it up with their Paki sympathizers, and there are plenty of them, believe me. But the Yanks won't have it. I've seen their hush-hush map of the mountains. It looks like a curved elongated grid with hundreds of squares, each containing dozens of pinpoints. You can guess what the pinpoints represent, can't you?"

"Caves?" Luke suggested.

"Better believe it. Hundreds of them, some of them not much larger than an elephant's ass, and others as big as cathedrals inside. We reckon the Yanks have filled in half of them so far with their bunker-busters in seven years of bombing, so at that rate they'll still be at it for another seven. Good business for the bomb makers but not so good for the poor bloody infantry who have to follow up and search the ruins. The Afghans don't take kindly to having their villages and hamlets taken out by stray weaponry, and resistance to the occupation is growing by the day. So far, the Yanks have lost well over a thousand men to the jihadis in this sector, and I hear we are now taking heavy casualties down south in Helmand."

"Why are we up here helping the Yanks out when we should be supporting our own boys down there, Steve?" asked Luke.

"It's a political thing, cooked up by Bush and Blair. The U.S. Special Forces had Bin Laden cornered in the Tora Bora mountains at one time, and they let him get away. Bush was hopping mad and asked Blair for units of our lot to help out, and we've been doing just that ever since. In the three years I've been here, we've traversed both sides of the border from Khost to the Khyber Pass a dozen times, but all we get is dodgy intelligence and fool's errands. Bin Laden's no mug. He's got hundreds of followers doing nothing else but creating bogus information and laying false trails relating to his movements. The hot line to our HQ is in action twenty-four hours a day, and every call is monitored. They used to check out every call and send a squad to interrogate the caller, but they packed it in when they discovered that Bin Laden was buying up stolen mobile phones and using them to call the hot line. One false call that sent a company of Delta Force and six Apache helicopters sixty kilometers up the mountains was traced to President Karzai himself, who'd had his phone stolen a few days earlier. They located the cave all right, but all they found in it was a U.S. flag stuck in a bucket of fresh shit. In another stunt, they shut in a half-starved tiger that mauled two GIs before they managed to kill it."

"How many searches have you been involved in?"

"Around fifty, I'd say. The last one was particularly annoying, as we found out we'd been there before through some graffiti one of our patrol had scratched on a wall. The U.S. bombing had completely altered the landscape around the cave, you see. That really pissed us off. We had spent six days marking the cave before we went in, hoping to catch some hostiles out in the open. Believe me, the cold in the Beacons is like a sauna compared with these mountains. And hard rations, no heat, and no smoking either."

"And the rest of the time?"

"Gathering intelligence, spotting for the bombers, listening in on local conversations, guiding the GIs most of the time. Boring. The first year was bad enough, but the last two have just about sent all of us around the bend. If it wasn't for the twice yearly R&R, we'd have been certified long ago."

"Much action, firefights?"

"Some. We've killed around two hundred hostiles all told, mostly Taliban and drug runners. We used to take prisoners and hand them over to the Yanks for interrogation, but then we began to hear stories of what they were doing to the poor bastards and called a halt. If we take a prisoner now, we just disarm him and tell him to bugger off back home. It's a dirty war, Luke, a war without end, and we can only finish it by pulling out and letting the Afghans do their own thing. They don't give a damn about Western democracy and Main Street USA. The only thing American they are interested in is the street price of heroin and how much the addicts are snorting today."

Luke laughed. "Add High Street UK to that, Steve. The way things are going, we'll soon be their best customer. You think the Yanks will pull out if they get Bin Laden?"

"Sure they will. Hell, I had a long conversation with my opposite number in Delta Force, and he told me Bush used to foam at the mouth every time he heard Bin Laden's name mentioned. The guy can't understand why the Afghans can't or won't give him up, even though he's upped the ante to $50 million, dead or alive. It's this Texas Ranger thing they copied from the Canadian Mounties. You know, they always get their man, dead or alive. He promised the American people he would get Bin Laden. Now the sands are running out, and if he doesn't pull it off by the end of this term, he'll go down in history as another bullshitting president who promised much and delivered nothing."

"So it looks like I'm stuck here till he's history?" moaned Luke.

Chambers laughed sympathetically. "Guess so, chum, unless you can capture Bin Laden single-handed and deliver him to the White House. Seriously, though, there's another aspect to this that I should warn you about, and this is from the mouth of the same Yank. Fifty million is a heap of loot in anybody's language, and especially to a three-star general in the U.S. Army. So if by some sort of miracle you should capture Bin Laden, quit the mountains and smuggle him down to our base in Helmand Province tout suite. Get General Alexander to assemble the world press and then put Bin Laden on show and claim the credit for his capture."

Luke was intrigued. "Are you serious, Steve?"

"Deadly serious. There is no way the top brass here are going to let a raggy-assed squaddie pick up that kind of money. They want it for themselves, and they'll stop at nothing to get it. I've heard that at least three Afghans who came forward with information have clean disappeared, and the same thing is likely to happen to any GI or Brit who gets lucky. If he's captured, Bin Laden won't be able to identify the informant because he'll be delivered DOA. That's on the express orders of Bush. There's no way he will let Bin Laden go on public trial. He knows too much about the Bush family and their good old boys in the Texas oil industry."

"What's the OC like? General Collins, isn't it?"

"That's him, Paddy Collins, commander of the 101st Airborne Division. Relieved the Marines here a few months ago. Came from Iraq under some sort of a cloud. Has to do with a fracas where a company of his men went berserk in a village and raped and killed dozens of civilians, like they did at Mai Lai in Vietnam. It's got to be political because the Marines had only served out a fraction of their rota. Collins absolved himself of any responsibility and set up his second-in-command as the fall guy. The investigation's still going on. Get this: The cowboy packs two pistols and wears cavalry gear like Old Blood-and-Guts Patton used to do. Did you read about the atrocities in Iraq?"

Luke nodded. "Yes, I did. Same old racist Yanks. Once they're in a foreign land, they pull up the drawbridge and treat the natives like they're some kind of subhuman race. What do the Afghans think of them?"

"Not much. They stay mostly holed up in their base camp and only venture out in battalion strength, supported by armor and Apache gunships, all excepting their Special Forces, who are all over the place. They ignore the government troops. They reckon half of them are Taliban sympathizers who would slit their throats, given half a chance. They also look on anyone with a beard as a hostile, and of course, all Afghans wear a beard, it's a sign of their manhood. That's no way to treat inhabitants of a country that you're supposed to be helping out."

"So that's why you're wearing one. It looks a beauty. How long did it take?"

"About six months. Everyone in my troop has one, and I'd advise you to grow one as soon as you can."

"Who gives out your orders?"

"Colonel Brad Pickens, Delta Force. Nice guy but out of his depth in the mountains. He's a jungle fighter, likes plenty of cover, and there isn't much of that here. He gives us some shitty assignments, but then again, he provides us with all the logistical support we need without asking too many questions. You'll like him. He's not a bullshitter like some of the Delta grunts.

"One more thing, look out for Collins. He's Irish-American and a big wheel in Noraid. Claims he's related to Michael Collins. Hates the British and flies the Irish flag alongside the Stars and Stripes. Pickens told me his office walls are covered with pictures of Adams, McGuinness, and all the rest of the murdering IRA bastards. Beats me how he puts up with us being part of his command. I can only think it's because he's in on the ransom scam and wants all the help he can get. Be doubly careful with him; to be forewarned is to be forearmed, as they say. By the way, I'm leaving Davvy Griffiths with you. He's only been here three months. Replaced a casualty. Good man to have, speaks fluent Pashto. I don't believe they've got anyone in the 101st can do that."

"Thanks, Steve, I appreciate the advice. What are your plans when you get home? Are you staying with the Regiment?"

Chambers shrugged his shoulders. "Don't know yet. I'll wait and see how I feel once I've been round the country to tell four wives and three mothers and fathers how their loved ones died. I'll tell you one thing, though. If that crazy bastard, Bush, and his poodle, bomber Blair, invade Iran like they're planning to, I'm off and so are the rest of my troop, if I hear right."

"Jesus Christ, Luke, I don't know what's worse, the potshots from the natives or this bloody awful paralyzing cold."

Sergeant Andrew "Kiwi" Bowman brushed away the ice that had formed on the edges of his beard and flapped his arms across his chest like one of the penguins in his native land. "Give me potshots any day; at least some of them are off target, but I've never known cold like this before; it's unrelenting, like being inside a freezer."

Luke tried hard to stop his teeth from chattering. He wished now that he had chosen a hideout a thousand meters farther down the mountain. At the very least, the lower altitude would have meant breathing would have been easier and the dull headaches less frequent. Their main consideration had been that the cave that served as their hideout was big enough to house the four-man patrol and their gear. Plus the fact that it was tucked away out of the path of the biting wind roaring down from the north, and instead of heading into the wind to get to the OP, it was at their back.

Once they had established the hideout, they moved on to set up the OP on the side of the mountain, facing their quarry's suspected cave across the valley. It had to be done under cover of darkness, and the best they could do was hunker down inside a small crevice and build a wall of ice and snow high enough to conceal themselves from any observer on the other side. It was cramped but at least it was sheltered from the wind and the driving snow that came with it.

They had drawn lots for the pairing-up. Luke had drawn Bowman, and they were on their second daylight watch.

Their orders were to observe a cave halfway up the mountain opposite. They couldn't see any evidence of a cave, but Colonel Pickens had shown him a video sent back by a drone plane that clearly showed a figure looking up at the sky and then climbing upward in the deep snow until it disappeared from view. There was no evidence that the figure had dug himself in beneath the snow, and it was highly likely that he had entered into a cave through a camouflaged entrance. His tracks were clearly visible, but Colonel Pickens said they would be gone within twenty-four hours, as proved the case when they were dropped off two days later.

Normally, Luke had the patience of Job when he was stalking a quarry, but he was finding this assignment as numbing to his brain as the weather was to his body. In a jungle watch, there would always be something to occupy the mind: a leafy tree, a bird, bugs, even clouds in the sky. The same was true of a hill or a mountain in fair weather. Craggy contours, an eagle or a buzzard, perhaps a mountain goat. But here there was nothing, just a vast carpet of blinding white snow and a lowering grey sky. Not once had he seen a snow eagle, which he had been told were plentiful in the area.

"Want me to take over?" asked Kiwi as he struggled to his feet.

"Sure thing," replied Luke. "Take it easy, though. I've heard of people going snow-blind looking at that stuff too long. I'm not sure that looking through glasses doesn't make it even worse. Already my eyes feel like they did one time after I woke up from a three-day piss-up."

"Right on," agreed the New Zealander. "Might be worth asking the makers if they can supply filters to take out the glare like they do with cameras. It doesn't seem to bother the Afghans any. Matter of fact, they wouldn't need these glasses at all. From what I've seen, their eyesight is incredible." Kiwi rubbed the eyepieces vigorously, as they began to frost over.

Luke sank to his knees and wriggled his body into his sleeping bag. The extra warmth felt luxurious, as did the darkness when he pulled the flap over his aching eyes. In no time at all, he was away like a baby.

Chapter 3

"What's up?" Luke muttered as Kiwi's boot ground into his ribs.

"We've got visitors," Kiwi whispered hoarsely. "Two of them."

Luke sat up sharply and looked at his watch. Thirteen hundred hours; he had slept for nearly four. He pulled on his white fleece headscarf and stood up alongside his companion. Kiwi sounded excited as he handed Luke the glasses and said, "Around a mile at two o'clock."

Luke trained the glasses on the targets then swept to their rear, searching for others. They were alone, one a tall figure wearing a white hooded robe and the other much smaller, dressed in a black burka. They each carried a large knapsack over their shoulders and held long staves, which they used expertly as they climbed the mountainside on a tangent, as if intending to reach the peak.

"Quick!" Luke exclaimed. "Get the laser ready. I can't see them going right to the top. Maybe halfway if we're lucky."

Kiwi pulled the laser out of its pouch and fitted it to the telescopic pole they had erected at the front of the hideout. He then covered it with a white cloth, which allowed the aperture to poke through, and carefully extended the pole until the instrument just cleared the parapet of the OP.

They waited, Luke with the glasses and Kiwi with the laser, both trained on the quarry as they struggled upward, ever slower as the exertion and the altitude took its toll. It seemed like forever, but Luke looked at his watch and saw that only fifteen minutes had gone by since they first set eyes on the quarry.

Kiwi broke the silence. "The one in front is a male and the other is a bint. See how she's trailing him by a good thirty meters and getting longer?"

"You're right, but she's tough, all right. I reckon I'd have a job keeping up with her. Wonder how old she is."

"Dunno," Kiwi replied. "She could be sixty even. They're as hard as nails, these Afghan women. I've heard they carry packs heavier than ours even and go places where even their bloody donkeys can't make it. And those who are packing poppies all carry an AK47 underneath their burkas. A Yank told me that after they've finished carving up a prisoner, they fight over who's going to get the liver and kidneys to eat."

"So I've heard but ..." Luke broke off suddenly. "Get ready, one's gone in. Spot her the minute she goes in."

Luke watched anxiously as the woman carried on upward.

"Now," he said sharply as she disappeared from view.

Kiwi said, "Smile please," and pressed a button. "Gotcha!" he grunted. "Phew! She had me going there for a minute. Be careful you don't knock the bloody laser. I don't want to spend another four days up here trying for another shoot."

"Wake up, wake up," muttered Luke impatiently into his headset as he waited for a reply from Trooper Griffiths, who he knew would be snoring soundly in his sack. The reply finally came over, and Luke ordered, "Come over with Williams, prepared for action."

Half an hour later, a voice called out the password, and the two troopers appeared outside the OP.

"What's the score then, boyo?" whispered Griffiths, his teeth chattering with the cold. "For Christ's sake tell me it's a no-go and we're on our way back home. I've never been this cold since I got pissed one night, fell off a canal bank, and went straight through the ice."

"Not so fast, Davvy," replied Luke. "We've got work to do. Follow my ass and no shooting unless you hear me call for it. Understood?"

Luke felt a momentary panic as he crashed through the heavy white curtain and came up against another, immediately behind it. He had not expected to find a second obstacle but his torch lit up a heavy Persian curtain a meter farther in. He immediately dropped to the ground, lifted up the bottom of the curtain, and rolled in, stopping with his chin on the ground and his rifle pointed menacingly forward.

There was no firing, as he had half-expected, not even a shout or a scream. He looked up to see a figure, sitting by a large oil stove, who stared at him in astonishment and waved a finger in front of his face, signaling silence.

The man's face was partly covered by a cowl but the eyes were visible and they seemed to blaze with anger. However, he made no attempt to get up, and Luke got warily to his feet and quickly surveyed his surroundings.

It was a typical Afghan cave he was now all too familiar with but with a difference. Instead of the usual graffiti, every centimeter of wall was covered with drawings of animals, flowers, trees, fish, insects, in fact just about everything that had to do with nature. Most of them were childlike but some were extremely artistic. He reckoned the cave was about fifteen meters square, with a ceiling height of roughly five meters. Many of the drawings at this level were of birds and butterflies. The floor was made up of compacted sand with a few rugs scattered about haphazardly, while around the side walls were stacked dozens of boxes and sacks of all sizes, interspersed with jerry cans, tables, and a large blackboard. In front of the blackboard was a desk with two chairs stacked upon it. Opposite it stood a long table with a chair at each end and nine tiny chairs on either side of it. But, it was the end wall that interested Luke most. It was curtained from floor to ceiling, and each of the two curtains bore a huge embroidered picture of a red dragon breathing smoke and yellow flames. Just up Welshman Davvy Griffiths's street.

Luke spoke into his headset, as he moved backward without taking his eyes off the Afghan. He lifted up the curtain, and within seconds, Trooper Griffiths crawled into the cave with his rifle at the ready.

"Ask the gentleman what's behind the curtain," Luke ordered in a low voice.

Griffiths looked sternly at the Afghan and spoke to him in Pashto.

The man looked surprised and again waved a finger in front of his face as he replied.

"He said please be silent, it's a dormitory and the children are asleep," whispered Griffiths.

"Tell him I want to check it out."

Griffiths spoke again, but this time the Afghan failed to answer. Griffiths repeated his question, raising his voice.

The Afghan shrugged his shoulders and got to his feet. He walked over to the wall and parted the curtains slightly.

Luke moved cautiously as he stood behind him and looked over his shoulder. The room was dimly lit by a small oil lamp hanging from the ceiling, and he could just make out two rows of tiny mattresses with a larger one at each end near the curtain. All of the beds were occupied, as was one of the two adult beds. Another pair of heavy curtains hung over the center of the far wall, and on either side of them were a number of washbasins with a towel hanging beneath each one.

"Check it out," he whispered to Griffiths, pointing at the curtains.

Griffiths moved quickly down the aisle between the beds and positioning himself well to the side of the right-hand curtain; he looked at Luke, nodded, and pulled the curtain smartly toward him. The interior was in darkness, and he shone his torch inside, circling it around the walls. He let go of the curtain, looked at Luke, and held his nose, pulling his arm up and down in the age-old sign for a lavatory. He closed the curtain as Luke beckoned him forward.

Luke walked over to the table and sat down at the head. "Bring that chair from the top end and sit next to me. Then ask the gent to come and join us," he ordered Griffiths.

The Afghan picked up his chair from near the stove and sat down at the table facing Griffiths, his arms folded and his hands concealed within the wide sleeves of his robe.

Luke looked at him warily. "Tell our friend to show his hands and put them on the table," he ordered Griffiths.

The Afghan responded by pulling out his right hand and placing it on the table.

"And the other," said Luke in a sharp voice, pointing at the left hand.

The Afghan sat immobile, his eyes staring straight at Luke.

Griffiths spoke to him again angrily, but still there was no response.

Luke stood up, pulled out his automatic, and pointed it menacingly at the Afghan's body.

This time he reluctantly obeyed the order, put out his hand, and placed it on the table alongside the other.

Jesus Christ! Luke felt his skin crawl, the sensation he sometimes felt when he narrowly missed slicing off a finger with a knife. It took him all his powers of self-control to remain calm, conscious that Griffiths had backed off in his chair and averted his eyes. The first three fingers and knuckles of the man's hand were missing altogether, while the thumb and little finger were mere stumps above the joints.

The man was a leper.

Luke pulled himself together, sat down, and re-holstered his automatic. He turned to Griffiths, who sat rigid, gaping at the deformed hand.

"Keep your voice low and ask him his name, what he's doing here, and does he speak English," he ordered.

The Afghan spoke for nearly a minute as he answered the questions.

Griffiths translated. "His name is Wasim Anwar and he's a schoolteacher. His wife is sleeping with the children, and they come from Kumara, a village eight kilometers down the valley. No, he doesn't speak any English but he sounds like he's well educated."

"Tell him my name is Luke Dryden and I'm very pleased to meet him." Luke held out his hand as his words were translated.

Wasim Anwar hesitated then slowly lifted his good hand, grasped Luke's hand, and shook it firmly before releasing it.

"Ask him if they actually walked here through all that deep snow in the valley."

Griffiths translated. "He says, of course. How else can they travel here at this time of the year? He wants to know why we've broken into his school and threatened him with guns. If the children had been awake, they would have been very upset."

Luke spoke directly to Wasim Anwar, and Griffiths repeated his words in Pashto.

"We are looking for Taliban insurgents, Mr. Anwar. We are under orders to do so from your government in Kabul."

Wasim Anwar pulled off his cowl, his eyes full of anger. Luke was relieved to see that there was no apparent damage to the face, although very little of it was visible through his full-length beard.

"We do not recognize the government in Kabul. We have our own government here, and our leader is Younis Khan. As for the Taliban, they have never come near our province, and they would be very unwelcome if they did. However, they would be much more welcome than the Yankees, who are destroying our beautiful country with their bombing and also killing hundreds of women and children. It is a far greater barbarism than that you accuse the Taliban of. Think of it, a beautiful day with not a cloud in the sky. Two young people getting married are receiving the blessing from their imam, when all of a sudden there is a great explosion, and death and destruction is everywhere. It was as through an earthquake had struck us. But it was not an earthquake, it was deliberate murder from on high. Unheard and unseen American barbarians, no doubt munching hamburgers as they go about their evil work, arrive over a target they cannot see with their own eyes. They watch their radar screens as our village is picked out by faceless people in a control center somewhere in America, and when the order is given, they press a button and presto, mission accomplished. Then they return to their base to be congratulated and perhaps given a medal for their bravery. And when they find out they have bombed the wrong target, they do not apologize for the error, and no one is punished for it. Our village died that day, and for what? To ensure that President Karzai and his corrupt government continue to salt away millions of dollars in foreign banks while our people starve."

Luke unwound the scarf from his face, and Griffiths followed suit. "Did the bombs kill anyone in your village?" he asked quietly.

"Many. Twenty-six people, twelve of them children, and the bride and groom."

"I'm very sorry to hear that, Mr. Anwar. We are British soldiers. We do everything we can to avoid killing civilians but sometimes things get beyond our control."

"Bah! The Afghan fighters do not wear uniforms. How can you Westerners tell who is a fighter and who is a civilian? Your big, arrogant commander in Jalalabad, the one they call Paddy Fatso, has said that any male Afghan over twelve who is found in a cave is to be taken prisoner and shot if he does not surrender. Even if they are found to have no weapons, they are handcuffed and taken away to be questioned. Many are never seen again. The caves used to give great pleasure to our adventurous young people, now they are too frightened to go near them in case they are bombed or taken prisoner."

"But you are living in a cave and with many children as well. Why is that?"

Wasim snorted. "If you were an American barbarian, I would refuse to answer your question but since you behave like a reasonably civilized person, I will tell you. All the children are under ten years old, and they are all lepers and orphans too. This is our own leper colony, blessed by Allah. And we are living in this cave because our school in the village was also bombed, killing a teacher and four children."

Wasim smiled as he saw the concern on Luke's face. He had witnessed the effect the dread word had on strangers a hundred times. "Don't worry, it is not contagious. My wife is the same."

Luke felt sheepish. "I'm sorry, Mr. Anwar, truly sorry. This is the last thing we expected to find when we saw you enter the cave. Our information was that you were suspected Taliban."

"And now you know we are not, are you going to take me away? I am over twelve years old, you know."

"Of course not. I must apologize if I have caused you any discomfort. We have no quarrel with the Afghan people."

Wasim's face hardened again. "But the Taliban are Afghan people, our people, just as the Scottish, Irish, and Welsh are British people. Some of us might not agree with their views, but they have every right to express them in their own country. What right have you to kill them and take them prisoner? You are thousands of kilometers from your home. What would you say if at this very moment Taliban people were dropping bombs on your villages and killing your people? President Karzai is a traitor and a fool, but even he did not invite you infidels to interfere in our affairs. You think that because we are a poor country and hidden away near the roof of the world that we are not aware of what is going on in the world around us. The Taliban are the VietCong of Afghanistan. The Yankees nearly destroyed Vietnam but in the end, the common people sent them home with their tail between their legs. The same will happen here. Read our history, it will tell you much. By the way, if you are British, why are you fighting with the Yankees up here? I thought the British were stationed in Helmand Province."

Luke shrugged his shoulders. *I'd like to know the answer to that one*, he thought.

"Search me, we're professional soldiers. We just follow orders. It's not for us to wonder why, it's just for us to do or die."

Wasim smiled knowingly. "Kipling, *The Charge of the Light Brigade*. Take heed of his words, my friend. Those who came to conquer us were vanquished time and time again, and so will you be if you continue to occupy our country." He stood up. "I think it is best if you go now. The children will be waking soon, and they will be frightened if they see you here."

Luke got up and struggled to pull his wallet from beneath his shirt. He took out all the money he had, around fifty pounds in Afghan currency plus thirty American dollars, and placed it on the table. He looked at Griffiths, who hesitated for a moment and reluctantly did the same.

"We would like you to accept this small donation to your school, Mr. Anwar, and hope that it will help buy something useful for those poor children in there."

Wasim nodded his head in appreciation. "Thank you, but they are not poor children. They are the chosen of Allah. Their suffering will be both our punishment and our redemption." He held out his hand, and Luke took it gladly.

"Good-bye and good luck," he said earnestly. "I hope this war will never touch your village ever again. For myself, I can only assure you that when I report back, no one will interfere with the refuge you have built here."

The two soldiers wrapped their scarves around their faces and joined Tommy Williams outside the cave. Dawn was breaking, and Luke signalled to Kiwi across the valley that they were coming in. The return signal came back, and they hunched their shoulders and set off down the mountain without looking back at the sanctuary that had humbled them all.

Chapter 4

T he guard stood aside as Colonel Brad Pickens—Delta Force OC—ushered Luke into the office and gave him a wink as he left and closed the door behind him.

Luke walked over and stood before the desk of the Officer Commanding U.S. Forces in Afghanistan and waited to be addressed by the three-star general seated behind it.

Paddy Collins had his head in his hands, looking down at a file on the desk, and did not look up.

A minute went by, and Luke spent it looking around the room. Chambers had not exaggerated. The walls were covered with framed pictures and photographs of every conceivable shape and size, relieved only by the flags of the United States, the Irish Republic, and the 101st Airborne Division propped up in the corners. The most prominent picture was a huge framed photograph of Collins dressed in cowboy gear riding an Arabian horse alongside George W. Bush, who was also in cowboy gear and mounted on a piebald. Both horses were reared up, and the two cowboys wore broad grins as they waved their Stetsons on high, Lone Ranger style. On the left of the picture was a photograph of General George S. Patton, and on the right one of a chin-up General Douglas MacArthur. A good number depicted Collins parachuting, riding horses, driving Jeeps and tanks, and posing grandiosely in the manner of the Italian dictator, Benito Mussolini. In almost every picture, he was immaculately dressed in U.S. cavalry uniform with highly polished riding boots and boasting two silver, ivory-handled pistols nesting in white leather holsters. Other photographs were iconic Americana; Washington crossing the Delaware, the capture of San Juan Hill, the raising of the flag on Iwo Jima, a leggy Betty Grable, and one he had never seen in his life before: a jagged signpost stuck in the snow with the name "Bastogne" scrawled on it. This last was flanked by the Stars and Stripes and the flag of the 101st Airborne Division.

But it was the Irish preponderance that raised Luke's eyebrows. Michael Collins was prominent, as were Eamon DeValera and Bobby Sands. Also in profusion were photographs of the general in full dress uniform consorting with the sinister figures of Gerry Adams and Martin McGuinness. One panorama even pictured a large crowd of smiling U.S. senators and representatives standing behind a row of masked Provos seated in front of the Capitol steps, each holding a U.S. flag in one hand and the Irish tricolor in the other. One picture in particular made him shudder with revulsion. It showed a masked Provo brandishing a Barrett sniper rifle above his head, standing with one foot on the body of a dead British soldier.

Seething with anger, Luke swore and crashed out onto a nearby chair. In a loud voice, he called out, "You sent for me, General?"

Collins raised his head in astonishment and nearly dislodged his glasses in the process. He righted them clumsily and scowled at Luke, momentarily lost for words.

Luke stared back with some astonishment of his own. The man was huge, massive, Orson Wellesian, totally at odds with the straight-backed military figure portrayed in the photographs. His bulk seemed to span the width of the desk. He wore a tie, and the pudgy neck sprouted from his collar like some outsized tuber seeking sun and air. But the face failed to match the torso. It was small and almost chinless, oval on the vertical, giving it a Humpty-Dumpty effect that made Luke want to burst out laughing. The eyes were brown and narrow, peering through ridiculously small wire bifocals that perched halfway up the bulbous nose. The hair was sparse and greying at the sides, complimented by a thin black moustache that looked as if it belonged to an old-fashioned French chef. But it was the pallor of his skin that intrigued Luke. It was the color of parchment but without the sheen, like blotting paper sprinkled with iron filings.

The words came out like poison darts: "I thought you fucking Brits said 'Sir' when you addressed a superior officer."

"That's right, we do, General," drawled Luke. "Always, when we're addressing a superior British officer."

Again, Luke could barely conceal his mirth. He had expected Collins's voice to be bass or even double-bass, but to his surprise it was high-pitched, almost falsetto.

Collins swore. "Is that so? Your attitude tells me you don't give a fuck for anything or anybody. Look at your filthy clothes and all that crappy fuzz on your face. If I didn't know better, I'd take you for one of those dirty ragheads always foraging round our cook-house."

"I got your message and came straight here, General. I've been mixing with the natives, as you know. Talking about beards, your General Grant sported a beauty, and he wasn't too choosy with his uniform either, if you ask me," retorted Luke, looking up at a photograph of the bearded Civil War general and his scruffy appearance.

Collins ignored the remark and looked down again at the file on his desk. "Your report states you apprehended a hostile and let him go. Is that correct?"

"I didn't apprehend him. I questioned him and decided he was no threat to the coalition. Then we shook hands, and I wished him good luck."

"*You* questioned him? Since when did you become a member of my intelligence staff? My express orders are that any hostile, male or female, over the age of twelve is to be arrested and handed over to Major Kleinwort for interrogation. You say you questioned him. Did he speak English then?"

"No, one of my men speaks fluent Pashto. I spoke through him."

"Is that so? Did you search him first?"

"I made him put both hands on the table while we talked."

"But you didn't search him?"

"No."

"Why not?"

"Because the man was a cripple. He was harmless. He was a schoolteacher and a leper."

Collins exploded. "Jesus H. Christ, are you crazy? Schoolteachers are the worst kind of hostiles. They are the ones who teach all this Islamic shit to the terrorists in the first place. This country is crawling with ragheads with no hands or feet, or missing an eye or an ear. Haven't you seen how many of them there are with Goddamn hooks for hands or walking with crutches? They got their wounds fighting the Russians. They're fanatics, call themselves mujahidin. Why, we captured one of them a month back. He had no arms but he had an RPG launcher strapped to his back underneath his Goddamn nightshirt. It was loaded, too, rigged so that it fired when he banged his chin on his chest, the cunning bastard. You were lucky to get out of that cave alive, mister."

"Nobody was armed, we weren't in any danger."

"Oh, yeah! It says in your report there were also nine children and one adult, all asleep. Did you search any of them?"

"No, they were all lepers, and they were all asleep. The adult was a woman. There was no point in waking them up."

"That was nice and genteel of you. So Afghan women don't fight, eh? Tell that to the Marines. Any one of our boys who was taken prisoner was given to the womenfolk, and they carved them up plenty. You can bet your life that woman had an AK47 under her blanket just waiting for you to make a mistake. Come to think of it, she might have been Bin Laden himself, since he's been known to wear a dress. What do you think of that? You could have missed out on capturing the most wanted man in the world, and the president would have had me crucified. The point is, Dryden, your orders were to search a designated hideout and bring in any hostiles for interrogation. You failed to do that, and in my book, that's a clear case of dereliction of duty. What does a genteel Limey say to that?"

Luke pretended not to see the sneer on the oval face. "I've already told you, they weren't hostiles, they were lepers," he persisted. "Jesus Christ, the poor beggars have got their fill of suffering as it is. There is no way I would hand them over to your persecutors. Without them, the nine kids would have starved to death. It's all there in my report. We have bombed them out of their sanctuary, and they have been forced to live in a cave. They pose no threat to coalition forces and should be allowed to live in peace."

"Persecutors!" Collins's face was now bright red. "Let me tell you, mister, our intelligence unit is the best. What they don't know about gathering information from the locals isn't worth knowing."

"Yes, so I've heard. I've also heard it's a close second to the Abu Ghraib prison in Baghdad. Seems your favorite trick is to take them up in choppers and toss them out if they don't say the right words."

"That's a dirty big lie. Nobody up here has ever been convicted of ill-treatment of prisoners, ever."

"There's a big difference between being accused and being convicted, if you ask me."

"Nobody's asking you," Collins fumed. "Who the hell are you to be talking about the niceties of war? Thanks to the British, there are thousands of fine Irish boys lying in their graves all over Ireland, tortured, mutilated, buried in prison graveyards."

"Who are all these fine Irish boys, General?"

"Cut the crap, you know who I mean. I'm talking about the Provisional IRA."

"And the Official IRA, the Real IRA, and the Continuity IRA?" asked Luke.

"All of them. All the patriotic heroes who have died fighting the British occupation of Ireland."

"You mean like the Taliban, who are fighting the American occupation of Afghanistan?"

"Bullshit, the Taliban are terrorists. We've only been here a few years. The British have occupied Ireland for centuries."

Luke sat up straight. "The partition of Ireland was agreed to by all parties before the last war and had the whole-hearted support of the Catholic church and, if I remember rightly, your namesake, Michael Collins. The last thing the bishops wanted was a million bloody-minded Protestants upsetting the stranglehold they hold on most of the country. The Irish government wouldn't take Ulster back if Britain offered to throw in £100 billion as well."

"Bullshit again," raged Collins. "The real Irish people were sold down the river. That's when the IRA was born, and they've been fighting for justice ever since and will do so until Ireland is all one country once again."

Luke was beginning to get tired of the argument. He knew that once an Irish Catholic got talking about the Troubles, they would cry in their porter for hours and twice as long as that when they were well and truly pissed. He glanced again at the offensive picture of the Provo and the dead squaddie and resolved to stick it to the fat bastard, rank or no rank.

"That's a lot of fighting. Does that mean you Yanks are going to keep supplying them with guns and bombs and booze forever?" he thundered.

"What the hell are you talking about?"

"The Provos have no friends except in the United States and Libya. Even the Irish Republic government regards them as psychos and terrorists. So where do they get all their weapons to keep on killing British soldiers and Irish civilians? From you Yankee cheerleaders, of course. Only a few years back, my troop blew up a cache of weapons in the Republic worth at least $2 million: M16s, Kalashnikovs, heavy machine guns, Barrett sniper rifles, grenades, plastic explosives, RPGs, you name it. They were all brand new and packed in boxes labelled 'Farm equipment donated to the people of Ireland by Noraid, USA.' The manifest even had the shipment date on it, November 2006, the time the IRA was supposed to be goody-goody upright citizens. It was put about that your government had severed all links with the IRA but they must have known about this shipment, and that means Noraid got the stuff from government sources. The whole thing stinks. Here's the British army fighting so-called Taliban terrorists side by side with your men while at the same time you're giving guns to the stinking IRA to kill our comrades with or, to put it in a way your Hollywood heroes might understand, Yankee renegades are selling the Comanches guns with which to kill the U.S. Cavalry."

Collins was dumbfounded by Luke's outburst. "Now you listen to me, Limey," he blustered, "I'm proud to be associated with Noraid. I've been with them since I was twelve years old. Used to take collections in my pa's top hat. We've sent millions of dollars over to the old country, all of it for good causes. Of course we've given money to the IRA, but it was never for guns, it was to help out the widows and families of the Provos killed by the British and the

Protestant Paramilitaries. And the money was never given directly to the Provos, it was given to Sinn Fein. It was up to Gerry Adams and Martin McGuinness how much they gave to the them."

"Jesus Christ! Adams and McGuinness?" swore Luke. "You must know they *are* the IRA. They've both served on the IRA Council, although they won't admit it. What a pair of scumbags. Can you imagine any army where the generals who give the orders to their troops remain incognito while the battles rage all around them? Phantom leaders holed up in the sewers ordering their zombies over the top and, at the same time, warning them that if they were ever taken prisoner, they must not reveal the names of any of their generals or they'd get a bullet in the back of the head. We took a Provo prisoner once, hung a grenade around his neck, and he squealed like a stuck pig. Told us the names of four of the Army Council, how they received the arms from Noraid, and also the location of the Noraid training camp for Provos up in the Adirondack Mountains in New York State. Noraid is up to its neck in the deaths of thousands of innocent people, and all the fancy words from people like you and your crooked Irish congressmen who are skimming millions off the top won't save you all from the fires of hell; that is, if the devil would accept you in the first place. George Bush complained that every time an American soldier is killed, the Iraqis pour out onto the streets, cheering their heads off. Well, I saw plenty of TV pictures of Irish-American sympathizers dancing in the streets and pubs of New York and Chicago every time a British soldier was killed by a cowardly Provo, more especially when the bullet came from a Barrett sniper rifle made in the USA."

Collins looked at Luke, open-mouthed. His face turned black as thunder as he stood up straight, sending his chair crashing against the wall behind him. "You've gone too far this time, you Limey bastard!" he shouted, and Luke saw his right hand drop to rest on the butt of his revolver.

Without even thinking, Luke flipped the flap of his holster and put his hand on his automatic, his blue eyes shading steely grey. He fixed his eyes on the pudgy face in front of him, keeping in view Collins's right-hand gun and ignoring the left-hand gun, which Chambers had told him was for show only. *Jesus*, he thought, *my gun's not cocked, hope he doesn't figure it.* He braced his legs, ready to take the only option open to him if Fatso called his bluff.

The general stood still, breathing heavily, caught in two minds. He had practiced the movement hundreds of times in front of the mirror, on targets, on horseback, on rabbits, on squirrels, and sometimes on mangy dogs. He was fast, very fast. He had been told that many times and had won prizes to prove it. On rare occasions, he would snag the gun as it came out of the holster, but mostly, it came out in a blur, hand and butt welded together. But he had never drawn against an opponent whose gun was loaded with live ammunition before, and what if, just this once, the gun should snag as it left the holster? He could use the other gun, of course, but he was hopeless with the left hand. And he had never practiced once with either of them since he had arrived in Afghanistan three months ago.

He looked down at the Brit crouched in his chair, his face inscrutable, only his eyes and nose visible through the mass of jet-black beard. He searched for the telltale signs of nervousness, but there were none. No moistening of the lips, a slight twitch, or even a bead of sweat. Just two blue, unblinking eyes fixed on his own, reading his thoughts, calculating the odds. *Holy cow*, he thought to himself, *he looks just like some of the Afghan prisoners we've picked up and who would rather die than utter a single word under torture.* The indecision was now beginning to draw beads of sweat from his own forehead and the nape of his neck. He looked at the steady, sun-tanned hand resting on the automatic. Was there a bullet in the chamber or would he have to cock it? He had heard that the British SAS were experts with the Walther automatic and could loose off a magazine with deadly accurately in less than five seconds. Also that they never parted with the weapon even when they went to bed. In that case, it was more than likely they would always have a bullet up the spout. They were ruthless, too, inhuman if some of the tales he'd been told by Provos were to be believed.

The tension became unbearable as he quickly figured his chances. Somehow, everything was wrong. He was used to drawing on standing targets with the gun on the level of the target's belly but Dryden was a full thirty degrees below his gaze, and although he would normally have plenty of space to take up a gunfighter's stance, he was restricted by the desk in front and the chair at his back. The desk too was a big problem on account of the large C-130 model airplane and the flags of the United States and the Irish Republic on either side of it, interfering with his line of sight. That meant he would have to Move at least two feet to his left to get an accurate shot in. Another thing, the Limey bastard may be wearing a flak jacket under his tunic, which meant he'd have to aim for the head. Everything now depended upon whether the Limey's gun was cocked. It was like Russian roulette. Was there a bullet in the firing chamber? And if there was, would there be plenty more to follow it? He felt the smooth ivory gun butt grow clammy as sweat from his wrists trickled onto it. His throat became parched and his legs began to feel weak, creating a longing to sit down and sip water from the glass on his desk. His hands began to tremble uncontrollably, and he desperately needed to take a leak.

He could stand the tension no longer, and he was about to take his hand off the butt when, to his utmost relief, the telephone rang, With his eyes fixed warily on the Brit's gun hand, he backed up to his chair and squeezed his bulk into it, taking his hand off his gun as he did so. Drawing himself forward to the desk, he picked up the water glass and drained it without pausing for breath. Wiping his mouth with his sleeve, he picked up the receiver. "What is it?" he demanded in a hoarse voice.

He listened impatiently for a few seconds and then thumped his fist furiously on the desk. "Fucking well take care of it yourself, you dickhead!" he shouted. "If you can't, I'll send somebody with half a brain to relieve you. Permanently." He slammed the receiver down, took a deep breath, and stared at Luke as if he had just come into the room.

"Captain Dryden," he snarled, "I am charging you with the crimes of disobeying a specific order, showing a total disrespect for your commanding officer, using insulting and degrading language, and impugning the integrity of members of the U.S. armed forces and members of Congress. You will be confined to a single cell in the base guardhouse until such time as arrangements for your court martial are put in place. I must warn you that any attempt to escape will be severely dealt with."

Luke got up and gave him a mock salute. "Whatever you say, General," he said quietly.

Collins pressed a button and the door opened almost immediately.

"You want me, General?" Colonel Pickens asked as he entered the room.

"Take this man down to the guardhouse, book him in, and tell the Provost Marshall to come down to my office right away," Collins ordered.

"Yes, sir. You want me to come back after?" drawled Pickens.

"No, no," replied Collins abruptly. "Book him in and go about your duties."

Pickens stood to one side to allow Luke to walk past him and then followed him down the corridor. They had barely gone ten paces when Collins appeared in the doorway and screamed, "If you're thinking of paying a visit to your leper friends, Limey, forget it. A B2 dropped two bunker-busters on their cave yesterday."

Luke stopped dead in his tracks and turned around, his face blazing with anger. He made to rush the door but Pickens and the guard grabbed him and held him back. "Don't take the bait, Luke," Pickens murmured. "The bastard's not worth it. Anyway, you'll have to stand in line, there's plenty of other guys on the base want a piece of him."

Chapter 5

L uke found himself in solitary. The only visitors permitted to enter his cell were officers from the division's legal department, seeking to clarify his account of operation Cave WMD307, as it was designated. They went over his four-page report with a fine-tooth comb, looking for discrepancies and comparing them with statements they had obtained from the other members of his patrol. Under orders from above, they sought to make changes to his version of events, at first cajoling him with promises of an immediate release and reinstatement to his troop and then, when he refused to alter a name or even a punctuation mark, they came up with threats of court martial, the stockade, or something even worse. Luke knew they were plotting a cover-up but he couldn't understand why they were so desperate to change his story.

It was Colonel Pickens who supplied the answer. Good old Brad, who had somehow bribed the duty officer one evening to let him visit and share a six-pack with the prisoner.

As Brad told it, a reporter for CNN who was embedded with the 101st Division had gotten hold of a copy of Luke's report and, reneging on his obligation to submit all such material for scrutiny and approval, had written up his own interpretation of the affair and presented it as a sensational scoop to his editor. The boss of CNN, aware of the seriousness of the disclosure, insisted on the army's verification before authorizing its release, and fearful of losing his cosy relationship with the defense secretary, he agreed to put a temporary hold on the broadcast pending an official release.

"When Fatso got the message from the Pentagon, he started shitting bricks," chortled Brad. "He was in enough trouble as it was from the cover-up in Iraq, and another mistake of this magnitude would surely cook his goose. He's out to bury it and you too, if he can arrange it. So do us all a big favor and refuse to retract a single word. Fatso's not a soldier's soldier, he's a political appointee because he was some kind of military adviser to Dick Cheney years back and used to wipe his ass. But be very, very careful. The guy's a snake, and they don't come any meaner. He'll try every trick in the book to offload this load of manure, and with you being a Limey, his legal eagles will try and baffle you with sections of the U.S. Army Code of Conduct that even 99 percent of us GIs don't understand. Savvy?"

Luke laughed. "Tell you what, Brad, if it comes to a court martial, I'll insist on you being appointed as my defense lawyer. How's that?"

Pickens looked serious. "Listen, pal, I've known this sonofabitch for a long time, and I know what I'm talking about. If it wasn't for him, there'd be at least twenty of my men playing baseball with their kids instead of pushing up daisies in Arlington. I don't mean the usual casualties of war, bridges too far, suicide missions, kudos for the general, you know what I mean. If you don't nail him to the mast, it will only be a matter of time before he gets a bullet. That's why I want you to be on your guard. I've had three of my guys watching the guardhouse round the clock since you went inside, but I'll have to pull them off Sunday. I suggest you get your boys to take over from them. You want me to get your number two to pay you a visit?"

"Many thanks, Brad, you can do that?"

"Sure can. What's his name?"

"Tom Jackson, Lieutenant Tom Jackson."

"Stonewall, eh? Okay, I'll make sure he gets to visit tomorrow or the day after."

"You got something going, Brad?" Luke asked.

Pickens made a face. "It's a big red. Fatso's been planning this operation since the first week he got here. Wants to impress his buddies in the Pentagon. He's been telling them a load of crap about how the Marines and our Special Forces got too defensive and allowed the Taliban to move back into Wazir and occupy a large stretch of hill country along the Pakistan border. His plan is to push them back over the border and establish a series of forward outposts to prevent them from ever returning again. We told him he's crazy taking them on in winter, when every possible advantage will lie with the Taliban, but he's deaf to our objections. Keeps on calling us chicken and brings out the saga of how the 101st beat the shit out of the Krauts at Bastogne, fighting in deep snow and similar terrain. Says the Krauts had hundreds of Tiger tanks shooting them up while the most the Taliban can muster are a dozen worn-out Russian T50s and a few 100mm mortars. I pointed out that the Russians had better tanks than the Tigers, masses of artillery, and hundreds of aircraft and choppers but were outfought and outmaneuvered by these same people but he won't have it. Says the mujahidins are all foreign Arabs, and the Taliban are just a bunch of dirty religious weirdos. The 101st are nowhere near ready for this kind of operation. They've only been here three months and have barely ventured out of barracks. You know what the terrain is like, it takes months to assimilate to it, yet these troops have come here from Baghdad, where the nearest you get to hills are the humps on camels' backs. Jesus, the switch was so fast, the 101st are still in their desert gear while the Marines went out and took all their winter clothing with them. I guarantee there'll be more casualties from frostbite than there'll be from enemy action."

"And you'll be up in front as usual," Luke remarked.

"Of course, but we're prepared for the weather. The snag is that this time of year, you get low cloud cover, and that limits the service the choppers can give us. If it's really bad, they don't fly, which means we hoof it or use specially adapted Humvees that the mujahidins can hear coming five kilometers away. Either way, we lose the element of surprise, and that gives them a big advantage."

"Is my troop involved in all this?" asked Luke.

"Sure are, everybody is. Even the cooks and shithouse wallahs have been ordered to fall in. Your neighbors in the cells next door will be sure to be released, and if the foul-ups are as dumb-ass as I think they will be, even the guards will be ordered to go with them."

Brad laughed. "That means you could be left cold turkey, so be sure and ask one of them to leave a key."

Luke liked the way Brad talked, or drawled rather. Old Virginia, if he wasn't mistaken. He was tall and straight-backed, a dead ringer for a bearded Gregory Peck. Add a drooping moustache, and he could have been one of Robert E. Lee's staff officers. He was obviously a West Point career officer with around twenty years service, most of them in one or more of the American Special Forces units. *What a waste,* he thought. A fine officer capable of leading an elite brigade into battle reduced to leading clandestine missions against insurgents, guerrillas, hostiles, terrorists, or whatever name the enemy was labelled with by Washington in America's ever-increasing number of dirty wars around the globe. He thought of his own experiences in Ulster and shuddered. And what the hell was he doing here, killing people in a country that Britain had gratefully pulled out of over a hundred years ago?

"Are you going for the full stretch, Brad?" he asked. "Thirty years, isn't it?"

Brad rolled his beer can back and forth across his forehead as he pondered the question. "Dunno, another OC like Fatso and I'm out of here. To tell you the truth, Luke, I like my uniform, I like its history and what it stands for. I feel good when I wear it on parade and even better when it's tested on a battlefield. But this cloak-and-dagger stuff, rags and burnouses and painted faces, is getting to me. It's nasty and it's dirty, especially when you're fighting an enemy without a uniform, and you can never be certain whether the guy you've killed is a hostile or a completely innocent civilian. I don't like the atmosphere either. We're supposed to have liberated these people, but when I'm among them, I've always got the feeling some of them would love to stick a knife in my back or put a bomb under my Humvee. And the way the mujahidins treat our prisoners is diabolical. Have you ever seen one of ours strung up from a tree?"

Luke shook his head.

"Well, I can tell you it's not a pretty sight. The men start off by giving them a hard time, kicking, beating, running the gauntlet, that sort of thing. When they're nearly half-dead, they hand them over to their womenfolk, all dressed in black and with only their eyes showing through the slits in their fucking burkas. They sharpen their knives in front of the poor bastard and then begin to carve him up and fight over the choice parts like they were a special from McDonald's. Jesus Christ, even the Nazis didn't treat prisoners like that if they were in uniform."

Luke shook his head again. "Looks like we've come full circle, doesn't it? Native American Indians torturing soldiers and settlers two hundred years ago, and the Fuzzy Wuzzies doing the same to our men in the Sudan over a hundred years ago. What a difference to the liberation of Europe, when every Tommy and every GI was king for a day."

"You're dead right," snorted Brad. "That was a soldier's war and so was the Korean campaign. But since then, they've all been politicians' wars, sticking their noses into other nations' business, bombing the shit out of them, and then expecting the locals to welcome us with open arms. Why, we can't go nowhere here or in Iraq without we're armed to the teeth, and if we want a broad, we've got to strip search her first and put barbed wire and guards around the whorehouse. Shit, Bill Clinton had the right idea. He took out Al Qaeda's training camps and weapons dumps with missiles. There was never any need to invade the Goddamn place and stir up a hornet's nest. Somebody ought to have told Bush to shove his head up his ass and tell him there ain't no such thing as a war on terror. It's a war on civilians, plain and simple, and every time we kill one, it makes three or four more itching to kill us. Why, we raided a village and found three kids no more than ten years old each packing an AK, and they would have used them, too, you could tell that by the look in their eyes."

Luke was beginning to feel the effects of the beer. He raised his can. "You should have been a politician yourself, Brad," he suggested. "I can see the day coming when the voters will finally revolt and ask the army to step in and clean up the mess on both sides of the Atlantic. When that day comes, we can put all the greedy, corrupt politicians in uniform, load their rifles with blanks, and ship them over here to find out how the Afghans deal with habitual liars and crooks."

Brad raised his own can and smacked it against Luke's. "Amen to that, old buddy," he said with a broad grin.

Pickens made one more visit and stayed for less than half an hour. "We're moving out at 0400," he explained, "and the division is following up two days later. Don't worry about a thing. I've spoken to Stonewall and he's leaving three of your boys behind to keep their eye on things. The big show is scheduled to last three weeks but I'll give it six at least. Stonewall told me to tell you that your boss, Wingate, is on his way over, so it's possible you'll be out of this shit-hole before I get back. I'm sorry I couldn't arrange for Stonewall to visit but I've got a message for you. Eat it and swallow it when you've finished reading it," he joked.

Brad held out his hand, and Luke could feel the cementing of a rare friendship as he clasped it.

"So long, Brad," he said, the sadness showing in his face. "Look after yourself and thanks for everything. By the way, where do you live in Virginia?"

Brad looked surprised. "Glen Allen, a small place outside Richmond. You know it?"

"No, but I'd like to visit one day before I get too old to travel."

"You do that and don't leave it too late. I'll show you some fox-hunting country that will make your English hair stand on end."

The message from Tom Jackson was brief. The troop was in on the big push but he was leaving three men behind to keep watch on the guardhouse. Any suspicious moves by the guards, and they would take immediate action. The good news was the boss was on his way over to sort things out.

Luke woke up suddenly at 0400 two days after Brad's last visit and sat on his bed, listening intently to the exhilarating sound of an army bestirring itself and preparing to move into battle. The powerful roar of diesel engines shattered a cold, brittle dawn, a noise accentuated by the low, snow-laden clouds that hemmed in the vibrations and made the ears ring. As the column clattered past the guardhouse, he could visualize the scene as the familiar sounds floated on the air. The awesome Abrams and the sleek Bradleys, the purposeful Humvees and the busy, speeding Jeeps. He could also hear bursts of machine-gun fire, as the crews primed their weapons, and curses as a gun jammed or a finger was injured. But there was no cheering and no onlookers. If it wasn't for the mechanical noise, it could well have been a cavalcade of ghosts exiting a mist and heading into another cloud farther down the road.

It took over an hour for the final vehicle to pass through the barrier, and when it was gone, the silence became almost as deafening as the noise that went before. Luke became aware of a strange atmosphere that now pervaded the guardroom and realized that the night light over the guard's table at the end of the corridor was switched off. The desk was out of his line of sight but he could always tell if the guard was at his post by the shading of the light as he moved around. He listened carefully for sounds coming down from the adjacent cell block, but there were none. No shouting, screaming, cursing, singing, tin mugs banging on the metal bars, not even the flushing of a toilet. It was eerie. He knew something was going on. And all he could do was stand up facing the bars, straining his ears until they hurt, listening for a clue, and praying for the dawn to come early this particular morning.

He was nearly asleep on his feet when he heard the familiar sound of a Humvee draw up outside the guardhouse. It was still dark and the light from two flashlights lit up the corridor as the owners came marching down and stood outside his cell.

Luke was partially blinded as one of the flashlights focussed on his face and a voice said, "Captain Dryden, my orders are to take you into our vehicle and transport you to Bagram Air Base. Please put your belongings in this bag immediately."

Luke obeyed the order, took the bin liner, and stuffed the few articles he possessed inside it.

"That's all?" asked the voice. "Good, now turn around, put both your hands through the feed aperture, and stand still while I cuff you. Don't you try ..." His words were cut off as he fell to the floor, spilling his flashlight, which rolled close enough for Luke to put out his arm and grab it. As he shone it through the bars, he was just in time to see another flashlight and automatic hit the floor and its owner's body crash down beside it without uttering a murmur.

"You okay, Luke?" a voice asked anxiously. "They both came in with their guns out, so we had to do something a bit desperate. We reckoned they were taking you for one-way ride."

Luke shone his flashlight upward and was rewarded with the sight of Kiwi Bowman peering anxiously through the bars. He moved the beam to the right and picked out the smiling face of Tommy Williams, holding his rifle at the ready.

"Good lads," he said. "I didn't think they were taking me down to the mess for a beer. Any more bodies lying around?"

"Just the driver," replied Kiwi. "Davvy's looking after him. Tommy, go and give him a hand to bring him in, and we'll put all three together in this cell. Shine a light over here, Luke."

Luke shone the flashlight on Kiwi's victim and watched as he searched for the keys to the cell. "Here they are," said Kiwi as he flourished them and quickly inserted one in the door lock. He cursed as he drew a blank three times, but on the fourth attempt, the tumblers clicked and he pulled the door open.

"Give me the flashlight, Luke, and get the big guy's coat on," said Kiwi. "It's perishing cold outside, believe me."

Luke stripped the heavy coat off the body and put his hand beneath his chin, searching for a pulse. "He's okay," he said. "How about him?"

Kiwi felt the other man's neck. "Okay too, but he's going to have one cracking headache when he wakes up. Let's get them in the cell quick."

They pulled the two bodies into the cell, propped them up against the wall, and stood to one side as Griffiths and Williams came down the corridor with the body of the driver and heaved him onto the bed.

"Is he okay?" asked Luke.

"Yes, I reckon he'll be out another half hour," replied Griffiths.

"Good," said Luke as he picked up the bin liner. "Lock the door and let's get the hell out of here. Anybody know where we're going?"

"We're all set for Camp Bastion," Kiwi said. "Tommy's made us a map we must keep to, and eventually a chopper will contact us and pick us up. I've checked the Humvee, the tank's nearly full."

"Any food in it?"

"No, I don't think so."

"There's a kitchen somewhere at the end of the corridor. Get in there and load up. Didn't anyone ever tell you that an army marches on its stomach?"

Chapter 6

Colonel Wingate stood up and held out his hand as Luke entered the office. "Good to see you, Luke," he said cheerfully. "I believe you've met General Alexander, haven't you?"

"Yes, sir, just long enough to toast the queen," Luke replied, glancing at the general seated behind his desk. *Jesus Christ,* he thought, *he's the exact antithesis of Fatso Collins.*

Britain's finest general was in shirtsleeves and looked as cool as a cucumber in the airless office. The clean-shaven, sun-tanned face with the famous clipped moustache and sparkling green eyes smiled up at him and immediately put him at his ease.

"Have a seat, Luke," said the general, pointing at a chair. "Can I get you a drink or something before we get down to business?"

"No, thank you, sir, I've just come down from the mess."

"Good," said the general. "It's over to you then, Jock."

Luke studied his boss as he shuffled the sheaf of papers he was holding. Unlike Alexander, he was smartly dressed in full uniform, the tunic of which bore three rows of ribbons, testimony to his many years of heroic service in the army. The leathery face was clean-shaven, with lines showing around his mouth and forehead, above which was a healthy crop of sandy hair, neatly trimmed with just a trace of sideburn. His piercing blue eyes and trademark boxer's nose signalled the message that he sought to instil into every member of his regiment: "Mess with me at your peril."

Wingate unfolded a paper he had selected and looked keenly at Luke. "Firstly, Luke, I must apologize for neglecting to get in touch with you sooner. I've been tied up in Iraq. Communications were fouled up, and I've been caught up in a shouting match with the foreign office and the ministry of defense. Secondly, this is not an inquisition. From the bits and pieces I have gathered from all sources, I am sure you are completely innocent of the charges brought against you, but I have to obtain the relevant facts in order to face down the allegations. Believe me, this thing has been blown up on both sides of the Atlantic, and in the eyes of the mealy-mouthed politicians, you are now regarded in the same light as Jack the Ripper in England, and Charles Manson in America. Now then, did you submit a written report to General Collins on your assignment?"

"Yes, sir, I did."

"Did your team members check its contents?"

"They did, all three of them."

Wingate made a note on his paper. "The report was written on your laptop?"

"It was."

"Do you still have possession of your laptop?"

"No, sir. I believe they trashed it."

"But it was among your possessions when you were arrested and taken to the guardhouse?"

"It was."

"Good. Now, Luke, we haven't seen your report, so we're going to record what you tell us and make a transcript later. Is that okay with you?"

"Of course."

Wingate looked at Alexander, who nodded, pressed a key on a desktop recorder, and settled back in his chair with his hands clasped behind his head.

Wingate put down his pen and paper and folded his arms. "Okay, Luke, when you're ready," he said.

Luke pulled his chair nearer to the desk and proceeded to relate the entire story from the time his team were dropped off at the chosen target in the White mountains up to the moment when they were picked up by a Lynx helicopter eighty kilometers from the UK base at Camp Bastion.

"That's it, sir," he said finally. "As far as I can remember."

"Good," said Wingate. "So you entered the cave and spoke to the leper teacher. How many of your patrol came in with you?"

"Just Trooper Griffiths."

"Did he speak to the teacher?"

"Yes, he did the interpreting."

"Of course. Speak to anyone else?"

"No, sir, they were all asleep, nine children and the teacher's wife."

"Did you see or find any arms?"

Luke hesitated. "No, but we didn't look all that closely."

"General Collins says his intelligence had positive information that Bin Laden's number two and twelve followers were seen heading for the cave eight hours before you went in, and they have aerial photographs to prove it."

"They must refer to another cave. It didn't snow all day, and the only tracks on that mountain were ours and the teacher's and his wife's."

Wingate shuffled his papers and turned over a page. "Okay, that gets the assignment, now for General Collins. The day after your return to base, Collins called you in to question you on your report. What was his attitude toward you?"

"Pretty shitty; he didn't take kindly to my beard, for starters." Luke stroked his beard fondly and both officers laughed out loud.

"I told him everything that I've told you, and he took me to task for not obeying his written orders to bring in any hostile over the age of twelve for questioning. I told him they weren't hostiles, and in any case, the two adults were lepers and without them, the kids would starved to death. He went into a rage and told me that every Afghan was a no-good, murdering heathen and their women were even worse. I contradicted him, and he went berserk and started lecturing me on the behavior of the British in Northern Ireland and the way we treated 'heroic rebels,' as he called them. He said he was a big wheel in Noraid and that he was proud to be associated with Adams, McGuinness, and their Irish friends in Congress. I guess I lost my rag and told him what I thought about Noraid and their friends. You know how I feel about the bloody Provos, don't you sir?"

Wingate looked thoughtful. "A big wheel in Noraid, eh? Now that's interesting. Anything else?"

"Not really, that's when he told me he was putting me under arrest for disobeying a specific order, showing disrespect for a senior officer, using insulting and degrading language, and impugning the integrity of members of the U.S. armed forces and members of Congress."

Wingate whistled. "Christ, he really threw the book at you, didn't he? You're lucky he didn't pull one of his famous guns on you."

"He made as if he was going to, but something held him off."

Alexander leaned forward. "The hell you say. Were you armed?"

"I was wearing my service revolver."

"Was it loaded?"

"Yes, sir."

"One up the spout?"

"No, sir."

"Did you know that he's been charged with striking an enlisted man in his own command on two occasions?"

"No, I didn't hear that one."

"Did you know they call him the fastest gun in the west?"

Luke laughed. "No, I just thought he had the fastest mouth."

Alexander exchanged glances with Wingate and shook his head. "Do you honestly think he would have drawn on you, Luke?" he asked.

"Hard to tell. He was hopping mad and his eyes looked mean enough."

"So what stopped him?"

"I think he had second thoughts and chickened out."

"If he hadn't chickened out, what do you think your chances were?"

"Fifty-fifty. I was sitting down. He didn't have a clean shot because of all the junk on his desk, and He would have had to move a meter to his left. I figured that would give me a chance to get beneath his desk and cock my gun."

Wingate swore. "The cowardly bastard, he had the drop on you but wanted 100 percent odds. You're damn lucky you're still alive, don't you agree, Rex?"

Alexander nodded his head. "I do. It's a bloody good job he wasn't a Serb, you'd have been dead meat for sure."

Wingate lit up a panatela and made a note, squinting through the smoke as he did so. "And that was it? You were arrested and taken to the guardhouse?"

"Not quite, he shouted after me that a B2 had dropped two bunker-busters on the cave."

"How did you feel about that?"

"Bloody awful."

"I'm not a bit surprised," said Wingate. "I was there when the Afghans were fighting the Russians. Nothing made them angrier than the indiscriminate slaughter of their women and children. It's counterproductive, The Russians should have known that after the treatment they received from the Nazis. Now then, tell us about your escape from the guardhouse."

"Nothing much to tell, really. My team played a blinder. Kept a twenty-four hour watch on the guardhouse for three days solid. They figured there was something fishy going on when the rest of the prisoners were set free and the guards left their posts and didn't come back. When the Humvee drew up with three soldiers wearing masks, they decided it was time to act, and they took all three of them out."

"How did they take them out?" asked Wingate.

"Chop-chop," replied Luke.

"So they were alive when you left."

"Of course. I checked one, Bowman another, and Griffiths the driver. We put them all together in my cell, locked the door, and left."

"You're absolutely sure all three were still breathing when you left."

"Absolutely."

"Did Colonel Pickens have anything to do with your escape?"

"No, sir, but he was a big help when I was inside. Told Lieutenant Jackson to keep an eye on things while he was gone. He left the base two days before the escape. I owe him a great deal. He's a fine officer and a credit to Delta Force."

Wingate scribbled on his paper and put it down. "Luke, this little 'incident,' as we'll call it, has developed into a full-scale international shouting match. It doesn't just involve our forces and the Americans, it's got to the top of government, Downing Street and the White House both. General Alexander has been taking all the flack, as I only got here myself yesterday. He'll give you the lowdown, and I'll take it from there, okay?"

Alexander put on his reading glasses and picked up a sheet of paper. "This is a copy of a report submitted to the chiefs of staff at the Pentagon by General Collins. I'll read out the salient points insofar as they concern yourself:

To General A. D. F. Ravensteiger:

The report concerning objective Cave WMD307 that is being circulated in certain quarters is a complete fabrication. The true facts of the matter are as set out below:

1. Captain Dryden failed to submit a report to my office on completion of his assignment, Objective Cave WMD307. He also failed to carry out my specific orders concerning the purpose of the mission and became abusive when I took him to task over his failings.

2. In my view, these failings may have cost us the priceless opportunity of capturing Bin Laden's second in command, Mullah Omar, who was spotted in the area by one of our surveillance aircraft.

3. This officer showed a complete lack of respect for my authority and used insulting and degrading language impugning the integrity of myself, the United States armed forces, and honorable members of Congress. With the help of three deserters from his own command, they murdered three guards and made their escape in one of our vehicles. We are searching for the killers but we will be unable to intensify our search until such time as we have completed our current operations against the terrorists in the Wazir region.

General Alexander tossed the report aside with a look of utter contempt. "By God, you've crossed swords with a real bastard here, Luke. General Brooker of the Marine Corps paid me a visit before he left for Iraq and warned me about Collins. It seems the man is a sort of Captain Queeg in an Army uniform. Keeps to his office and relies on his subordinates to run the show. Takes the kudos when things go right but blames everyone except himself when they go wrong. Brooker says he's halfway over the edge and to be careful how we deal with him. He says he should never have been promoted, and it is only because of his friendship with Vice President Cheney that he's still in command of the 101st Airborne. As far as NATO is concerned, he might as well be over in Iraq with his division for all the help they get from him. We are in a real shooting war down here with the Taliban, and our position is getting more desperate by the day. We're taking very serious casualties now, and there is no sign that we're going to get any reinforcements this side of March."

"But I thought the prime minister had promised Washington that five thousand troops were on their way weeks ago," Luke complained.

"Bullshit. Window dressing for inaction," said Alexander, angrily.

"As a matter of fact, the Canadians have lost so many men recently that there's a great danger they will be pulled out altogether, especially since the other NATO countries won't commit any more troops. If that happens, then the Taliban will swamp us. We desperately need some help from the Americans up north but Collins won't send us so much as a bent rifle. He says he needs all his resources for his big push against the Taliban. Jesus Christ! Everybody knows there aren't any Taliban up there, they're all down here in Helmand. All he's up against are a few jihadis and mountain bandits, who will disappear over the border into Pakistan as soon as they hear the tanks coming. They'll suffer needless casualties, not from the enemy but from the weather and terrain. But then the most important American objective in Afghanistan is the capture of Osama Bin Laden, and you can be sure Cheney has impressed this on his blue-eyed boy, Collins, whether it's for the reward or for the honor. Colonel Wingate has asked me to pull 3Troop out of his command as soon as his so-called offensive is over. What do you make of Collins's allegation that you did not submit a report, Luke?"

"Unbelievable. I took it into the main office the day after we got back. In any case, if there was no report, why did three of the division's legal beagles visit me in jail with the report and ask me to alter some specific points?"

"Which you refused to do?"

"Not even a comma."

"Good for you," Alexander said approvingly. "Now then, I've been ordered by our pansyfied minister of defense to assist in your apprehension and that of your three accomplices, and if we succeed in doing so, we are to deliver you up to our friend General Collins. Imagine! This is the devious bastard who told the House of Commons that I had assured him that we were winning the battle against the Taliban and he would be able to withdraw two infantry battalions in time for Christmas. He has refused point blank to send in any more troops and is delaying the announcement of deaths and refusing to publish figures of the wounded altogether. Naturally, I told the minister to shove it and said that if I caught General Collins snooping on my sector, I would arrest him instead and throw him in the slammer. That remark hasn't gone down well with the chiefs of staff who, as no doubt you know, are munching cheese inside the minister's pocket every day. So what do I do with you? That's for your boss to decide. Right, Jock?"

"Afraid so," replied Wingate in a funereal-sounding voice. "Luke, Bob Thorpe of 4 Troop resigned last week, and I need someone to take his place immediately. I want that someone to be you. Any objections?"

"No, sir, none at all. What about Bowman, Griffiths, and Williams?"

"Bowman and Williams will go with you, Griffiths will stay here. General Alexander badly needs someone who speaks the language. What about Jackson; do you think he is capable of taking over 3 Troop? We're desperately short of fully trained officers at the moment, you know."

"He's a good man, likes responsibility. I'm sure he'll fit in nicely."

"Right, this business with the Americans is not going to go away, I can promise you that. However, since you'll be based in the British sector in Iraq, General Montgomery will see to it that there won't be any trouble. We shook hands on it."

"Excuse me, sir, why did Bob Thorpe resign?"

Wingate made a face. "Same reason all our best men in Iraq are thinking of following suit. He's been out there for three years now, with just a few R&Rs in Cyprus. His wife and kids want him home, and every time a Brit gets killed in Iraq, the wanting goes up a notch. You know Jim. He's a fine soldier, loves the regiment, but like all the men out there, he's not getting a square deal from our lousy government. We're now fighting against impossible odds with inferior equipment against insurgents who want us out so that they can sort out their own problems free of interference from outsiders. The Shia have turned really nasty now. They won't cooperate with us and don't want us in Basra and the towns, with the result that we're sitting targets hunkered down in bases and forward outposts all over the south. It's now turned into a full scale civil war. There are four or five competing insurgent armies fighting each other for control of territory and the oil fields, and we're caught right in the middle of it. It's similar to the situation we had in the Catholic areas of Northern Ireland, where every squaddie had to watch his back at night when the Provos came out of their holes, but in Iraq it's a hundred times worse, twenty-four hours a day. They have to guard against attack when they're asleep, patrolling on foot, or inside a Warrior or Challenger, and particularly when they're riding in supply convoys. The enemy has an unlimited supply of arms coming in from Iran, while we are having to rely on worn-out equipment that isn't being replaced by the cheap bastards at the ministry of defense. Now the insurgents have started to employ a new tactic: starving us of gasoline. Every tanker we have is a target, as is every storage tank on our bases. That means we're running out of gas for our vital supply convoys, and that is causing plenty of hardship, believe me. And while all this is going on, and we are losing men at the rate of twelve a day on the average, those lying bastards in Whitehall are telling the nation that we are winning the war and all troops will be out in twelve months. They've been saying that for six years now, and they keep getting away with it. It's crazy. The only reason we are still there is to save the faces of Blair and his gang. You agree, Rex?"

"One hundred percent," thundered the general, "and when I leave here, I am going to devote my every waking hour to bringing our cowardly, duplicitous rulers to book. They got away with sacrificing the lives of nearly a thousand British soldiers, including my two sons, on the altar of Catholic appeasement in Northern Ireland. By God, I will not allow them to escape the wrath of the new generation of thousands of men, women, and children who grieve for their loved ones as the jackals slink away and seek profits for their foul, inhuman deeds. Do you still want to go to Iraq, Luke? It's more dangerous than it's ever been, believe me."

"More than ever, sir," Luke replied.

Alexander stood up, put his arm around Luke's shoulder, and led him to the door. "I guarantee you'll make a big impact over there, Luke, but make sure you come back fit in mind and body. Our movement is going to need every soldier, serving or ex, when the time comes to save our country from the hands of those who seek to destroy it."

Chapter 7

Colonel Wingate had arranged to fly back to the UK the next morning, and Luke commandeered a Land Rover to take him to the airfield.

"No, Luke," said Wingate, "let's walk down to the plane. I feel like the exercise and besides, there are a number of things I want to discuss with you on the way. Tell the driver to meet us by the plane, will you?"

Luke spoke to the driver and caught up with the colonel. As he walked with him, he couldn't resist asking him the question that had been niggling him all night. "What did General Alexander mean when he talked about a movement, sir?" he asked.

Wingate stopped for a moment, looked at his depleted cigar, dropped it on the ground, and crushed it with his foot before answering.

"Luke, Rex Alexander is the finest judge of a man's character I've ever met. He wouldn't have even mentioned the word if he had not been 100 percent sure of your confidence, and of course, the fact that you're Jack Dryden's grandson does weigh heavily in your favor. The movement is a meeting of minds between a growing number of senior officers in the army, the navy, and the air force. Rex, Grant Montgomery, and myself are founder members of the organization. We all have different reasons for belonging but Rex's motivation is stronger than most. If you remember, he lost two sons in Northern Ireland, both to a sniper's bullet."

"From a bloody Barrett's rifle," Luke said bitterly.

"Just so. The killers have been rewarded with an amnesty by our pathetic government but Rex will never rest until they have been brought to justice, and his kind of justice means the hangman's rope. The rest of us are appalled at the total disregard the politicians have for the safety and well-being of our armed forces: the fake wars, the mendacity, and the cruel, needless loss of life that is growing by the day. Just as these creatures have destroyed the impartiality and integrity of the civil service, the courts, and the police service, so they are now seeking to suborn the last enduring institution of our once great nation, and I regret to say, they are succeeding. We happen to know that the three chiefs of staff have been secretly guaranteed peerages and gold-plated pensions on retirement, and they are all too likely to accept them. As a result, any serving officer who criticizes the government can forget about promotion, and that includes complaints about the shortages and faulty equipment that are now costing us serious casualties, especially in Iraq."

"Is it as bad as it is here?" Luke asked.

"Worse. I've been there for three weeks, and believe me, the troops are stretched to the absolute limit, with no prospect of things getting any easier. Montgomery told me that he asked for an additional three battalions of infantry, and they sent him two companies, one of which was the Royal Engineers. He is now so stretched that he has had to withdraw units from the Iranian border and the main oilfields. Result? Arms and volunteers are pouring in from Iran, and the insurgents now control most of the oilfields and refineries. Our troops are now in a very dangerous, no-win situation and must be withdrawn immediately if we are to avoid a catastrophe. Everyone from field officers to war correspondents is shouting out this undeniable fact from the rooftops, but the chiefs of staff have gone stone deaf. They prefer to put on their hearing aids and listen to what their lords and masters in the government tell them to do. And as if this is not enough, our own Intelligence Corps is picking up nasty little bits of information that movements are afloat to take on the Iranians."

Luke shook his head in bewilderment. "But that's madness. They might destroy the Iranian cities and nuclear facilities, but their armies on the frontier would join up with the Iraqi insurgents and massacre our troops in double quick time. It's unthinkable, insane."

Wingate swore. "Not when you've got two bloody megalomaniacs running the show like Bush in the White House and his ass-licker in Downing Street. Look what happened after Bush came to power and how they softened up a gullible public with lies and innuendo and patriotic blandishments. Now they're at it again, only this time it's much more serious. The big lie this time is that Iran will have the bomb in less than one year, yet only a few months ago, the best brains in the business were telling us that it would be eight years before they were able to make a deliverable H-bomb. How can all those experts be proved so wrong on the say-so of proven liars? I quite believe Iran will build a bomb eventually, but not inside five to ten years, and that will give us plenty of time to get the hell out of the Middle East and let the Arabs sort out their own problems. In any case, why should Iran be singled out for punishment? Every sovereign nation has a God-given right to defend itself, and if I was living next to an aggressive, American-backed nation like Israel, I wouldn't rest until I achieved parity with their stock of H-bombs, which now exceeds that of our own country."

Luke looked at his boss intently. He had never seen him so angry and disillusioned, and it worried him. "But sir," he asked, "have we got any hard evidence or is it just conjecture?"

"I feel it in my bones, Luke. I've never forgotten the public warning President Eisenhower gave his nation about the danger of the U.S. military-industrial complex shaping up to take control in America and eventually the world. Their new, unwritten foreign policy is, 'If they're not with us, bomb 'em back to the Stone Age.' Thanks to Bush, they are now totally in control, the military arm through its acquisition of trillions of dollars worth of armaments, and the industrial arm through the manufacture and supply of those weapons. They are practically giving away unwanted or obsolete weaponry to countries that should never be trusted with them. All they have to do is sign up to Bush's line on his so-called war on terror, and the sky's the limit. God knows how many dictators like Saddam Hussein this crazy policy has created and sustained. How we ever got so close to America, I will never know. I wouldn't trust them as far as

I can spit tobacco. Look at the way they cut and run in Vietnam when the going got tough. They will do exactly the same in the Middle East, once they have bombed the hell out of Iran. Their Achilles' heel is body bags arriving regularly, day and night, at airports in the United States. Once that happens, they'll pull the plug on all their much vaunted commitments to the rest of the world, leaving a trail of destruction in their wake. By God, if there is one power in the world that is capable of destroying our civilization, it is America, and it is only a matter of time before one of their lunatics finds a way to press the doomsday button. Only a miracle can save the world from that fate. To answer your question about hard evidence, the answer is no. Any other questions?"

"Just one. If we do come across Yanks cooking up some nasty business, what do we do?"

"Good question. I'll give you answer to that when it happens."

"Yes, sir, understood."

Wingate smiled at Luke and held out his hand. "Good luck and take care of yourself, Luke. Your grandfather has every reason to be proud of you."

Luke felt a lump in his throat as he watched Jock Wingate walk up the steps of the plane and disappear through the door without looking back. The shoulders were not so straight anymore and the eyes not so bright. He carried a responsibility few men are called upon to shoulder. The Regiment was his family, and as tough as he was, the old soldier would mourn the loss of an SAS member as he would his own son. His love of the army and its ideals was legendary, and an example of his compassion was revealed right here before Luke's very eyes. For instead of a chartered plane or an executive jet to take him home in comfort, Jock had chosen a C-130 transport. And his companions inside the plane were the latest batch of dead British servicemen, killed in action and on their last journey home.

"You mean to tell me you let that fucking Wingate pull those murdering squaddies of his out of Afghanistan altogether and send them into hiding? Jesus Christ, man, what the fuck do you think you were playing about at? I told you how important it was to get them under lock and key and ship them over to America."

Alastair Campbell suffered fools badly, and in his opinion, there was no other person in the cabinet dimmer than Dudley Cantwell Coward, the defense secretary.

The most powerful man in Britain was in a foul mood, and the minister of defense cursed his luck at being first choice for what he knew would be a torrid day for a goodly number of ministers and civil servants. He knew that Campbell had been seething for hours about the latest development in the pursuit of Luke Dryden. Now, he was about to receive a telling off comparable to the one he had given the chauffer who had, without permission, taken his beloved Bentley on a pub crawl with his mates and returned it minus the front end and windshield. Furthermore, the last tirade he had received only a week ago had been accompanied with the threat that the next cockup would surely be the last.

Coward looked up at the most hated face in Whitehall and searched for the slightest hint of compassion, but there was none. The tall figure seemed to tower over him, and the elongated chin appeared to wag stronger with every word he spoke. He was no longer the handsome political fixer who had anyone who was anybody eating out of his hand. His curly black hair was now streaked with grey and his eyes bore the hollow look of a person who had suffered much angst. He was coarser and rarely smiled anymore except when he was in the company of his own kind in Lancashire or with his friends in the unions. But the one characteristic that the public and his associates remembered him for was his long, pointy nose, the organ that had marked him out as Fleet Street's number one journalist for sniffing out political scandal when he worked for the *Mirror* tabloid.

However, that was before he was unceremoniously dumped by Tony Blair as a sop to those members of the party who were intent on replacing himself as prime minister.

Dudley Coward's reply was surly and defensive. "Good God, Alastair, we did our best. We had over a hundred military police searching for them but our field officers in Afghanistan are as thick as thieves. They hid them from us until Wingate arrived on the scene, and then they all disappeared."

Coward was lying through his teeth. He had sent a squad from Special Branch hot-footing it over to Afghanistan, only for them to be told by General Alexander that if they were still on his base by nightfall, he would have them taken to a Taliban stronghold on the border and left to enjoy the tender mercies of their womenfolk.

Campbell looked at him suspiciously. "Wingate landed at Northolt two hours ago. He came in a plane full of dead bodies and was picked up by a chopper. Went straight back to Credenhill."

"Dead bodies, you say?" said Coward excitedly. "That's it! Don't you see, the bugger is using corpses to get his men back to the safety of his base. Pound to a pinch of shit the four murderers have used body bags as cover. Maybe even pulled dead bodies out to make room for themselves, the sacrilegious bastards."

Campbell stared thoughtfully at the minister for a moment, went to his desk, picked up the phone, and dialed a number. "Check on the C-130 that landed at Northolt two hours ago," he ordered. "Undo every body bag, and check to see if they are well and truly dead. Then count the bodies and check them off against the manifest. Any discrepancies, call me back immediately."

There was the sound of a voice protesting in the earpiece, and Campbell shouted, "Just fucking do it!" and slammed down the receiver.

"Good grief, Ali, what's all the fuss about?" The noise had woken the prime minister, who had dozed off on the sofa, his empty mug still grasped in his hand.

Campbell glowered at the sleepy figure. "Those SAS soldiers who murdered three Yanks have slipped through our fingers, and this useless idiot here is trying to bullshit his way out of accepting responsibility. One of these days, Dudley and his ministry of cockups are going to do something right, and I'll have three heart attacks and an ejaculation."

Tony Blair sat up straight, concern showing on his tired, unshaven face. "Is that true, Dudley? They really got away?"

"I'm afraid so, Tony. Those bloody SAS know every trick in the book. That's why every government in trouble comes asking for their services, don't you know."

"Good Lord, what am I going to tell Cheney? He'll be hopping mad. He was counting on us delivering them into his hands so that he could placate his favorite general in Afghanistan."

"Tell the creep to go fuck himself," swore Campbell angrily. "Either that or tell him to send his boys over here and extract them from Credenhill. I know the SAS act rough but the story Fatso Collins put out about their crimes stinks to high heaven. I've read it three times, and it's as full of holes as my fishing net."

"Don't talk like that, Ali," scolded Blair. "I'm going over there next week, and I'm in the dog house with Cheney as it is. It would have helped a lot if I could have told him he can pick them up. He's as mad as hell with me because we aren't patrolling the border in our sector effectively enough, and the insurgents are infiltrating the American sector with Iranian arms and jihadis."

"Another cock-up by the ministry of defense," snorted Campbell. "Dudley publicly promised two thousand fresh reinforcements, and all they got was two hundred. The loony left in Parliament count for more in his calculations than the poor bloody squaddies being shot up around Basra."

"Not true," squeaked Coward. "We've hit a crisis in army recruitment. It's dried up completely, now we're taking heavy casualties and the body bags are piling up at Northolt. Bad news travels fast. Some traitorous bastard from the *Mail* worked out that a squaddie on a twelve-hour watch under fire from the insurgents gets exactly £2.40 an hour and pays tax and council tax, whereas an ex-soldier riding shotgun in Baghdad picks up £2,000 a week, tax free. Result, no serving squaddie in his right mind is going to sign on again, and there is no chance of recruitment here when the minimum hourly wage is £5.50 and unemployment benefits nearly as much. I've worked my tail off trying to get more money out of the Treasury but it's like getting blood from a stone. In fact, they are talking about cutting our budget like everybody else's."

"What a load of bullshit," swore Campbell. "You people waste more money than what goes out to the men in the field. All you do is make grandiose promises and then stuff your little empire with thousands of bean counters, consultants, and PR personnel. I've seen the figures. You could cut fifty thousand jobs off your establishment and still have the same number surplus to requirement. Promises, promises. Two years ago, you promised that all C-130 transports would be fitted with explosion-suppressant foam, and so far you've only done one, and that's still in this country. Since then, two more have crashed and burst into flames. Who do you think is going to volunteer for the army if they're going to be transported around the Middle East in flying coffins?"

"That was Robert Reid did the promising. I wasn't with the ministry of defense then."

"That's no bloody excuse. You've had a year to do something, and you've done sweet fuck-all."

The PM broke in hastily. "Now, now, chaps, that sort of talk will get us nowhere. What's done is done. Now we've got to do something positive about these SAS murderers. Why don't we get the army to storm the base at Credenhill and bring the fugitives out forcibly?"

"No way," replied Campbell. "The top brass might allow it, but the lower ranks will refuse point blank to carry out the order. We'd have a mutiny on our hands."

"Well, what about Kruger and his Paramilitaries? There's thousands of them, and they've done absolutely nothing since the force was formed. It's time they earned their corn."

"I've already asked Kruger when he will be ready to sort them out, and he told me it would be another six months at the earliest. Said it was a very difficult operation, and his men were intent on receiving the same type of training the SAS used so they could fight them on equal terms."

"Good God, Ali, equal terms?" Blair protested. "Why, there are a hundred thousand Paramilitaries, and there can't be more than five hundred SAS personnel on base. What's he playing about at?"

"He's a loudmouthed, arrogant Boer, and he's got a yellow streak a mile long. He's scared shitless about taking on the SAS. He'll stall and stall until half his force is pensioned off."

Blair scratched his head. "Well, something's got to be done and quick. Tell you what, let's bomb the bastards out like we did in Baghdad. Flatten the place completely. Don't leave a brick standing. I never did like the SAS. We'd be better off without them. They're becoming a menace. It's a well-known fact that if the army ever did attempt a coup, the SAS would be right up front. Jesus Christ, the first place they would go for is 10 Downing Street, and they wouldn't give a shit if they blew it to pieces."

"But if you bombed Credenhill, you would probably kill the fugitives. I thought you said Cheney wanted them alive," protested a frustrated Campbell.

"Well, if we're not going to get them alive, the next best thing is corpses. Cheney will have to settle for that. You know what he says about terrorists: get them, dead or alive."

"And who are you going to get to drop the bombs, Tony?" asked Campbell patiently.

"Why, the RAF of course. That's what we pay them for, isn't it?"

Campbell watched as Coward edged away to the window and stood open-mouthed, afraid to say anything in case he became implicated in the fantastic plot unfolding before his very eyes.

"Come off it, Tony, nobody in the RAF would contemplate such a thing, even Air Chief Marshall Plantagenet."

"Well, we'll get the Yanks to do it. They've got plenty of bombers down at Fairford. Credenhill is right on their doorstep. I'm sure Cheney would okay it."

"No way, Tone," Campbell said, looking pityingly down at the prime minister, who was staring at the bottom of his empty mug. "The country would go berserk. They worship the fucking gung-ho SAS. Anyway, you can bet your life the survivors would come looking for whoever ordered the bombing, and that would mean curtains for every member of our government."

Good God, Campbell thought to himself, *Tony's lost his marbles since his return. Looks like he's been praying with Cheney and his neo-cons again. But the scary thing is that he's deluded enough to believe his actions are justified, and moreover Cheney would agree to the bombing without batting an eyelid.*

The remark seemed to unsettle Blair. He hated physical violence of any kind, especially violence directed at his own person and that of his family. "Well," he said plaintively, "we've got to do something pretty damn quick before I go to Washington. What do you suggest, Ali?"

Campbell was silent for a moment. The issue was far too important to be settled here and now. It needed to be kicked into the long grass or directed into the hands of a master of guile and obfuscation. His eyes lit up. "Sorry, Tone," he purred, "this one is just too big for me. I suggest we give it to Mandy. He'll come up with the right answer, I'm sure of that. Don't you agree, Dudley?"

Chapter 8

S AS B Squadron was charged with patrolling the 120-mile stretch of the Iraq border between Al Ahmara in the north and Abadan in the south. Their purpose was to halt the flow of arms and insurgents from Iran and, in addition, protect the oil pipeline and oil facilities in the immediate area.

Luke felt at home in the desert. After all, it was where the SAS had its origins, where its unique techniques were developed and its elite reputation was established. The terrain in Iraq was similar to that of the Western Desert, Oman and Arabia, it was only the tactics that had changed. Whereas David Stirling and his Special Forces made do with modified Jeeps armed with light machine guns, Luke's troop boasted the latest long-base Range Rovers, armored and fitted with a fearsome range of weapons including twin 50mm heavy machine guns, Milan-5 anti-tank launchers, Stinger anti-aircraft missiles, H&K automatic grenade launchers, and anti-personnel RPGs. It also carried a copious amount of diesel and stores and something that David Stirling would have given his eyeteeth for: a state-of-the-art satellite guidance and communications system. On top of that, the patrol could normally call on back-up in the form of ground support Tornados or Apache gunships, support that Stirling rarely enjoyed.

But these were not normal times. The British army was fighting with its back to the wall in a vast, inhospitable sector teeming with insurgents hell-bent on driving the infidels out of their sacred land. The battle for the hearts and minds of the Shia population had been lost. Now it was a war of attrition, a battle to hold the line until the devious Labor government deemed it could no longer survive in office as the public clamor for the extraction of the army grew stronger and stronger. There were those in the ministry of defense who feared that the casualty figures now being desperately massaged or held back were sucking the effectiveness out of the force as recruitment collapsed and reinforcements became nonexistent. And as the fighting strength of the army deteriorated, the enemy increased alarmingly in numbers and modern weaponry, much of it smuggled over the border from Iran.

Thank heaven for small mercies, thought Luke, *at least they were spared the menace of air attacks, but it would surely be only a matter of time before the insurgents acquired aircraft or the Iranian air force openly supported them.*

For eighteen long months, Luke's "Pinkies" roamed the southern border of eastern Iraq, setting up ambushes at crossings identified by satellite surveillance. They bore down on endless convoys of gun-runners, scattering their columns and making them easy meat for picking them off at their leisure. The SAS appeared out of the blue, in the blazing heat of the day and sometimes in the bone-chilling cold of the desert night, catching the insurgents off guard and giving them no chance of forming a rearguard or mounting a counterattack. They tore along the vital oil supply lines, intercepting gangs of saboteurs and scaring off insurgents who were preventing oil crews from repairing damaged pipelines. Appeals for help from British troops in forward outposts were given top priority and many lives were saved by devastating raids on the rear of the attackers and their supply lines. So successful did 4Troop become that Luke was given another troop after four months and then another two months later. Deprived of weapons and explosives, the insurgents were forced to reduce their attacks, giving the British forces time to reorganize and devise a new defense strategy: employing mobility rather than fixed positions, which had been the basis of the "hearts and minds" policy forced on the army by the politicians in Whitehall.

Casualties among the SAS were surprisingly light considering the intense attacks they were subjected to night and day. In fact, there were only sixteen deaths altogether. Four of them, the entire crew of a Pinkie, were the result of an attack from the air by an American A10 tank-buster. These last cruel deaths were the ultimate nightmare of a commander in the field—the so-called friendly fire syndrome.

Luke was in the lead vehicle of 4Troop when the A10 Warthog was spotted approaching the column head-on at around three thousand meters high. The troop was not within a fifty-mile radius of any base or forward outpost on his map, and he had certainly not requested back-up from any U.S. command. "Get in touch with him immediately and find out what's he's looking for," he ordered his radio man. "At the double."

He stood up and focused his glasses on the plane as it came closer, seeking some sign of recognition from the pilot and his intentions. "No reply!" the radio man shouted. "No recognition sign of any kind."

Luke swore. "Shit, keep on trying, Pete. I don't like the look of this bastard at all. Tell all crews to prepare to take evasive action and ready their Stingers."

He swept his memory for the instructions he had received on the Warthog battlefield tactics. Over enemy territory, any vehicle that moved would be attacked unless it carried a recognition symbol: orange-colored panels. Over disputed territory, a friend-or-foe signal would be sent to any prospective target, asking three times for a password. Only if the target silhouette was definitely identifiable was the second requirement to be ignored. The Warthog pilot would spend around five minutes seeking the recognition signal, and if none was received, it would lock on to the target and attack, letting off anti-missile flares as it came down and got within range for its own missiles.

"No luck!" shouted Pete. "Either his radio is down or he's deaf as a jock on a piss-up."

"Right," said Luke. "I've got a nasty feeling coming over. Tell the others to spread out. At the first sign of offensive action, I'm going to leave the line, hare up the road two hundred meters, and make a U so that I come belting back fifty meters clear of any other Pinkie. If the plane targets us, give it the works; number one crew on its approach, number two amidships, and three crew up its ass. Got that?"

"Yes, sir."

"Good. Kiwi, make ready to burn rubber. Tell me something, squire. If you were out duck shooting, which bird would you shoot at, the ones sitting on their asses or the ones on the wing?"

"The ones on the wing every time. There ain't no fun shooting a sitting duck unless you're desperate for grub," replied Kiwi, a fanatical game hunter.

"That's what I thought. Let's hope the Yank isn't a city-bred dimwit who doesn't know a duck from a bald eagle."

Luke trained his glasses on the Warthog again as it came directly overhead and began to circle their position, once, then twice. At the start of the third circle, it straightened out and started to come down, releasing an anti-missile flare as it did so.

"Let's go, Kiwi!" shouted Luke, and the Pinkie leapt forward, churning up the sand as it sped forward and turned into the U return. The Warthog came screaming down, throwing out flares every ten seconds, hell-bent on destruction.

"Bloody hell," swore Luke, "he's refused the bait. He's heading straight for number two." Rising to his feet, he shouted into his headset, "Take evasive action, Jimbo, he's onto you! All crews, fire your missiles now."

Luke saw the missile leave number two vehicle but it was too late. It had barely left the launcher when a missile from the Warthog slammed into it, turning it over and setting it on fire. The Warthog leveled off and began to gain altitude, having apparently evaded three missiles chasing after it. "Hold on and take it coming back!" Luke shouted at his gunner.

The instruction was unnecessary, for at that very moment, the Warthog exploded in midair, and the resultant fireball came tumbling down no more than two hundred meters from their own position, sending out explosions that continued for a full minute after it hit the ground.

All three Pinkies converged on the stricken Pinkie, their crews jumping off before the vehicles had come to a full stop. They sprayed foam on the flames until it looked as if it was buried in snow and then began the harrowing task of looking for survivors.

Luke stood alone in his Pinkie, grim-faced, watching every movement as his men searched the wreckage. Ten minutes later, Kiwi came up to him, shaking his head. "Sorry, Luke, no survivors," he said sorrowfully. "Okay to bag them up now?"

"Yes, put them all in the same Pinkie and cover them with the flag."

"What about the Yanks? You want us to go over and check them out too?"

"No," replied Luke with a degree of bitterness he had never experienced before. "Let the gung-ho bastards burn. And if they go to hell as they deserve to, then I hope they burn there too."

Major Tunney got up as Luke entered the office of General Montgomery and laughed at the startled look on his face. "Sorry to surprise you like this, Luke," he said as he held out his hand. "I thought it's about time I came over and checked up on what you chaps are up to."

Luke really was surprised. Harvey Tunney was the top spook at Credenhill, and he had never seen him off the base, let alone out of the country.

"Have a seat, Luke," said General Montgomery. "You're going to need it when you hear what the major has to say."

Tunney sat opposite Luke and cleared his throat. "Luke, what I have to tell you is so bloody confidential that I couldn't trust any of our normal lines of communications, coded or otherwise, to convey it to you, hence my visit in person. It has to do with signals we have been picking up from an area in the Iranian mountains forty kilometers southeast of Ilam. As the crow flies, that is directly across the border from Al Kut. Have you noticed any unusual activity in that area at all?"

Luke thought for a moment. "Across from Al Kut? Sorry, we don't operate that far north. Our sector ends just north of Al Amarah; from there on, it's American territory. It's around seventy kilometers from there to Al Kut."

Tunney looked extremely disappointed. "Nothing at all? No stories of unusual air traffic, troop movements, strange things that go bump in the night. That sort of thing?"

"Sorry, Harvey, we don't come across much traffic coming down from there. Mostly our traffic goes north as we close out the border crossings and force the insurgents to try their luck up there. Maybe I could give you something better if I knew what it is you're after."

"Very well, I'll tell you but I must warn you that I am speaking in the strictest confidence. What you hear from me must not be repeated outside this room. Understood?"

Luke smiled inwardly. Tunney was a brilliant intelligence officer, but he was inclined to go over the top on occasions. He was like a boffin who would go to any length to conceal the six-digit combination of his bicycle lock. But this had to be big to bring him out to Iraq and insist on holding the meeting in the OC's office. He put his left hand on his heart, raised his right hand, and nodded his head in acknowledgment.

"Take a look at this." Tunney pointed at a map spread out on the general's desk, and Luke got up and studied it.

"You see this mountain area over the border in Iran? It's called 'Ten Peaks' in English, all huddled together with only narrow inhospitable canyons separating them from each other. For the past two weeks, we've been picking up unidentified signals coming from this area. The signals are encrypted, and they are being transmitted to and from the U.S. Skynet military satellite system. At first, we didn't pay much attention to the chatter. We know U.S. Special Forces are working inside Iran, have been for the last five years. Also the chatter we picked up was similar to that exchanged between both our own and U.S. Special Forces, except that this source does not move on to a new location after a period of time. The chatter is fixed in one location and is increasing in intensity, leading us to believe that there are a lot of bodies out there engaged in some kind of secret project. We have asked for an explanation for this activity from our opposite number in the Pentagon, and they assure us that it is consistent with their policy of seeking out secret nuclear facilities throughout Iran and refuse to divulge any more information than that. It's bullshit, of course, and an insult to our intelligence. The Iranians are putting all their facilities underground. The idea that they would build something important in such an inhospitable locality is simply ludicrous."

"But surely you've got photographs of the site, Harvey," said Luke. "I thought we had a satellite of our own specifically aimed at Iran."

"Not any more. It's kaput. Went on the blink six months ago, and the cheapskates in the ministry of defense say it will be another year before they have the funds to put up a replacement. Can you beat that! The one place in the world where World War III is liable to break out at any time, and we haven't got a clue what's going on below."

"Well, we've got spy planes in reserve, haven't we?"

"Yes, but we can't use them either. After the fiasco when the Iranians captured a Royal Navy patrol boat in their waters and humiliated both the navy and politicians, all services are under strict orders not to infringe on their territory by land, sea, or air."

Luke swore. "Jesus Christ, you couldn't make it up! That means you're going to disobey orders and send in the SAS, right?"

"In a nutshell, yes," replied Tunney. "That's why you're here and I'm here, as far away from our rotten politicians as it's possible to get. The boss has picked you for the job because (a) you are in close proximity to the target and (b) the topography is very similar to the White Mountains in Afghanistan."

"Plus the fine job you've been doing along the border, I might add," General Montgomery said, nodding his head in agreement. "Luke, I don't like the smell of this. As a matter of fact, I've got a very nasty feeling that won't go away. There's a madman out of control in Washington who will stop at nothing to achieve a regime change in Iran, just as he did with Saddam Hussein. The man has completely lost touch with reality. He's been ranting and raving about the threat posed by the ayatollahs for years, and now he's preparing for just one last throw of the dice. The fact that the lives of all the coalition forces in Iraq may be put into jeopardy by his actions means nothing to him. In fact, our occupation is a sideshow to his messianic war on terror and his guardianship of the state of Israel. Of course the Iranians are supplying arms to the insurgents, they are allies of the Shia, after all. But there is no sign that they are about to up the ante, despite all the provocation from Washington. Have you seen any troop movements or armor massing on your stretch of the border?"

Luke shook his head.

"Nor will you. The Iranians are playing a waiting game. They know that as the economic crisis hits rock bottom, the United States will be forced to withdraw its forces and leave the Iraqis to sort out their own problems. And that is how it should be. But if they are attacked, they will react violently, and if they supplement the Shia with heavy armor and air support, there is no way we can hold the fort without suffering heavy casualties and eventual defeat. And by God, I am not about to let that happen. Are you up to the job, Luke?"

Luke glanced at the pale, earnest face of Harvey Tunney and broke into a wide grin. "Of course I am, sir. If Major Tunney can find the time to come all the way out here to spy on us, I'm sure I can find the time to do likewise to the bloody Yankee trespassers."

Chapter 9

It was nearly midnight when the four-man patrol crossed the border into the Iraq province of Ilam and made for the mountainous region of Bakhtaran. Luke had handpicked the other three members: Kiwi Bowman, Tommy Williams, and mountain man himself, Ghurkha Corporal Kulbr Rai, or Sunshine, as he was known to his comrades.

Bowman was his number two. He would have trusted the lanky New Zealander with his life in any situation and then some. Taciturn and self-effacing, Kiwi was the epitome of his country's fighting men. Luke's grandfather had regaled him with tales of the bravery of New Zealand and Australian troops in the Western Desert campaigns, which had impressed him to the extent that he would probably base his selection on nationality alone. On top of that, Kiwi was adept at communications equipment.

Williams was a hard-drinking career soldier with almost twenty years of service under his belt. A fitness fanatic, he could have made top grade in any country's army but he seemed to be satisfied with the two stripes he had worn now for over eight years. Luke suspected that it was his argumentative nature that had held him back, but his record with the Paras was excellent, and he had passed the SAS induction test at the first attempt.

Sunshine Rai was an automatic pick on the basis of his upbringing in a mountainous region of Nepal. He was an expert in field craft and had been recommended to Jock Wingate by the OC of the Ghurkha

Brigade based in Wiltshire. Small in height and wide of body, Sunshine was a favorite in any formation on account of his cheerful nature and capacity for prolonged surveillance operations.

Kiwi and Sunshine had studied the contour map of the target area and settled on a journey time of four days to reach the mountain, travelling during the hours of darkness. In fact, they made such good progress that they reached the foot of the target at 0100 on the third day and set up a hideout within a nest of boulders a few hundred meters farther up the slope.

Luke left the hideout and walked a meter back in order to take a look at the top of the mountain from a new angle, but when he came within sight of it, there wasn't the slightest hint of any activity at the top, not even the glimmer of any artificial lights. He took another sighting farther on and was disappointed once more. It was too late for another try, and he hurried back to the hideout to give the news to the others just as the sun announced its entry into the eastern sky.

"You got a good look at the hill, Sunshine," he said to the Ghurkha. "What's your estimate now for getting up there? I'm talking about all of us, not just you with your mountain-goat legs."

Sunshine smiled broadly. "For me, three hours; for you chappies, maybe five hours," he said in his cheerful, sing-song voice.

Luke was impressed. "Good, only we might not have to climb that far. The spooks have pinpointed the Source as eight thousand meters up, so for starters we'll go up to six thousand and take a look-see. We'll kip here till dusk. Until then, I want no careless movement or smoke of any kind. I'm pretty sure there will be American Special Forces around, and if they are doing something secret up there, they are bound to have a spy satellite in a stationary orbit. Those babies can spot a pair of grasshoppers mating under a fig leaf, believe you me. What puzzles me is how they are hiding their activities. The Iranians are bound to have a military plane fly over at some time or another, or even a civilian aircraft might spot something. Any ideas, anyone?"

"They could be doing it under cover of darkness," suggested Tommy Williams. "Civilian aircraft would keep well clear of these mountains at night, and I don't suppose the military do much night flying anyway. Did the spooks give you any specific times for the radio transmissions they picked up?"

"Yes, haphazard during the hours of daylight only. They must think that if work is going on, it would be wiser to do it in daytime, as noise travels much farther at night."

"Well, it beats me unless they have some kind of black-out gear up there," suggested Williams.

"Okay," said Luke, "we'll find out tonight. I suggest we have some breakfast and a well-earned rest. Standard two-hour watch. I'll take first, and then Kiwi, Tommy, and Sunshine."

The patrol halted some two thousand meters from the top, and Luke swept the visible area above him with his NVGs. "Nothing up there," he said to Kiwi after a long scan. "We'll do a lateral until we come back to this point. Make a note of our bearings now."

They moved on, picking their way carefully through the jagged rocks and gullies with the aid of their NVGs, cursing silently if they disturbed a stone or caught a limb on the shards of rock sticking out like bayonets in the most unlikely places. They had covered more than half the distance from their starting point when Sunshine, the lead man, came to a sudden stop and pointed his hand at something ahead of him. Luke hurried to the front and trained his glasses on the area indicated. Tracks, unmistakable vehicle tracks, coming up from below and disappearing into the gloom directly above.

"Jesus Christ," whispered Williams. "How in the hell does a vehicle get up there, even if it's fitted with tracks?"

"Easy," Kiwi replied. "I've seen one operating back home. It's called a Mountaineer and carries a crew of three. It can climb at an incredible angle, and when the going gets too rough or too steep, the crew get out and haul a cable up to a spot farther up and spike it into the rocks. Then the driver starts up a winch, and the machine hauls itself up to the anchor point. A bit hairy but very effective."

"How far up this mountain would you say it could climb?" asked Luke.

"About three-quarters. I can't see it going any farther. If it gets too steep, the machine would likely start swinging on the end of the cable."

"Well, it looks like they're building something big up there but we haven't got time to check it out before daylight. We'll follow the tracks down and find out what the score is, and then it's back to the hideout and an early start as soon as it gets dark. Spread out, two either side of the tracks."

"See anything?" whispered Kiwi as Luke came to a halt and took out his glasses.

Luke didn't answer right away as he concentrated on the spot where the tracks came to a sudden end.

"Take a look and tell me what you see, Hawkeye."

Kiwi took the glasses and took his time surveying the tracks. "They go nowhere. Looks like that rock-face is the end of the line to me."

"What if the rock-face is a fake, you know, a curtain hiding a cave like up in the White Mountains?"

Kiwi trained the glasses on the wall again. "If it is, it's a bloody good bit of camouflage. Can't tell really in this light; want me to go and take a closer look?"

"If it was a cave, what would you expect to see outside?"

"A guard. Maybe two."

"Correct. Go down and take a look, we'll wait here till you come back."

Luke signaled for Sunshine and Williams to cross over and join him. "We think the tracks end up in a cave," he said quietly. "Kiwi's checking out for guards. I reckon it'll be an hour before he makes it back."

Kiwi did better than that, by at least fifteen minutes. "There's two," he said, panting with exertion. "They're in a dug-out about ten meters away from the rock-face. Looks like one's awake and the other's asleep. If I came over the bank at their rear, I could take them easy. Still can't see an opening, though; it's too bloody dark. Something else. The tracks don't end at the wall, they curve left and run down into a ravine."

"Good man, Kiwi, we'll break off now and come around lower down next time. If there is a cave there, we've got some preparations to make. Who's going to volunteer to make himself invisible and see what happens when they change the guard?"

"I will, boss-man," answered Sunshine. "I'd rather kip down here in lovely fresh air than spend the night choked up by you fart-asses."

"Okay, Sunshine," laughed Luke. "Lie low and don't forget there might be a satellite spying on you. Meet us at the bottom around twenty-one hundred. Pleasant dreams."

"It's a sure thing now that they only work in daylight," Kiwi suggested as they made their way down to their hideout. "That means we have to make a decision now whether we take on the bottom cave or the top cave first. I say we take on the bottom cave. If they're feeding stuff up to the top, then that must be where most of the bods are. If anything goes wrong, we'll have a better chance of escaping."

"I'm with you on that. How about you, Tommy?" asked Luke.

"Me too, but what about communications? If we take them out down below, it's going to take at least two hours to climb to the top. What if they try and communicate with each other in the meantime?"

Luke looked thoughtful. "Good point but we'll have to take a chance on that. We'll go for it at midnight and hope that the lazy bastards are kipping down in both caves, okay?"

"Okay," replied Kiwi.

"Me too," agreed Williams.

"It's a cave all right," Sunshine said excitedly as he returned to the hideout. "The wall is just piece of canvas that they must roll upward to about three meters from the inside. Just inside is a tracked, camouflaged machine with a big wheel on front that looks something like a tractor. It never came outside. Maybe it's their day off."

"How many bods?" asked Luke.

"Can't be sure; I counted eight all day including the two on guard."

"What's the rota?"

"Four on, four off, last change 1800."

"What units were they?"

"No can tell, all in khaki fatigues. Could not savvy shoulder flashes. Think they are like engineers."

"So they're probably Army then," remarked Luke. "What were they doing all day if the tractor was idle?"

"Sweet FA," Sunshine replied disgustedly. "Play cards, drink beer, read funnies. Never come out in open. Only the two guards, and they make it very snappy. Must have lavatory inside cave, I think."

"Were they armed?"

"Yes, M16s. One with sidearm. Officer I think."

"Anything else?"

"All keep very quiet, nothing else."

"This canvas. When they closed it, did it just hit the ground or did they stake it down from the inside?"

"Don't think so, no noise or movement after come down."

"What about up top, any movement there?"

"Nothing, no see nothing all time."

"Good work, Sunshine," Luke said, appreciatively. "Now let's get our heads together and figure out exactly how we're going to tell these people to stop trespassing on other people's property."

It took Kiwi and Sunshine less than ten minutes to overpower the two guards; tape their mouths, hands, and feet; tie them back to back; and prostrate them inside their dug-out. All four of them then crept silently up to the canvas curtain, where Luke bent down and grasped the edge touching the ground, feeling for its strength and its thickness. He took out his combat knife and held it high, just touching the canvas, as Kiwi and Williams stood on either side, hands ready to take hold of each flap as Luke prepared to slice through the canvas and open it up. Behind Luke crouched Sunshine, his rife at the ready with its flashlight switched on. "Now!" whispered Luke as he jabbed in his knife and, using both hands, sliced rapidly through the canvas until he reached the floor. Kiwi and Williams jerked the flaps open and Luke went in, closely followed by Sunshine and then Kiwi and Williams.

Their lights were not needed, for the cave was quite well lit by two overhead lamps hanging from the roof. At the rear of the tractor, in an untidy line, were six single iron beds, all of them occupied.

"Quick, close the flaps," Luke whispered to Kiwi. He moved up to the bed on the left, and when he was satisfied the other five were being covered, he jabbed his rifle hard into the body of the sleeping occupant.

"Wake up," he said menacingly. "One false move and I'll blow a hole in your chest. Sit up slowly and put both hands through the bars of your bed head."

Half-asleep and visibly frightened, the soldier did as he was told, and Luke quickly stepped round the bed and fastened his hands together with a plastic handcuff. Simultaneously, the other five occupants were woken up and dealt with in a similar fashion until all of them were sitting upright like invalids in a hospital ward, amazement and fear showing on their tired faces as they stared back at their masked captors. All six of them were wearing plain khaki fatigues with no visible insignia except for shoulder flashes.

"Check them for ID," ordered Luke, and Kiwi went down the line, patting them down, looking under each pillow and mattress and then their backpacks resting at the bottom of the beds. "Nothing!" he shouted. "Not a bloody thing."

Luke pulled up a chair and sat down facing his captive, placing his rifle on the bed with the muzzle rammed into the man's groin. The soldier looked frightened and kept rolling his tongue around his lips.

"Where's your dog tags, mister?" Luke snapped.

"I don't have any," came the reply.

"Why not?"

"Orders, sir."

"Do you have a name then?"

"Faraday, sir, Brigham Faraday."

"Are you a Mormon then?"

"No, sir."

"What is your rank?"

"Corporal, sir."

"And your outfit, Corporal?"

The soldier hesitated.

"And your outfit, Corporal," Luke repeated.

"C Company, 1st battalion, V Corps, United States Army Engineers."

"Is there an officer among you?"

"Yes, sir, Lieutenant Knox in the next bed."

Luke directed his gaze onto the officer who had gone red in the face trying to free his hands from the handcuffs.

"What's a U.S. engineering officer doing in these parts with an oversized tractor?" he asked pleasantly.

"None of your Goddamn business, and who the hell are you?" came the truculent reply.

"Why, I'm your captor, Lieutenant, and I'm asking you again. What are you doing in these parts?"

"Go fuck yourself, I'm not answering any Goddamn questions until I know who you are."

Luke put his hand in his shirt, took out a pistol, aimed it at the lieutenant's chest, and pulled the trigger.

There was a curious "phut," and the officer half-raised his body into the air before collapsing back onto his bed.

Unable to believe his eyes, the corporal froze and gaped in horror at the lifeless body, whereas the other soldiers screamed out loud in protest, one even bursting into tears.

"Take the stupid bastard outside and dump him with the others," Luke ordered. "I don't like corpses staring at me when I'm asking questions."

Kiwi and Williams freed the officer's hands and carried him outside. When they returned, Luke turned his gaze on the corporal, who had forced himself up against the bed-head, his fearful eyes darting at the empty bed beside him.

"Now then, Brigham," Luke said evenly, "you seem like a reasonably intelligent person. I asked a very simple question of your late superior, and I'll ask it again of you. What are the U.S. Engineering Corps up to in this neck of the woods?"

Brigham Faraday looked pleadingly at his frightened companions, all of whom nodded their heads vigorously in his direction. "Well, sir," he gulped, "we are part of a team charged with supplying materials to a project being undertaken further up this mountain."

"How far up this mountain?"

"Three thousand meters or thereabouts."

"And what is this mysterious project being undertaken?"

"I don't know, sir, none of us do."

"We've been up the mountain. We didn't see anything going on up there."

"No, sir, you won't unless they are taking in materials. They're working in a cave ten times as big as this one."

"How long has this been going on?"

"Nearly five weeks. We started on my birthday, which was four weeks last Friday."

"How old are you, Brigham?"

"Twenty-five, sir."

"And do you want to celebrate your twenty-sixth?"

"Yes, sir, I surely do," Brigham replied uneasily.

"Well then, tell me what the fuck you are doing here then, soldier," Luke shouted impatiently.

"Really, sir, none of us know what we're here for except to expedite materials," Brigham replied in a frightened voice. "We telephone them we are coming and take the goods up the mountain and stack them up outside the cave. Then our orders are to return to our post and wait for further goods to arrive. We have been ordered not to discuss our work with anyone, even our folks back home. They've confiscated our cell phones to make sure we don't."

"But you do know where these goods are coming from."

"Yes, sir, they're coming from Iraq, same as we did."

"How is that, by choppers?"

"No, sir, on foot and on donkeys."

"Donkeys! Did you say donkeys?" Luke said incredulously.

"Yes, sir, donkeys. The ravine runs all the way back to the border. It's an old smuggler's route, and only donkeys can negotiate it now."

"How did you get the tractor up here then?"

"In bits and pieces. We reassembled it in less than three days," Brigham said proudly.

"It must make a hell of a racket, draw attention to this place."

"No, sir, it's all electric, quiet as a golf cart."

"But there must be locals about, don't they use the trail?"

"Very few. Any who do are taken out by our Special Forces, who are alerted by our spy satellite."

"Nice people, your Special Forces," Luke said darkly. "When is the next shipment coming through?"

"There isn't one, we're out of here on Monday."

"With the tractor?"

"No, we've got orders to take it up as far as it will go and leave it."

"How do you communicate with the cave up top?"

"A land line."

"No satellite communication then?"

"Not here. That's done from up top. Can I please have a drink of water, sir? My mouth is like sandpaper."

"Where do you keep the water?"

"Stacked up against the back wall."

Luke looked at Kiwi and nodded his head. Kiwi went over and came back with an armful of half-liter bottles and handed one to each of the prisoners.

"Shit," Kiwi swore in disgust. "Here's me thinking I was in for a cold beer, and all that's there is bottled water."

"Open your mouth and take it down slowly," Luke said as he screwed off the top and put it to the corporal's lips. He let him take down half the bottle and then wiped the top with his sleeve and drained the rest himself.

"How many people are there at the top cave, Brigham?" he asked.

"Can't tell, sir. We're a relief unit, and nobody has come down from up there as far as I know."

"Any of you lot see anyone from up top?" Luke asked, looking at the other captives. He was rewarded by four heads all shaking negatively.

"Right, now listen up, all of you," Luke said harshly. "We're going to trash your land line and ditch your weapons. Then we are going to tie you up good and bring in your buddies from outside and do the same to them. We'll give you a drink of water before we leave, enough to last you until we get back in a few hours' time. If you've been good boys, then we will release you. If not, prepare to say your prayers."

Chapter 10

T he patrol took control of the top cave without firing a shot. Once again, the outside guards were taken by surprise, and the personnel inside were caught sleeping in their beds.

The cave was much larger than its counterpart down below, and twelve single iron beds were arranged in neat rows in the area at the rear. Not all of them were occupied, and Williams reported a total of ten bodies altogether. Luke and Kiwi kept watch as Sunshine and Williams tied up the prisoners one by one, resorting to duct tape for some of the hands as their stock of plastic handcuffs ran out.

"Okay, now turn out their pockets and wallets," ordered Luke.

Sunshine and Williams searched every captive thoroughly and failed to find any ID, dog tags, or information of any kind. "Sorry, nothing at all," shrugged Williams. "These people don't exist."

Luke walked over to an object standing almost dead center in the cave. It looked exactly like a large aluminum coffin, tapered at one end, and resting on a concrete base. It was made up of a series of small brass plates, all bolted together and forming an oblong shape some four meters long by one meter square. There was something futuristic about the thing, and Luke could not help but think of some of the monolithic stone works Henry Moore was famous for. However, the sleek symmetry was spoiled by a rectangular black box at the larger end, from which protruded a mass of multicolored cables that trailed over an upright and disappeared into a large box bolted to the cave wall. Looking closer at the aluminum squares, he saw that each one was stamped with a series of letters and numbers in Arabic or Farsi, which he could not decipher. As he stood back and looked again at its silhouette, something supernatural flashed before his eyes, and he felt a strange twinge of fear run up his spine.

"All right!" he shouted angrily as he turned his attention to the prisoners. "What the fuck is it and sixty-four dollars to the lucky bastard who gets it right."

There was silence in the cave as the prisoners fidgeted among themselves, casting glances at each other or looking down in an attempt to escape the notice of their captors.

Luke picked out a burly figure who was desperately trying to free his hands. "You there," he shouted, "I didn't hear you call. Are you deaf, or don't you understand a word of English?"

The man struggled to sit upright and glared at Luke. "I understand English perfectly," he said defiantly. "Who the hell are you?"

"I ask the questions here," snorted Luke. "Give me the big four."

"Like hell I will," came the reply.

Luke pulled his pistol out and pointed it at the captive's chest. "Look, I know you're Army. I'm warning you, answer my question right now or you're dead meat."

The captive stiffened and was about to give a reply when he thought better of it and shook his head instead.

Luke raised his voice. "Last chance, dickhead. What is the purpose of that heap of scrap metal over there?"

Again the captive shook his head, whereupon Luke took aim and fired his gun. The big man jerked violently, fell forward, and hung there, his bound hands preventing him from slumping any farther.

A great commotion broke out, and Luke had difficulty in making his voice heard above the screams and curses of the other prisoners. "Take him outside and put him with the other bodies," he ordered Kiwi and Williams, as he turned his attention to a prisoner who was wearing wire glasses and had tears running down his cheeks. He was a good-looking but rather nerdish youngster, wearing gaudy Hawaiian-type pajamas.

"How about you, are you going to tell me you're not Army then?" he demanded.

"No," sobbed the prisoner, "really, I'm not in the Army at all, I'm a civilian. My name is Henry Parnell."

"What sort of civilian are you?"

"I'm a scientist."

"What sort of scientist?"

Parnell swallowed hard. "I'm a physicist."

"Doing what exactly?"

"Nuclear fission."

Luke was silent for a moment as the momentous words sunk in.

"Jesus Christ!" he shouted. "What's a nuclear fission physicist doing in this godforsaken place? Are you working for the Iranians then?"

Parnell looked appealingly at his fellow captives and was rewarded with a deafening silence. He blinked the tears away from his eyes and gave his answer in a barely audible voice. "No, I work for the U.S. government."

"And you're working on that thing over there, is that correct?"

"Yes."

"So, now I'll repeat the question I asked your dumb, dead associate. What the fuck is it?"

The scientist gulped audibly and said, "It's a prototype atomic bomb."

"A prototype atomic bomb. A prototype atomic bomb," Luke repeated. "Are you telling me it's something new, something you're testing?"

"No, it's the type of bomb we dropped on Nagasaki. They called it Fat Man, only we've made the casing different for ease of assembly."

"Is it ready to go off?"

"Yes, sir, the day after we have evacuated the base."

"And when is that?"

"Tuesday, the Fourth of July, 1100 Eastern Standard Time."

"Jesus!" Luke exclaimed excitedly. "How are you going to detonate the thing, by timer or satellite?"

"By satellite."

"Who is in charge of this operation?"

Parnell glanced sideways at his companions and muttered a name. "Speak up," Luke said sharply. "I didn't hear you."

"Colonel Schroder, he's the chief of operations."

"And which one is Colonel Schroder?"

All eyes focused on a lean, athletic-looking individual, who turned his head away as Parnell pointed him out.

Luke moved down four beds and addressed the shy officer. "Okay, Colonel, I know what the thing is. Now I want to know why in God's name you intend to set off this bloody great firework on your Independence Day in a country thousands of kilometers away from your own turf."

The colonel yanked at his taped hands and refused to answer.

"Have it your way, Colonel," said Luke, pointing his automatic. "I'll ask you just one more time. Why are you setting off an atomic bomb inside Iran?"

The colonel looked away, and just as Luke was about to take aim, a voice shouted, "For God's sake, don't shoot him! I'll tell you what you want to know."

Luke lowered his gun and looked at the owner of the voice, a tall, willowy figure with a long, sallow face and a striking crop of flaming red hair.

"Okay, what's your name?" demanded Luke.

"Perkins. Oliver Perkins," came the reply.

"And your position, Olly?"

"Middle East Section Director, CIA."

"Uh uh," Luke said, nodding his head knowingly, "the plot thickens. Any connection with Colonel Oliver North?"

"No, none at all."

"Then what is the purpose of this secret operation, Olly?"

"Our plan is to detonate the device and draw the attention of the world to Iran's nuclear bomb-making capability. We know they are years away from making a bomb but we've been telling the world lately that they are now on the verge of creating one. The UN inspectors will inspect the site and determine that it was a crude device they were testing, but it will nevertheless establish Iran as a nuclear power. The UN will condemn the test and impose draconian sanctions on Iran. Then the United States will use violations of the strict embargoes as an excuse to take out all nuclear-oriented sites in Iran with the help of its ally in the region. The president himself approved the operation."

Luke shook his head in wonder. "Jesus Christ, I know your outfit has cooked up some screwball schemes in its time, like poisoning Fidel Castro's cigars, but this one takes the biscuit. Do you really think you can get away with such a crazy operation, playing around with nuclear bombs?"

"We got away with it in Iraq," the CIA chief replied defensively. "Anyway, there won't be any civilian casualties; there aren't any people within fifty miles of this place."

"Of course not, that will come when you shower your shock and awe blessings on Iranian cities, won't it? You mentioned you were working with an ally, surely it can't be the UK."

"No," Perkins said, taking a quick glance at the second bed on his left. "I said an ally in the region."

Luke took a look at the person Perkins had identified, a young, swarthy-looking individual with black, curly hair and a trimmed beard circling his mouth and chin. "What's your name?" he asked politely, waving his gun at the new target. "Mustapha or Fagan?"

"It's Levy, Mordecai Levy," came the surly reply in perfect English.

"And you're on loan from the Israeli government, right?"

"I'm an observer, nothing more."

"Yes, and I'm Peter Pan and you're one of the Lost Boys. I wouldn't like to be in your shoes when the Iranians find out you're an Israeli spy, Mr. Levy."

Luke grabbed a couple of chairs and beckoned Kiwi to follow him as he squeezed past the Fat Man bomb and set up the chairs against the wall at the rear, well out of earshot of the captives.

"What do you think, Number Two?" he asked.

Kiwi scratched his head. "I saw a picture once called *Doctor Strangelove* that reminded me of George Bush. It ended with a whooping cowboy riding an H-bomb down onto a Russian city, starting off World War III. All the characters were a bunch of weirdos, just like some of those over there. I can't believe what I'm seeing, but we've got to do something quick. Come daybreak, their HQ is bound to communicate with them."

"Sure, but it's too big for us to decide. I've got to get in touch with Tunney immediately and get instructions."

"You can't use your cell phone from here, Luke, the Yanks will intercept every word you say," Kiwi protested.

"I know, I'm gambling on their satellite focusing on this mountain alone. If I can get to the top of a higher mountain, I figure I can home in on our Comsat without them picking up my signal."

"Jesus Christ, Luke, that means you've got to go down this mountain, across to the next, up that one, and then the same coming back." Kiwi did some counting on his fingers. "God, that's marathon stuff. You sure you're up to it?"

"I'll pretend it's the Brecon Beacons in Wales," laughed Luke. "We both licked them, didn't we?"

"Will you take Sunshine with you?"

"No. You'll need all the help you can get keeping guard over this lot. Keep them handcuffed at all times, and only let them loose one at a time when they want to go for a piss or a crap. Drag the CIA guy's bed over to the radio console and make sure he gives the right answers to any calls coming in from their command center." Luke took out his pistol and handed it to Kiwi. "Take my stun gun and scare the shit out of them if they give you a hard time. Ration their water and feed them once today and again tomorrow. Get Sunshine to do the same for the prisoners down below. Also go through the place with a fine-tooth comb and destroy any arms or munitions. And while you're at it, go through that pile of high-tech stuff and log it," Luke said, pointed to a long table piled high with laptops, calculators, and video and communication equipment."

"What if we get visitors?" asked Kiwi.

"You've got plenty of hostages. Use them as cover even if you have to drag them over the border. If you have to leave the cave, be sure you hack through that load of knitting coming out of the bomb before you go. Use a grenade if you have to. I'll keep in touch over the two-way as much as I can, so tell Tommy to keep his radio on standby all the time, okay?"

Kiwi nodded slowly, unhappy that Luke was insistent on going it alone.

Luke smiled at the forlorn expression on the New Zealander's face. "Cheer up, for Christ's sake, comrade," he chided. "I've got the easy job. I wouldn't like to be responsible for looking after that shower in there for a day even. If you pull it off, I'll put you in for a medal, I can promise you that. Now let's get back there and read them the riot act."

"Listen carefully, all you people," Luke began. "Your lives will depend on what I'm about to tell you. I'm going to be away for a while, sorting out the mess you've got us into. While I'm gone, you will be treated humanely by my men, but anyone who attempts to escape or raise the alarm will be signing their own death warrant. Let me tell you this. If your commanders suspect that this operation has been compromised in any way, they will send a B2 over here from Diego Garcia or Fairford in England, and flatten this place with bunker-busters before you can say George W. Bush. There is too much politically at stake, and they will never allow this bomb to fall into the hands of the Iranians come what may. If you don't believe me, just ask your CIA boss. I've figured a way out of this mess but I need to get new orders from my OC first, so be good boys and don't give my men a hard time. Any one of you who doesn't cooperate will be left handcuffed to his bed when we leave, counting the minutes left in his miserable life. There is no way we are going to allow your fruitcakes in the Pentagon to start World War III, believe you me."

The next two days was the most nerve-wracking period he had ever experienced in his entire life, Kiwi told Luke when it was all over. He hardly slept a wink in over thirty hours, and the only relief he got was when he set up a roster with Sunshine and Williams, whereby they each spent an hour outside, where they were able to expose their faces and bodies to the fresh mountain air, during the hours of darkness only. Apart from that, the only other pleasure he got was sampling the excellent foodstuffs from the large stocks the captives had accumulated at the back of the cave. This was offset by the constant attention the three of them had to pay to the sanitary needs of the individuals, who seemed unable to hold their water for much longer than an hour and the other function for more than four. This meant they were constantly unshackling the captives, escorting them to the large chemical latrine at the rear, and tying them up again. On top of that, they had to feed them, wash their perspiring faces, and listen to their incessant moaning and groaning night and day. The CIA chief, the Israeli, and the Army people accepted their confinement pretty well but the scientists were a constant pain in the ass and affected to suffer from every illness known to man, although there was little evidence of medicines lying around to validate their claims. The only one of them Kiwi felt any twinge of sympathy for was Friesland, a drug addict who began to suffer withdrawal pains on the second night and begged, without success, for a stash of heroin he had hidden beneath his mattress. In the end, Kiwi was driven to rearrange the beds to face the small digital TV screen and feed it with a constant supply of DVDs, consisting mostly of pornographic and horror films, with the sound option on mute.

But the most nerve-jangling moments came when the red light over the communication console flashed and the buzzer sounded. It was easy to forget Perkins, the CIA man, almost hidden behind the Fat Man, amid Kiwi's rush to hurry over, pick up the phone, and hold it to his mouth with one hand and dig his gun into Perkins's ribs with the other, ready to pull the phone away at the sound of one false word and sweating about whether he had managed to convey any inkling of the predicament he was in by a coded word or two. As time went by, Kiwi got so nervous that he would have Sunshine standing near the bomb's harness with his Kukri, ready to cut through it if necessary whenever the phone rang.

There was a recorder plugged into the console, and after every conversation, Kiwi would play it back over and over again, searching for clues, for any indication that the takeover had been rumbled. So far, there had been eight such calls, all of them mainly concerned with the welfare of the team and congratulatory messages on a job well done. But there were also items concerning the imminent evacuation date for the team, the arming of the bomb, and the current setting for the explosion: 1100 precisely, on Tuesday, July 4, Eastern Standard Time.

It was a very relieved son of New Zealand who received the primary call on his two-way from his troop leader; Kiwi stepped outside to listen to it in private.

The voice was breathing heavily. "Doctor Bowman, is everything all right at your end?"

"One hundred percent. Where are you now?"

"I'm on my way back to the hospital and will be with you shortly. In the meantime, I want you to line up all the occupied beds in the ward in front of the new X-ray machine. Also fix a placard to the X-ray machine with the manufacturer's name on it. Then make another placard detailing each patient's name and profession and date of admission in large print. Prop each patient up in a sitting position and fix the cards to the foot of each bed. Using a camcorder, take a panoramic of the group and then take a snapshot of each individual patient. Keep yourself and the other doctors out of the picture at all times. Finally, get Dr. Williams to transfer the film onto my laptop in preparation for transmission to my Web site. My very best regards, Professor Dryden.

"Very good professor, will do."

Re-energized by the contact with Luke, Kiwi set about the task with gusto and achieved all that was asked of him on the stroke of midnight. He then drew up a chair in front of the row of beds and watched in amusement as each of the "patients" tried to outstare him but failed to do so and dropped off, one by one, until the only sound in the cave was that of the snorers and his own heavy breathing. He sensed rather than heard Luke's presence outside the cave, and he got up and watched anxiously as the bottom of the canvas was carefully lifted and Luke's head appeared in view. He pulled him in and helped him to his feet.

"About time too," he whispered with a feeling of relief. "I was just about to send out a search party in case you'd lost your way. Fancy a hot chocolate or something stronger?"

"Coffee will be great, comrade. Anybody give birth while I was gone?"

Kiwi laughed. "No babies but plenty of shitty blankets. I'm almost beginning to feel sorry for the stupid bastards."

"Don't. The boss told me the assholes are within a whisker of starting World War III. It's the Israeli connection that's made it critical."

"What's our orders? Do we blow the fucking thing up now?"

"No, we play it smart, show the world what a bunch of desperados Bush and his cowboys really are. But we've got to act fast. Did you manage the video stuff like I asked?"

"And some. I've got a scoop that would make CNN's boss weep in his beer. It goes on for nearly an hour. You'll never believe it but I had to tell some of them to stop yakking. You know what some Yanks are like once they get their faces on TV. They start acting like they were famous Hollywood actors."

"Good, much traffic with their command satellite?"

"Not too bad, I think we've got away with it all right."

Luke was relieved. "Thank God for that; the boss and the spooks aren't so confident about my communication with the base. They give the Yanks full marks when it comes to eavesdropping. He wants us out of here like yesterday."

"What about the bomb?"

"We make it safe, trash all the electronics."

"That's easy, Sunshine's got his Kukri sharpened up all ready. What do we do with the mad professors?"

"We tell them there's a B2 on its way, and it's every man for himself. We'll escort them down to the bottom base and collect the prisoners down there. Then we'll force them to scatter downhill to the east; I don't want any of them getting in our way as we head west."

"The Army guys might be okay but I'm not so sure about the nerds."

"That's their problem. I've been given a secure channel to transmit your video to base, and then we're off with the DVD for insurance. Also pack up some rations while I watch Sunshine do his work. Then release the prisoners, and we're on our way home. Now let's make tracks, what I said about the B2 might just be bloody well true."

Chapter 11

The Persian Carpet Project, or PCP as it became known to its creators, was to be the catalyst for the last defining moment in the months of George W. Bush's presidency, the last battle in his messianic war on terror that would crush the jihadis and roll back the tide of Islam, which he claimed threatened to engulf the Western world. At the same time, he believed it would establish himself as one of the truly great presidents of the United States of America, in recognition of which a grateful country would surely present him with a chair alongside Lincoln in the Memorial and a bust above Teddy Roosevelt in the Dakota Hills.

It was Theodore Bendover, the director of the CIA, who had come up with PCP, the installation and explosion of a Fat Man atomic bomb inside Iran itself. The UN Security Council had put in place sanctions against that nation but the resolution ruled out the use of military force unless it could be proved that Iran had tested a nuclear device, verifiable by UN inspectors. Despite all the official warnings put out by the United States about Iran's bomb-making capability, the president's own experts had told him that it would be at least five years before they could assemble and test a bomb, and eight years before they could deliver it to the United States. This meant that unless he could implicate Iran as a direct threat, the only thing he would be remembered for would be the fiasco in Iraq that was now threatening to end in a humiliating cut-and-run withdrawal comparable to that of Vietnam. After all the prestige he had invested in the war, that was something George W. Bush would not allow to happen. He knew the American people were in no mood to accept another regime change war in the Middle East, especially now that Congress was controlled by the Democrats. But if they could be persuaded that the mullahs actually possessed the bomb, it would be a simple matter to arrange for an incident on the lines of the Gulf of Tonkin incident in Vietnam, and use it as a pretext for an all-out bombing campaign. Furthermore, the deepening recession was causing havoc with the economy, and a full-blown war with Iran would get the ordnance factories booming again and put a halt to the horrific unemployment figures, as the unemployed were absorbed into the military and its attendant industrial complex. A keen student of American history, GW was well aware that, starting with the Spanish-American War, every foreign conflict in which the United States was involved— even including Vietnam—had enriched the nation and extended its domination over the rest of the world.

Theodore Bendover—a fellow Texan—had become his closest advisor now that Rumsfeld was gone, shutting out even his old pals, Cheney, and his chief of staff, Colonel Derry Pinkerton. Bendover was at pains to point out that dropping an H-bomb on some remote part of the country was a nonstarter, even if they managed to persuade the Israelis to do the job for them. The UN inspection team, still in Iran and led by an Arab-leaning Pakistani, would smell a rat and inevitably come up with the evidence that the bomb was a plant, and that would rule out any hopes of invading Iran before his term of office expired.

One of Bendover's staff had proposed that a prototype Fat Man bomb could be made and dropped instead. The explosive characteristics of the bomb would be analyzed by the UN inspectors, and they would conclude that the Iranians had at last advanced to the critical stage of making a bomb. But the plan was fraught with danger. The Fat Man prototype had been bedeviled with problems from the start during World War II, and had malfunctioned at least six times during tests. In fact, the scientists at Los Alamos had given the Hiroshima bomb only a fifty-fifty chance of success, and everyone had breathed a sigh of relief when it did explode on target. But what if the bomb should fail to go off and fell into Iranian hands? Even the president balked at the idea and ordered Bendover to come up with something much less hazardous.

And so was born the infamous Persian Carpet Project. The Fat Man bomb would be used as first proposed, but it would be assembled inside Iran on a site chosen by a CIA agent who had once trained as a geologist at Esfahan University in Iran. In order to eliminate any possibility of the bomb falling into enemy hands, an explosive charge was to be included that would automatically destroy the bomb if it failed to go off, leaving only a few odd scraps of metal bearing letters and numerals in Farsi for the inspectors to pick up, plus a few particles of fissionable material contaminating the site. As further insurance, Special Forces would be sent in beforehand to place three relay boxes around the chosen site. These would then be subjected to a signal sent down by satellite, and if the return signals confirmed that all three relays had been readied, then the decision to go ahead with the detonation of the bomb would be made.

Bendover appointed an Intelligence Colonel, Siegfried Schroder, as field commander of the operation, and he in turn chose six Army-sponsored nuclear physicists to undertake the task of assembling a Fat Man bomb from scratch. He also picked the Army units that would establish the site, transport the components, and set up communication with a secret satellite that would be fixed in a stationary orbit over the site for the duration of the operation. Security was to be provided by an elite company of Delta Force, who would surround the mountain and eliminate any unwelcome intruders. The entire project was subject to the utmost secrecy, and all personnel involved were obliged to sign sworn affidavits to that effect. Financing would be arranged through a special fund set up by Israeli Intelligence and deducted from the latest appropriation for U.S. military aid to Israel that had been inflated for the purpose.

The preferred date for setting off the bomb was 9/11, but with the situation in Iraq worsening by the day, the president insisted that the date be brought forward, and in the end, the Fourth of July was chosen. This was to be his last throw of the dice, the event that would decide whether history would remember him as a truly great president, in the mold of Washington and Lincoln, or place him in the ranks of losers like Carter and Nixon. And if the war with Iran went well, would a grateful American public be foolish enough to change horses in midstream while the nation was involved in a life-and-death struggle against the forces of evil? Surely they would amend the Constitution and offer him another term in office and, perhaps, yet another after that.

It was a tight schedule, but the team put together by Bendover outdid themselves, and on the second of July, they sent a message to the CIA chief confirming that it was all systems go for 1100 on Independence Day, subject to his confirmation.

Only five people were present in the White House war room on July the fourth. They were Theodore Bendover, White House Chief of Staff, Colonel Derry Pinkerton, Assistant Chief of Staff, Colonel Ronan Kennedy, Hermann Zimmermann, the new defense secretary, and the president himself. On the table in front of each person was a fixed communications console and, at the side of that, a laptop and a notepad. Directly facing them was a huge TV screen, which was blank, waiting to be switched on by any one of the consoles.

The president drained the glass of branch water in front of him and settled back in his chair with his hands clasped behind his head. He was in an especially good mood. He had retired early and slept solidly for nine hours, showered, dined on a large portion of ham and eggs, and read the sports section of the *Washington Post*. The meeting was scheduled for 8:30 AM but he always liked to arrive at least half an hour early. It gave him a chance to blow the cobwebs away and make a few notes on the agenda and familiarize himself with the minutes of the last meeting. If there was one thing he hated about meetings, it was being reminded of something he had promised to take care of and had let slip his mind. Besides, it was Independence Day, and boy, would he have something to tell all the good old boys from Texas who were joining him for dinner later that evening, if all went according to plan.

Derry Pinkerton was already busy with papers at the head of the table and had laid his brief out on the table in front of him. Ronan Kennedy was the next to arrive, and he bowed gracefully as he said, "Good morning, Mr. President," and took his seat two places to his left.

Smartly dressed, Colonel Kennedy exuded the confidence of a top-drawer officer who could do no wrong. He had been recommended by the defense secretary for the post of ground operations officer. A West Pointer, he had served two tours in Iraq with the Army Intelligence Section and was reputed to know the border country in the north like the back of his hand. It was only after the third meeting of the group that the president discovered he was married to a sister of the defense secretary. The man was obviously a social climber but so far, he had done a good job. The operation was on schedule, and total secrecy had been maintained.

Next in was Theo Bendover, his friend for nearly twenty years. Good old Theo, he was showing his age now. The hair was thin and grey, and the weather-beaten face was showing the effects of his fondness for rye whisky. As far as the president was concerned, the riotous drinking bouts were a thing of the past, but their relationship was as close as it had ever been. The fact that he was president never seemed to register with the former chief of the Texas Rangers baseball team. He'd never wanted the job at the CIA in the first place, and he'd only agreed to take it after Dubya had begged him for old time's sake and limited his term of office to two years. The president's so-called friends in Washington were deserting him, left, right, and center, but as long as he had Theo to watch his back, he felt confident enough to take on the jackals who were gathering in Congress after his wounding in the mid-term elections.

Last in was the new defense secretary, Hermann Zimmermann, successor to Donald Rumsfeld, whom he had been forced to fire against his wishes. True to form, the 280-pound general came in ten minutes late, a deliberate ploy designed to signal his contempt for a president in his last months in office. Bush hated the gross figure with a bloated face, three chins, and a pair of piggy eyes that almost merged with each other when he was angry. He was a Goering look-alike whom even the finest tailor in Saville Row would be hard-pressed to cut a uniform for. Both sides of his jacket were plastered with ribbons and medals and gold braid, and his cap, which he never removed in public, was more Russian than American. Nevertheless he had insisted on wearing his full dress uniform at his daughter's wedding, even though he demanded top hat and tails for everyone else. Short of friends, Bush had acceded to the demands of the military and appointed Zimmermann against his wishes. The oaf was the Pentagon's revenge for the Rumsfeld years, when the overstaffing, incompetence, and obscene waste that had become endemic was challenged and sometimes reversed. Many of the top brass had been dismissed or retired but they were now waiting in the wings, plotting, confident of an early return to power. The only reason he put up with them and their stooge was because they were unanimous in their support for war with Iran, a war that they calculated would be ten times more profitable than the sideshow in Iraq.

"Sorry I'm late, Prez," boomed Zimmermann, "I was halfway out the door when Baghdad called. Took me nearly an hour to sort them out."

Lying bastard, thought Bush. "Sit down, Hermann, we're anxious to get through to control," he said impatiently. "All set, Theo?" he asked as he turned to Bendover. "Let's see what's going on in mad mullah country, shall we?"

Bendover pushed a button and the screen lit up, displaying a panoramic view of the now-familiar snowcapped mountain bathed in sunshine. There was a collective gasp from the viewers as they noticed movement on the lower reaches of the east side of the mountain.

The president looked at his watch and swore. "What in the name of Sam Houston are all those people doing on the mountain in broad daylight?" he shouted. "I understood that the evacuation of our people is set for as soon as it gets dark over there. Theo, find out what the hell is going on."

"Yes, sir, you're dead right," Bendover said as he pushed another button.

A harassed-sounding voice answered, "PCP control."

"What's going on, Harry?" Theo asked testily. "We're in the war room right now and there's people crawling all over the mountain in broad daylight. Has somebody jumped the gun, for Christ's sake?"

"Search me. We haven't given the go-ahead yet."

"Well, who in God's name are those people then?"

"We don't know, we lost all contact with the base three hours ago."

"Lost contact! Three hours ago! Jesus Christ, why wasn't I informed sooner?"

"Sorry, Theo, we've been too busy trying to regain contact. Everything is dead, the base console and computers and every cell phone listed. The only contact we can get on the site are the three relays we used for testing, and they aren't the slightest good to us anymore."

"Oh my God, you mean to tell me you've lost control of Fat Man as well?"

"I'm afraid so. Like I said, we've lost touch with everything. It's like we were trying to pick up an electronic signal on Saturn."

"So we can't blow the Goddamn thing up?"

"Not unless someone goes up there and does it manually."

Bendover gasped and looked at the president for guidance. His friend's face was not a pretty sight. It was as pale as the notepaper on the table, and his pupils looked as if they had disappeared into their sockets. He seemed unable to speak, even to mouth some of the mangled syntax he sometimes spouted when he was under pressure. Bendover felt a sudden fear. It reminded him of the time when news was brought to the president of the 9/11 catastrophe, and Dubya was momentarily paralyzed and unable to speak. What if he was to collapse and die at such a critical time and left him holding the baby?

"George!" he shouted, taking hold of his arm and shaking it, spilling the glass of water he was holding into his lap as he did so. "For Christ's sake, we need your advice fast."

The shock of the cold water seemed to jolt the president out of his stupor. "Jesus!" he screamed. "It's got to blow up! If it doesn't, we'll all be hung, drawn, and quartered. For crying out loud, we've spent millions on the project. You mean to tell me we can't raise any one of our people on the phone and find out what the hell's going on?"

He turned to Kennedy. "You're in charge of ground operations, for Christ's sake. Get hold of one of your men and tell him to round up the nerds and order them to call us."

Ronan Kennedy shifted uneasily in his seat. "No can do, Mr. President," he whispered. "Everybody except Delta Force had their cell phones confiscated in case they are intercepted by the Iranians."

"What! Then how in Jehosophat's name did the top base keep in touch with the lower base?"

"They laid a land line between them," interjected Theo Bendover.

"Excuse me, Prez," boomed the defense secretary, "can I get a word in here?"

"Go ahead, Hermann, see if you can make any sense of this fucking awful foul-up."

"Well, if the nerds and Delta Force boys are unable to communicate with each other, what is to stop our boys from shooting up the nerds? They've got orders to eliminate anything that moves outside the two bases. It will be a turkey-shoot, believe me."

"Good question. What do you say to that, Kennedy?" growled the president."

The ground operations officer squirmed again. Up to now, it had been first names at every meeting; now he was in the mire, right up to his neck in it. "Mr. President, the plan was for the nerds to assemble after dark at a designated point in the pass a thousand meters up the mountain. They would be met there by Delta Force and escorted down and then across the border."

"Do the nerds know their way back to the border if they don't use the pass?"

"I doubt it. Delta Force escorted them up the mountain and helped them set up their bases."

"So now they are wandering about like drunken sailors liable to get shot up at any minute. I hope they do catch a bullet. I don't give a shit about any of them. They've ruined our plans completely, and now it looks as if the mad mullahs are going to get their first atom bomb, courtesy of the White House!" roared the president. "I've a good mind to tell Delta Force to shoot the lot of them."

"Let's hope they do," remarked Bendover. "It would be better than letting them fall into the hands of the Iranians."

"My God, please don't let that happen," the president whispered, a frightened look on his face. "That would be an absolute disaster."

"Mr. President, we've set up a base camp two kilometers from the border. If we can get a chopper ..." Ronan Kennedy broke off as Theo Bendover's console buzzed again, and an urgent voice came over the speaker: "Theo, please switch your console to TV reception and select channel 87 right now."

Bendover sat bolt upright and pressed two buttons. The mountain picture disappeared and was replaced by a picture showing the distinctive Al Jazeera–London logo in the top left-hand corner. The audience gasped as the picture focussed and revealed a large silvery object in the background, bearing a banner with the words "U.S. ARMY FAT MAN ATOMIC BOMB" in large black letters scrawled on it. In the foreground was a row of iron beds, occupied by men wearing white overalls or Army fatigues. Every person was sitting awkwardly, bolt upright, with their arms behind their backs, and at the bottom of each bed was a card bearing the patient's name. A voice off camera was speaking:

"You, third from the left, Joseph Schneider, what is your occupation?"

The man replied, without hesitation, "I'm a physicist."

"What kind of a physicist?"

"I'm a nuclear physicist."

"What are you and your companions doing here in the Iranian mountains?"

"We're assembling an atomic bomb."

"A Fat Man bomb, the same bomb you dropped on Hiroshima?"

"Yes, sir."

"Are all the people around you engaged on the same project?"

"Yes, sir."

"What is the name of the project?"

"Persian Carpet Project, or PCP for short."

"Is the person in charge of the project among you?"

"Yes, sir, he's Oliver Perkins of the CIA."

"Oh my God!" whispered Bendover. "It's Olly."

The camera focused on the fifth bed from the left. "You are Oliver Perkins, American CIA Director, Middle East, are you not?" demanded the voice."

A haggard-looking Perkins licked his lips and answered in a barely audible voice.

"Speak up, Mr. Perkins, millions of people all over the world are very interested in what you have to say," urged the voice.

"Yes, I am." This time, the voice was audible but only just.

"And you are in charge of Project Persian Carpet, are you not?"

"I am."

"Will you explain, what is the purpose of PCP?"

"It's to set off a nuclear explosion that will incriminate Iran in the eyes of the world."

"You mean in the eyes of America."

Perkins shrugged his shoulders. "If you like."

"And then what?"

"Search me, that's up to the politicians."

"Can't you take a guess?"

Perkins shrugged his shoulders again. "Could be the president wants a pretext to bomb the shit out of the mad mullahs."

"What is an Israeli Intelligence officer doing mixed up in all this?"

The question took Perkins by surprise. "Um, he's—oh shit, why don't you ask him yourself?"

"I will, Mr. Perkins, indeed I will," came the laconic reply. "Mordecai Levy, you heard the question. You told us you were an observer. Now why would an Israeli be observing an American plot to start World War III?"

There was silence. The Israeli tucked his head into his chest and refused to answer. The same question was asked three more times, and each time Levy refused to answer.

"Very well, Mr. Levy, suit yourself. Your refusal means that you will be left here to the tender mercies of the Iranian authorities when they arrive, while your more cooperative companions will be set free. Mr. Perkins, would you care to tell us why he's here or would you like to keep him company when we leave?"

"I honestly don't know; if I did, I'd tell you. None of us like the Jew bastard. He gives us the creeps sticking his nose in everything and getting in the way."

"Okay, I'll let you off that one. What time is the bomb set to go off?"

"1100 Eastern Time, July Fourth."

"American Independence Day?"

"Yes."

"So you will be celebrating Independence Day by killing thousands of innocent Iranian citizens?"

"I don't think so. There's no life for miles around."

"But what about the radiation? It kills people for God knows how many kilometers around, and for years afterward, doesn't it?"

Perkins looked uncomfortable and did not answer.

The camera focussed on another captive and then another, until all except the Israeli had disclosed their particulars and knowledge of the project. Then, as suddenly as it had first appeared, the transmission ended and the screen returned to the main Al Jazeera-London logo.

The presenter's voice said, "Please do not switch off your set, our normal service will resume in a few moments."

There was a pregnant pause, and then the president exploded. "Goddamn, Goddamn, Goddamn!" he screamed, turning on his shell-shocked staff. "I can't believe this is happening to me." Never in his entire life had he felt such embarrassment and fear. His whole body shivered and seemed to shrink to half its normal size, as if seeking to hide itself from the horror that had appeared on the screen. His eight-year role as the most powerful man in the world had made him immune to personal and professional attacks from the pigmies in the world outside. He only ever read the funnies and sports pages in the newspapers and only watched news programs on TV that were presented by good old boys like Rush Limbaugh, who could be trusted to present him in a good light, come what may. Even the midterm elections debacle had failed to shake his belief in his own invincibility. He was the president, and he would use the immense clout of his office to overcome the present difficulties and ride into the sunset with a reputation at least on a par with, or even greater than, that of Washington and Lincoln.

But that dream depended on the success of Persian Carpet. Iraq was now an unholy mess and would continue to be so as long as Iran was allowed to dictate events through the Shia majority. There was no way he could withdraw U.S. troops with honor in his last year, and if the bloodshed was still going on, the Republicans would be massacred in the elections and his name would forever be linked with that of Benedict Arnold. Iran was the hub of Islamic extremism.

Destroy that country, and the hostile Arab states would fold like a pack of cards, broken-backed, unable to export their murderous Sharia law throughout the civilized world. Such a victory would earn him the everlasting gratitude of moderate Arabs and Christians everywhere and, at the same time, ensure that cheap Middle East oil would continue to underpin the continuing prosperity of America. Even more exciting was the prospect that if America was engaged in a major war of liberation, the American people might be persuaded to forgo the November elections and reward him with an undisputed third term.

Persian Carpet! Persian Carpet! How in God's name could things have gotten so bad? He felt the color return to his cheeks and the heat that went with it extend around to the nape of his neck. He looked at his officers through a red mist, and the person of Ronan Kennedy caught his fiery gaze as the man sought to draw his body out of view behind the ample frame of the defense secretary. Colonel Ronan Patrick Kennedy, the man handpicked by Zimmermann to do the job and the braggart who had told him he would deliver the heads of the three mad mullahs to him on a plate if so ordered. Goddamn bull-shitting sod-buster. He should have known better than to have approved another Irishman to a job of such importance after the trouble Fatso Collins had caused in Iraq.

"Kennedy," he raged, "your men were supposed to be looking after the nerds! How in God's name did the Iranians manage to capture the lot of them and put them on show without showing up on our spy satellite?"

"God's honor, Mr. President," Kennedy protested, "we had men all over the mountain and also guarding the two bases. Nothing could have gotten through our cordon. I know for a fact that my men eliminated thirty-odd people who were moving across the mountain, but they turned out to be peasants or mountain men and were unarmed. Like I said, nothing could have gotten through unless they came down from above by parachute."

"Well, something or somebody did get through and must have killed or captured your men on the bases, tied up the nerds, made a picture show, and then stampeded them down the mountain like a herd of longhorns. Now you get through to your big Delta Force chief and get him to round up the nerds right now and chase them over the border fast. Don't let them stop for a leak even. Make them piss their pants if they have to go. The first nerd they find, put him on the phone to me. While that's happening, tell him to lead a squad himself up to the top base and find out what's going on. Keep him on the line all the time until every last one of them is over the border. Understood?"

"Yes, sir, Mr. President."

"And nobody leaves this room until we get to the bottom of this thing. Understood?"

"Yes, sir, Mr. President," came the chorus.

"Now then, Theo, will Control have made a recording of that film?" he asked.

"Of course. They record everything."

"Right, tell them to replay it, freeze every frame, and blow them up until their eyes bug out. I want them to search for clues, voice recognition, signals from the hostages, the state of the bomb, anything else they can think of. Get them to put it through here as well so that we can see what's going on. Goddamn it, Theo, I could swear the speaking voice on the film was John Howard, the ex-Australian PM."

Bendover spoke into his module, and within seconds, the dreaded Al Jazeera logo reappeared and the picture came up. The review went on for three hours, during which time the president called for six coffee refills with sandwiches. The viewers found their eyes boggling as the experts in Control went to town, zooming in and out, switching angles, freeze-framing every face, and enlarging it until the minutest scar or imperfection became visible. They targeted the mouths, hoping to get a lip-read, and then the body and feet, seeking language in that direction. They viewed the end of the bomb, where the control box was fitted, and found that it was obscured by the large body of Colonel Schroder, who was staring straight ahead as if hypnotized. They sought desperately to try and bend the picture to bring the box into view, but without success. Then they concentrated on the audio track, synthesizing the speaking voice, reducing the sound level to a whisper, and then increasing it to an ear-splitting frequency.

Gradually, the eyestrain and soporific imaging took its toll, and the viewers dozed off one by one. The president was sprawled out in his chair with his arms dangling over the armrests, Bendover was sitting up straight with his chin on his chest, and Zimmermann and Pinkerton were slumped over the table, their heads in their arms. Only Kennedy was awake, staring bleary-eyed at his console, mindful of the president's order, and waiting desperately for a friendly voice to come through from an Iranian mountaintop.

Chapter 12

"George, George, wake up, we've got contact with the mountain." Theo Bendover shook the president's shoulder, and he came-to instantly.

Ronan Kennedy spoke into his console. "Hold on a minute, will you? The president is waiting to speak to you."

He looked at the president. "His name is Henry Bradshaw, he's one of the nerds," he said excitedly.

The president cleared his throat and spoke into his console "Henry, I don't want any horseshit, give me the facts straight up. What the hell are you doing out on the mountain when you should be inside the base?"

The voice was reedy and timid. "Mr. President, we were taken hostage by four very nasty armed men. They handcuffed us to our beds and then started cross-examining us. They tried to kill one of us and then forced us to spread out and climb down the mountain on the eastern side. Jesus Christ, all I have on is my overalls. I'm half-frozen to death."

"Who did they nearly kill?"

"Captain Brown, he refused to give them the big four."

The president looked puzzled, and he looked enquiringly at Ronan Kennedy.

"He's in charge of the top base security, sir. The big four are the only four questions an enemy is allowed to ask a prisoner under the Geneva Convention: name, number, rank, and date of birth."

"Anybody else get hurt, Henry?" asked the president.

"No, I don't think so, but they left the Israeli behind in the base, still tied to his bed."

Oh my God, thought the president as a shiver ran down his spine. "Now why would they do that, Henry?"

"Because he refused to answer any of their questions."

"But they didn't kill him."

"Nuh-nuh-nuh-nuh-no, Mr. President. Jesus Christ, I can hardly speak, I'm so fucking cold."

"Now bear up, son, just a few minutes more, and I'll tell your rescuer to help you out. You know they made a film of you all. Did you get a good look at the cameraman?"

"Yes, he was also questioning us as he filmed. But I didn't see his face. He was wearing Arab clothes and had a scarf around his face."

"Jesus! You said there were four men; were they all dressed the same?"

"Yes, sir."

"Did they all speak English?"

"Yes, sir, only two of them had accents, one like an Aussie and the other Chinese. The big chief spoke perfect English, like they do at Oxford."

"How do you know that?"

"I was at Oxford. Rhodes scholar, class of '96."

"You don't say," the president said sarcastically. "Did any of them have names?"

"They called their leader 'Boss' and sometimes, 'Luke.' The others were Sunshine, Kiwi, and Williams."

"Who took the pictures?"

"That was Kiwi."

"Okay, now listen carefully, Henry. Did they interfere with the bomb in any way?"

"I don't know, sir. They started trashing all our gear when we were outside, and they had the Chinese guy standing by with a bloody great knife he called a kukri ready to cut the wiring every time Control contacted us."

"The hell you say! Tell me straight, Henry, do you think they cut the controls before they left?"

"No doubt about it. The boss man was very angry. He told us there was no way we were going to start World War III while he was still alive. Holy cow, Mr. President, I think I'm going to pass out. There's no feeling in my feet anymore."

"All right, Henry, thank you for your help. If you run into any of your colleagues, be sure and tell them to contact us, won't you?"

"But Mr. President, they can't contact you. They trashed all our cell phones."

"Shit. Pass me over to your rescuer."

"Hello, Sergeant Cassini here, Mr. President," said an eager voice.

"Sergeant, do you know where the top base is?"

"No, sir, I don't."

"Well, Henry does. Give him your coat and get him up there as fast as you can. Tell Henry to check the bomb and call me back immediately. Understand?"

"Yes, sir, Mr. President. I don't know if he can make it, sir. He's lying on the ground like he's going to die it any minute."

"Goddamn it, man, give him your coat and resuscitate him. Then move ass like a Yeti is after you both. Use your bayonet if you have to."

"But I don't have a bayonet, Mr. President, all I've got is a Swiss Army knife."

"Jesus! Use that, then. I want an answer inside half an hour, now get going." He turned to Bendover. "Theo, call Control and tell them to contact every Delta Force grunt on the mountain. I want every man off that mountain before midnight their time, and that's an order.

"God help us all," the weary president said as he slumped back in his chair. "Where the Sam Houston do we go from here?"

"There's only one thing we can do, Prez," boomed Zimmermann. "We've got to destroy the bomb, vaporize it, and bury it under half the mountain. Two SXB bunker-busters would do the job nicely. There is no way we can allow the bomb to fall into the hands of the mad mullahs."

"Come on, Zimmer, that would stir up a hornets' nest," Bendover said. "The Iranians would win the sympathy of the whole Islamic world, and that would be the end of Uncle Sam in Iraq and the whole of the Middle East." Theo Bendover despised Zimmermann. The dickhead's answer to any problem in a foreign land was "bomb the shit out of them."

"I didn't mean us, I meant the Israelis. We sent them forty SXBs when they bombed Lebanon. I'm sure they have at least four ready to go," Zimmermann replied peevishly.

"Fuck the Israelis!" roared the president. "I don't want nothing to do with those Jew bastards ever again. Their PM promised me he was going to keep bombing the shit out of Hizzbollah until every terrorist was either dead or kicked out of Lebanon. Then as soon as those lefties in the UN put some pressure on, he caves in and they go slinking back home with their tails between their legs. Now Hizzbollah are stronger than ever. How in God's name can we ever win our war on terror with chickenshit allies like them and the Brits? Make no mistake, the next time they come begging for more shekels, the only thing they'll get is a load of buckshot up their asses. And what the hell is an Israeli doing in our operation, Theo? Bin Laden is going to piss himself laughing when he gets to see a Jewboy sitting among our fellahs."

"He was part of the financing. They would only agree to forgo $80 million of their military aid package if they were allowed to send an observer. It was all in the final agreement you okayed, George," said Bendover quietly.

"Yeah, well, we should never have allowed him in. Didn't Henry say they'd left him tied up to the bomb when they left?"

"Yes, he did."

"Good, serves the bastard right, sticking his nose where it don't belong. Now then, check with Control and find out what they've discovered among that Mickey Mouse stuff they did on the screen."

Bendover spoke into his console.

"Sorry, Theo," came the reply. "We can't add anything to what Bradshaw just told you, but here's something interesting. At 0706 on July 3, we picked up a message originating from the top of Mount Hazzan, which is 22 degrees northwest of our base. A Professor Dryden sent a message to a Dr. Bowman. They are discussing a new X-ray machine, and the professor asks the doctor to line up some patients in front of the machine, place an ID card in front of each of them, and take their pictures. The professor signs off by saying he will return to the hospital sometime soon, and Bowman says 'Roger boss, will do.' That's it. There was a lot of static but we managed to enhance the diction enough to determine that the professor is a well-educated Englishman. One of our NATO officers says that he sounds just like a Sandhurst graduate."

"So he's a Goddamn Limey then," swore the president. "Jesus Christ, I thought they were supposed to be on our side. Don't tell me they've taken up with the mad mullahs."

"Mr. President, Mr. President!" Ronan Kennedy shouted excitedly. "I think I've cracked it. These people are British Special Forces. You know, the SAS. I would swear to it. In the first place, they always team up in fours and wear scarves to hide their faces. Then they always call their team leader 'boss.' There's lots of Australians in the SAS, and I'd say the Chinese guy is really a Ghurkha. There's a lot of them too. What did they say the names were, Theo?"

Bendover looked down at his notepad. "Luke, Kiwi, Sunshine, and Williams," he replied.

"No, no, the two doctors."

Bendover put the question to his console.

"Dr. Bowman and Professor Dryden," came the reply.

"That's it!" Kennedy screamed triumphantly. "It is the fucking SAS. Dryden was the name of the SAS captain who escaped from our base in Afghanistan and killed three guards. And Bowman was one of the others. You remember that, don't you, Mr. President?"

"Damn right I do. Anything that concerns Fatso Collins is something I can't ever forget. What you don't know is that the SAS didn't kill the guards, they only knocked them out. The inspector general told me that a relief guard found them alive and well but he was ordered to join the main body of the division that had just left. The base guards were knifed in the back. He volunteered the information when he heard about the case later. The investigation is still going on but the IG told me the finger points at Collins. Tony Blair promised me that if they caught the 'SAS bastards,' as he called them, he would ensure that they would be extradited here to face trial."

"But that can't be right, Mr. President," said Kennedy. "When I was in Iraq a month ago, there were plenty of stories going round about Dryden and his border patrol troop down south. He's a hero. One story has it that it was his lot downed one of our Warthogs when it wiped out one of his vehicles by mistake. Naturally, we put the loss of the plane down to engine trouble. They quote Dryden as saying that if he had the choice of shooting a GI or a raghead, he'd top the GI every time."

"Well, I'll be damned. Blair told me he had hundreds of military police out looking for him at home and abroad. Said they were being treated as deserters. Looks like his army isn't trying too hard to catch them, don't it?"

"He must know, Mr. President. Blair was visiting Basra when I was there. If he didn't hear Dryden's name mentioned, then Bin Laden's Jesus Christ. Anyway, there is no way they can catch him. I'm told the colonel in charge of the SAS won't let any government men or policemen into their base in England. If that's true, then Blair's a Goddamn liar."

"Sonofabitch. Wait till the next time he comes brown-nosing. I'll blow so much smoke up his ass they'll think Sherwood Forest is on fire. And if he thinks he's getting that Congressional Medal he's been too chicken to accept, he's in for a big surprise."

"You'll get the chance sooner than you think, Mr. President," broke in Derry Pinkerton. "He's down for a visit on July 22."

"July 22? Why, that's my other dog's birthday. Cancel Blair and don't give any reason. Shit, forget about him, what in God's name are we going to do about the bomb?"

"Bomb it, Prez, take the whole mountain apart. Don't even leave a pinch of paint for them to find. Get rid of the evidence, and what have they got? An Al'Qaeda propaganda film, pure and simple," trumpeted the defense secretary.

"And what about the missing mountain?" Bendover asked, testily.

"They get earthquakes in Iran all the time, for Christ's sake," Zimmermann retorted angrily, "especially in the mountains."

"How long would it take to get a B2 over there from Diego Garcia, Zimmer?" asked the president.

"Around four hours, like it was with Baghdad. Course, they would need to prepare the planes and load the bombs first. Eight hours tops, I would say."

"That's a long time; the place will be crawling with Iranians long before then."

"Mr. President."

"Yeah, Kennedy."

"Israel is less than two hours away. They could be there in less than half the time. Why not get them to do it?"

"Because like I said, I don't trust the money-grubbing bastards, that's why. Anyway, there's nobody there who could make a big decision like that. They are all fighting each other like ferrets in a sack after the war in Lebanon. There's no one to talk to."

"There's General Halutz, the chief of staff," argued Kennedy. "Tell him you'll suspend all military aid to Israel for five years if they don't agree. Like you say, money talks with them, and $15 billion is sure to make Halutz bang a few heads together. Anyway, they're already implicated, with that guy Levy being identified on the film. They've done this thing before when they bombed an Iraqi reactor, so the Arabs will naturally fix the blame on them, and that could take the heat off us. Zimmer is right, we just can't let them have the bomb intact. It's unthinkable."

The president looked at Kennedy with a new respect. *Sure, there would be plenty of fallout over the film, but there would be a lot more manure on the head of the actual bomb dropper*, he thought. Kennedy made sense, but was it doable?

"Yeah, but how is the world going to know it was an Israeli plane dropped the bomb?" he reasoned. "There's a lot more of us in that picture than there are Israelis."

There was a pregnant silence as the others chewed on their pencils or stabbed them into their notepads. "I've got it," said Bendover, "at least I think I have. We'll let them drop their bombs, and as they are turning back for home, we'll shoot them down well inside the border. We'll scramble a couple of F16s from Baghdad and have them waiting for them. The Israelis will think the Iranians shot it down, and the world media will go to town picking through the wreckage, looking for evidence."

"Very good, Theo, very good," the president said, beaming at his friend. "The more I hear, the more I like it. You said two bunker-busters would do the job, didn't you, Zimmer?"

"I did," replied the defense secretary, "only four would really put the icing on the cake. Jesus Christ, it would be like finding Tutankhamen's tomb, it would take them years to dig out any pieces."

"That would mean two bombers then, wouldn't it, Zimmer?" asked Bendover."

"So we zap two instead of one. Our guys need some practice anyway. They haven't fired an air-to-air missile in combat since the invasion in 2003."

"Two hours you say," mused the president.

"Well, three at the most. They had plenty of practice in Lebanon, and it looks like they're going to get a lot more shortly."

The president looked up at the screen. The picture seemed to give him a sudden thought. "Listen up," he said, "did anybody notice whether the film gave away the location of the bomb site?"

They all pondered the request and then shook their heads.

"Right. Theo, get Control to examine the film again and see if there was a mention, right quick! Time to take a leak. I'll be back in half an hour."

He stretched his arms and legs as he stood up and made for the door.

"Any news?" he asked as he returned and took his seat.

"No," said Bendover, "they had already checked that possibility and the answer is negative."

"Great, that's good news. It'll be night-time over there soon, and they don't know where we're at. That should give us plenty of time to get all our people over the border. Don't you agree, Ronan?"

"Yes, sir, Mr. President," replied Kennedy, relief showing in his weary face. "Stacks of time."

"Okay, that settles it then. All those in favor of Ronan's suggestion, raise their right hand."

Three hands shot up immediately and were followed soon after by the reluctant hand of Theo Bendover.

"Good," grunted the president, raising his own hand, "that makes it unanimous. Zimmer, get through to that Israeli General What's-his-name. Ronan, clear everybody off the mountain. Theo, give Control their instructions and also tell them to keep that mountain showing on our screen for evermore. Jesus, I need to take another leak. Hold the fort; I'll be back tout suite."

He was coming out of the toilet door when Derry Pinkerton called out to him: "Mr. President, I've just had CNN and Fox News on the line. They've just received the Al Jazeera film from their London offices, and they want permission to broadcast it. What do I tell them?"

The color drained from the president's face. "Tell Murdoch and Walton that if they show so much as one frame of that crap while I'm in office, I'll have them locked up in Guantanamo for spreading Al Qa'eda propaganda over our great country. And that goes for all the rest of the lousy, muck-spreading networks, savvy?" he shouted angrily. "Jesus, now I need another piss."

Ten minutes later, the president was again emerging from the toilet when Theo Bendover came charging down the corridor and nearly passed him by in his haste.

"Come quickly, George," he panted. "We've got a problem, and we need you right away."

It wasn't often Theo became agitated, and the president hurried up to the war room as fast as his chubby legs could carry him, his mind full of foreboding.

All eyes were fixed on the big screen, and not a word was spoken as he settled in his chair.

Bendover was the first to speak. "I'm afraid they're on to us, George. Those flashing lights you see at the bottom of the mountain are paratroopers with lights fixed to their helmets, and if you look closely, you'll see dozens more floating down to join them. Control have picked up at least twenty transports flying over the area, and they calculate that with a capacity of fifty troops per plane, there will be a thousand men on the ground within ten minutes. There's also a pattern to the drop, they're surrounding the mountain and distributing men down the pass all the way to the border. Even worse, there is a long column of armor coming up the road from Ilam, with helicopter gunships ahead of them. I'm afraid the game's up. All we can hope for is that our people managed to reach the border before them."

"Well, let them take the fucking mountain," boomed Zimmermann, "the more there is up there when the bombs come down, the more casualties they will take. And if any of the nerds catch it, so much the better. We don't want any of them falling into the hands of the enemy."

"Don't listen to him, George," begged Bendover. "It's over. Abort the bombers and call it a day. If they start taking casualties, it might provoke them into mounting a full-scale invasion of Iraq. Our forces are no longer strong enough to resist such an attack. The Shia will join them, and they'll drive a wedge between our units in the north and those in the south. That will make our position untenable. It will become a rout."

"Not so!" shouted Zimmermann. "We've still got two hundred thousand or so men in Iraq, and every one of them is worth ten ragheads. They wouldn't get within a hundred miles of Baghdad."

The president stared at the crimson face of the bellicose defense secretary for a few seconds and then returned his gaze to the screen. He shuddered as the flickering lights merged into a mass of illumination stretching back as far as the camera could see. The Iranians must have been tipped off hours ago and were reacting to the situation with military precision and speed. He was never a quitter; every neuron in his brain urged him to face them down and follow Zimmermann's advice. But when he turned again to his friend Theo and looked at the earnest face of the man whose advice he valued above that of all the generals and politicians in his administration, past and present, he froze. Just as he did on previous occasions when a decision of great importance was asked of him.

He sat staring at the screen as if in a trance for a good two minutes and then suddenly leapt to his feet. "I'm going down to the Oval Office to consult the oracle," he said to Bendover. "Stay here, I'll call in my decision within the next half hour."

Ronan Kennedy looked at the door, open-mouthed, as it closed behind the president. "What was that all about?" he asked Bendover in a whisper. "And who the fuck is the oracle?"

Bendover shook his head sadly. "It's God," he answered, "and he has to be alone when he talks to him. But we will get a decision, I can guarantee you that."

The rain was falling fast as the president stood looking out of the center window of the Oval Office, flanked by the Stars and Stripes on one side and the Lone Star flag of Texas on the other. He could not see them but he knew they were there, blanketing Pennsylvania Avenue and every available public piece of land adjoining it. Thousands of rabid, raucous, chanting protesters, with their huge banners and pulsating megaphones, oblivious to the weather; like wolves circling their wounded prey in the knowledge that in the end they must prevail. "Goddamn the unpatriotic bastards," he muttered.

The sound of the rain beating on the windows made him shiver, and he went to his desk, unlocked the right-hand bottom drawer, and took out a whisky glass and a bottle of Southern Comfort. He poured out his customary two fingers of the golden liquid and settled down in the executive chair, savoring the first long pull that caressed his throat and set a warm glow spreading down to his chest. He felt exhausted. Never in his life had his brain been in such a turmoil or the siren voices so clamoring and insistent. Now the intermittent buzz that had appeared just over a year ago became more prevalent, confusing his train of thought, raising doubts and diluting the macho image that had made him famous. Only the other day he struggled to recall whether it was Mullah Rafsanjani who had tried to assassinate his father and if it was Saddam Hussein who had taken the Americans hostages in Teheran, or was it the other way round. It terrified him to think that he was becoming reduced to the antithesis of the cool, calm western sheriff he aspired to, a pitiful caricature of a drunken layabout, begging for the means and despised by the town folk he had sworn to protect with his very life. Theo had warned him the game was over but he would never accept that, not in a million years.

He knelt down beside his chair and prayed, as he always did when he was unsure of a situation and needed divine guidance. He spoke in a low, reverent voice and raised his eyes to the domed ceiling, again and again, as the Lord answered him. Finally he said amen and crossed himself. As he got to his feet, his eyes alighted on the portrait of Richard Nixon that took pride of place in its position over the fireplace, and he walked over and raised his glass to the enigmatic, shadowed face. Speaking out loud, he said, "Here's to yuh, yuh sad old bastard. They wore you down and kicked you out but I won't let that happen to me. Right now they hate my guts but one day, when the Islamic bombs start falling on New York and Chicago and LA, and millions of Americans die and the oil stops flowing to the West, they will remember George W. Bush, the president who sought to protect the country he loves from the greatest threat to its existence since the Civil War. Then they will finally recognize the sacrifices I made and reward me with the Congressional Medal of Honor, a place among the greats in the Dakota Hills, and a chair alongside Lincoln in his Memorial. God bless you, my friend, and may the good Lord watch over you."

His eyes misted over, and he went back to his chair and sat down. His glass was empty, and he poured himself another two fingers and took it down slowly. As he put the glass down on the desk, he nudged the photograph of Laura and the twins. His favorite, the one he took himself on a glorious summer's day down on the ranch. He leant on the desk and cupped his chin in his hands, staring at it for an age before averting his eyes. Then he opened the center drawer of his desk and took out a red leather gift box. He placed it carefully on the desk, opened it, and looked at the inscription inside.

To our illustrious president
George W. Bush on his 50th birthday
May God reward you with many more

U.S. National Rifle Association

He traced his fingers over the golden letters, smiling as he did so. The Smith and Wesson magnum glinted as he took it from the box and held it in hands that trembled slightly as he felt the weight. He thumbed the cylinder open, inserted a single cartridge, and spun the cylinder. There was a moment's hesitation, and then he picked up the remaining rounds, completed the load, and snapped the cylinder shut. He placed the gun on the desk, flipped the switch on the intercom, and spoke into it. "Theo," he said, "it's go ahead with the bombing. I'll be up directly."

He flipped the switch, picked up the gun, spun the chamber another three times, and placed in on the desk, staring at it for a good two minutes. The rain hammered against the window as he picked the gun up once more and held it against the side of his head. He closed his eyes, put his forefinger on the trigger, and began to squeeze it softly, as he had been taught many times by the hired hands on the ranch. He grunted as his finger froze and refused to complete the movement, and he took his finger off the trigger and tried again. Beads of sweat appeared on his forehead as the refusal was repeated. He tried again and again but without success, and at last, angry and frustrated, he took the gun away from his head and banged it down on the desk. Tears dripped down his face as he stared at the object of his anger and made as if to pick it up once more. But this time, he was unable to move even his arm toward it. He looked up appealingly at the ceiling dome and began to pray, pleading for forgiveness and a blessing. He drew comfort from the reply, and drying his eyes with his handkerchief, he emptied the bullets from the revolver, put the items back in the box, and returned it to the drawer.

Chapter 13

The troop had passed by the Wadi Halfa at least forty times in the course of their patrols along the border, and it was now as familiar to them as the Iranian border post two kilometers east, the post that flew a huge Iranian flag that was larger than the building itself. Wadi Halfa was a deep gash in the desert floor one hundred meters wide and nearly two kilometers long. Twice when they had passed it going north, his patrol had been fired on by insurgents well concealed behind its banks. The next occasion they were fired upon, Luke had sprung a trap by sending two Pinkies well to the west of the Wadi, and when they received the signal that the main troop was under fire, they charged in and caught the enemy unawares. After that, there was rarely any hostile action but in order to protect his flank, Luke would always dispatch a Pinkie to reconnoiter the opposite side of the position.

On his second-to-last patrol before taking his first leave in over two years, Luke was at the wheel of the reconnaissance Pinkie when it hit a mine. The explosion ripped through the offside floor of the Pinkie, turned the vehicle on its side, and killed the co-driver outright. Luke was lucky. He was knocked unconscious and was pulled from the wreckage by the two rear troopers, who were unhurt. Two days later, he awoke in the military wing of a Birmingham hospital to find himself covered in bandages, minus his left leg, six broken ribs, a punctured lung, and a dislocated shoulder.

Although he was fortunate enough to have visitors two or three times a week, it was nearly a month before the person Luke wanted to see most of all came to see him.

"Good to see you again, Luke," spoke a cultured voice as Luke looked up in astonishment at the bearded, bespectacled figure who hung up his coat and hat and came toward him with his hand held out.

"Do I know you?" he asked, wondering if the visitor was yet another consultant. "The voice sounds familiar."

"What if I was to tell you that I'm your employer, and I'm here to offer you a new position in the company?" the visitor said mischievously, pulling off the composite mask and revealing the smiling face of Colonel Wingate.

"Crikey!" Luke exclaimed as he took the hand and shook it nervously. "The boss himself. Very nice to see you again, sir. It's been a long time."

"It certainly has, Luke. Too long. Let's hope it won't be like that in the future. I'm sorry I'm late visiting but I've been out of the country and only returned yesterday."

Luke grinned and pointed to the mask. "Is that your latest party trick or have you come to examine my broken bones?" he asked. "Everyone except the hospital cook has."

"I think not, old man, I'm told you're making good progress. What's your own honest opinion?"

"Bloody slow, I've hardly been off the bed since I got here. It's not the leg, it's my lung. They still haven't got the bits out. Now they're telling me the ribs will have to mend before they dare have another go. That will take weeks, and I'll be right round the bend and not worth saving by then."

"What about the leg?"

"The pain's gone, but they can't send me to the rehab for fitting an artificial until my lung has healed. They're right, of course, there's no way I could do any exercising, I haven't got the breath to blow out a candle."

"Patience, lad, just remember how lucky you are and look on this as an extended R&R without the swimming pool and the ladies.

You're in good hands, unlike some of the poor patients in the National Health Service wards next door."

"What's with the disguise?" asked Luke. "Was that a joke?"

"Hardly," Wingate replied in a serious voice. "If I was recognized by the Section Four police, I'd either be arrested or shot. When I tell you that we're under siege at our base, I'm not exaggerating our position. Either Section Three or Section Four are bugging us all the time. We hardly ever attempt an exit or entry in broad daylight anymore except for exercises in the Beacons or picking up supplies. In those cases, we form a convoy with a Warrior front and rear."

Luke was amazed. "Section Three and Section Four? Jesus Christ, I've been away too long, what do they do for a living?"

"Section Four is our equivalent of the Stasi. They're the ones in long black leather coats who knock on your door in the middle of the night and take you away for questioning."

"And Section Three?"

"Paramilitaries, one hundred thousand of them. We call them 'Pinkoes' because that's the color of the beret they've been kitted out with. They were supposedly formed to protect us from our naughty homegrown terrorists. If a Pakistani passenger even breaks wind in flight, the pilot is on to airport security and there will be a battalion of them on the tarmac complete with tanks and choppers to form a welcoming party. They are also responsible for breaking up strikes and protests or anything else the government judges to be against the public welfare. We are the latest to be added to their list of undesirables. The OC is a General Kruger, ex-Boer and ANC turncoat."

"Whatever happened to the old-time coppers?"

"Oh, they're Section One. They still excel in chasing motorists, locking up old ladies who don't pay their council tax, and harassing our red-coated fox hunting friends in the country."

"My God! Don't tell me there's a Section Two as well."

"There is. They call it Intelligence, the old MI5, MI6, ID, and Passport Control knocked into one. Some call it BBSS: Big Brother's Secret Service. All four sections form Blair's new Department of Homeland Security, a carbon copy of Bush's brainwave but without any of the personal safeguards. Of course, it's all a gigantic Labor plan to control and regulate every aspect of a British citizen's life from cradle to grave, just as they have done with the Health Service. Oh! I forgot, there's also a Section Five."

Luke groaned. "Don't tell me, let me guess. It's an age-related termination unit."

Wingate laughed. "Worse than that even. CDMC: Control and Dissemination of Media Content."

"Good God, why did I leave Iraq?" moaned Luke. "There's more freedom there if you can avoid getting shot up by the bad guys." He paused for a minute and brought his voice down to a whisper. "If you are right, then somebody will be bugging us this very minute."

Wingate laughed again. "Don't worry, they do plenty of that next door but not here. Our boys sweep the military wards twice a day, once before visiting hours and again when they've gone. After that, a fly would have a hard time avoiding detection. Of course, the hospital is under surveillance from the outside, and every visitor is checked out by the Stasis, hence the disguise."

"How did you get out of the base then?"

"Chopper and then shank's pony. See! I've still got the mud on my boots."

Luke shook head. He wouldn't have been a bit surprised if the old warrior had dropped in by parachute.

"How are they looking after you? Any complaints?" asked Wingate.

"Not a one, I'd give every one of the staff a medal for competence and humanity."

"That's good, you're in for a DSC yourself. Oh, and I nearly forgot, it's Major Dryden as from yesterday."

Luke couldn't hide his amazement. "Major? A squadron?" he blurted out. "What in heaven's name have I done to deserve that? I screwed up. I got my number two killed, wrote off a Pinkie, and crippled myself. I should have used a different route. The insurgents made a note of my previous pass and laid a minefield a rabbit couldn't navigate. It was an unforgivable error of judgment. I deserve a demotion, not a promotion."

"Nonsense," Wingate snorted, "after the number of passes your troops made around the wadi, a hit was inevitable, sooner or later. It's the work you've done along the border that's got you your promotion, not to mention the Fat Man assignment in Iran. Now don't get carried away, I said nothing about a command. I've had a word with the hospital OC, and he tells me there is no way you could play an active part in a Sabre Squadron right now. He estimates you could be ready for light duties in six months and normal duties in another six, assuming everything goes well with your treatment."

"Bloody hell," Luke protested, "I heard Jim Garfield lost a leg and was back in Afghanistan in less than six months. If he can do it, so can I."

"Jimmy didn't suffer any other injuries, Luke," said Wingate patiently, "and he's not been posted to the front line yet. Your main problem is your lung. They are only able to operate in stages to remove all the foreign bodies. Until this is done and your lung is fully functioning again, they will not send you down to rehab. It takes a lot of physical effort to adapt to an artificial leg, and exposing a weakened lung to that kind of demand could lead to serious complications. Take the doctor's advice, my friend; the people here are tops. Best in the world, I would say."

Luke looked downcast. "I'm sorry, but there's no way I could take a desk job, even a support job. I'm a country boy, open-air fiend, if you like. I'd be useless, staring out of the window at bricks and mortar all day long. I wouldn't last a month."

"That's not true, Luke. The General told me you used to spend hour upon hour up in his stuffy attic war games room. He said you would sometimes stay up until you fell asleep, and he would have to lay you down on a couch for the night. And what about the time you spent inside during officer training? You were inside learning tactics every bit as much as training outdoors."

"Yes," Luke said ruefully, "that was before the action started. Right now, there's no place I'd rather be than in the desert. It's in my blood. Like David Sterling said, once you've experienced its magical mystery, you're its prisoner for life."

"I agree with that, since I've experienced the same feeling myself. But as they say, all good things come to an end. And as it happens, your misfortune is for us a blessing in disguise."

At that moment, there was a knock on the door, and a huge trolley appeared in the doorway, guided by two nurses in trim blue and white uniforms.

"Morning, sirs," trilled the taller of the two, an attractive blonde with rosy cheeks and pink-lacquered eyelids. "What would you like to drink: coffee, tea, cold milk, or lemonade?"

"One tea without sugar and one black coffee with sugar," she called to her assistant, repeating Luke and Wingate's preferences.

The assistant's eyes never left Luke as she felt for a cup and overfilled it.

"Look out what you're doing!" the blonde snapped as tea slopped over the trolley. "No, don't use the same cup, for God's sake, use a new one."

She waited impatiently for the drinks and then delivered them, first to Wingate and then to Luke.

"Sorry about that, Captain," she smiled as she held Luke's hand and fitted the mug into it before slowly releasing her grasp. "Is there anything else I can get you? There's biscuits, mince pies, grapes, and sausage rolls; oh yes, and chocolate éclairs."

"No, thanks, Mavis," said Luke, "just coffee is fine."

"Are you sure, Captain? Perhaps another coffee then."

"Thanks again, Mavis, I'm fine. Perhaps this afternoon."

Luke rolled his eyes as he saw Wingate grinning at him, and he waited impatiently as the nurses mopped the floor thoroughly before taking their leave.

Colonel Wingate drank half of his tea, placed the mug on the bedside table, and folded his arms. "Luke," he said, "do you remember the talk we had when I left Camp Bastion two years ago concerning General Alexander's movement?"

"I certainly do. I've been waiting for something to happen ever since, but if it has, I haven't heard about it," Luke replied.

"Of course you haven't, it's not a topic that can be aired in the officer's mess even, let alone among the rank and file. Unfortunately, it is the need for absolute secrecy that has forced us to delay any worthwhile decision making time and time again. However, I can tell you now that things are coming together rapidly, and our plans envisage a military takeover before the end of the year."

Luke struggled to sit up straight, excitement showing in his eyes as the enormity of Wingate's words sunk in.

"The Chief of the General Staff and the General Officer Commanding cannot be trusted to become involved in our plans, and Alexander and Montgomery have agreed that I should take charge of the operation since they are in no position to take a hands-on approach from their posts in Iraq and Afghanistan. The position with the navy and air force is somewhat difficult. Both Admiral Cunningham and Air Chief Marshall Harris are sympathetic to our cause but they can't do much to help since what forces they have left after their commitments in Iraq and Afghanistan are swallowed up by this damned new European Defense Force that we've signed up to. However, they have given me their categorical assurance that under no circumstances will they take any action against any of the forces belonging to Union Jack, which, at the moment, consists of the Special Forces Regiments and the Rapid Reaction Force based in France."

"Excuse me, sir, you said regiments. Does that include us and the 21st and 23rd as well?"

"It does. We completed the final transfer of 23SAS to Credenhill only two weeks ago."

Luke whistled. "Blimey, all three under one roof. How the devil did you manage to fit them all in?"

"Not too badly really. Seventy percent of effective personnel are overseas, so billeting was relatively easy. It was the equipment that caused most of the problems. It is amazing how much ordnance we have acquired from various sources. At the last count, we had eighteen Challenger 2 tanks, thirty-six Warriors, sixty-odd PCs, thirty artillery pieces, twelve Lynx helicopters, plus more than a thousand ground-to-air missile launchers and countless mortars and RPGs."

Luke whistled again. "That is unbelievable; how on earth did you manage to get hold of the stuff, let alone transfer it to Credenhill?"

"Let's say we purloined most of it from our sympathizers in the Scottish Division, the Queen's Division, and the Light Division, and of course, the Royal Artillery and 3rd Mechanized Division, and leave it at that. It is nowhere near enough for our purposes but we estimate that in the next six months, we will have trebled our strength and will be combat ready in October at the latest. A great deal depends on the Rapid Reaction Force in France. 2Para and 3Para are vital to our needs; without them, we could be in a lot of trouble."

"What if the Paramilitaries mount a full-scale attack on Credenhill? We wouldn't have a prayer against a force of fifty thousand men attacking such a small perimeter."

Wingate sighed. "That's our Achilles' heel, I'm afraid. Section Three have only been operational for just over a year and are not yet fully trained. But they are catching up fast. Pretty soon they will have armor and air cover, and that is really bad news. If it is soon, they will be able to blockade us in our base and prevent us from building up our strength."

Luke looked puzzled. "But sir, why are you telling me all this top-secret stuff? There's nothing I can do to help. All I want to do is get out of here as fast as possible, pick up a new leg, and get back to my troop in Iraq before the balloon goes up. The situation there is on a knife edge since that maniac Blair pulled out two battalions. The Shia are going take that as an invitation to remove the rest of our army, and they aren't going to do it using blank cartridges."

"Luke, as I've already said, we are well on our way to achieving our objective, but there is one strength we haven't got that every army needs in a situation like this, and that's why I'm here. I want you to set up a fifth column, an undercover army to counter the advantage they will soon have. An army that will play havoc with the enemy's war capabilities, lines of communication, and relations with the civilian population."

Luke was astounded. "Me, a fifth columnist?" he cried. "Working underground? That's fantasy stuff. I wouldn't last a week."

"I disagree," said Wingate. "Many of the reports you sent back from your patrols were incredibly detailed and informative. Ask anyone in intelligence, and they will tell you the same. On top of that, the descriptive accounts you sent in of actions in Iraq and Afghanistan were snapped up by the *Mail* and *Express,* and they are constantly asking for more. As for the Fat Man exercise, there has never been a sabotage operation anywhere, at any time, that could compare with the magnitude of its influence on a theatre of war. Luke, the job I'm offering is tailor-made for a man of your experience and capabilities. Your contribution to the success of Union Jack would dwarf any performance a troop or even a squadron could make on the battlefield, no matter how heroic and derring-do it might be. It could even make the difference between victory and defeat, I'm sure of that."

"But sir, I'm a cripple, a wheelchair warrior. What on earth could I possibly do that a junior officer with all his faculties couldn't do better?"

"It's your brain we want right now, Luke, not your body. We have no one in the Regiment who can match your organizational skills, and there is no way I would look outside of it for a candidate. I hope you don't mind, but I've talked to your grandfather about this, and he is 100 percent in favor. He told me you know the particulars of every battalion, brigade, division, corps, and ancillary unit in the modern British army as well as their bases and training grounds."

Luke laughed. "If I do, it's because the old devil crammed it into me since I was five years old. He's the one you want, not me."

"He did volunteer. Said he would report for duty at Credenhill at twenty-four-hours' notice."

"There you are, the man himself at Credenhill. Seriously, though, how could I be expected to carry out such a monumental task from a hospital bed?"

"Look, beneath this section of the hospital is a very large, empty store-room that I have got permission to use. I can set this room up with communications, computers, and anything else you think you might need. I'll also send up two of our best hackers, four communications experts, and a pair of ladies to take care of the filing and paperwork. You will be in complete charge of the operation, and you will report directly to me. Goddamn it, man, you'll go out of your mind sitting here wondering how things are going on down at the base. This way, you'll be an important part of the action, you'll be in contact with all personnel, and you'll have a big say in the setting up of the interim government when we've finally achieved our aims. What do you say?"

Luke stared at the kindly face of the man he respected more than any other, and he felt ashamed. To think that he had obliged one of

Britain's greatest soldiers to practically beg him to perform a task that he was honor-bound to carry out as a member of the SAS sent a shiver down his spine. He did his utmost to sit up to attention and look seriously at his commanding officer. "Colonel Wingate, sir, can I ask you just two questions?"

"Of course. Go ahead."

"One, how many men do you think I would have to recruit to suit your purpose?"

"I had in mind twenty-five thousand. Thirty thousand would be admirable. And the second question?"

"How soon can I start?"

Chapter 14

The message was personal and designed to appeal to an ex-soldier's sense of duty. It read:

Dear _____

Our country is now facing the greatest threat to its existence since the Second World War. Only an immediate change of government can halt the calamitous slide into anarchy and economic collapse that the politicians in Westminster have brought about through their incompetence, greed, and total disregard for the welfare of the citizens who voted them into office.

My officers and I have decided that it is the solemn duty of those entrusted with the defense of our nation in war to extend that trust to fight the corrosive totalitarian influences that now seek to destroy us from within. Our aim is to throw out and punish the charlatans who have betrayed us and replace them with a caretaker government composed entirely of military personnel dedicated to the restoration of law and order, free speech, and economic competence. We shall also withdraw from the European Union and repeal all laws imposed on our nation by that undemocratic body. Finally, we will restore the precious freedoms our nation has long enjoyed thanks to the sacrifices made by our brothers in arms who are no longer with us.

We face a duplicitous enemy that will use every means possible to retain their power and riches, including treason, murder, torture, and genocide. We regret to say that these creatures have suborned the highest echelons of our three services, and we are unable to count on their full support. We are therefore building a volunteer army at our base at Credenhill that is gaining in strength day by day. But we do need many more volunteers, and we are contacting qualified ex-servicemen who have served in Northern Ireland and abroad. Our records show that you are one of these proud people, and we ask that once again you will answer the call to duty and join us in our fight to save our country.

We must warn you that the task will be highly dangerous, and you may be called upon at any time to embark upon operations that will bring you into conflict with the well-armed paramilitary formations that the government has created in order to enforce their will upon our people.

If you do decide to sign up to our great cause, please reply immediately by e-mail to: www.saveournation.uk.co when further instructions will be sent to you.

Yours sincerely,

Colonel J. C. Wingate
Commanding Officer
SAS Regiment, Credenhill

The "Kitcheners," as Luke's new team was christened (after the surname of the great World War 1 recruiting officer) reckoned that if they were to recruit volunteers, the first thing they would have to do was to organize a network of receiving centers within easy reach of recruits, many of whom would have to return to their homes each day after receiving training.

Their main target was the Territorial Army (TA), a body that had become increasingly disillusioned with their treatment from a cost-cutting government that expected them to provide cover for the troops in Iraq and Afghanistan and treated them like second-class citizens when they returned home, often to find that because of high unemployment, they had lost their jobs and, in many cases, their good health.

Negotiations were at an impasse, until one day a sympathizer in the ministry of defense leaked a document recommending that the TA should be removed from its present supporting role with the army and amalgamated with Section Three Paramilitaries under the command of General Kruger. The paper was addressed to the defense secretary and signed by his first minister.

From that day on, the TA became a powerful supporter of the Union Jack movement and unreservedly dedicated its nationwide network of drill halls and training facilities to the cause, in return for full funding and replacement of equipment and supplies lost to the regular army. Fifty strategically placed TA sub-facilities were placed at the disposal of the Kitcheners, along with ten TA super-facilities that would be the depositories for all the heavy armor, transports, and artillery forming the spearhead of each unit that would be sent out to confront the enemy. All bases were to be commanded by officers from the SAS and other Special Forces units.

The response to the appeal was immediate and overwhelming, so much so that Luke's team were forced to divert many of the respondents to Credenhill and regional TA recruiting offices. Each favorable reply automatically prompted a request for further information on health, family ties, present address, and a specific reason for wanting to enlist. From these new details, a final intake of fifty thousand volunteers was drawn up, and forty thousand were instructed to report to the designated base nearest to their home at staged intervals. The remaining ten thousand were asked to remain on standby, ready to report for duty at a moment's notice.

A supplementary statement was also e-mailed to every respondent advising them to check their entitlements for regular pensions, war widows pensions, disablement payments, housing allowances, and other ex gratia emoluments. This move was initiated because the Kitcheners had accidentally discovered while trawling through the ministry of defense databases a huge scam involving underpayments amounting to hundreds of millions of pounds to current and former servicemen dating from the year 1997. A proviso was inserted guaranteeing that the criminals involved in the scam will be punished and the stolen money refunded with interest within one month of Union Jack taking over the reins of government

The next task for the Kitcheners was financing the operation. Advertisements in the remaining independent newspapers—the *Daily Mail*, *Telegraph*, and *Daily Express*—attracted donations from business and private individuals at home and abroad of over a billion pounds in the first month alone, with promises of further help if a second appeal was launched. Supplementing this advertising were the efforts of the high-tech experts in the team, who succeeded in breaking into local radio broadcasts around the clock without incurring any costs to themselves.

But the biggest prize of all was a no-strings-attached secret donation of £2 billion from the French government. The gift was authorized by the president, who desperately wanted Britain out of the European Union. He let it be known that it was his cherished aim to re-establish French domination of the EU, and with a recalcitrant Britain out of the way, his task would be made that much easier.

Even the government was forced to contribute indirectly. When the ministry of defense threatened to cut off all funding to the SAS and Special Forces, they were given an ultimatum: withdraw the threat or all Special Forces operating abroad would be recalled. Faced with this counter-threat, the supine chiefs of staff, aware that this would cause havoc among the armed forces in Iraq and Afghanistan, forced the ministry of defense to back down. But that was not good enough for Jock Wingate. He immediately put in a requisition for the replacement of worn-out or damaged equipment, to the tune of nearly £1 billion.

Another important task was arms procurement. A healthy-looking war chest was the easy part. Purchasing the armaments was a lot more difficult. Jock Wingate had intimated he would like to treble his existing stocks, but since the army chiefs had closed the door on any further transfers, other avenues had to be explored. Standard items such as uniforms, small arms, and light transport were easily acquired. It was the heavy armor, artillery, air transports, and helicopters that were the big problem, and it was causing plenty of headaches for the team. Then along came an unlikely benefactor in the person of Victor Anatoliyevich Bout, the notorious Russian arms dealer. Although officially embargoed in most countries, Bout had put together a huge package of arms for the Iraqi government, which was resigned to the prospect of the United States and the UK quitting the country sooner rather than later. Included in the package were one hundred Challenger tanks with transporters and two hundred Saxon APCs, which the UK had agreed to supply at a knock-down price. These, along with an American contribution, were to be delivered to a secret airbase outside Moscow. They were then to be delivered to Iraq in Bout's fleet of Antanov cargo planes, in one batch, when called for.

Everything was going according to plan, and about half the package had been committed when all of a sudden, supplies dried up with no explanation from the U.S. and UK governments. The Iraqis refused to accept a reduced package, and Bout was left high and dry, holding more than £4 billion worth of C-130 transports, Apache gunships, Challenger tanks, Saxon APCs, howitzers, and tons of ammunition and spares.

Bout quickly found out that the person responsible for cancelling the British order was the newly appointed foreign secretary, a rabid left-winger who, in turn, had persuaded his American counterpart to do the same. When he became aware of the Kitcheners' search for arms, he immediately offered them the whole consignment at cost price, delivery included. All they had to do in return was pay cash up front in dollars and provide a landing strip big enough to land the Antanov cargo aircraft.

The Kitcheners agreed to the sale and immediately set about finding a suitable airfield. They settled on one at Shobdon, an ex-RAF airfield eleven kilometers north of Credenhill. Colonel Wingate immediately ordered three mobility troops and a unit of engineers to take over the field and secure it.

One month later, the last of the package was delivered from Russia, and the Kitcheners set about allocating the armaments they had obtained from all sources and dispersed them to the ten TA super-bases. By the end of August, Luke was able to deliver to Colonel Wingate a fully trained, well-equipped army of forty thousand volunteers with another ten thousand in reserve.

Luke would always look back in pride at the achievement of his team and the vital part it was destined to play in the downfall of Blair's hated government. At the end he was worn out, but in the midst of the tremendous feats of planning and organization, as well as his own recuperation, there occurred a blessing that more than compensated for the long hours and sleepless nights he had endured week after week.

On a brilliant sunny morning he would never forget as long as he lived, he was awakened by a hand shaking his shoulder. He looked up through bleary eyes at an angel standing over his bed.

"What time do you get up in the mornings, Major?" the angel asked, smiling down at him.

"0600," he replied dreamily.

"Well, it's 0630 now and you've overslept. Time for your early morning exercise. It's a lovely day. Just your dressing gown will do."

The voice was firm but gentle, the face small and exquisite. And the smile? There was only one way to describe it. It was a sunbeam lighting up the world.

Still half-asleep, Luke spoke distantly.

"Excuse me, but are we going somewhere? I haven't been told of any appointment."

"No, Major, your appointment is with me, and I'm taking you out for some fresh air. I'm told you haven't been outside the building since you were admitted."

She had a lovely speaking voice, low but clear as a bell, from the South. The Home Counties, he guessed. "I'm sorry, but I'm due down in my office in half an hour. Maybe later, this afternoon perhaps."

"That means not today or even this week, Major Dryden," she scolded. "I've been warned that you would fob me off. You're a workaholic and you're damaging your health."

"Now who's been telling tales out of school? Someone after my job, maybe."

"No, the one who gave you your job: Colonel Wingate."

Luke was amazed. "You mean to tell me the boss ordered you to turf me out of bed and cart me out into the freezing cold?"

Her laugh was musical. "No, of course not. I work for the Women's Royal Voluntary Service and I'm just following their instructions. Would you rather I left and got on with something else?"

"No, no," Luke said quickly, "please don't do that. Orders are orders. Will you please pass me my dressing gown and hold on for a minute while I brush my teeth? By the way, what's your name?"

"Carol. Carol Sanderson."

"Nice to meet you, Carol. Mine's Luke."

Carol was right, he had been abusing his body, working eighteen hours a day, seven days a week, down in the basement. As she pushed him slowly down the pathway and into the hospital gardens, the arboreal setting and the warm sunlight on his face reminded him of his open-air upbringing and his affinity with nature. He felt ten years younger, full of the joys of spring and in sync with the world once more. But it wasn't just mother nature that had made his spirits soar, or the sudden lifting of the burden of office. It was the beauty and the nearness of the caring young woman who had entered his life so suddenly and captured his heart—hook, line, and sinker.

Carol Sanderson was a war widow, married for eight years with two children, a boy and a girl. Her husband, Lieutenant Robert Sanderson, was killed in Iraq when a roadside bomb blew up his vehicle. She lived in a quiet cul-de-sac at the south end of Grove Park, roughly a mile from the hospital, where she worked as a radiographer. Her sister, Kate, also worked at the same hospital and boarded with her. The children's names were Elizabeth and James, and there was a dog that sometimes answered to the name of Troy.

Luke asked her what she was doing, helping out at such an ungodly hour of the day, and she told him she loved the purity of the unspoiled break of day, and it was really the only time of day she could spare, two hours before she had to take the children to her mother and then clock in for work. She had been doing the voluntary work for over a year and was well practiced at dealing with injured soldiers, particularly amputees. There was nothing clinical about her duties. She devoted all her time to putting the patients at ease and taking their minds off their afflictions and personal problems. More often than not, she would write letters for them, read newspapers, and shop for toiletries, snacks, and CDs. Altogether, Carol devoted fourteen hours to her voluntary work—two hours on five weekdays and four hours on Sunday afternoon. Luke was fortunate to be the next patient allocated to her care after the discharge of her last patient, another amputee.

Never had a Tuesday morning brought such anticipation into Luke's life. To most soldiers, every day of the week was the same, especially abroad on active service. Now one particular day had become something special for him. He would wake up at five or even earlier, shave, and put on his best dress uniform. Then he would get into his wheelchair and face the door, waiting impatiently for it to open and reveal the vision that was beginning to take hold of his life. He began to envy the marine sergeant on the floor above, who enjoyed the second hour of her presence, and also the patients she visited on the other weekdays and more especially on Sunday afternoons. He no longer felt that the daily routine down in the basement was the most important part of his life, and he began to take more of an interest in his health. They had removed the final piece of shrapnel from his lung and given him the all-clear to prepare himself for the fitting of an artificial leg. This he set out to do with a vengeance in the hospital gym, and within a month, he transferred to the army rehabilitation center at Headley Court for the fitting.

His progress was remarkable, a fact that he put down to his eagerness to get back to see Carol again. His work with the Union Jack team had not been affected too badly, as he had kept in touch through a video link set up in the rehab center. The fitting of his artificial leg went without a hitch, and after a seemingly endless regime of physical exercises, the doctors pronounced him fit for light duties and gave him his discharge.

On his first day back at Selly Oak Military Hospital, he spent the day with the team in the basement, and at 7:00 PM, he walked across the hospital grounds and leaned against a large chestnut tree bordering the access road leading to the accident and emergency block. He took out his mobile and spoke into it. Within seconds a Warrior personnel carrier roared out on to the main road. It charged across the road and smashed into a black saloon car parked halfway onto the pavement and shunted it into the adjacent grass verge. It then reversed onto the road and charged into a four by four parked twelve yards farther on and did the same before reversing back and driving through the entrance into the hospital.

Luke grinned as he watched the occupants scramble out of both vehicles, and gather together, waving their arms and screaming obscenities. He waited for a few minutes until they turned their attention to their wrecked vehicles before stepping out onto the pavement and walking in the opposite direction, marveling at the ingenuity of the unit charged with clearing the way for military personnel to visit or exit the hospital and evade the attention of the Section Four goons.

It was a short distance to Carol's house and he knocked nervously on her door. The welcoming smile on her face said it all. They embraced, and he entered a magical world inhabited by the most beautiful woman in the world, her equally beautiful sister, two enchanting children, and a happy-go-lucky golden Labrador called Troy, who grabbed his hand in his soft, moist mouth, and refused to let go until he was bribed with a biscuit by one of the children.

They were married in the hospital chapel by the Regimental Chaplain. The General, his wife, and the rest of Luke's family were in attendance, as were members of Carol's family, four of them from the U.S. and two from Canada. It was by far the happiest day of Luke's life. Even his artificial leg seemed to join in the celebrations, as he never experienced even one twinge, despite all the activity he indulged in.

The honeymoon was short and sweet. Urgent messages from his team made it imperative that he return to Selly Oak hospital, and he reluctantly gave up two days of blissful enjoyment that he swore could never be replicated for as long as he lived.

Chapter 15

L uke Dryden woke up with a start. He could have sworn he heard the familiar sound of a 200mm shell screaming through the air and exploding with a terrific bang somewhere over his window. He lay still for a moment or two, convinced he had been dreaming, and recalled the experience during training when he crouched head down in a foxhole listening to shells screaming overhead, followed minutes later by the deafening roar of the Challenger 2 tank that had launched them as it passed directly over his foxhole.

There were other noises coming from down below, and he switched on his bed-light and swung his good leg over the edge of the bed. Before he could reach for his crutches, however, he heard the scream of another shell coming, and this time he dropped to the floor and stuck his head and shoulders beneath the bed only moments before the window blew in and showered the room with glass and brickwork. The room was lit up by flames pouring out of a window on the floor above. Now he could identify the noises down below: rifle and machine-gun fire interspersed with RPGs and voices screaming and shouting out orders.

The door burst open, and a figure came charging in, shining a flashlight. "Jesus, Luke, where in the hell are you?" a voice shouted in a pronounced Welsh accent.

"Under the bed, looking for my leg," replied Luke. "That you, Kinnel?"

"Thank goodness for that. Looks like someone's got it in for you, boyo."

Sergeant Parry knelt down and gave Luke his arm as he dragged himself up and sat on the bed.

"What's going on, Kinnel?" Luke asked as he shook the debris off his clothes.

"Dunno. Someone shouted they're shooting at us. From across the park, I think."

Luke swore. "Jesus, give me a hand to strap my leg on; we're sitting ducks up here, and we've got to get out right quick. I heard RPGs, but they didn't sound like they were coming this way."

"No, there's a real battle going on outside, and I'm itching to get out there. You think you're fit enough to join in, Luke?"

"Try and stop me. Round up the team and gather them in the basement. Get Gerry to break out the armaments. And try and raise Sergeant MacDonald. Give me your flashlight, and I'll meet you down there right away."

Luke moved to the window as he dressed and looked out over the park. There was some activity going on the other side, and he could hear the sound of a heavy machine-gun opening up. He also thought he could see a big blaze behind one of the trees. It was brightly lit down below, and he spotted a number of figures running into the park, all with rifles in their hands. "Right," he said, looking down at his left leg, "now we'll find out how good you are. Don't let me down, or I'll sell you off for scrap iron."

It was practically all over when Luke and his team reached the other side of the park. The firing had stopped, and Luke stood and stared in amazement at a tank transporter pulled up on the road at the park's edge. It was on fire throughout its length, including the Challenger tank it was carrying. As they watched, there was an explosion beneath the tank, and the troops facing it edged back to avoid the sparks and debris thrown up into the air.

"Thank God, we thought you'd caught it, Luke!" a tall figure shouted, striding toward him. "Take a look at that," Sergeant Neil MacDonald boomed, pointing at the hospital.

Luke turned and looked back at the hospital. He could see his own shattered window on the second floor, and above that to the left was a huge, gaping hole in the brickwork, with smoke and flames pouring from it.

"Jesus!" Luke moved involuntarily forward but MacDonald checked him. "The medics are up there, and the hospital firemen are tackling the blaze. There's nothing you can do, Luke; leave it to them."

Grim faced, Luke turned and looked at the transporter. The gun was side-on, pointing up at the hospital and looking like a flaming torch in the night sky. He shook his head and said, "Firing off a transporter? It's unheard of, Mac. Tell me what happened."

"It's the Pinkoes. Pulled up around 0500. I was on watch at the time, and we heard an almighty crashing of gears and went to investigate. It was the Challenger's gearbox making the racket, not the transporter. The driver couldn't move it a centimeter. As we approached, we saw the turret swing around and fire a round at the hospital. Trooper Ronson was carrying a 203, and he took out the cab and then put another round into the gas tank section. The flames engulfed the tank but they managed to get off another round before the hatch opened and a Pinko came up with a revolver in his hand. Bridges topped him, and he fell back inside. Seconds later, three crewmen scrambled out, screaming, and jumped off with their clothes on fire. We doused the flames, and all three of them are lying on the ground over there. I've sent for the medics; they should be here any time now."

Luke walked over to the three Pinkoes and stood over them, shining his flashlight on each one in turn. Two were shivering and making moaning sounds, while the third looked up at him with the hollow eyes of a man in great pain, licking his lips constantly. "For God's sake, can't you keep the bloody kaffirs quiet?" he croaked. "The crybabies are driving me crazy."

"You sound like a South African," said Luke. "Are you?"

"I was."

"Army?"

"Yes."

"What are you doing over here?"

There was no answer.

Luke walked back to join Sergeant MacDonald. "Where's the one who got shot, Mac?"

"Over there, by the Pinkie."

"Dead?"

"Yes."

"White or black?"

"White."

"Looks like a South African crew, two white and two black. Strange, eh?"

"That's how they do it nowadays," growled MacDonald. "Like in rugby, half the team has to be black, even if they're dickheads."

"So we owe our lives to a defective gearbox, do we? Are you sure it was the gearbox?"

"That's what Jonesy says. He's ex-engineers, and he says the earlier Challenger 1 had problems with the gearbox in the Gulf War."

Luke looked scornful. "Looks like we're not the only ones kitted out with shitty equipment, doesn't it? Let's hope the rest of the Pinko army is equipped like that."

"Better evacuate quick if you ask me," urged MacDonald. "The magazine's liable to go off any minute now. There will be some fireworks then, believe you me."

Luke was on first-name terms with the editor of the *Daily Mail*, John Gibbons.

"John," he said as, after a long delay, a sleepy voice answered the phone, "this is Luke Dryden speaking from the Selly Oak Military Hospital. Are you looking for a good story to start off the new day?"

"Good God, Luke, you're up early," came the reply. "How's it going, and how's the leg?"

"Couldn't be better. And you?"

"Half-dead at this time of the morning. Let's have it, Luke."

"Get a crew down here right away. The Pinkoes have been shooting up the hospital with a Challenger tank. We've got three prisoners, and I want you to photograph and interview them as quickly as possible."

"The hell you say. Any casualties?"

"Two in the military wing and some in the civilian wing at the rear. I want you to give this the max, John. Will you do that for me?"

"You'd better believe it." There was a pause. "Anyone else getting the story, Luke?"

"I'll give you fifteen minutes before I call the *Express* and the *Telegraph*, no more. This place will be crawling with the law any time now."

"Forget the *Telegraph*, Luke, they're in Campbell's pocket now. They'll shit on you for sure."

"I'll give them this one last chance. If they do, so be it."

"What about the TV channels?" asked the editor.

"You must be joking, I wouldn't touch any of them with a barge pole. I might try Al Jazeera, but I don't think they've got a crew outside London."

"More fool them. I know their London director. I'll get him to contact you at the hospital, okay?"

"Thanks, John."

"No, Luke, my thanks to you. Don't forget to buy a paper, will you? It will be in the second edition, all being well."

Luke put the phone down and sat back in his chair. John Gibbons of the *Mail* and David Beaverbrook of the *Express* were a dying breed. Every other ethical editor of the center-right dailies had been hounded out of their profession by a combination of New Labor apparatchiks and the combined efforts of Section Four and Section Five. Faced with trumped-up legal challenges orchestrated from the spin doctors in Downing Street and rapacious demands from the labor unions, their operating costs had risen to such an extent that they were forced to reduce their output, which inevitably led to a drop in circulation and profits. The two papers were just about managing to keep their heads above water, but both editors had told him that another few weeks of the present government would mean the end of their famous papers. The editor of the *Telegraph* had just been arrested and charged with printing inflammatory articles exposing the greed of all MPs in their plundering of public funds. This was deemed as liable to cause a public disturbance, and the writing was on the wall for that paper now that he was gone. John and David were men of principle and courage. Their demise would mean the end of any meaningful opposition for the millions of Britons who yearned for an end to the Orwellian dictates that were rapidly turning their beloved country into a hideous totalitarian state.

He had hardly put the phone down before his mobile rang. It was Colonel Wingate, and his order was brief: "Arrange for the immediate return to base of all team personnel and equipment, the Guard Troop, and Regiment patients. The bodies of Hughes and Willoughby are to be included in your party. A chopper will make ERV in park, 0800, Tuesday. I advise you to be prepared for enemy action while evacuating."

"Are you lot out of your tiny, fucking minds? You go and blast a hospital like a bunch of Nazis in Warsaw, kill six National Health Service patients fast asleep in their beds, and then tell you me you did good because you killed two SAS squaddies. Jesus Christ, man, the *Mail* and *Express* are carrying pictures that would make a sadist weep buckets."

Alastair Campbell was livid, and his crimson face showed his anger. As a professional journalist and Britain's top spin doctor, he knew the power of the front page, and no newspaper in the world could match the eye-catching imagery produced by the two tabloids. Millions of Britons would be damning the government for weeks to come. Why, even the *Times* and *Guardian* had been forced to condemn the incident, though they were careful to make their comments on an inside page and without pictures.

Things were going badly for New Labor and the strain was showing in Campbell's angular face. Even the carefully coiffured brown hair had lost its luster, as he neglected his personal appearance in his messianic pursuit of the New Labor project. He had become insular and intolerant; as a result, many his old friends avoided him like the plague. He had also lost his sense of humor and would take offense at the slightest criticism. The job of carrying the increasingly useless prime minister was taking its toll, and any one of the ministers who added to that burden was likely to feel the full effects of his bile. And Moses Mandella, the home secretary, was high on his list of dickheads.

"They weren't to know the target was part of the main hospital," replied Mandella defensively. "They were given a picture of the eastern face of the hospital and told to fire at a ground-floor window thirty meters in from the left-hand side."

"Some shooting," sneered Campbell, "just like England taking penalties. The nearest they got was two floors up, and who did they think they were going to eliminate at five o'clock in the morning, for Christ's sake?"

"They needed darkness for cover; the place is crawling with SAS."

"How many SAS?"

"Oh, I don't know. A troop or two."

"How many in a troop?"

Mandella scowled. "How the fuck should I know? Ask Dudley, he should know."

Dudley Coward, the defense minister, was standing, looking out of a window, trying to make himself as inconspicuous as possible.

"Dudley," snapped Campbell, "how many squaddies in an SAS troop, for Christ's sake?"

"I really don't know, Ali. I've never spoken to an SAS person since I was made defense minister."

"Well, can't you make an educated guess?"

Coward hesitated. "Er, um, perhaps twenty, maybe thirty, maybe even forty."

Campbell exploded. "Goddamn it, man, how do you expect to eliminate the bastards if you don't know their strengths and formations? If they've got a hundred troops and there's twenty in a troop, that means we're faced with two thousand men. If it's forty, then they've got four thousand men. How are you going to plan a battle with them on that kind of guesswork?"

"We're not planning anything at our end, Alastair," Coward replied. "That's Moses's department. Our agreement was that Moses and his Paramilitaries would deal with the SAS, and the army would deal with any attempts within its own ranks to join their revolt. We just haven't got the men and resources to do both, as you well know. Moses has bled us dry setting up his own private army. You've just seen a sample of their handiwork. Good God, I wouldn't like to be within a hundred kilometers of Credenhill when Kruger attacks their base, assuming he ever will."

"Fuck you, Dudley," Mandella said viciously. "A thousand kilometers would be too close for you and your armchair generals if there was any action going on. Kruger tells me he'll be ready to take Credenhill in less than three months. Then we'll show you assholes what soldiering is all about."

"Okay you two, cut it out," Campbell said shortly. "There's too much at stake here for you to be arguing about who is to blame. The point is that bastard Dryden has made a fool of us once again and is by now safely holed up in Credenhill, planning more trouble. Don't you realize the man is fast becoming a cult figure with the masses? Both the *Mail* and the *Express* now refer to him as Dryden of Arabia. Mark my words, this latest cock-up is going to cost us dearly, I can feel it in my bones."

Normally, Campbell would enjoy the spectacle of two ministers going at it, hammer and tongs. It exposed weaknesses that he could profit by at later meetings of the cabinet. He looked upon government as he did the Premier League football club where he was the chairman, manager, and coach all rolled into one, totally in control, answerable to no one, except perhaps the fickle fans, whom he would appease with the sacking of an unpopular player or sometimes the promise of more investment at the annual board meeting. Since his return to power, he had been instrumental in the sacking of six members of the cabinet, and he intended to wipe the slate clean with the remainder before the next election. Coward was definitely the next one for the chop.

"But Alastair," whined Coward, "I can't hold off the army brass forever. There is already unrest in the lower ranks, and it is beginning to percolate through to divisional level. This Dryden character is beginning to assume the image of a national hero in the country areas outside the city swamps. What with his dispatches from Afghanistan and Iraq, his role in the Iran atom bomb plant, his humiliation of a sadistic general, and now his narrow escape from death in a military hospital, artificial leg and all. Why, there are more paparazzi parked outside the Credenhill base than there are Paramilitaries blockading it at the moment."

"All the more reason why Kruger should get his finger out and blitz the bloody base then!" Campbell shouted angrily. "Look, Moses, what is it going to take to get Kruger to move and concentrate all his forces on the main objective?"

Mandella smiled thinly. Campbell's tone was now conciliatory, conceding the argument without quite getting down on his knees and begging for his help.

"I'll give it to you straight," he purred. "Kruger is in no position to take on the SAS right now. All right, he's got one hundred thousand Paramilitaries under arms but most of them are tied up dealing with race riots up north, council tax riots, firefighting, waste-disposal duties, and ambulance services. I quite believe him when he tells me the most he can muster is twenty thousand as things are, and that is only a third of the number he says he wants to take on the SAS."

"So what do you suggest?" asked Campbell.

"One of two things. We enforce a curfew on all riot areas and shoot on sight any rioters and looters breaking the curfew. The other, five thousand men from the army's Home Division based in York to help us out."

"No, Alastair," protested Coward, "the Home Division is on twenty-four-hour notice to proceed to Northern Ireland should fighting break out between the Protestants and the Provos. Those are your own orders. You can't break up a combat division just like that. It reduces its effectiveness by 75 percent or more."

"What is the latest intelligence from Ulster, for Christ's sake?" sighed Campbell.

"Things are on a knife edge. Two more bombs in Belfast and one in Armagh. At least thirty casualties. Also six Catholics shot dead in Londonderry today. That makes over twenty this week."

"So who cares?" shrugged Mandella. "Let them kill each other off if that's what they want. The more Provos get killed, the better for us. No more bombings, and an end to all the security apparatus we have to provide, sorting the psychotic bastards out. That suits me fine. It's plain common sense, we either let them clobber each other or we let the SAS clobber us. Which is it to be?"

Campbell scratched his chin thoughtfully and looked at Coward. "Moses is right, you know, Dudley. I'm up to here with the fucking Provos trying to blow the shit out of London again. Also, I hope the Prots do give them a taste of their own bloody medicine and bump off Adams and McGuinness in the process. Yes, Moses is right, let them sort each other out. After a while, they'll get the message and come begging us for help. Then we'll only need half a division to bring them to heel. Get cracking and tell the Home Division to prepare to move half their troops down to Credenhill without delay. Have their OC liaise with Kruger and make plans to eliminate the fucking SAS once and for all."

Coward bit his lip. "Good God, Alastair, General Sherman will be spitting bullets. He hates the Paramilitaries, calls them shag's army or words to that effect."

"If I remember right, Dudley, you told me the general hated the SAS. Something to do with Kosovo."

"That's right, I did."

"And does the angry one still want a lordship when he retires?"

"Of course, that's why he's still on our side."

"Well, you tell your pussyfooting, shag-hating general that he'll be red carded if he doesn't do as he's told. Not only that, he'll be out of a job and think himself lucky if he makes private in shag's army. Got that, Dudley?"

Coward knew that the argument was at an end; the frosty look in Campbell's eyes told him that.

"Very well, Alastair, I'll put my foot down and tell him what you say. But don't blame me if Sherman winds up outside Credenhill with barely enough men to provide a guard for Buckingham Palace."

Mandella waited until Coward had closed the door behind him before addressing Campbell. "Jesus Christ, Alistair," he hissed, "you and Tony are tossing these medals and peerages around like they were prizes at Goose Fair. You'd better make sure my peerage is in the bank, otherwise when I decide to pack this job in, you'll both wish you'd never heard of the House of Lords."

"For heaven's sake, Moses," Campbell said soothingly, "yours is solid gold and packed in a casket, just like mine and Tony's. The ones we are giving out to the top brass are plated. Once they've served their purpose, there is no guarantee they will even get one. After all, unlike your agreement, there is nothing in writing, not even a promise. Just a little nod and wink. When you're dealing with the morons in the military, they can work wonders, believe you me."

Chapter 16

The violent thunderstorm that had ruined a perfect summer day grumbled irritably in the distance as Alastair Campbell peered through the window overlooking the rose garden at the rear of 10 Downing Street. A carpet of delicate rose petals caressed the newly mown lawns, prematurely torn from pastel blooms that were now reduced to a shadow of their former magnificence.

He was in a pensive mood, and as he looked back, he wondered if the desolate scene mirrored the fortunes of New Labor as the political storm clouds gathered once more and threatened to wash away the promised renewal of the party's fortunes following the incredible events of the past two years, when it lurched from crisis to crisis.

He had become resigned to the fact that he would never again play any substantial part in New Labor once Tony had departed and Brown replaced him at Number 10. He and the chancellor had never got on, and many of the enemies he had made within the party when he was in charge now sat around the cabinet table. As a result, he had busied himself with part-time jobs: journalism, sports activities, speech-making, and the like, which enabled him to enjoy a comfortable life-style, bolstered by the knowledge that when, at some propitious moment, he published his precious diaries, he would acquire riches that would make the eyes water of every dirty, corrupt, rotten, pox-ridden minister who had conspired to cast him into the wilderness, and that included the increasingly ludicrous figure of the globe-trotting Anthony Charles Lynton Blair

Following Blair's enforced departure, Gordon Brown was duly anointed as the new prime minister and had barely gotten used to the trappings of power before the roof fell in, as Campbell had repeatedly warned it would.

It was a well-known fact that the new incumbent was being handed a poisoned chalice but no one expected the seismic upheaval in the political landscape that was about to overwhelm New Labor. In any case, many of the problems that cropped up were of the ex-chancellor's own making. The long-overdue financial crash that he had avoided for so long by means of dodgy forecasts, empty promises, double accounting, and downright political larceny came soon after he entered 10 Downing Street and installed a stooge as chancellor. All of a sudden, the recession became the great depression, and the ugly head of inflation was raised once more. This was the signal for public sector unions to demand wage increases of 10, 15, and sometimes 25 percent. Not to be outdone, the private sector unions demanded similar terms plus commensurate increases in pension rights already enjoyed by civil servants. The new chancellor offered 3 percent, an offer that was turned down flat, as was his final offer of 5 percent.

The strike that followed was universal, making the "dirty jobs" strike of 1979 look like a little local difficulty. Frightened investors rushed to sell shares, while big business promptly moved their funds offshore or overseas. There was a run on the banks similar to that of Northern Rock, and the pound fell 50 percent against the dollar and 60 percent against the euro. The bank rate was hiked to 14 percent, and inflation hovered around 18 percent. Worst of all, the housing market collapsed completely, and over 9 million property owners found themselves with negative equity. Unable to secure loans from the IMF, the chancellor appealed to the EU for help to shore up the pound, only to be rebuffed again, as happened with the Tories on Black Wednesday. Unable to endure the pressure he was under, a dithering Brown called on the party to either back him to the hilt or face a general election and another twenty years in the political wilderness.

But the union bosses were having none of it. They were now the only substantial backers of the party, and without their largesse, New Labor would be hard-pressed to fight a local election, let alone a general election. They called his bluff, and to their great surprise, the dour, stubborn Scotsman defied them all and called an election.

Alastair Campbell was having a beer with some friends in his local working-man's club when the news came through. The national executive had sacked Brown and put out a short list for the election of a new leader. And on that list was one Peter Benjamin Mandelson, ex-MP, a onetime EU trade commissioner and now a Lord.

"Never, never, never!" Campbell shouted at the top of his voice, as he banged his tankard down on the table, splashing himself and his comrades with Thwaites best bitter. He lowered his voice. "It's a setup. That snake would never risk his neck if there was any chance of losing. Just look at the other candidates: two journeymen, a black number-cruncher, and an Indian guru who can hardly say 'good morning' in English. Not one union man had been nominated to give him a run for his money. How the sly bastard has wormed his way back into favor, I'll never know."

"You should have stood yourself, Ali," Tom Boulton, one of his companions, suggested. "He wouldn't stand a chance against you with all your experience under Tony Blair. Besides, who's going to vote for a faggot like him, and him being a crook into the bargain?"

"That's not how it works, Tom," replied Campbell. "Mandelson's always got away with murder. You know how crooked some of the union bosses are, particularly those with interests in Europe. I know how he operates. He's got the goods on one or more of them. I wouldn't stand a chance. Anyway, it's too late now. I was in Barbados when all this happened, and I never got one phone call from anybody on the national executive. That tells its own story, doesn't it?"

"Bloody hell, Ali, we'll be lucky to come in front of the British National Party, if he's in charge. It's not just his sexual orientation that gets up people's noses, it's his fascination with the moneyed classes, champagne, and high living. I've heard he puts on rubber gloves before he shakes the hand of a working man these days. You're not going to let him get away with it, are you?" Tom pleaded.

"What can I do, for Christ's sake? Nobody in the party will listen to me. All my old comrades have left or got the push. None of them would want to get involved in the shambles that is now New Labor."

Tom Boulton got up and stood on his chair. "Listen to me brothers!" he shouted. "We've got two candidates for our new leader. Raise your hands for your preference of the two names I'm going to give out. One: Alastair Campbell!"

A forest of arms shot up into the air, accompanied by a chorus of "Ali, Ali, Ali!"

"Right!" shouted Boulton. "Now, number two: Peter Mandelson."

There was a chorus of boos, with not a single hand being raised in favor. Tom looked across at a table where two young men were seated, holding hands. "Are you sure or are you two abstaining, Cecil?" he asked.

"Shame on you, Tommy," replied the taller of the two. "Didn't you see me hold my hand up for both of us when you called Ali's name?"

There was a roar of laughter around the hall, and many of the drinkers banged their glasses repeatedly on their table.

"Come on, Ali!" one of them shouted. "Let's show those Notting Hill fairies what we think of them. Throw your hat in the ring. You'll walk it."

Campbell took a long, slow draught from his tankard. The cheering and shouting had electrified him, as it did whenever he was on the campaign trail. It sparked the germ of an idea that at first tickled his fancy and then grew into an outrageous stratagem that he could ignore no longer. It had to be tested. He could hold his curiosity no longer.

He drained his beer, stood up, and made an exaggerated bow to his audience. "Brothers, I thank you from the bottom of my heart for your kind vote of confidence which, I'm sorry to say, won't make the slightest difference to the party shenanigans going on in London. We all know it's a setup, and there will be only one winner, the right honorable Peter Benjamin Mandelson, the darling of the Bloomsbury and Islington sewing circles."

There was a chorus of boos from around the hall, and Campbell raised his hand for silence. "I wouldn't stand a chance but there is one name I could put forward who would give them a run for their money and also beat the shit out of Cameron and his creepy Tories. Come on, somebody, who do you think I'm talking about?"

"Bejesus, it's got to be Tony. Tony Blair!" shouted an excited Irish voice.

The hall erupted. "Tony, Tony, Tony!" came the chorus. "Three election wins in a row. Who else could come near that?"

Campbell sat down and smiled mischievously as the shouting reached a crescendo and the slogan changed to "Five more years with Tony."

Tom Boulton stood up again and called repeatedly for silence until the hubbub came to a stop. "Great sentiments, comrades!" he shouted. "But what about the reality? We haven't heard or seen Tony for months. He could be dead for all we know. Let's find out what Alastair knows that we don't know."

Campbell stood up and cleared his throat. "I spoke to Tony some time ago. He's hiding out somewhere in Europe. You've read the papers. Every country he visits, there's a fruitcake waiting to take a potshot at him, especially now that Bin Laden has put a £5 million price on his head. He's had a charmed life so far but the last attempt in Boston was traumatic. He told me that he is not showing his face in public again until Bin Laden's killed off, and even then he'll stay under cover until the government restores the protection unit Brown decided he should forgo because he was making shedloads of moolah from his speaking engagements. Sure he was, but what the public never realized was the cost of private protection, especially in the States. It far exceeded what was coming in, and he's now in debt up to his eyeballs. He told me that he thinks Brown told Scotland Yard to check up on his movements and prevent him from coming back home. He's had a really rough time, believe me. Same with Cherie. She's had enough of the rotten Yanks and their bloody Irish-American psychopaths. Tony said he's sorry about the way things have turned out badly for the party and cannot believe Brown called a snap election. He was quite willing to go the whole term himself but the Brownites put so much pressure on him that he had no option but to go early. He also said that Brown covered up the bad state the finances were in and told a bunch of lies that everyone in the party believed. Tony's and my own warnings that Brown lacked prime ministerial quality and would buckle under pressure have come true, but no one believed us at the time."

"Yes, but will he want to come back after the way he's been treated?" asked a voice. "I wouldn't."

"I'm not sure," replied Campbell, "but I'm willing to ask him. You know Tony, he'll do anything to help the party and the country if he's called upon. But the thing is, would the party and the party members want him back?"

"Of course we would!" shouted a voice. "Wouldn't we, lads?"

There came a roar of approval, and in one corner they started to chant, "We want Tony, we want Tony, we want Tony Blair!" over and over again. The chant caught on and soon every person in the room was on their feet chanting and stamping their feet in time to the refrain.

Campbell looked around and studied the expressions on the faces of the excited crowd. *Just like the old days*, he thought to himself, *only better*. Last time around, Tony needed him to sort out the media and the party apparatchiks. This time, he would need him to do better than that. He would need him to run the whole shooting match.

It was close to 8:00 PM when the Gulfstream touched down on the tarmac at a small airfield near Winchester and taxied up to an end parkway. Campbell was sitting alone in his car on the apron next to a hired limo, and he heaved a big sigh of relief as he got out and waited for the passengers to disembark. It had been a long wait, made all the longer by the fact that that he had been unable to contact his visitor on his mobile and faced the unwanted prospect of another cock-up. The aircraft door opened, and a lone figure appeared, hesitant, looking warily at the ground below. Campbell waved his arms and shouted, "Tony, Tony, over here! It's Ali."

Tony Blair shot a glance in his direction and limped down the steps, looking furtively left and right as he did so. He hurried toward Campbell and practically fell into his arms.

"Ali, Ali, good old Ali," he whispered, "it's so good to see you again, my old mate."

"Likewise, Tone," Campbell replied, hugging him closely. "I was beginning to think you weren't going to turn up. But where are all the others, for Christ's sake?"

Blair looked troubled by the question. "Quick, let's get inside and on the road, Ali. I'll tell you why when we're on our way." He opened the passenger door and slumped down low in the seat.

Campbell was shocked as he followed suit. "But where is your bodyguard? There's plenty of room for them in the limo."

"I'm on my own and I haven't got a bodyguard. That's why I want us to get a move on. Please, Ali, let's get on the road."

"Of course, old son, but where's your luggage?"

"This is it," Blair replied, patting a small briefcase. "Toothbrush and all."

"Good God, I can't believe what I'm hearing. Give me a minute to tell the limo driver about the change of plans, and then you can tell me all about it."

Campbell went up to the limo and spoke to the driver for a few seconds.

"Right, here we go," he said as he got in the car and started up the powerful engine. "Comfortable, Tone?" he asked as he put it into gear.

"Yes, thanks, Ali, where are we going?"

"My place, if that's okay with you."

"Of course, Ali, anywhere you say. You know I'd trust you with my life. You're the best friend I ever had."

Sure I am, you two-faced, lying bastard, thought Campbell. *That's why you dumped me over the Kelly suicide. It doesn't look like the friends you've got left have done much for you.* He took another sideways look at his passenger. *God, he looks like shit*, he thought. *At least ten years older than when I saw him last.* The famous bright-eyed countenance that once beguiled friend and foe alike was now ashen and heavily lined, testimony to the fearful pitfalls and assassination attempts that had been his lot from the day he had been forced to resign as prime minister and seek fame and fortune in foreign lands. The carefully sculpted hairdo was now a limp, receding clump that had given up the struggle against baldness, and in doing so, it had made his ears more bat-like than ever. The irregular teeth had lost their sparkle, and his jowls appeared to tremble when he spoke. Now, the very best of beauticians would have his work cut out to make him look half-presentable. Dorian Gray would have been proud of him.

"Now then, Tony," Campbell barked, "where the hell are Cherie and the kids, not to mention your bodyguards?"

"That bastard, Brown, withdrew them when I was on vacation with Berlusconi in Sardinia. Said I wouldn't need them, as Silvio has got a small army guarding his holiday villa. The cheapskate even had the nerve to tell me he would review my bodyguard arrangement when I was back in the UK. Had the nerve to tell me I would have to fund my own security when I was out of the country."

Campbell smiled to himself. *Talk about the pot calling the kettle black*, he thought. The Scrooge-like ex-chancellor and the free-loading ex-prime minister.

"What about Cherie?" he asked.

"She changed her mind at the last minute. Said she wants me to go home first and make sure it's safe. That's why I'm late. We had a big argument, and she took off with the kids and all the luggage."

"Good grief, what made you change your mind, Tony? You weren't very keen on the idea when I first brought it up."

"That's true. Silvio has got a lot of guards at his villa, Ali, but I didn't like the look of any of them. There's this film I remember where two Italian bodyguards were bribed to disappear when a bomb was fitted under the car of their American employer and it got blown up. Sometimes, I wouldn't see a guard all day, and it made me really nervous. Then I realized how safe I used to feel at home with bodyguards I knew and trusted and who were always at my elbow. It's been like that from the time the first bomb went off in my hotel in Jerusalem."

Campbell shook his head. "Tell me about it, Tone, right from the start, but before you do, I must take a leak. There's a good place just ahead."

Chapter 17

"That's better," breathed Campbell as he climbed back in the car. "You're sure you don't need to go?"

Blair shook his head and looked anxiously at the speedometer as Campbell pulled out and raced through the gears. Campbell had the reputation of being a reckless and devil-may-care driver.

"Now then, Tony, I've heard so many different accounts about your lucky assassination escapes, especially the one in Boston, I could write a book about them. Your friends in the tabloid press were having a glorious time, believe me. Most of them were bloody disappointed when you came out in one piece."

Blair swore. "I'm sure they were, just like the yellow press in America. I'd only just arrived there when the FBI told my bodyguards that they were not going to provide us with protection because we were over there in a private capacity and not on official government business. I heard later that it was done on Bush's orders because he's still smarting over the Iran thing and is giving all British politicians a hard time. Not only that, the White House started feeding the press with some very uncomplimentary stories about my years in office and how I was supposedly kicked out by public demand. We had arranged a lot of public and private speaking arrangements for both Cherie and myself, but suddenly many of them were cancelled for no reason, and new opportunities dried up. I tell you, Ali, Bush is a ruthless bastard. Once he gets his knife into someone, he never lets go. Cherie hates both him and his bloody snooty wife. Then to cap it all, Brown strips us of our bodyguards, saying the same thing as Bush, that we were on private business. That meant we had to hire bodyguards at our own expense, and that costs plenty, I can tell you."

"How many did you hire?" asked Campbell.

"Twelve, we couldn't afford any more. Anyway, out of the blue comes this invitation for me to make a speech at an Irish-American dinner in Boston celebrating an event concerning Ireland around two hundred years ago. You know, the one I apologized for on behalf of Great Britain. I was to give a talk on the Good Friday agreement and all the progress that had been made since then. I wasn't too keen on the idea at first. As you know, we fell out with Adams and McGuinness shortly before I left office, but I was told that neither of them had been invited and that two friends of ours, Bono and Bob Geldof, were to be the guests of honor at the gig. But what staggered us was the size of the check: $250,000. As you can imagine, Cherie was all for it, and I fell in, despite being uneasy about being surrounded by hundreds of Irish sympathizers. After all, we were short of cash and we needed the money."

"You were a fool, Tony," Campbell said reproachfully. "I would never have let you take it on. The bloody Irish in Ireland are bad enough, but those bloodthirsty, jingoistic Irish-American bastards are something else again. You should have let Cherie bring home the bacon. The audiences she gets wouldn't say boo to a goose."

"Sure, I'm a lot wiser now, but that was then. There were eight of us sitting behind the lectern, and I was half-asleep when I was called up at number eight. They started heckling me before I had even got a word out, and I was waiting patiently for them to quiet down when it happened. Something heavy fell on my shoulder, bounced off, and landed on the floor in front of the lectern. There was a tremendous explosion, and that's all I remember until I woke up in hospital all bandaged up. The police told me I was lucky to be alive. If the bomb had landed on the lectern instead of on my shoulder, it would have been curtains. As it was, the blast blew the lectern backward, with me hanging on to it, and sandwiched me against the rear wall."

Campbell snorted. "Most of the red tops here said a guy in the audience stood up and threw a grenade at you, and others said that the bomb was hidden inside the lectern."

"Not so. Cherie saw it drop from the ceiling, and so did three of the other speakers."

"Was Cherie badly hurt?"

"No, but it scared her to death. She still talks about it in her sleep and shakes with fear every time she hears an Irish accent. That's why she insisted on taking up Silvio's offer to fly us all out to Sardinia to recuperate."

"You weren't badly hurt, though?"

Blair shook his head. "No, it was shock more than anything. I still get rumblings in my head from time to time, but they don't hurt, just make me feel dizzy. And my ankle hurts like hell sometimes. You know I've got a bad heart, it's a wonder I didn't have a seizure."

"They haven't caught the bombers yet, have they?"

"No, and they never will. It was a setup from start to finish. Silvio got some Mafia friends of his in New York to make enquiries, and they found that Noraid put up the cash for my fee and withdrew it minutes after the deed was done. Of course, I never got a penny out of it, only some horrific bills from the hospital."

"You've had it rough all right, old son," Campbell said soothingly. "That would never have happened if your Uncle Alastair had been in charge. Serves you right for getting rid of me when the going got tough."

Blair went crimson. "Gosh, Ali, I hope you don't hold that against me still. Honest, I did it for the good of us both. They were calling for both our heads when Kelly was found dead. One of us had to go, and if it had been me, then I would not have been able to close down the inquisition like I did. Otherwise, they could have hung us both out to dry, you know that."

"Okay, okay, that's your version. We'll let it go at that for the time being. Now tell me, have you thought about what I told you over the phone?"

"Indeed I have, Ali. That's why I'm here. You said you were going to make some more enquiries. Do you still think I'd stand a chance of being re-elected party leader?"

"More than ever, son. I was thinking it would go to a second or even a third ballot when I last spoke to you, but now I'm absolutely positive you'd walk it on the first. Those morons on the executive are running around like headless chickens trying to sort out the mess they're in. At the last count, there were eleven candidates, all of them swearing to run on the first ballot. But I've spoken to nine of the executives, and now they are all for Tony Blair. You probably know who they are, and I can assure you I've got enough on every one of them to guarantee they'll switch their vote to you. I could do it the easy way and shame Mandelson into withdrawing his name, but I want to humiliate him and bounce him out of the party altogether. There's no way I would let him take up his cushy number in Brussels again, believe me."

"That sounds great, Ali, but there's just one thing I'd like to know. Will I have to do a lot of electioneering? I don't think I'm up to it any more. Besides, I'm scared of crowds since Boston; I've always got it at the back of my mind that some evil person is stalking me, waiting for the chance to throw a bomb my way. Now, Cherie would never accompany me on the campaign trail, even for a cuppa with a group of blind people. Another thing, I've heard that there's a movement afloat in England that is determined to have me hauled before a court in The Hague and charged with war crimes. Do you know anything about that?"

"Can't say I do," lied Campbell. "Don't let it worry you, Tone, I'll see to it that you get more security than George Bush even. As for electioneering, we'll do most of the important stuff on the box and let the wannabe ministers take care of the rest. We've got the BBC, Sky, and most of commercial TV in the bag. That's where the battle will be won. Door-to-door canvassing and village hall meetings are out of fashion now. What you say doesn't matter a shit anymore, it's all image and cult of the personality. You could put Einstein up for election for a professorship by the student body at Oxford against a bit player from *Coronation Street* who couldn't count how many toes he's got on one foot, and the bit player would win hands down. All because he's on the box every night and looks good, while Einstein looks weird. That's TV today. A plain-looking singer with spots who has a voice like Frank Sinatra wouldn't stand a chance against a handsome, curly-haired croaker who couldn't stay in tune with 'Three Blind Mice.' Let me tell you something else, Tony. If you were half as presentable as you were in the old days, nobody would bother to stand against you."

"But I'm not a shoo-in now, am I, Ali?" moaned a sorrowful Blair.

"No, you look like shit and you talk like a fucked-up fairy. But I'm going to fix all that. I've booked you in for a month's stay at the Heritage health farm in Croydon. You've heard of the place, haven't you?"

"Isn't that where Princess Diana used to go when she disappeared from the public eye?"

"That's it. They do a marvellous job, not just physically but mentally as well. They employ one of the top shrinks from Zurich at close on a thousand pounds an hour. They boast that if you go in pretending you're Napoleon, you will come out speaking French, and acting like the little corporal himself."

"Sounds expensive, Ali, who's going to pay for it all?"

"You are, mate."

"But Ali, we're broke. All I've got coming in is what little Cherie earns."

Campbell laughed derisively. "Come on, pull the other one. Cherie's loaded, everyone knows that. Anyway, you can sell that pile you own in Cambridge Square and the other one in the country. You've no business being in the property market. That's for creeps like Mandelson, not the prime minister of Great Britain. Anyway, once you're back in office, you'll have no financial worries. I wouldn't be surprised if the Heritage refused to accept payment."

Blair smiled for the first time. "Just like old times, eh, Ali?"

"Better believe it. Now then, let's get down to business. I'm not doing this out of the goodness of my heart, believe you me. I've had enough of being the loyal servant, the indispensable employee, the tail-end Charlie. This time, I'm selling my services to the highest bidder on my own terms. No verbal agreements or airy-fairy promises. I intend to make you king again, restore you to your throne. Your financial worries will be over, you'll be settled in at Number 10 again, and more importantly, you will be able to take the pick of Scotland

Yard's finest to look after the safety of you and the family. But this comes at a price. You must agree to every one of my conditions, or there is no deal. Each and every one of them is interwoven and crucial to the success of the whole. If you want to see them, say yes. If not, say no."

Blair was too shocked to answer right away. Alastair had a rough-and-ready tongue and always spoke his mind, especially when he knew he was in the right. But he had never, ever faced him down and was always deferential to his position as top man in government. Now he was a complete stranger, hostile, demanding, and vengeful to boot.

"All right, Ali," he said guardedly. "I'll listen to what you have to say, but I'll not promise anything until I've weighed up each and every condition and talked it over with Goldy."

Campbell exploded, "What? Are you seriously asking me to submit to questioning from that fucking university roommate of yours? No fucking deal. The conditions are in plain English, for God's sake, and require a simple yes or a simple no. Give them to that prat and you'll wait six months for the answer to just one of them."

"Very well," Blair said wearily, "let's hear what you have to say, and we'll take it from there."

Campbell opened his glove compartment and took out a sheet of paper. "These are the conditions on this one sheet," he said as he handed it over. "Take your time reading them."

Blair took the sheet, put on his glasses, and started reading. When he finished, he dropped the sheet into his lap and turned to Campbell, his face red with anger.

"Good grief, Ali!" he shouted. "Is this one of your bad jokes? You might as well stand for election yourself as ask me to agree to this crap. Do you honestly think I would lower myself to even consider prostituting myself to any of your demands? I may be in a bit of a bind at the moment, but I'm still the only Labor leader to lead the party to three consecutive election wins. I thought you were a friend of mine, yet you've brought me over here under false pretenses, pretending you were doing me a favor, and all the time you intended to feather your own bloody nest. Heck, I don't need your help to win an election, I can go before the executive myself, and they would fall over themselves to select me over all the others."

Campbell laughed. "Like hell they would, they wouldn't even let you in the building. You've been living on a different planet, Tony. Old Labor took control of the party before you left, but you couldn't see it. They only tolerated you because Brown didn't want anyone crapping on his patch. Now you're fair game for every MP who holds a grudge, and believe me, there are plenty of those in Parliament today."

"If that's the case, what makes you think you can do better then?" Blair asked contemptuously.

"Because I'm a fixer, and you know Goddamn well that I was the driving force behind all three those election wins. There's a great deal of apprehension among the hierarchy about the prospects for the election. All the polls show that the Conservatives will win big, and we're in danger of coming in third behind the Liberal-Democrats. Now, that's not because our voters are going over to the Tories, it's because they are going to ignore the party machine, especially if Mandelson is declared leader. I've taken soundings at the grass roots, and believe me, the findings are unbelievable, something like 70 percent in your favor as things stand at the moment and 80 percent-plus if you are adopted. Despite the manner of your leaving and all the shit thrown at you by the media, you're still very popular with the ordinary Labor voter. All we have to do is get them to vote. Add that to the captive vote we enjoy with 7 million civil servants and another 6 million on benefits, and we're home and dry. When I present my research to the executive and have a quiet word with nine of the creeps, they'll come begging at your door."

"So if all this is true, why do I need you? Why don't I get a good public relations guy like Ralph Richardson and have him get me elected?"

"Because he doesn't have the goods on nine crooked electors like I do. And if you did do that, I'd back Mandy and give all the juicy bits in my diaries that relate to you and Cherie and Berlusconi to the *Daily Mail* as a Christmas present."

Blair shook his head sorrowfully. "I can't believe I'm talking to the friend I confided in for more than twelve years. Why, I made you the second most powerful man in government. Doesn't that mean anything at all to you, Ali?"

Campbell laughed. "Jesus Christ, you really are up there with the fairies, Tony. Without me pulling the strings, you would have been out on your ear long before you dumped me overboard. I took all the flak while you were prancing around the world like a bloody pop star, and I kept your enemies at bay. It was me and Brown who won your elections for you, and you delude yourself if you think otherwise. I held my nose while you shit on the good guys in the government and betrayed all the principles we were elected on. But my own betrayal was the last straw for me. I went out on a limb for you when I produced those dodgy dossiers on Iraq so that you could ingratiate yourself with that asshole Bush. I warned you time and time again you were backing the wrong horse, but you wouldn't listen. And what did you do in return? You set me up as the scapegoat for Kelly's suicide in order to save your own skin, just like Judas did with Jesus. Now the boot is on the other foot. I'm the king of the castle, and you can either face up to the fact or spend the rest of your life pissing your pants whenever you hear the sound of an Irish accent. Use your head, man! Fall in with my plan, and you can enjoy the limelight once again with all the crappy champagne socialists and pop stars knocking on your door. I'm offering you a chance to redeem yourself, and all you have to do is carry out my orders. Let me tell you something, if Cherie hears you turned down a golden opportunity like this, she'll kick your ass from here to Barbados and back."

Blair cupped his chin in his hands and stared at the paper in his lap for what seemed an eternity. "Do you really think they'll take me back, Ali?" he asked eventually.

"It's a cast-iron certainty if I'm running the show."

"And is there a chance we can win the general election as well?"

"No doubt about it."

"And I'll be back at Number Ten with all my family and friends and partying at Chequers as well?"

"In spades, son, only this time you'll have a new neighbor of your own choice next door, instead of that bastard, Gordon Brown."

The last remark made Blair beam. "Sounds great, Ali." He searched his pockets for a pen but drew a blank. "Lend me a pen, will you? I don't seem to have one with me."

"Sorry, friend, I don't have one either. Not to worry, you can sign it when we get to my house."

Campbell put his foot down on the accelerator and got in the fast lane. Teflon Tony hadn't changed a bit. His schizophrenic mind had gone into overdrive. He could almost hear the wheels whirring as a fantastical combination was selected and the tumblers fell into place. Campbell glanced at Blair's face. It no longer bore the harassed look of a deeply troubled human being. It reminded him of one of Tom the Cat's expressions in the famous cartoon series; the cunning look that spelled plenty of trouble for Jerry. Poor Tony. The presence of four signatory witnesses waiting at his home would wipe off his self-deluded smile, he was sure of that.

Alastair Campbell was true to his word. Tony Blair was welcomed back into the fold with open arms and crowned leader of the party once again. A slick electioneering campaign masterminded by Campbell saw New Labor regain their lead in the polls, and Election Day dawned with all the major pollsters predicting an overall Labor majority of twenty-one seats over all other parties. But the grasping politicians had completely misread the mood of the nation. Sick and tired of a decade of Labor misrule and the puerile posturing of the two main opposition parties, the voters stayed away in droves, and the end result was that only a derisory 29 percent of the electorate had bothered to cast their vote. While the low turnout made little difference in the safe seats of all the parties, it played havoc in the crucial marginals, where nearly two hundred seats changed hands, some of them registering a plurality of less than fifteen votes. New Labor emerged as the largest party but lost its overall majority, while the Conservatives and Liberal-Democrats lost ninety-eight seats between them. The big winners were United Kingdom party, the Scottish and Welsh Nationalists, the BNP, and the independent parties, who won a total of eighty-four seats between them. But the biggest winner of all was the "spoiled paper vote," consisting mainly of the write-in, "None of the above."

As the largest party overall, New Labor claimed the right to govern and was duly sworn in with Tony Blair as prime minister.

Chapter 18

L uke Dryden studied Jock Wingate as he entered his office and took a chair. It was his first day at the base, and the boss had asked him to report immediately on his arrival.

Wingate had aged considerably since he last saw him. The weather-beaten face was paler now, and the hair showed grey around the temples. Even the ramrod back seemed to have lost some of its rigidity as he sat forward with both elbows on the desk, hands clasped together, fingers touching the tip of his nose. The price of high command, thought Luke, and the responsibility of life-and-death decisions that affected the men whose lives he valued far above his own. But the eyes still showed a steely blue, and the famous boxer's nose that legend held could smell a fight fifty kilometers away was as prominent as ever.

As was his custom when he was not at a training ground, on maneuvers, or in a war zone, the colonel was immaculately dressed in a uniform that looked as if it had just arrived from a bespoke tailor. The rank and regimental insignia were highly polished, as were the buttons, but it was the ribbons that caught the eye of a knowledgeable observer. Three colorful rows indicated the possession of every major award the British army was able to bestow upon one of its bravest officers. Luke's eyes were also drawn to the watch he was wearing. Unlike the solid gold Rolex watches affected by the top brass and government officials—courtesy of the taxpayer—his was simplicity itself. A silver-plated, old-fashioned watch with a brown leather strap and a dial marked with neat Roman numerals. Surely an heirloom, as perhaps was the faded gold ring on his finger.

"Have a seat, Luke." Wingate smiled. "I don't want you putting too much strain on that leg of yours. It cost the ministry of defense a bomb, I can tell you. Nothing but the best for my boys, you know."

Luke laughed. "It's so damned good I'm thinking of entering the Olympics, and I don't mean the Paralympics version either."

"Good for you. Any pain at all?"

"Nothing to speak of. Just a bit of soreness in the knee joint now and again."

"So you would consider yourself as 100 percent fit for duty again, would you?"

"Without a doubt, the MO will confirm that. Have you got me in mind for Iraq again, sir?"

"Whoa there! Not so fast. No one from here is going anywhere. As a matter of fact, I'm gradually pulling men out of all assignments abroad. We've got a big war to win here at home, and we're going to need every man we have to win it. I've cleared this with Alexander and Montgomery, and they have agreed to ensure that the ministry of defense will be no wiser. Now then, I am so impressed with the great job you and your team achieved at Selly Oak that I'm putting you in charge of an even greater challenge here at the base."

Luke shifted in his chair and leaned forward expectantly.

"Now that we have the men and resources outside of our base, we are in a position to go on the offensive, and not before time, I can tell you. Of course, we have many friends all over the world who support us secretly. Our paymaster tells me that we have enough funds coming in to keep us in operation for a year without receiving a penny from the government."

"Have they cut off your funding, then?"

"No, they dare not. I've made it clear that if they reduce our allocation by as much as a penny, I'll withdraw or suspend all SAS operations overseas. That was good enough to have Blair, or should I say Campbell, shitting bricks. Blair's master in the White House would go through the roof if he suspected he was compromising the safety of his troops, and our absence from the battlefield would surely do that. No, we still get our funding, but it's limited. We need every penny we can get to purchase equipment and munitions, and we've only got a few months to prepare for Union Jack. I intend to set up a special unit within Planning and Intelligence, with you in command and an officer of your choice as your number two. He will take over in the event of any rough stuff you do not feel you are able to undertake personally. Melvyn Dickinson is your Second in Command, and Jim Farnsworth will be your liaison officer between D Squadron and Signals. How does that appeal to you?"

"Sounds spot on."

Wingate leaned forward. "Luke, we have got to hurt this venal government of ours. We've got to expose every nasty, dirty lie that has enabled them to pull the wool over the eyes of our shell-shocked voters time and time again. We've got to put the wind up every single member of Parliament, their wives, partners, and even their children, so that every one of them is looking over his or her shoulder, wondering when they are going to get the chop, run over, or submit to the tender mercies of Section Four. I want you to hack into the assets of these bloodsuckers and screw them up. Stay clear of hospitals, doctors, anything that would hurt the old, the young, and the genuinely infirm.

"Hack into the databases that service the wages and pensions for MPs and ex-MPs, civil servants, and trade unionists. Screw up shady housing benefits and benefit payments. Hack into the Treasury and foul up payments to the EU and handouts to third world dictatorships. As you pointed out in one of your articles, databases are the Achilles' heel of the modern state. Paralyze them and you are halfway to your goal. But you wrote of this in a military context, didn't you? I believe it can work even more effectively in a civil confrontation. Just think what would happen if we compounded these attacks on the establishment with a massive assault on the very foundations the working population depend on to maintain their illusions that as long as they are in work and Labor is in office, their way of life is safe. Just as in Orwell's *1984,* they have been brainwashed into believing that as long as they keep their head down and accept the blatant lie that all the new regulations pouring out of Brussels are for their long-term benefit and will hasten the dawn of a brave new world in which everyone is equal and poverty has been abolished forever.

"Just think how the lotus eaters who voted New Labor into power in four successive elections will feel when the corruption and sleaze at the very top is finally exposed before their very eyes; how all the grandiose promises are revealed as no more than cynical bribes and worthless spinology. How will they react when the lights go out at night and the power fails in the daytime? When the traffic systems go on the blink and snarl up the traffic in towns and cities, as well as dozens of accidents involving juggernauts blocking motorways. How will they feel when their favorite TV programs are blacked out nightly or their morning papers fail to appear? When food shortages cause prices to rocket and when the price of a gallon of gas reaches £15 and the cheapest flight to Spain starts at £5,000. Why, they will bear it grudgingly for a month or two, and then all hell will break loose, with mild-mannered Britons exploding with a pent-up fury that will bring them out onto the streets in their thousands."

The colonel paused for a moment as if to let the gravity of what he was proposing sink in.

"This is the scenario I want you to work on so that when we are ready to make our move, the whole country will be a great seething mass of disenchantment and resentment, a populace so worked up and anti-government that if Adolph Hitler himself offered himself up for leader, they would welcome him with open arms. How does that sound to you?"

Luke searched for the right word and finally found it. "Magnificent, absolutely magnificent. If we could translate all those words into positive action we would be home and dry, no doubt about that. Do you really think we could do all those things with the limited resources we have?"

Wingate leaned back in his armchair and clasped his hands behind his head. "I believe we do. There are many historical instances of revolts that succeeded against impossible odds. You picked out some of them in your book *How to Bring Down a Tyrant*. Put it all together as if we were members of the French underground plus all the other resistance movements rolled into one, and I don't believe for one moment that we can fail. This government and Parliament are so corrupt and full of their own importance that it will never entertain the notion that their days are numbered. Blair and at least two of his ministers are megalomaniacs, firmly believing they have been chosen by God to create a socialist Utopia, not only here, but in Africa as well. They seem to think that because they have the army chiefs in their pocket and boast a politicized police force that can rival that of any banana republic, they are immune to criticism from any quarter. Like Bush used to say, we're either with them or against them, or so they believe. What do you think, right here and now? This very moment?"

Luke hesitated. To be asked for his opinion from a legend in his own time was akin to Jesus asking him the way to the gates of heaven. But then the very ethos of the Regiment was that every operation undertaken by its members was carefully discussed and debated by those directly involved and whose lives were dependent upon its success or failure. "I think ..."

He broke off, and jumped to his feet as a huge explosion rattled the windows and caused bits of plaster to fall from the ceiling. For one moment, he was tempted to dive beneath the knee-hole in the colonel's desk but when he saw that Wingate had barely moved a muscle, he was persuaded to compose himself and walk over to the window to check out the cause of the explosion. He saw a column of smoke rising over the vehicle maintenance buildings at the north end of the parade ground, and then came the scream of a siren from the control tower and yet another as a fire engine came roaring past, with two Land Rovers not far behind. They headed for the building and then disappeared from view.

Luke returned to his seat. "Good God," he said, "that was an AS90, if I'm not mistaken. Half a degree lower, and it would have been curtains for us."

Wingate did not reply. He was looking at his watch and mouthing numbers at the same time. When he reached seventy-five, there was a loud crump from the other side of the aircraft hangars, followed by three more at intervals of thirty seconds. "Good," he murmured, "that's the best effort yet. I don't think we'll get any more deliveries today."

"Some delivery!" laughed Luke. "fifty kilos of high explosive, I believe. Were those AS90s sending some back?"

"They were. We've got four batteries dug in around the base, one of them manned twenty-four hours a day."

"But how did the gunners fire back so quickly? It couldn't have been more than two minutes. Were they firing blind?"

"Not likely. The flash was spotted immediately and the signal sent immediately to the Gun Laying System and alarm. The response time was one minute, fifty-six seconds for the number one gun."

"Who was doing the spotting?"

"A TA reconnaissance unit. There are dozens of them circling the base, screwing up Kruger's siege plan. As you know, Section Three Paramilitaries forced out the garrison of the army base at Andover, and they have made it their main HQ in the south. As it happens, the base was home to two regiments of the Royal Artillery with around sixty-five AS90 self-propelled guns and some L18 light guns. They started shelling us with the light guns from a range of around seventeen kilometers, but we made mincemeat of them with our AS90s. Then they extended their range with their AS90s and caused some considerable damage before we formed our early warning systems and forced them to break up their batteries and resort to using single gun positions. That was their big mistake. We take one and they get four back in reply. Mind you, their gunners aren't up to scratch. There are hundreds of craters in fields up to two kilometers forward and back of the base to testify to that. Not surprising really. Most of the crews are South Africans who left when the ANC took over, and they must be rusty as hell."

"So the battle's won. Just some mopping up to do," said Luke.

"Not quite. We have just learned that Kruger is seeking to get hold of ERA shells stocked by NATO in Germany. As you know, this ammo doubles the range of the AS90, and if they succeed, they will be able to shell us with impunity with the guns they've got left. That's where you come in. Your first assignment here will be to ensure that ammo never crosses the Channel. I understand you've got good contacts inside NATO; make use of them. We just cannot afford any more destruction to all the heavy equipment we have stored out in the open, in particular our ammo dumps.

"Now then, where the devil were we when we were interrupted?"

Luke settled down in his chair and waited patiently as Wingate lit a panatela. "I believe that whatever we do, the whole rotten edifice will collapse within a year, maybe two," he said. "The finances are in an appalling state. I'm told that if things continue as they are, the Treasury will have to renege on its international debt payments by the end of this year. They will no longer be able to pay the salaries or the pensions of the bloated civil service, which now comprises one quarter of the working population, and these people are, of course, the very ones they depend on to vote them back into office year after year. Our manufacturing base is almost nonexistent, and the much-vaunted service sector is struggling to keep its head above water. On top of that, our balance of payments deficit is now so bad that the IMF will no longer bail us out, and creditors are threatening a sterling crisis now that our fair-weather partners in Europe have turned their backs on us. It's a classic banana republic comedy. The revolutionaries drive a dictator out, they then promise the earth and deliver nothing while they empty the Treasury and salt away the loot in Swiss bank accounts. The military step in to prevent anarchy, and the cycle starts all over again."

"What are your aims once we take over, sir? We must not make the same mistake the dictators do, time after time," Luke declared.

Wingate dumped his cigar in an ash tray. "Firstly, we have to clear out the scum who have brought Britain to its knees. The cruel bastards who regularly incarcerate poverty-stricken ninety-year-old pensioners for failing to pay their council tax while allowing rapists and murderers to roam the streets at will. Blair and all the members of the cabinet, past and present, who voted for the invasion of Iraq and its continuation are to face the death penalty. Sitting members of Parliament will be expelled, and they and their next of kin forbidden to apply for public office, even down to the lowly rank of dog-catcher. They will also be stripped of their bloated pension pots and forced to perform certain public duties without recompense for a minimum of five years. Sections One to Five will be abolished, and a new county-based police force established, with MI5 and MI6 reverting back to their former roles. There is to be a total ban on immigration for one year, and setups like the Race Relations Board and Aid to Africa will be ended. It is of the utmost importance that we wake up and organize the silent majority who have been marginalized by New Labor and who are the true representatives of our country. We must remove the scales from their eyes and proclaim from the rooftops the unbelievable damage these vandals have done to the nation in the name of multiculturalism, their version of a one-party state. I want them to witness the precious freedoms New Labor has stolen from them as they slept and instill in them such a demand for vengeance that they call for the culprits to be not only hung but also drawn and quartered as well.

"We anticipate two years maximum military rule. Then a new-style Parliament sited in the countryside, with two elected chambers of no more than one hundred seats in each. The royal prerogative will be restored, secession from the EU given top priority, and a cast-iron Bill of Rights introduced. We will then create a truly independent judiciary and civil service, put an end to regional authorities, and restore the old counties that have been abolished. A complete overhaul of the public services with priority directed at the old, the very young, and the genuine infirm. We must aim for an end to the obscene culture of rewarding mediocrity and failure that is draining the public purse and driving talented people abroad. The name of the game will be accountability in both the public and private sectors. For a start, we will get rid of the discredited honors system and all the outdated class privileges that have made a mockery of honest government.

"I could go on forever but I intend to deliver my full treatise to you when I have cleared it with Alexander and Montgomery. Then I want you and your team to develop it further, so that we can deliver to our people a government that will restore to them all the benefits of free enterprise they once enjoyed and drive a stake into the heart of the socialist dogma that has brought us to within a whisker of a full-blown totalitarian state. And bear in mind that we, as administrators of the treatment, will be subjected to a period of vilification that will test our ingrained sense of patriotism and discipline to the very limit. Do you think all this is achievable? We'll need plenty of help from you as we go along. I'm told no one knows the political scene better than yourself."

"I'm not so sure about that, sir. As you know, I quit the Conservative party years ago, and a lot of sewage has flowed out of Westminster since then. I expected the Tories to provide the main opposition after the election of a hung Parliament, but lo and behold their policy is to back every act laid before Parliament—in the interest of the country, as they put it. So now we have a situation where most of the constituencies have a wafer-thin majority and elect six hundred and fifty desperate MPs who will murder their own mothers in order to hang on to their seat and the mouth-watering perks that go with it. The Conservative party of Winston Churchill and Margaret Thatcher no longer exists. It has been replaced by a bunch of self-seeking public school fops and university geeks who would faint if they got grit on their hands or ventured out into the real world. There is not one MP with a military record in Parliament, 70 percent are dodgy lawyers, and the rest are number-crunchers or spivs. I'm sorry, but there is not one member of the party I would recommend you take into your confidence. They really cannot be trusted anymore. What can you say about members who go around pleading that they are no longer the nasty party and beg us to give them a chance to double the handouts New Labor has promised? Cameron is a Blair clone and a bastard one at that. The rot set in when they garroted Margaret Thatcher, and the writing was clearly on the wall when the party gave that oaf, John Major, a standing ovation at the party conference following the 1997 general election. Imagine that! He leads them to the most humiliating defeat in history, and they cheer him to the rafters, just as they cheered Blair when he left Parliament. And to top it all, they voted overwhelmingly to support the invasion of Iraq."

Colonel Wingate swore. "My bloody sentiments too, by God. So the great party of Winston Churchill, Margaret Thatcher, and you and me are a bunch of nasties, are we? I wonder what would have happened to our country if we had been nice to Hitler and the Argies? What about UKIP?"

"It has possibilities, but at the moment, it's a one-issue party. The one to keep our eye on is the Freedom First party. It's basically an Internet movement at present, but the way it is picking up support from every walk of life is quite astonishing. Apart from them and UKIP, we must avoid dealing with all other politicians like the plague.

As you say, we must forbid any current or ex-MP from applying for election to the new Parliament, and that goes for lawyers too. Wipe the slate clean and start anew. Show volunteers the flag and reward those who follow it handsomely. Promise them hard times like Churchill did and offer them a vision of a resurgent Britain at peace with itself, self-confident and a beacon of hope for our European friends as they too struggle to shake off the yoke of stagnation and creeping socialism."

Wingate was impressed. "Let's see, Luke. Although you've left the party, have you kept in touch with like-minded contacts since then?"

"More so than before. I've had hundreds of calls from the old guard begging us not to give up the fight. There is a huge pool of despairing patriots in the country yearning for a savior to come forth and lead the fight against the criminals who have destroyed our way of life. It's incredible how many civil servants in high positions are swamping me with leaks from every department of government. If there is a fight, we would know about every move they make, even in Downing Street itself."

"Will this silent majority support a military coup?"

"Without question, as long as they can be assured that Parliament and the rule of law will be re-established within a reasonable period. In this respect, I would advise you to seek out Peter Halstead. What he doesn't know about constitutional matters isn't worth knowing. He's now living in Switzerland, hounded out by Section Four."

Wingate made a note. "Anyone in mind for the top job?"

"Only Jack Churchill of Freedom First. But he's getting on a bit, and I'm not sure he could stay the course."

"Okay, Luke, let me ask you once again. Do you truly believe the country is ready for a coup?"

"Yes, sir, I surely do. But it has to be soon, and it can't be allowed to fail. Only you can give the answer to that question."

For a split-second, Wingate looked despondent. He pushed back his chair, got up, and went to the window overlooking the parade ground. As he stared out, with his shoulders slightly bent and cigar pointing straight ahead, Luke could not help but think of Winston Churchill, alone in his study in 1940, looking out over the green lawns of Chartwell, pondering the telephone call that had just informed him his country had called upon him once again in its hour of need.

Without turning around, he spoke in a voice that sounded uncharacteristically pessimistic. "Luke, the Regiment is now down to half-strength, and half of that is overseas supporting actions in Afghanistan, Iraq, Syria, and now Iran. I've got exactly three hundred seventy-six men on base, and that includes fourteen cooks, two accountants, and twelve medics. We're now working on a plan that will enable us to secretly withdraw 90 percent of our overseas operatives by November at the latest and hide them in the ranks of our Rapid Reaction Force based in Versailles. But that does not help us here. At best, we can pull out a hundred of these men to add to our strength but that does seem adequate enough for the job in hand. I …"

Luke could not help interrupting the colonel at that point. "Do you mean you actually set a date for the operation?" he asked excitedly.

The colonel wheeled round and returned to his chair. "We have indeed. The provisional date for Union Jack is November 12."

The date rang a bell, and Luke rummaged around in his brain until the answer came to him. "Why, that's the date set for the G8 summit with Blair in the chair. Leeds Castle, isn't it? What day is that on, sir?"

"The Monday after Armistice Sunday. Do you think the summit will go ahead as planned?"

"Without a shadow of a doubt. Blair is so hung up on playing the big shot in front of his admirers, he would still go ahead if only one of the heads of state turned up. There is something fishy about this summit. We last held it in 2009, and now we're hosts again. Seems like some of the other members are afraid of holding it on their own soil. It's rumored that the anarchists are planning their biggest demonstration ever, something five hundred thousand, minimum. They've really got the bit between their teeth after the chaos they caused in Canada. If this one's just as bad, I wouldn't be surprised if the G8 decide to call the event a day. About bloody time too. All they do is wine, dine, and hand out our money to third world dictators. Do you think the anarchists will help or hinder our operation?"

The colonel smiled. "We did think of going in beforehand and saving the country the enormous cost of cleaning up after the wreckers had their day. But then we perceived we could turn their unwashed presence to our own advantage. Blair will be so concerned about the safety of his guests, he will demand that the army provides an impenetrable guard around the castle and the airfield chosen for their arrival. There are rumors that the army will commit the entire Household Division to the operation."

"Good God!" Luke was flabbergasted. "The whole division? That means there won't be a squaddie left within fifty kilometers of the capital."

The colonel smiled again. "And it also means good cover for us. The anarchists are planning a protest outside Parliament on that same Monday. What better excuse do we need than to turn up as they are tearing the place apart and chase them off before we storm our objectives?"

"Blimey, it gets better all the time. But we can muster little more than four hundred men. How can you expect to capture London with such a small force? The police can muster at least twenty thousand, plus the Paramilitaries."

"That is a problem, I agree," replied Wingate. "A problem for you and your team to solve. The Rapid Reaction Force are committed to our cause but we will need all our TA units to coordinate with them and pave the way for the big push on London. We don't want to get into hand-to-hand fighting with the police; that will cause casualties among the population. We want to put a hundred Chinooks over the city and simultaneously drive in with the same number of tanks. Shock and awe, without the devastation, is our strategy. When they see what they're up against, they will lay down their arms, we're convinced of that. The Metropolitan Police Force is not what it used to be; now it is composed of 60 percent ethnic minorities with mostly black officers, some of them Yardies. They will hesitate to fire their guns when they see the Paras exiting the Chinooks. Our biggest headache is the Household Division. We are not sure how we stand with them. As you know, most of the top brass are in Blair's pocket, and we don't know exactly how far down the chain of command the bribery extends. As long as the division is stuck outside Leeds Castle, we are okay, but if they get wind of our plans and move back into the city before the twelfth, then we are in trouble, big-time trouble. They are bound to become suspicious once we start moving troops around, so it will be your job to penetrate the ranks and find out where their loyalties lie. Spread the word around that there is a coup in the offing but not until the New Year, and when it comes, it will be from the north or maybe Ulster or Wales, even."

The mention of the north prompted a question from Luke. "What about the Homeland Division in York? They are on twenty-four-hour call to move into Ulster in the event of a Protestant move against Sinn Fein or IRA."

"I know. This is something we're working on hard. It's crucial that the division elects to join us or, at the very least, stays in barracks. Unfortunately, the O.C. is a glory hunter and is fond of mixing with the Islington crowd. However, I understand that his staff are very unhappy with his position and may even dump him at some stage."

"What about the navy and air force?"

"The navy's okay but we're still working on the RAF. They'll be crucial. We can't have Euro fighters picking off our choppers. Are you close to any ranking officers in the ministry of defense, Luke?"

"I know an air vice marshal and a couple of commodores. If they saw one of their planes fire one shot at us, they'd ground every plane under their command, I'm sure of it."

"Good, pass that information on to Jim Farnsworth, plus anything else you might think will help. God, what 'The Few' would think about the bunch of shysters running the RAF today doesn't bear thinking about. Mind you, the army isn't that much better. They're down to sixty thousand men now, and there are still a hundred brigadiers on the roster. One brigadier for every six hundred men. Makes the mind boggle, doesn't it?"

Luke nodded. He knew of two field marshalls who had been made life peers in the past month alone.

Wingate got to his feet. "Well, that gets it for now, Luke. We'll set up a weekly progress meeting in the war room starting a week from today. Right now, we'll adjourn to the mess and drink a toast to the return of the prodigal son. We've got a mountain of work to do, and I'm counting on you and your team to soften up this godawful government of ours to such an extent that when we hit them hard, they won't know if their fat asses are punched or bored."

Chapter 19

Moses Mandella sat at the end of the oval table and glared at the four people facing each other on opposite sides. Only one of them ventured to meet his eyes, the rest preferring to stare at their clipboards or glance sideways at their neighbor. They all knew that the home secretary was in a foul mood, and when Moses Mandella was in a foul mood, the safest way to escape his anger was to make oneself as inconspicuous as possible and say as little as possible.

"What a fucking, ass-holing balls-up you useless, skiving bunch of retards made of that simple little job I gave you on Friday!" he shouted, beads of sweat beginning to run down his face. "Why, my two-year-old grandsons could have done better with both hands tied behind their backs. You had over fifty men at your disposal, plus satellite surveillance, and yet you let a one-legged SAS bastard make you look like the Keystone Kops. Do you know what Campbell said to me this morning? He said the next time he wants a job done, he's going to enlist the help of the Women's Institute, with me bringing up the rear. I've never seen him so mad. He was foaming at the mouth and jumping up and down with rage. Said one more shambles like that and he's going to get me deported back to Jamaica. Now it's my turn. What have you all got to say for yourselves, and don't give me any lying excuses or I'll have you picking polluted condoms off Hampstead Heath for the rest of the week."

"Moses, we did all that was asked of us. What more do you want?"

General Otto Von Kruger, commanding officer of Section Three Paramilitaries, was determined to get his answer in first so that he could sit back and watch his three companions squirm. He looked at the black face of the thickset home secretary. His eyes were as black as his skin, unfathomable and unblinking, and his furrowed brow signaled that he was in the mood to give the boot to someone even if they were entirely innocent.

"We were in position exactly as planned," Kruger said defensively. "It's not our fault the Challenger's gear box broke up. Blame that on the ministry of defense. The cheap bastards supplied us with a tank out of mothballs they knew was faulty. Our armaments officer has been checking on the hundred and fifty tanks they supplied us with, and so far, he's found three out of five are crap. Our guys did good. They fired off the transporter, shot up the hospital, and didn't surrender until the tank and transporter was burning up."

"They shot up the hospital all right," sneered Mandella, "only it was the hospital wing behind it that took most of the flak: killed six patients and wounded God knows how many more besides. You've seen the pictures in the *Mail*. Not one SAS bastard in them but plenty showing your bloody stupid tank crew crying their eyes out. And to cap it all, you let Dryden and his gang fly away in a chopper like they were going off to Blackpool for the weekend. That's what Campbell is really pissed off about, and so am I."

"We didn't let them fly away," protested Kruger. "Section Four are responsible for keeping tabs on Dryden. They've staked him out ever since he entered the hospital. They should have nabbed him before he got anywhere near the chopper."

Hans Hoffman, the chief of Section Four, took offense. "That's a load of crap, Kruger, and you know it. When your lot fouled up with the tank, the hospital grounds started crawling with SAS, some of them bloodthirsty Ghurkhas. We were outnumbered and outgunned. Section Three were nowhere to be seen. It would have been suicidal for us to take them on. Not only that, their escape chopper had two Apache escorts."

Kruger snorted angrily. "Bullshit, the SAS don't own any Apaches. All they've got is some worn-out Lynxes. Did your lot see any Apaches, Shipman?" he asked, glaring at the director of Section Two.

Harold Shipman raised his head and looked furtively at the home secretary. "Sorry, I can't answer that one, Kruger. I've checked with my satellite crew, and their camera wasn't focused on the hospital at that particular time."

Mandella exploded. "What? I gave you explicit instructions that you were to keep sight of Dryden until he was apprehended by Section Four. Don't you morons take any notice of what I tell you to do anymore? I made it top priority, and nothing comes before that, ever."

"Sorry, Moses," replied Shipman. "We switched coverage to the PM when he left Downing Street. He's our top priority whenever he goes on the road. Those are your instructions to us, if you remember."

"Jesus Christ, you mean you've only got one lousy camera on a satellite costing millions of pounds?"

"No, we've got four. The other two are providing twenty-four-hour surveillance on the SAS base in Credenhill and the other for your house in Kensington."

Mandella squirmed uncomfortably in his seat and quickly turned to Robert Crippen, the chief commissioner of Section One—the National Police Force. "What about your part in all this, Crippen?" he spat out. "You've got hundreds of police manning road blocks around the hospital, yet when Section Four need help, there isn't one to be seen. What do you think we give you guns for, target practice?"

Crippen went red in the face, and he struggled to get his words out coherently. "That's not fair, Moses," he said. "We never got a call for help from either Section Four or Section Three. Seems to me they were both too busy evacuating the area than making a fight of it."

"Cut the crap, Crippen!" Kruger shouted angrily. "You know bloody well ..."

Mandella folded his arms and shook his head sorrowfully as he watched his four security chiefs go at each other, hammer and tongs. He believed he had more intelligence in his little finger than all four of them put together. There was no love lost between any of them. They could not even bring themselves to address each other by their first names. Still, it was he himself who had encouraged the hostility between them. Divided, they posed no threat to his position. United, they could make his life very scary indeed, especially if they were to appoint the sinister ex-Stasi, Hans Hoffman, as their leader.

Moses Mandella was the son of a Jamaican immigrant who arrived in England on the SS *Windrush* in 1948. Ostensibly, Zach Mandella was penniless like the rest of the passengers in steerage, but unknown to the others, he had packed the diapers of his three-month-old twin boys with cocaine, and from the proceeds, he was able to purchase a small tobacconist shop in Tower Hamlets in London. This enabled him to lead a life superior to those of his fellow immigrants, who filled the menial jobs spurned by native Londoners at that time.

Moses and Zeke were the names of the two boys, and the initial connection with cocaine was to follow them for the rest of their lives, as they grew rich importing and distributing drugs in the East End of London. Like the Kray brothers in Shoreditch, they built an empire in Tower Hamlets and ruled it with an iron hand. But they were a lot smarter than the Krays, for they reached their fiftieth birthday without a single conviction between them, although they were hauled before the courts regularly by frustrated law officers. Money talked in those days, and the brothers had plenty of the stuff to bribe witnesses, police officers, mayors, jurors, and sometimes even the judges themselves.

Unlike Zeke, Moses had political ambitions, and egged on by his pushy wife, Arabella, he set his cap on gaining a peerage in order to put himself on a level footing with several black men in London who had been ennobled and bore impressive names like Lord Abuwalla of Brent Common or Lord Bulawayo of Mile End. He realized that although New Labor was dishing out titles to anyone prepared to donate a million-plus to the party coffers, they would reluctantly draw the line at any award to a drug dealer since drug suppression was now a key part of Labor's election manifesto. And so he hired an expensive PR consultant who specialized in defending the nefarious exploits of the current members of Parliament.

The consultant advised him to gain a seat in Parliament and spend two or three years ingratiating himself with the New Labor hierarchy until he was able to win a place in government as a junior minister. After two years in that position, he could feign ill health, whereupon he would, subject to a sizeable donation, be given a seat in the House of Lords.

The PR consultant was well aware that a new party rule made it mandatory that half the seats in any city with a large ethnic population must be given to candidates according to their ethnic background. This meant that in the last election, twenty-eight of the New Labor winners were nonwhite, making it an odds-on bet that one of them could be persuaded that he should sacrifice his seat in the interest of the party, sooner rather than later. The consultant had no trouble finding a suitable sacrificial lamb. Zeke provided the muscle, Moses the cash, and in less time than it takes to organize a betting coup at the racetrack, a by-election was called, and Moses was duly elected as the honorable member of Parliament for the safe seat of Hackney.

However, Moses Mandella was not content to sit on the back benches forever. He resented being at the beck and call of the whips and looked down upon as lowly cannon fodder to be drummed into line and told how to vote on nearly every motion that came before them. Using the methods and streetwise acumen that had made him king of the drug dealers in London, he set about organizing the ethnic MPs into a group that eventually became a party within a party and made it a force to be reckoned with in the Commons. So powerful did it become that within a year, it was the New Labor whips who were doing the bidding for Moses's support on contentious legislation, conscious of the fact that as they were a minority government, he could force an election at any time of his choosing. And as he wrung concession after concession from the cabinet in favor of the ethnics, so did the anger of the white MPs of all parties increase, until it became open warfare on all fronts in the Chamber.

It was a situation that the chief whip could not allow to continue, and he sought out Moses and asked him on what terms he could be persuaded to turn his back on his fellow ethnics and quit the sinister group he had created.

He offered him the post of junior minister in half a dozen ministries, but Moses refused them all, saying he would settle for a peerage instead. This was refused on the grounds that only a term of at least three years as a junior minister would enable him to qualify for such an honor.

He was then offered an ambassadorship to Washington or Paris, and these he also refused. Next came trade commissioner for the EU, and after that the office of deputy prime minister, but again he refused them both.

"Listen," he said, "I'll settle for a junior office but only if you guarantee I'll get the peerage as soon as two years are up."

The weary chief whip pondered the offer for a week and then capitulated. The current holder would be promoted sideways, and Moses Mandella would be made a new junior minister at the home office.

The PM, vacationing in Sharm el-Sheikh, rubber-stamped the appointment, but when the home secretary heard the news, he went berserk. "After all the bloody hard work I've done to rid Britain of its shameful reputation as the drug capital of Europe," he screamed in private, "they go and lumber me with the cocaine king himself. Now the bastard will do his best to re-label us as the drug capital of the world."

As a consequence, Moses found himself shunned by the decision makers in the ministry, all of whom had been handpicked by the current home secretary, most of them white, gay, and Oxford educated.

Finding himself with little to do, Moses resumed his business affairs, strengthened by the knowledge that he was now in a position to acquire critical details of home office operations against drug traffickers like himself. He would serve the required two years, get his peerage, and retire to the secluded mansion in Buckinghamshire that Arabella had set her heart on.

All went well until one morning, he switched on the TV to be greeted by the news that a chartered Boeing 747 on its way from Heathrow to Buenos Aires had disappeared from the radar screens and was feared to have crashed into the South Atlantic some six hundred kilometers from its destination. On board were the home secretary and twenty-eight senior officials of his ministry bound for a meeting of the International Conference on the Suppression of Narcotics. Six Royal Navy aircraft had been dispatched to the scene on the express orders of the prime minister, but they were unlikely to arrive there until after first light.

Moses was mortified. He hardly spent ten minutes away from the TV set as the rolling news grew bleaker and bleaker by the hour, until at 2400 BST, a bulletin announced that no trace of the aircraft or any survivors had been found and the search had been called off for the day. He was on his sixth daiquiri and about to retire when the phone rang. It was the PM.

Moses had never talked directly to Tony Blair or heard his voice except on TV and the one time he had bothered to turn up for Prime Minister's Question Time. Usually, Tony came over as the cocky, self-assured version of a man who looked in the mirror every morning, tipped his hat, and winked wickedly as he reluctantly dragged himself away from his reflection. Or he could be like one of his own rich customers, a celebrity who had just snorted two lines of heroin and sat at the head of a table, basking in the admiration of a gaggle of socialites. However, the voice that came over the telephone was anything but. It sounded more like the voice of a funeral director at a burial.

"Moses, have you heard the news?"

"Yes, Prime Minister, I have. Can't believe it. So sudden and all."

"Yes, yes, it's a pity of course," Blair said sympathetically, "but life goes on, and we must move with it at all times. I've checked with the cabinet office, and I'm told you are the only person with any authority left in the ministry; is that correct?"

"I don't know, Prime Minister, I don't know who was on board the plane and who wasn't."

"Call me 'Tony.' 'Prime Minister' sounds a bit stuffy in this day and age, don't you think, Moses?"

"Yes, Tony."

"I can tell you for certain that you are the only one left. Bloody hell, what was Graham Stewart thinking about taking that many of his staff on a bloody junket? Alastair tells me there were eighty-six passengers on the plane, forty-four of them Scotties and sixteen by the name of Stewart. Plus it's Mardi Gras week in Brazil. Fucking Scots, always on the look-out for booze and freebies. It wouldn't surprise me a bit if they weren't all as pissed as assholes, pilot included. Now I'm in deep shit. I'm off to Washington tomorrow, and I need someone to brief me on this top Al Qa'eda bastard we've got locked up in Bellmarsh."

"But Tony, I know nothing about any Al Qa'eda prisoner. As a matter of fact, I know very little about anything that goes on in the ministry. As far as my superiors were concerned, I was as welcome as a double dose of the clap."

"Because of your color?"

"Naturally."

"The racist bastards. Here's me doing everything I can to make Britain multicultural, and my own ministers keep stabbing me in the back. You know I think a lot about black people and that I'm pushing for at least a hundred when we fight the next election, don't you, Moses?"

"Sure, Tony." Moses wondered why there were never any blacks close to home in Downing Street. If there were any, they must be in hiding in the attic.

The voice became cool and confidential. "Listen to me, my friend, you don't have to know a bloody thing about anything that goes on in the ministry. The mandarins do all the work and plan all the cock-ups. At the moment, they are all running around like headless chickens, and I need you to go in there and sort things out. I know you can do it because you've got the reputation as a very hard-headed businessman and have made shedloads of money. Do me a favor and take them on. You'll be well rewarded, I can promise you that."

Moses hesitated. He knew Blair's promises were about as sincere as an alcoholic promising to go teetotal after just one more drink.

"I don't know, Tony, I don't think I want all the hassle. Anyway, I'm a junior. The mandarins aren't going to take any notice of what I say."

"The hell they won't. Tell you what, Moses, I'll make you temporary home secretary till all this blows over. Then if you like the job, you can keep it. Just think of the prestige you'll gain from the position. The first ever nigg—sorry, first black home secretary. That will surely be something to write home about, won't it? Think of all the perks: big salary, big car, gold-plated pension, and a place in the history books. Why, even your namesake will come calling."

Mandella hesitated again. "Sounds good, Tony, but I'm not really interested in the perks. I'm considering retirement in a couple of years, and there's really only one more thing I want before that happens."

"Mind telling me what that is, Moses?"

"I'd like a peerage, you know, a lordship like Kinnock and Mandelson."

There came a sharp intake of breath. "You mean that's all you want from me? Golly, would you take the job if I can fix it?"

"I'd be tempted. I'm sure the wife would say yes."

"And she'd be right to do so, bless her. You know of Baroness Amos and BaronessVaz, don't you? You and Lady Mandella could take your seats right between them on the front bench. Sounds great, doesn't it?"

"Yes, it does, and I'm sorely tempted. It's the responsibility that worries me. I have never liked to take on a job unless I know exactly where I stand. I've got a business reputation to uphold, and I certainly don't want to retire with the label of a failed politician tied around my neck."

"Look, Moses, we've had our eye on you for a long time now," lied the PM. "I wouldn't offer you the job if I didn't think you could do it. If it's any help, I'll send Alastair over to your office in the morning, and you can get your heads together. Ali's a good man, and he loves nigg—I mean black people. Goes to Barbados every Easter. He'll put your mind at rest straight away. By the way, my friend, I wouldn't be a bit surprised if you could find a way to even the score with SAS once you've learned the ropes."

Moses nearly dropped the phone in surprise. How much did the PM know about the devastating blow he suffered when the SAS had boarded the MV *Maracaibo* loaded with £25 million worth of cocaine off the Colombian coast and scuttled it with all its cargo? He had paid cash in advance for the consignment, and its loss had nearly bankrupted his organization. Holy Jesus, what an opportunity to get even, and with the PM's blessing, too.

He ignored the remark. "Very well, Tony, I accept your offer. Two years max, okay?"

"Good man, Moses, I knew I could count on you from the moment I looked at your record. Alastair will be over to you shortly. Make sure you give him every bit of information on the Al Qaeda prisoner, won't you? And by the way, Cherie is throwing a soirée at Chequers on the fifteen of this month. I'll get her to send you and yours an invitation, if that's okay with you."

"Thank you, Tony, I'll accept your offer, but there is one little thing you can do for me, if you don't mind."

"Of course, fire away."

"Put it in writing. I never accept an offer unless I've got it down in black and white. Good business practice, you know."

There was a pregnant silence, and for a moment, Moses was afraid that he had gone too far. But then he remembered the promises the PM had made to all and sundry over the years, and the casual way he had neglected to keep many of them.

The answer, when it came, was brief and decidedly unfriendly. "Very well, Alastair will bring it with him when he comes. Make sure you reciprocate with the information I require."

The prime minister put the phone down, his face flushed with anger, and at that moment, Alastair Campbell came into the office, a mug of steaming coffee in each hand.

Campbell looked at him and frowned. "What's up now?" he asked. "Don't tell me Moses turned you down. That's good news, as far as I'm concerned."

"Worse than that," replied the PM angrily. "He accepted but only if I promised him a peerage and put it in writing. The black bastard tried to talk down to me, for Christ's sake. Two years as an MP and he thinks he's Martin Luther King already. I nearly told him to shove it, and I would have, if time wasn't so short. Blimey, Ali, what else could I do? Six refusals for the job so far. What in God's name is going on?"

"We don't do God 'round here, if you remember, son," joked a laconic Campbell. "Hell, nobody in their right mind would take the bloody job on. Eight appointments in ten years, one suicide, and now what looks suspiciously like an assassination. Would you take it on, Tone? Seriously, though, do you mean to tell me he signed up for a lousy peerage? Why, he could get two for the price of one if he handed over a mil. All he had to do was contact the party treasurer."

"He's tried that. Seems like the treasurer draws the line at drug barons."

Campbell whistled. "Times sure have changed, haven't they? Mind you, you asked for it, packing the House with all those niggers. Give them a yard and they'll take a mile or, as they say in South Carolina, give them a grape and they'll stick you for a melon. So it was the peerage that clinched it? You should at least have asked for a donation. A mil would come in handy right now, I can tell you."

"No, it wasn't really the peerage," the PM replied wearily. "The clincher was the *Maracaibo* caper. He wants revenge."

"You're joking," gasped Campbell. "The fool actually wants to mess with the SAS? He must be off his rocker."

"Serves him right. Like I say, if you accept being chucked in at the deep end, then you have no one else to blame if you don't come up after three."

"Bloody hell, he's in deep, all right," chortled Campbell. "You know something, Tony, maybe some good will come from this, after all. While Stewart was farting about chasing invisible terrorists and druggies and letting the SAS run wild, this guy might just do the opposite: see the light, take the job seriously, play the hero, squash the bastards. Even if he makes a balls of it, we can always give young Ian Ponce the job. Another three months and the public will have forgotten about his bloody daft activities, and we can slip him into the post without anyone noticing."

The words seemed to cheer the PM up. "Christ, I hope you're right there, Ali, but I can't ever see Mandella turning his back on the drug trade."

"Maybe not," replied Campbell, "but stranger things have happened. I seem to remember a young socialist who once carried a banner for the CND. Now that same young man is a prime minister who will bomb the shit out of any country that does not toe the line."

Chapter 20

L uke Dryden lost no time assembling the best team of experts he could find at the base for his new assignment. The buzzword was sabotage, and there was no shortage of that kind of talent in the SAS. With the help of Captain Jim Farnsworth of B Squadron, Luke pored through the records of every serving officer and selected the twelve he needed to plan and carry out the first operation, code-named "Good News," an operation designed to deprive New Labor of their stranglehold over one of the most vital organs of a democracy: a free press, or the Fourth Estate, as it is sometimes called.

During Campbell's enforced absence from Downing Street, some sections of the media had begun to reassert their independence, with the result that stories of sleaze, incompetence, and corruption at the highest levels of government, which had been ruthlessly suppressed when he was in charge, began to see the light of day and led to a universal hatred and contempt for the governing classes that was unparalleled in modern times.

Far from showing any humility for his past misdemeanors, Campbell set about restoring his exalted status and that of his nominal boss, Tony Blair, with a vengeance. The minnows of the national press, the *Guardian*, the *Observer*, and the *Independent*, were the first to feel his wrath for stepping out of line, and they were quickly brought under control by the simple threat of depriving them of any governmental advertising. Since the government payroll now constituted a quarter of the entire working population, such massive advertising had become the lifeblood of these privileged papers, and without it, their days would be numbered.

Rupert Murdoch's papers—the *Sun*, *Times*, and *News of the World*—which had been flirting with Tories, were quick to step back in line, raising the question once again of what kind of secret deal had been made between an arch-conservative like Murdoch and a champagne socialist like Blair. The *Mirror*, Campbell's old paper, had never really left the fold, and that left the *Express*, the *Mail*, and the *Telegraph* facing the music.

The editors of these three papers were summoned to Downing Street and were read the riot act. Any articles critical of government policies, government ministers, and the Labor party in general were to be submitted to Downing Street for approval before publication, or else.

The three editors refused to be intimidated, and within days, wildcat strikes began to plague their papers and were allowed to continue unhindered by the authorities. Major advertisers began receiving threats that if they continued placing advertisements with the papers, they were likely to be visited by any number of tax inspectors, health and safety inspectors, employment inspectors, police inspectors, and most dreaded of all, Hans Hoffman of Section Four. As a result, advertising revenue started to dry up, and circulation numbers nearly halved within months. The *Daily Telegraph*, already in financial difficulties, was on the verge of bankruptcy, and it was only a matter of time before the *Express* and *Mail*, under tremendous pressure from their shareholders, would be forced to do the same. As it was, they were obliged to rein in their sensational investigations into corruption at the highest level of government, plus the evil activities of Moses Mandella and his secret police.

These crude methods of intimidation were unnecessary, as far as the broadcasting media was concerned. The BBC was gently reminded that a reduction in their license fee would be well received by license payers, while the commercial channels were told that a resolution put forward by one of Labor's bolshie MPs, limiting advertising slots to a maximum of one minute in any one-hour period, was still being considered at the highest level. By the end of his first year back in office, Alastair Campbell was master of all he surveyed. As he once remarked to his partner, when they stood on the balcony of their luxurious apartment overlooking Horse Guards Parade, he could now instruct the *Times* to publish cartoons depicting the Prophet Mohammed raping twelve virgins in the Garden of Eden and not even the BBC, ITV, Channels Four and Five, or even the Muslim press would raise a single objection. He calculated that sooner rather than later, the *Mail* and *Express* would either capitulate or go into liquidation, and when that happened, the power of New Labor would be absolute, ensuring re-election into the distant future and beyond.

But as every dictator in modern history had found out to their cost, seizing control of the media was the easy part. Maintaining control was another matter altogether. And Luke Dryden was a keen student of history.

There had not been a greater series of targeted destruction in Britain since Hermann Goering sent his bombers over in the Second World War. The targeting was, however, far more precise. At exactly 0300 on a bitterly cold Sunday morning in March, a series of huge explosions destroyed 60 percent of the newspaper publishing industry in Great Britain and Northern Ireland. Only the *Mail, Express, Telegraph,* and their associated publications escaped the blitz, and the Monday morning editions of these same newspapers revealed the scale of the destruction.

From Southampton and London in the south to Birmingham and Manchester, to Glasgow and Edinburgh and across the sea to Belfast and Dublin, the pattern was the same. Explosives and mines had been expertly placed around the support structures of the main buildings housing the printing presses in such a way that when they were detonated, the entire roof structure fell in from the center, damaging or writing off the machinery beneath it. The same method had been applied to the newsprint warehouses and office blocks and even some garages housing delivery trucks.

The *Mail* likened it to Fred Dibnah's speciality—collapsing factory chimneys—while the *Express* explained that if the attack had been made against the *Telegraph* premises in Canary Wharf Tower, the whole building would have been brought down.

The effects of the blitz were catastrophic. Shares in the targeted companies nose-dived. In the case of the *Guardian*, the *Observer*, and the *Independent,* they achieved negative equity. Thousands of employees were laid off, including correspondents, columnists, sports writers, and fortune-tellers. For regular readers of the papers, the most devastating effect on their lives was the abrupt loss of the sports pages, the racing columns, and the TV guides. As a result, they stormed the newsagents for copies of the *Mail* and the *Express,* only to find that the shelves had been swept clean. The two papers were forced to print extra copies throughout the day but had to call a halt in order to prepare the presses for the Tuesday edition. On that day, they doubled their circulation but still could not satisfy demand. Huge lines built up outside newsagents all over the country, and fights broke out as regular readers clashed with interlopers demanding a copy of the proscribed right-wing papers. Fights also broke out in Parliament as it dawned on Labor and Lib-Dem MPs that all the attacks were concentrated on left-wing publications, and they accused the Tories of colluding with fascist elements in the army.

And as the circulation of the *Mail* and *Express* soared and the profits trebled, so did the spirit of free speech return to their investigative journalists, with the result that damning articles and leader columns began to appear again, even in the *Telegraph*, exposing the sleaze and incompetence at the heart of a government hanging onto power by virtue of the shameful acquiescence of the equally dishonest and self-seeking Tory and Lib-Dem MPs.

Jock Wingate was delighted with the success of the mission and rewarded all members of the Kitcheners with three-day immediate leave.

Luke was over the moon with the concession. The cloak and dagger stuff he was forced to use to protect Carol from the attentions of Section Four thugs, even for a few hours visit, was beginning to tell on his nerves. He had tried to persuade her to join him at Credenhill but she was reluctant to leave the children and her job at the hospital. She was right, of course. Some of the officers and men had brought their wives in but they were mostly childless. A camp under siege was no place for youngsters, and tough and fearless as Elizabeth and James were, it wouldn't be right to expose them to the shelling the base experienced from time to time. He was determined to make the best of this opportunity. Things were moving so fast now that it could even be the last.

They met up in Grasmere in the Lake District, at a guest house close to the lake itself. Carol had been there many times and knew the lake and its surroundings like the back of her hand. The setting and its memories seemed to bring out the youthful exuberance of her youth and Luke marveled at her passionate love of nature and the extra beauty it brought to her face. He was reminded of his own youth in Shropshire and the equally glorious bounty nature had bestowed upon the hills and dales there. They were kindred spirits, and the more he saw of her the greater became the foreboding that, considering the hard times ahead, such happiness could not endure.

They were sitting alone on a wooden bench overlooking the lake on a twilight night that reflected the myriad stars in the still waters when he finally broached the subject."

"Carol, I've been thinking it would be a good idea if you and the children went to stay with your parents until the New Year. It's winter in Canada now, and the kids would have a wonderful time, and so would you. You haven't seen them for three years, and it's time you went."

"Good lord, are you trying to get rid of me, Luke Dryden?" she said, laughing. "Only this morning you were telling me that you couldn't live one day without me."

"That's true, darling, I meant every word I said. But the change would do you good. You've been working too hard lately, especially with the amputees. Too much work can damage your health, you know."

Carol had stopped laughing, and her face took on a serious look. "What's gone wrong, Luke? You promised me the war would be over for Christmas. What's happened? Is the Regiment in trouble? Are you losing the war then?"

"No, we are winning the war, and I'm sure it will be over for Christmas, God willing.

"It's this hide and seek business that's got me worried. Staff Sergeant Barnes went home last Tuesday, and we haven't seen him since. Intelligence are pulling all the stops out to find him but so far no luck."

"Well, maybe he's had enough of being cooped up in the base, and has gone awol. You said yourself that some of the men are grumbling about the inaction."

"No, no, Barnes is a thirty year man, he'd never go awol. Besides, his wife has gone too and intelligence say his house was broken into and there were signs of a struggle, and there was blood about. They told me it's a classic Section Four snatch and we'll be lucky if we either of them again. We just haven't got the resources to track down every snatch."

"So you want me to leave our home, give up my job, desert my sister, and take the children out of school when they've only just started back. No thank you, I'm not giving up on account of the scum in Section Four. I'm counting on you to eliminate every single one of those bastards and the sooner you do it the better."

"But, darling, don't you see, every time we meet the odds are against us. They are getting closer all the time, and if they ever found out where we live they will snatch you and maybe the children and Kate as well if they're at home when they come."

Carol was silent for a moment, and Luke thought he had frightened her. But the look on her face when she looked up at him was anything but. "Look here husband," she declared. "If this business is going to affect your work at the base, then there is only one solution to the problem. There will be no more visits until you have defeated Mandella and his bloody army. And that's my last word on the subject.

"What is the government going to do to help us in our hour of need?" asked a plaintive voice. "After all, it is the fault of you lot that these bloody mercenaries are allowed to roam the country at will, blowing up anything that takes their fancy. One hundred thousand Paramilitaries in Section Three, yet not a single one of them on duty within a kilometer of any of our presses. It's a bloody disgrace. A few hundred SAS cooped up in their base in Credenhill making fools of both our security services and the army. Good God, Alastair, many of us are looking bankruptcy in the face, and we must be given financial help immediately or go under."

Alastair Campbell stared at the speaker sitting directly across the table as he would a cockroach emerging from his underwear. Of all the publications that had benefited from New Labor, the *Guardian* was first to the trough. Every year, it was given the cream of the hundreds of thousands of classified ads for government departments in return for its unswerving support for New Labor. He was the one who had set it up, and now, lo and behold, the editor who had benefited most of all had the temerity to demand yet more largesse from the hand that fed it. Timothy Bottom was a disgusting, greedy, unscrupulous little queer, and Campbell made a mental note to exclude the *Guardian* from any further ads as long as the treacherous rat remained its editor. He knew instinctively that it was Bottom who had instigated the call for a meeting with himself and the Newspaper Publishers Association. He looked around at the editors and press barons seated around the table. He knew every single one of them by their first names. They had wined and dined him in their homes, in the swankiest of restaurants, and even in the apartments of their glamorous mistresses. They had deluged him with gifts and promises of directorships when he retired from office. Rupert Murdoch had even offered to pay him millions of pounds for his precious diaries (although he had yet to put the offer in writing). Now here they were, baying for blood and asking for taxpayer's money to cover their losses. Not Tony's blood, the home secretary's blood, or the defense secretary's blood, but his blood only. The man who had made more money for the bitching press than any politician in history.

"I don't do home office, I don't do defense, and I don't do God, Timothy," he replied sarcastically. "If you complained to Moses Mandella, he'd tell you to piss off, the army would threaten to shove a bayonet up your ass, and God would give you the biggest kiss-off since he sent the Israelites into exile. You people have made billions out of our government, and if you had put a fraction of those profits toward protecting your own property, you wouldn't be in the position you're in today. You're a money-grubbing bunch of hypocrites, always preaching to your readers how they should behave and be charitable, while all the time you're coining it in by filling what you call a newspaper with more advertisements than there are in the Yellow Pages. As for your staff, I'm told you have laid all the poor buggers off without pay until you're back in business again. That's a pretty shitty way of saying thank you for years of loyal service, if you ask me."

"Hang on a minute!" screamed Farley Rusk of the *Observer*. "My paper has done all it can to get the *Mail* and *Express* to take on our redundant staff, but they refused to hire a single employee. Said they didn't want our lefties contaminating the purity of their middle England readership, the fascist bastards. Anyway, you're in no position to preach to us about loyalty. You were Maxwell's right-hand man on the *Mirror* when it went bust and everybody lost their job. Not only that, he raided the pension funds too and left them empty. Don't tell me you didn't know that sort of shitty business was going on."

Rusk spoke bitterly. His paper was on pretty shaky ground before the bombings. Now, with only half the plant covered by insurance, the future looked very bleak indeed.

Campbell shrugged his shoulders. "That's old potatoes, Farley, and you know it. I repeat, I was editorial. I had absolutely nothing to do with the financial side. The inquiry proved that."

Another voice broke in. "Well, if you've no intention of helping us out over the plant destruction, what are you going to do about our loss of business? It will take us years to tempt back our lost readers. The *Mail* and *Express* are soaking them up by the millions. At the last count, the *Mail* circulation was up by over 150 percent to over 8 million copies, and the *Express* up by the same amount to nearly 6 million copies. At this rate, they'll be the only newspapers in circulation by the end of the year and stinking rich in the bargain."

"What do you want us to do, Tom?"

Campbell had a soft spot for Tom Hudson, the editor of the *Independent*. They had worked together on the *Mirror* and turned out some good stuff before Captain Bob Maxwell screwed up.

"Well, find a way to close them down. Get the union boys to call their men out on strike or bust up their machinery or both."

"We've tried that; most of their staff is nonunion, and the ones who are union aren't going to risk losing their jobs when there are thousands of laid-off printers waiting to snap them up. As for sabotaging their machinery, they've got security systems that would make our system around Parliament look amateurish, so I'm told. They've even got ex-SAS guards around their plants, the cheeky bastards."

"So get 'em for what they're printing, for God's sake!" shouted Tidsley Blenkinsop of the *Times*. "Have you bothered to read any of the unspeakable garbage they are putting out? Why, last week the *Mail* cartoonist lampooned the Islamists by printing five cartoons of Mohammed enjoying sex in his harem, and on page three, at that. Now both papers have reverted to calling blacks niggers, Arabs wogs, homosexuals faggots, and lesbians lesbos. They're actually substituting racist words for swear words wherever possible, the fascist swine. What does Mandella think he's playing at? He can use at least a dozen laws to put the editors in jail for what they're printing."

"And if you're reading the papers like I do, Tiddly, you will learn that we have got sixteen writs issued against them, and these are printed every day in both papers like some badge of honor. They are sticking two fingers up to us, daring us to close them down and making sure their readers know that if we close one down, the other will follow suit. Just think of it, 14 million readers plus their families, most of them white, deprived of their news stories, sports pages, page three boobs, women's pages, children's pages, arts pages, horoscopes, holidays, crosswords and Sudoku puzzles, weather forecasts, and the classified columns. Why, these are the kind of people who go raving mad if their paper is delivered ten minutes late in the morning."

"So let them eat cake. There's always television to turn to. A lot more enlightening and informative than those two dirty rags, I can tell you."

"If you believe that, you'll believe anything, Tiddly," Campbell replied wearily. "People who can think for themselves will never substitute their read for the crap that appears on the small screen, and not many people have a set in the lavatory either. A lot of them would rather go on the Internet and download news from Australia or Canada or even the United States."

"That's right," came a chorus from around the table, as all eyes focused on Rupert Murdoch, the only UK newspaper proprietor to own a TV station, "none of them will settle for boring TV chat shows."

The owner of the *Times, Sun,* and *News of the World* looked cross. His losses exceeded that of all the other publishers put together. He put two fingers up, mouthed an obscenity, settled back in his chair, and closed his eyes. "Tell them, Alastair," he murmured. "Give it to the poor saps straight."

Campbell acknowledged the advice with a grateful nod. "Now listen carefully," he began. "We are a minority government, and we can only stay in power by pitting the Tories and Lib-Dems against each other or threatening to call an election, which they are shit-scared of facing. Now I have it on very good authority that the two papers have already prepared proofs of the final edition they intend to publish if we close them down. It consists of one page only with the banner headlines 'New Labor closed your paper down. Reopen it by voting Conservative or Lib-Dem in the forthcoming election.' You can imagine what the reaction will be. The Tories and Lib-Dems will call a vote of confidence, and we'll be forced into an election without one daily newspaper to back us up. We'll be lucky to win a hundred seats, and half of those will be Scottish. It will be a massacre, and we'll never recover from it. My advice to you all is to cut your losses any way you can. Get our friends in Europe to print limited editions for you and fly them over. That should keep some of your readership happy."

"Happy my ass," snorted Farley Rusk, "there is no way they would pay five pounds for a copy of the *Observer*, and that's the price per copy the French have given us. They know we're in a hole, and they intend to make a mint out of it, the cheap, profiteering bastards."

"What about us then?" shouted a voice that set off a series of groans around the table. It belonged to Fergus O'Toole, the editor of the *Irish Times*. "We've got nothing to do with your country yet your bloody SAS savages have razed our fine establishment to the ground. This is an act of war, and my government will be demanding full reimbursement of our losses, plus payment for every lost copy until our presses are rolling again."

Campbell could barely conceal his contempt. "There will be no reparations from us, O'Toole, any more than there have been from Dublin for all the damages the IRA have caused to Britain with explosions planned, financed, and armed within the Republic. As far as the government is concerned, the IRA are now beyond the pale and will be treated in the same manner as the SAS."

"Hear, hear," came a voice, "serves you right for printing inflammatory articles urging the IRA to kill British soldiers. If I knew the SAS man who set the explosion at your works, I'd recommend him for a medal, you Fenian prick."

Campbell was quick to intercede. "Come, come, people," he implored, "we are all in this together. We must forget our rivalries and pool all our resources for the common good. The chancellor wants me to tell you that the government is too strapped for cash to bail any of you out directly, but he assures me that he will put pressure on the banks to finance your rebuilding costs as well as waiving all VAT demands."

"What about the army?" whined Timothy Bottom. "They're sitting on their asses all day playing poker. Why don't their engineers rebuild our premises and take it out of the ministry of defense budget?"

"Not a chance; they're all out in the war zones."

"Like hell they are. There's at least twenty squaddies refurbishing a stately home for the minister of defense and another ten doing up Mandelson's new pad in Chelsea," replied Bottom.

"First I've heard about it," lied Campbell. "They're probably home on sick leave." He knew all about the defense minister's project but was in the dark about Mandelson's. "Now then, gentlemen," he said abruptly, "I'm afraid I'm going to have to call this meeting closed. I'll keep in touch with you individually and give you any further help I can."

The meeting broke up, and the disgruntled representatives filed out, most of them looking balefully at Campbell as they passed by him.

Campbell remained in his seat, studying his notes, for a full ten minutes before the door opened and Rupert Murdoch came striding back in. The tycoon slammed his briefcase on the table and took a seat opposite Campbell.

"Look here, Alastair," he drawled in his Americanized Aussie accent, "I'll get straight to the point. I'm really scared about what's coming next. Wingate isn't going to go on vacation after what he's done to us. He's on a roll, and I guarantee that his next move will be against the broadcasting media. I don't give a shit about the BBC and the others, but I'm sure as hell worried about what's in store for Sky. My organization has backed New Labor to the hilt, and that makes us a sworn enemy of the SAS. Now it's payback time, and I want the government to pull out all the stops and give our UK broadcasting facilities round-the-clock protection. Damn it all man, it's in your own best interests to see that we don't get hurt. Look at modern history. In every revolution or coup d'état, the prime target for the rebels has always been the broadcasting stations. Their capture gives them immediate access to the public and the opportunity to substitute their lies and propaganda for what has gone before. Very few uprisings have failed when that first objective was attained, believe me. It's bad enough hanging around watching the *Mail* and *Express* stealing all our business cost free, but if the SAS foul up our satellite broadcasting, viewers will go back to reading, and that will make them richer still. I don't mind telling you I can just about cover the cost of rebuilding our plants, unlike some of the other poor buggers, but if Sky is damaged, it will put an end to my operations in the UK forever."

Campbell was astonished. "Jesus Christ, Rupert, I could understand it if you were ground-based like ITV or the BBC, but most of your stuff is up there in space. How could they possibly put you out of business?"

Murdoch frowned. "Look Alastair," he said impatiently, "I thought you knew better than that. The satellites are only a part of our operation. We've got broadcast centers all over the UK, and Ireland as well. There are forty-four facilities at least where they can give us a lot of pain, and those are the ones I want protected."

Campbell was lost for words. "Forty-four! Christ, Rupert!" he blurted out. "How on earth do you expect us to do that?"

"Get the army to do it. That's what they're paid for, isn't it?"

"No way, they're scraping the bottom of the barrel as it is."

"Use the Territorial Army then, they're trained up enough for guard duty, aren't they?"

"There ain't no TA. They've all resigned."

"Section Three then, or have they all resigned too?"

"I dunno, Moses treats them like they're his own private army. Maybe he's plotting to use them to take over the media himself." It was a weak joke but Murdoch failed to see the funny side of it.

"Fuck Moses, that jumped-up nigger wouldn't raise a finger to help me if I was dying on his doorstep. And all because the *Sun* exposed his wife's sexual appetite on their wedding anniversary. You'll have to call a national emergency to cover all broadcasters. That he cannot refuse."

Campbell looked unhappy. "I'll do my best, Rupert, but you know what a contrary bastard he can be. I wish to Christ Tony had never given him the job in the first place. He's the only one who can top him. I'll have a word with him this afternoon."

"Make sure you do," Murdoch said ominously as he picked up his briefcase and made for the door. "Remember, if we go down, you and New Labor won't have a prayer of winning another election this side of 2050, if ever. And Tony and Cherie will be lucky if they get an invitation to speak at a negro spiritual meeting anytime they come begging in the USA."

Chapter 21

Moses Mandella had been thrown in at the deep end in the government's most incompetent and despised department: the home office. Alastair Campbell had given him no more than two or three months before he would be on his knees, begging to be reassigned. But Moses was made of sterner stuff. Unlike the suits in the ministry, he had come up the hard way, battling his way to the top, whether it was dealing with the drug families in Colombia or the murderous dealers in Tower Hamlets. Compared to them, the public schoolboys and Oxbridge graduates who populated the ministry were like a bunch of delinquent choirboys. It took him only a few short weeks to rumble their cosy little world of tea and biscuits, sickies, short-time working, extended holidays and junkets, expense accounts, freebies, and overstaffing. But the one thing that baffled him more than anything was their complete disdain for the citizens they were paid to serve and their arrogant belief in their own superiority. Among such people, he was king. They would do anything he told them to or face the sack, from the most senior mandarin to the lowliest office boy. With over 5 million people on the dole, there was no way they would jeopardize their jobs and the gold-plated pensions that went with them.

It didn't take Moses long to recognize that although the ministry of the late Graham Stewart was even more of a basket case than when that useless idiot took over, there was no reason why it could not be restored to its former greatness. All it needed was a man of vision and a man with an insatiable appetite for power; in other words, a man like himself. And why not? He was in charge of a vast ministry employing close on two hundred thousand people, a ministry that impinged in one way or another on practically every government department of any importance. All it required was a leader who was not afraid to defy the unions, the judges, Parliament, and even the prime minister himself. A leader who was brave enough to sack every useless, self-seeking police chief and judge; shut down a newspaper or TV station; build dozens of new prisons; and bring back the death penalty. He realized now that this was the calling that God had chosen for him all along and, like his namesake, Nelson, he was determined to take up the challenge and reshape the country in his own image.

By a stroke of good fortune, Tony Blair had appointed as chancellor a graduate of the London School of Economics, a fellow Scot by the name of Angus MacTavish. It was an appointment that was celebrated by Tony's left wing pals, not because Angus was renowned for his financial acumen but for the more important reason that he was black; Tony having decided to take up the white man's burden once again. Furthermore, Angus's parents also hailed from Jamaica, having arrived in the UK around the same time as his own parents. They had docked in Glasgow and settled there after taking the prudent step of changing their surname, by deed poll, from Abudabuabu to MacTavish, the name of the first mate on the SS *Windrush*. Alastair Campbell was dead set against appointing him but Blair insisted that he take the office. After all, the lad had followed his own hallowed path to Parliament: Fettes College, Edinburg, St. John's College, Oxford, and membership of the Labor party. And the fact that he was black would surely cancel out any doubts about his suitability for a job of such vital importance. As had been the case with Moses Mandella, Campbell tried hard to change his mind but gave up after Blair threw one of his notorious tantrums.

The two sons of the Caribbean hit it off right from the start and formed an alliance that would frustrate their cabinet colleagues and lead to more than one unhappy resignation. They both recognized that with Alastair Campbell in charge, their chances of survival would be far greater if they stuck together and faced down the white men; Moses, because he needed funds for his ambitious plans, and Angus, because of the fearsome reputation he enjoyed as a protector of the downtrodden black minority.

The unprecedented powers Graham Stewart had sought in his vainglorious war on terror were but a prelude to Moses's secret aim of establishing an all-powerful police state in Britain. However, it was a good start in the right direction, and he wasted no time in expanding its importance. Hardly a day went by without an incident of treasonable activity turning up, as if by magic. Terrorist plots were uncovered regularly, airports were closed and surrounded by tanks, mosques were raided, and alleged terrorists arrested until at last public hysteria reached such a pitch that a frightened Parliament unanimously granted him full powers of arrest without charge and imprisonment for indefinite periods, without right of appeal. This authorization was the key to the establishment of an all-powerful Homeland Security setup, embracing five newly named departments:

Section 1. An expanded regular police force, with county police chiefs appointed by, and responsible to the home office.

Section 2. A police intelligence unit combining the existing MI5 and MI6 spy agencies.

Section 3. A paramilitary force with an initial establishment of one hundred thousand men armed and equipped to the standards enjoyed by the U.S. National Guard units.

Section 4. A special unit designed to maintain a compulsory ID system and database on every British citizen, with unlimited powers of arrest.

Section 5. A new unit (CDMC) for the control and dissemination of media content.

It wasn't difficult for Moses to find suitable people to run the new agencies. He placed a simple advertisement on TV and watched as the applications came pouring in. He set up a special database and personally chose the grading that would bring the short list down to a manageable figure. The applicant's age was set at between thirty and fifty-five; sex: male only; nationality: unimportant; education: unimportant; experience: minimum ten years in police forces, correction centers, private surveillance, and security companies plus the three services. Applications from public school and university graduates, MPs, royalty, religious freaks, schoolteachers, TV personalities, politicians, lunatics, and drug addicts were not to be considered.

Moses interviewed each applicant for section head personally and chose Robert Crippen and Harold Shipman as heads of Section One and Section Two, respectively, General Kruger for Section Three, Hans Hoffman for Section Four, and Charles Henry Drake for Section Five. He gathered them together in his private office and laid out his plans before them, plans that would be trumpeted as a call to arms in the war against terrorism but which, in reality, would transform a country groaning under the yoke of an incompetent, wasteful, and authoritarian socialist Utopia into a full-blown totalitarian state.

Alastair Campbell returned to Downing Street in a foul mood following his meeting with the press and the altercation with Rupert Murdoch. After less than two years back in office, he enjoyed the reputation of being the most powerful man in Britain, yet now, after one incident over which he had no control, Murdoch had the temerity to make ominous threats against him. All because of that crooked black drug pusher in charge of the home office, Moses Mandella. The man was impossible. He had been too busy lately to take in all the complaints that were flying around from his cabinet colleagues, but his latest dealings with the man had revealed to him the true extent of Mandella's malign influence on government and the fear he seemed to have instilled in the minds of even the most senior ministers. It was true that Graham Stewart had laid the foundations for the Homeland Security Department, which was formed to protect Britain from attack by Islamic terrorists, and that he was the man responsible for introducing some of the most draconian and oppressive laws in the country's history. But in the incredibly short time that he had been in charge, Mandella had built himself a surveillance empire to rival that of J. Edgar Hoover or even the Stasi or KGB. Campbell admitted that it was his own fault for allowing such a thing to happen; he had taken it upon himself to oversee the workings of the foreign office, Europe, and overseas development personally, aims he identified with himself more than any other. As a result, he had taken his eye off the ball, and the chickens were now coming home to roost. Like Tony Blair, he hated economics, and he shunned anything to do with the home office, which had become a graveyard for aspiring politicians throughout the ages.

Now he was under threat in his own back yard from an unholy alliance of Mandella at the home office and Angus MacTavish at the Treasury. And on top of that, he was faced with a worldwide economic meltdown, a looming war in Iran, a National Health Service on the brink of collapse, and the emergence of the Freedom First party, which was taking the country by storm. But it was the tongue-lashing he had received from Rupert Murdoch that had hurt him most. He was a journalist first and foremost, and the media was his passion. Rupert Murdoch should have recognized that fact, but he had treated him like a sleazy politician on the make. Worse still, it made it unlikely that the mogul would offer to publish his precious diaries when the time came to retire from politics. However, there was one ray of sunshine to lighten the gloom. Murdoch and most of the press were hurting like hell, and the person who was responsible for guaranteeing their safety and well-being from internal terrorist activities was Moses Mandella himself. Murdoch already hated Mandella's guts. How much more would the great man hate him if the SAS were to damage his greatest asset: Sky TV? There was no more a formidable enemy than Rupert Murdoch when he was on the warpath.

Immediately after he read the contents of the chancellor's red book detailing Treasury expenditure over the past year, Campbell called a meeting of three of his closest allies in his own private snug at 10 Downing Street to discuss its implications on government policy.

"Jesus Christ," he complained, "the bloody madman's spent more on his bloody war on terror than defense and the National Health Service combined. No wonder the army, doctors, teachers, and taxpayers are screaming blue murder. What on earth does his private army of layabouts, illegal immigrants, and Pinkoes do to justify all that money? The police have locked up practically everybody wearing a turban or a beard, and there hasn't been a real bomb attack for two years. The only time I've seen them in action is when there's an alert at an airport or when they're in a gay parade with their pink helmets and pink shoulder flashes. If any one of them has ever fired a shot in anger, I've yet to hear of it. There are a dozen regular army men coming home in body bags every day of the week, yet these impostors are living off the fat of the land. It's a bloody disgrace, and it's about time we took him to task on it."

"I should be very careful if I were you, Alastair," Dudley Coward whispered, looking around the room nervously. "Walls have ears, you know."

"Not these walls, they don't. I've had a private firm de-bug it, defuse it, and render it audio repellent. Don't think Section Two haven't tried it, though. My security boys have found more bugs in Number 10 than there are in your mattress, even in my own house, for Christ's sake."

"Good grief, Alastair, I never knew that," Coward said, blushing deeply. "Do you suppose the blighters are listening in on me at home?"

"Without a doubt, son," Campbell replied, smiling inwardly at the gay minister's embarrassment. "That creepy Shipman has bugged the houses of practically everyone in government. Hell, I've been told he's even bugged the archbishop of Canterbury and listened in to his private prayers. You be careful when you go to bed tonight and watch what you say to that mate of yours." He grinned at the other two ministers as Coward's face turned even redder.

"Now, back to business. Moses has increased the strength of Section One to three hundred ten thousand policemen, Section Two to twenty-five thousand snoopers, Section Three to over one hundred twenty thousand Paramilitaries, Section Four to twenty thousand-plus secret police, and Section Five to twenty thousand TV and press regulators. That's a total of four hundred ninety-five thousand security operatives, four times the combined total of the armed forces. And what has he got to show for all this expenditure in money and manpower? Absolutely nothing. The country's in turmoil; strikes, race riots, the stock market in free-fall, and now this Stalinist treatment of the public. It's come to the point when you can't spit in the street without being thrown in jail and held there until you've forked over a bribe. Where the public used to complain about never seeing a policeman on the street, they now complain about there being one around every corner waiting to pounce if you so much as stare in their direction. A lot of motorists are too frightened to take out their cars for fear of being stopped and served an on-the-spot fine for some triviality, and the more expensive the car, the bigger the fine. And a sure way to get arrested is to take a picture of their ugly mugs, in or out of uniform."

"Hell, I know," groaned the foreign secretary, Ed Fowler. "A friend of mine was reported for saying nigger at a prayer meeting. He was arrested three months ago by Section Four, and we haven't seen him since. No charge, no bail, no nothing."

"It wouldn't surprise me if he wasn't incarcerated in Smithfield," said Peter Plum, the Northern Ireland secretary. "They say that there are hundreds being held there on all sorts of trumped-up charges, mostly terrorism. Those who have been released say it's only because there's a shortage of cells they are freed at all, and then they never get an apology or redress. They say there are torture chambers there and a crematorium at one end, which is always fired up, just like Belsen. And there are more such places in other parts of the country. The problem is that it is impossible to get in touch with anyone placed under arrest since Parliament granted Homeland Security the right to deny habeas corpus and hold a prisoner indefinitely without charge. They just disappear. The lawyers go to Section One police stations and are told no one of that name is being held there, and they suggest they try Section Two. The same answer is given to enquiries there, and they refer them to Section Four or Section Five. It's a merry-go-round. The trouble is that there are very few lawyers left who are willing to do more than go through the motions."

"That's not all," moaned Coward. "Hoffman's got it in for gays and ignores all the laws protecting us. Nowadays you can't even go near a public toilet without being pounced upon by one of his goons."

"Well, something's got to be done about it and fast," said Campbell. "The man's gotten far too powerful. Christ, every time someone mentions his name, they speak in a whisper. As for some of the freaks he's gathered round him, half of them can't speak English, and if you're white, they treat you like you're shit. I didn't save New Labor for it to be trashed by a bloody black dope dealer. The bastard doesn't go through me anymore, he goes straight to Tony. He knows he's only half there, and he butters him up and tells him the whole world hangs on his every word."

"But you're the real leader of the party, Alastair," said Ed Fowler. "Tony relies on your judgment for everything, inside and outside Parliament."

"If that was true, Moses would never have been appointed home minister in the first place. There are times when Tony digs his heels in and won't budge a centimeter. There's something weird going on between him and Moses. Cherie thinks the sun shines out of his ass, and he's at their home for tea and crumpets two or three times a week. It's like Rasputin and the tsarina. Whatever he says, she laps it up."

"Maybe she's on drugs," suggested Ed Fowler. "I'm bloody sure Tony is, half the time; Moses will see to that. So what are we going to do about it, Alastair?"

"I want Dudley to sound out the chiefs of staff. The army's still more than a match for Section Three, and they all hate Mandella's guts. Feed them on that. Tell them he's starving the three services of cash because he's spending billions on the Paramilitaries. Frighten them with rumors that they are next to be purged and their wives and children and mistresses too, just like Stalin did. Mention that it's no good wearing a bloody coronet on their head if there's no body to support it. Concentrate their tiny little minds. Even suggest they might call in the SAS if they have to. Let me tell you this straight: The black bastard doesn't scare me none. I was brought up in the mean streets of Glasgow, and I know there's always a way you can bring down someone who's got too big for his boots. If Dudley isn't successful, I've got a plan B that will cook his goose good and proper, but it will take a bit longer."

The three ministers looked at him expectantly, and Peter Plum took the cue. "What's that, Alastair? Be a good mate and tell us, please, please."

Campbell scratched his nose and kept them waiting before replying. "I'll have a word with the head of the Colombian cartel. You know, Pedro Martinez, the father of the girl Moses is alleged to have raped and left for dead in Tower Hamlets six years ago."

Chapter 22

"I want to know what the hell all your useless idiots at the home office were doing yesterday besides screwing, boozing, sleeping, scoffing pizzas, and dancing naked on the filing cabinets."

Alastair Campbell stood, legs apart and arms folded, glaring at the home secretary, who sat on a sofa, sandwiched between Tony Blair and Peter Mandelson, and waited impatiently for an answer.

Blair and Mandelson looked uncomfortable and averted their eyes. Both of them had agreed with Campbell beforehand that Mandella was to blame but they had never expected him to voice his criticism so harshly. After all, Moses was in charge of the most powerful ministry in government and should be treated with respect.

But Campbell was hopping mad, not just on account of Murdoch but because he owned a shed-load of shares in the Mirror Group and they were now as worthless as the rolls of newsprint in the warehouses, ruined by the sprinklers that came on to damp out the fires.

"The newspapers have got their own security staff. It's them that was doing all the screwing, boozing, sleeping, and scoffing pizzas," snarled Mandella. "That's what they get paid for."

"Of course they do!" shouted Campbell. "But they're not trained to deal with explosives. It's your job to anticipate attacks like this and issue the appropriate warnings. After all, never a day goes by that you don't bang on about imminent terrorist attacks that never materialize. The SAS must have had hundreds of squaddies flying around the country planting those explosives, yet your intelligence people never said a word. Jesus Christ, man, they set off more explosions in one night than the IRA managed in thirty years and got away scot-free. We spend millions on intelligence, and all we seem to get out of it are half-baked attempts to blow up the Dome or the Arsenal football ground."

"The Yanks spend billions on intelligence, and they never got a warning of the Trade Center attacks either," Mandella shot back. "These SAS bastards have had sixty years or more training in their work. Most of my people are amateurs compared with them. Anyway, the papers should have anticipated the attacks. The ones they blew up are the ones who have been pushing for years for the SAS to be closed down. They had it coming. Serves them right, I say."

"Jesus Christ, what a bloody stupid remark that is, coming from someone who is supposed to uphold the law of the land. Can't you bloody well see what we're up against? The SAS have become a law unto themselves. They'll feed on their success, and this is only the beginning, I warn you. Their next step will be to close down the broadcasting media, and if we allow them to do that, we really are up the creek. Just think of it, man, no viewing except the crap you get from Sky and the porn channels from Europe. Why, we'd be out of office before you could say *Coronation Street.*"

"They won't close down one program," Mandella replied coldly. "I've given Section Three orders to guard every broadcasting studio and transmitting station in the country until I tell them to stand down. I can guarantee their safety, even your favorite program. *Tom and Jerry*, isn't it?

"Now, now, chaps, let's not get personal," pleaded the PM. "We're all in this together. United we stand, divided we fall, as they say. Moses, I'm very impressed how quickly you've reacted to the dangerous situation that we're in. I want you to know that whatever resources you need will be provided without any questions being asked."

Campbell was not about to let it go at that. "Who is in charge of the operation, if you don't mind me asking," he said, glaring at Mandella.

"General Kruger. He's taken personal charge of everything."

"Is the guy experienced in this sort of thing?"

"I don't know. I never asked him."

"So how do you know he can do the job?"

"He's a general, for Christ's sake. What do you want, a fucking field marshall?"

"I don't trust generals. Give me a colonel any day, they're much closer to the men they command, like Wingate. This Kruger guy will likely delegate the job to his second in command and carry on with his wining and dining. He won't be aware how deadly serious the job is or how we cannot allow it to fail. Have you made it clear to him?"

"I intend to do just that," snapped Mandella.

"Might I put in a suggestion, Alastair?" The words were silky smooth. Peter Mandelson's voice had prompted many people to ask whether he had been the voice-over for the snake in Disney's *Jungle Book*, hence the nickname "Kaa." He was yet another crony that Blair had secretly appointed and made deputy PM.

"Go ahead," muttered Campbell. There was little love lost between the two main contenders for Blair's affections.

"Why don't we ask Colonel Chevalier of the French Sûreté to come over and advise us? He did a marvelous job for President Chirac when the students were threatening to burn down Paris. Not one broadcaster was affected, and neither were any of the newspapers, come to that."

"Jesus Christ, are you suggesting that we need a bloody frog to help us protect our own country? Next thing you know, you'll be calling in the Foreign Legion."

"I had thought about that, Alastair," purred Mandelson, "but I understand they've got their hands full in Chad right now."

"Well, we've got to do something, and fast," said Campbell. "As far as I know, Section Three have never been really tested. Sure, they've been called in to slaughter bird flu chickens and sort out a riot between Liverpool and Manchester United football fans and, of course, the race riots. But God knows how they'll make out against trained saboteurs like the SAS. Talk about the Foreign Legion, I'm told there are more foreigners in Section Three than there are Brits, a lot of them illegal immigrants. As for the Brits, they're a rag-bag of ex-cons, army deserters, and druggies. If that's true, we need someone like Kaa's frog to whip them into shape. Hasn't anyone thought about recruiting ex-SAS, Paras, and Guardsmen? There's plenty of them about. Look how many there are doing security jobs in Iraq." Campbell was getting impatient; he also had a shed-load of shares in ITV, and if those went down the tubes, he'd be looking bankruptcy in the face.

"We can't afford recruits like that," snorted Mandella. "They get twenty times as much as we can pay them."

"And they're ten times more likely to catch a bullet. Bloody hell, what does money matter? It's only for a short spell. Sign them up and sack them when it's over. Don't you agree, Tony?"

"Eh, what's that you say?"

"I said we'll pay whatever it takes to sign up some good recruits," Campbell said irritably. He was getting tired of the PM's latest habit: ducking out of debate and waiting to be asked for his comments.

"Yes, Ali, sounds like a good idea. Never do things on the cheap, that's my motto."

Mandelson and Mandella looked uncomfortable as the PM settled back on the sofa. They both knew that Blair was losing it and that Alastair Campbell was effectively in charge, but they were unwilling to admit it, even to themselves.

"Right, then; is that it?" asked Campbell.

"Just one small item," said Mandella.

"What's that?"

"We believe we've already got an SAS bastard in Section Three. Someone has been leaking information, mostly top secret. We think he must be an officer."

"Holy cow!" cried Campbell. "You call that a small item? That's all we need, a bloody rotten spy in our midst. Can't you get intelligence to ferret the bastard out?"

"They're doing their best. There are over eight thousand officers in Section Three, and some of them can't even speak English properly. He could be one of them."

"Their best isn't good enough. Put a price on his head. Offer £500,000 for the first man to expose him. Tell him he'll even be given a part in TV's *Big Brother* if he wants. There's nothing like moolah to get results, believe me."

"Five hundred thousand?" whispered Mandella. "Are you crazy? Where am I going to find that kind of money?"

"Easy. Sack two of your ministers. Nobody will miss them. In fact, you'll probably find the department will run a lot smoother without them. Now then, when is your General Kruger going to do us all a favor and sort out the SAS once and for all?"

Moses Mandella frowned. "I spoke to him yesterday. He told me his plans are well advanced."

"How well advanced is well advanced, may I ask?"

"Four to six months, all being well."

Campbell looked at Mandella unbelievingly. "Four to six months to clean out that nest of vipers? Are you fucking serious? Christ, man, it took less time than that to sort out Saddam Hussein and his entire army. You've got a hundred thousand against five hundred, that's two hundred to one. What are you waiting for, one thousand to one?"

"It's not men, it's materials. Section Three don't have any Apache gunships, and Kruger won't move without them."

"How many gunships?"

"Twenty minimum."

"Well, appropriate them from defense. We'll authorize their transfer."

"There aren't any available; every single one they have is on the battlefield."

"So? Has the bloody factory burned down?"

"No, the production line is at a standstill, waiting for parts from America."

Campbell was exasperated. "Bloody hell, you mean to tell me we can't get the parts off the shelf?"

"The U.S. Army has commandeered all the spares for six months, minimum. That's what has determined our own timetable."

"Holy shit, Moses, that takes us into November. We can't have fighting going on in Credenhill at that time. We're hosting the G8 summit at Leeds Castle in the second week. What in God's name will our partners think?"

Mandella shrugged his shoulders. "Cancel it, then; it's only a bloody talking shop and an excuse for self-important nobodies to get their faces on TV, for Christ's sake."

"Hang on there, Moses, I'll have you know that the eyes of the world will be on Leeds Castle this November," Blair protested. "The decisions made there will affect the well-being of millions of people for years to come, especially the poor devils in Africa. I didn't get to bed until gone midnight on any one night of the last meeting, believe it or not."

Tony Blair was fuming. That one of his own ministers should suggest that his friends were nobodies was unforgivable.

Mandelson was quick to step into the breach. "Look," he exclaimed, "our Rapid Reaction Force in Europe is equipped with Apaches. Surely they will lend us twenty for the short time we shall need them."

Alastair Campbell reacted angrily. "Good God, Kaa!" he shouted. "You know bloody well the frogs won't allow it. They control the EU Defense Force, and our RRF is now an integral part of it. Only last week, we asked them to cannibalize ten Challenger tanks for spares for our forces in Iraq, and they turned us down flat. Bloody frogs. We can't even call on the RRF anymore without their permission, so Kruger will just have to go in without them. The SAS don't have any Apaches, so what the hell is he so afraid of?"

"They've got at least one Lynx gunship, and that's the one that shot up the Section Four HQ in Oxford," said Mandella. "How do we know they haven't got a dozen or more?"

"How the fuck should I know? Get your intelligence people out of bed and tell them to get their finger out. All I'm saying to you now is that Tony wants the SAS destroyed by the end of October at the latest. If Kruger won't take it on, then tell the Boer bastard to piss off back to the jungle and get someone else who will, even Kaa's Maurice Chevalier if necessary. Am I right, Tony?"

"Yes, Ali, we must have things tidied up before the G8 summit. I've invested a lot of capital in this meeting, and if the American security men suspect there are SAS thugs going around planting explosives, they might advise the president to stay away. We can't have that, can we?"

It was too much for Mandella. "Jesus Christ, Tony, Obama comes swaggering over here with a security force bigger than our RRF and shuts down half of London for a week. Why don't you suggest he gets them to do the job? Bomb the shit out of the SAS, like he does everybody else on his terrorist list."

Mandella hated Obama's guts. The president had been instrumental in closing down one of his operations in Colombia, which had cost him millions.

"Now, now, Moses, I won't have you talking about our closest ally like that. Just do what we ask and wipe out the SAS before they do the same to us. Money is no object. Give General Kruger all he wants, including Apaches, if you can locate any. We are all depending on you. Just think of the prestige victory will bring you. The son of a black slave defeats the finest special operations regiment in the world. Why, you'll make Colin Powell look like a hump-backed shoeblack. All Africa will be singing your praises, just as they do for your illustrious namesake."

Mandella was somewhat mollified by the PM's flattery. "All right, Tony, I'll give it my best shot, but I still think I've been given the shitty end of the stick. I took on this job to look after home affairs, not fight a bloody war. Why the hell aren't the ministry of defense and their snooty generals sorting this one out? What are we paying them for? Wait until I take my seat in the Lords, I'll soon sort out the goose-stepping bastards who hang out there, believe you me."

There was a deathly silence as his colleagues looked uneasily at each other and averted his gaze.

God, Mandella thought to himself, *I'm the only one in the cabinet who tells it straight up. All the rest shit bricks when it comes to dealing with the army top brass.* It made Mandella feel pleased with himself. But what he did not know, and the other three did know, was that the House of Lords appointment committee had turned down the PM's nomination of Moses for a peerage. Failed politicians, crooks, jailbirds, dykes, gays, pedophiles, rapists, footballers, pop stars, prostitutes, jockeys, and TV cooks were normally acceptable to their lordships. But a drug baron, and a black one at that? Never in a million years.

Chapter 23

Jock Wingate took his place at the head of the table and beamed at the thirteen officers gathered around it. "Brilliant," he said, "absolutely bloody brilliant. A classic operation to rival anything we've done before, and with the added bonus that we did not suffer a single casualty. Luke, my congratulations to you and your team. You've shown the country the way forward. From now on, 'Union Jack' will be on the tongues of every soldier, sailor, and airman who believes in the principles of freedom and love of country that he or she signed up for. Not only that, you have silenced an important part of the monstrous propaganda organs of a socialist state that has demoralized honest working people and encouraged the millions on the government payroll, cheats, ethnics, and the work-shy to believe that for as long as they do as they are told and vote Labor, their corrupt indolence can last forever. Now then, how long do you think it will take Campbell's mouthpieces to get back in business?" he inquired, looking at the ex-Royal Engineers officer sitting next to Luke.

Sam Duffell took his pipe out of his mouth and looked at his notes. "I would say at least six months. First, the sites will have to be cleaned up and then contracts placed before they can lay a brick. We don't make any of that kind of machinery anymore, so it will have to come from Germany or the United States. Then they will have to re-engage specialist engineers to run the plant. Yes, six months minimum for the first serious daily run. As a precaution, I would suggest placing a few explosives among the building supplies that arrive on site. There's nothing quite like an unexploded bomb to delay construction work of any kind."

"And some great crested newts," volunteered one of the officers. "The eco-warriors will be delighted protecting them, believe me."

Everyone laughed at the suggestion.

"Do you think Campbell will order the Royal Engineers to undertake some of the work, Sam, move things on a bit?" asked Luke.

"Not a chance. They're all in Iraq or Afghanistan. In any case, the OC, General Broomhill, would never allow it."

"I've heard rumors that some of the papers are going to be printed in France and Germany and flown in. Is that a feasible option?" asked Wingate.

"It's feasible," replied Luke, "but very expensive. Only Murdock could afford to do such a thing and for a limited time at that. I think the threat of a few bombs over there would put an end to ideas like that. They will bear in mind what happened to the Irish publishers."

"Good, now let's hear what's happening on the street. What kind of feedback are you getting so far, Stretch?"

Robert Holliday, the lanky intelligence officer, allowed a smile to cross his face. "So far, so good," he drawled. "As you would expect, Campbell and his stooges in the broadcasting media are screaming blue murder and blaming us for everything from genocide to the shortage of AIDS medicine and condoms in the Congo. The *Mail* and *Express* are doing a great job. After the first day, they've now put all comment about the destruction in the back pages, making it difficult for the government to make its case. It's great to see them exerting their independence once again and putting two fingers up to the apparatchiks. Littlejohn in the *Mail* has even gone so far as to suggest the IRA could be involved, since a box of unexploded Semtex found at one site bore the unmistakable marking of a consignment bought by the IRA from Libya in the seventies, and Peter Hitchens backs him up on this. Of course, it's rubbish and the two columnists know it. No one in their right mind would play about with forty-year-old Semtex, even the dickheads in the IRA. But the rumors have put the spotlight on the Provos just when they least need it. Adams has been on the BBC every day this week, crying with rage and protesting their innocence. I almost feel sorry for the creep. For once in his life, the poor sap is telling the truth and nobody will believe him. By the way, Sam, I hope you're going to discipline the trooper who set the charge that didn't go off," he added jokingly.

Sam Duffell made a face. "I know who it is, and I've decided his punishment already. I'm going to order him to plant a dummy bomb in Adams's bed and pay out of his own pocket for the psycho's laundry bill afterward."

The officers all laughed at the joke and relaxed as a steward knocked on the door and came in, carrying fourteen mugs of tea on a huge battered tin tray.

Colonel Wingate waited until the empty mugs had been cleared away and the door had closed behind the steward.

"Right, gentlemen," he began, "I'll now put you in the picture as to the public reaction to recent events. First, the good news. I've been inundated with letters, phone calls, and e-mails pledging support for our cause. Of course, none of the parties can be sure that the Regiment is on the march, but people aren't stupid, they can read the signs, and they desperately want us to know they are with us come what may. The most important pledges are from Air Chief Marshall Harris and Admiral Cunningham. They will not move against us under any circumstances and will resign if ordered to do so. The CBI will support us any way they can, as will the Merchant Navy and British Airways. Barclays Bank are with us plus TESCO and Waitrose. Warren Buffett is backing us, as are Margaret Thatcher and Norman Tebbit. Just about every ex-SAS member still alive is begging to re-enlist, and applications from ex-servicemen and the regular army are simply pouring in. Of course, we cannot process all these volunteers but they could be used as auxiliaries if the going gets rough. I will see to it that we have weapons available for them in that eventuality.

"Now for the bad news. The army chief of staff is dead set against our plans, and I think you all know the reason why. Blair has promised him a dukedom and peerages for six members of his immediate staff if he stays loyal. Not only that, they will each receive a golden handshake of a million pounds and given early retirement in two years' time, complete with gold-plated pension rights. Their perfidy makes me want to vomit. I can hardly believe these jackals are members of the British army we belong to. They even have the gall to proclaim they are acting in the best interests of the British people and her majesty the queen. But there are stirrings in the ranks, and this is something I want you all to exploit at every opportunity. We will win our fight for freedom, I am sure of that, but the last thing I want to have on my conscience is that we were forced to fire upon our comrades in arms.

"Sadly, I have had to add another thirteen names to the list of our comrades incarcerated by Section Four in various concentration camps around the country. That now makes a total of forty-six men in captivity after we allow for the sixteen who have been liberated by our rescue squads and are now back on base. The deaths from enemy action overseas has now risen to forty-eight. I intend to increase the strength of our rescue units from two troops to four, and I would ask that you provide the best men you can offer for this purpose."

Wingate took out a slim cigar and lit it carefully, mouthing a thick smoke-ring that all eyes followed as it wafted slowly upward, until it broke up on a section of strip lighting.

"Now then, I am informed that this bloodthirsty bastard at the home office, Moses Mandella, has been ordered by Blair, or Campbell if you like, to instruct his Section Three Paramilitaries to surround our base and either starve us out or, preferably, attack us until there isn't one of us left. If I know Mandella, he'll take the latter option. He'll squat with his henchmen in his bunker in Whitehall, his eyes glued on CNN or his own satellite cameras, cussing if things go wrong and whooping and cheering if they cause us pain. He won't care about casualties; as far as he's concerned, the Paramilitaries are as expendable as the poor bastards who are hooked on his drugs and can no longer afford to pay for them. I estimate they outnumber us by about two hundred to one, so he will be looking for a quick victory. This brings us to the quality of the enemy we are facing, Stretch. What do you know about this General Kruger? Our survival will surely rest upon our knowledge of his military training, his tactical planning, and his battleground experience."

"Not a great deal, really," replied the intelligence officer. "He's around sixty years old, was awarded his commission after graduating from the Bloemfontein Military Academy, and spent most of his years fighting the ANC. Rose to the rank of colonel leading a South African force sent to help Savimbi's Unita rebels in the Angolan civil war. Went over to the ANC and fought against his former comrades. Promoted to general by Nelson Mandela. Along with other ANC ranking officers, he was accused of taking part in a multimillion-dollar scam involving the purchase of new jet fighters for the air force. He disappeared for three years and finally surfaced in London in the nineties. Bought his way into Section Three, and a year later was made commander in chief. Is credited with making Section Three into a formidable, but as yet untried, fighting unit."

"That's it?"

"Yes, sir, that's it."

"Right. Stretch, I want you to find out more about this man. Make some enquiries with old soldiers he once commanded. Establish whether he's a fighter or a quitter, ruthless or magnanimous. At the same time, find out the present-day strength of Section Three. Last time I heard, it was one hundred ten thousand and growing. Strip out the cooks and bottle-washers and latrine diggers, and get me the true fighting strength. Identify their armor, artillery, mortars, and especially choppers. I don't think they possess any bombers or fighters but check it out anyway. Make up a list of their ranking officers so that we can send their wives and dependents a good-will message.

"Just one other thing, have you got a mole in the ministry of defense records department?"

"Yes, I have."

"Can he get access to the database on all Regiment servicemen, past and present?"

"I'm sure he can. You want them to disappear?"

"Indeed I do, right down to the regimental mascot. I want to stop those bastards in Section Four knocking on the doors of ex-members and carting them off to the Smithfield."

"But that will mean losing all wages and pensions coming to us from the ministry of defense. It will cause tremendous hardship," protested the intelligence officer.

"I brought that up with our paymaster, and he assures me we can take care of such expenditure until this is all over. We have the original records, and he tells me that if funds keep coming in like they are doing, he'll be able to slip a little extra into the packets of the poorer pensioners and widows. Now then, Luke, tell us, what have you got in store for the BBC?"

Luke held up an A5 photograph of a studious-looking man in his early forties and held it up for all to see. "Anyone recognize this man?" he asked.

There was a pause as Sam Duffel took hold of the photograph and studied it closely. "He's a scientist," he stated. "I can't remember the name but he was in the news about five years ago. He's an American, rated top in the world in radar and laser technology, a real whiz-kid like Einstein. He disappeared while attending a scientific symposium in Paris and hasn't been seen since. The Americans put out a statement saying that he had been kidnapped by the Russians. There was a huge row over it but it soon died down."

"You're right, Sam," said Luke, "but not for the likes of a freelance investigative journalist I know in London. He got on the trail and traced the scientist to a ranch in Wyoming, where he is being held under house arrest by the CIA. That's as close as he could get, but when he started questioning the scientist's friends, he was told that the man had turned pacifist and refused to carry out any more work on some top secret military project. One of them hinted that he was thinking of leaving the country and that he was being prevented from doing so by the government. My informant is writing a book about it, and he asked my advice on how to approach it. I told him to delay publication for a while and I might be able to present him with the final chapter."

"Why did you do that?" asked Wingate.

"Because we need him. I've got big plans for him. He could make all the difference between success or failure of our plan to deal with the broadcasting media."

"And you want us to snatch him, right?"

"If that's possible."

"How do you know he'll come willingly?"

"I'm sure he would. What we'd ask him to do would be nonmilitary, no one will get hurt, and he'd be taking on an oppressive government like his own. I think it would be a small price to pay for his freedom."

Wingate pondered Luke's words for a moment and looked around the table. "Anyone disagree with that?" he asked.

There was not one dissenting voice.

"Well, Luke," he said, "you could not have brought this up at a worse time. We've pulled all our men out of the Americas for duties in the Middle East. How soon do you want the job done?"

"Like yesterday."

The colonel looked enquiring at the adjutant, Major Dawson, who shook his head. "Sorry, Luke," he said. "It would take weeks to get anyone back on their own turf. Months even. I can try but I can't guarantee quick results."

"I think I might be able to help."

The speaker was Captain Jake MacKenzie, one of the longest-serving members of the Regiment. A Canadian, Jake looked like a rough, tough lumberjack and, indeed, that had been his profession before he sought adventure in the Canadian Special Forces and then transferred to the SAS. Tough he might be, but he was soft spoken and always had a ready smile on his face.

"Fire away, Timber," urged Luke.

"You've all heard of Delta Force, I presume," MacKenzie began, and smiled broadly as everyone laughed good-naturedly. "Well, my outfit did some cross-border exercises with a Delta company once, and I made friends with Captain Bruno Walters, the company commander. He hails from Montana, and as I lived pretty close over the border in Alberta, we used to visit each other regularly and chew the cud. Nice guy, beautiful wife and kids. It was his turn to visit us but he never turned up, and when I called him, the phone was disconnected. No answer to e-mails either. Eventually, I got in touch with one of his neighbors, and he told me that he been court-martialed, discharged from the Army, and sentenced to two years in jail. He'd apparently shot and wounded a deputy who was messing around with Elena, his wife. While he was inside, Elena left home and took the kids south somewhere. When he came out, Bruno was really cut up and immediately sought out the deputy and beat him up. That cost him another two years in jail. Well, to cut a long story short, Bruno ended up running an America First militia training camp just outside Fort Peck. You've heard of them: ultranationalists who hate foreigners, anything to do with government, and especially the law. They've tried to close him down a number of times but apparently he's still there, and his camp is bigger than ever. If I'm not mistaken, Bruno would jump at a chance of a cloak-and-dagger job like this. Do it for nothing, in fact."

Luke was impressed. "Yes, I've heard about America First. Fruitcakes, most of them, but not all. You're sure he's reliable after all he's been through, hasn't allowed it to cloud his judgment?"

"No, Luke, he's not that kind of a guy. CIA means government to him, and he'd be tickled pink to kick their ass."

"Sounds good, Timber. You willing to go talk to our new friend Bruno?"

"You bet. I might even persuade him to come and join us if he's not too busy."

Luke turned to Wingate, who was looking at Timber thoughtfully. He smiled and nodded his assent.

"Good," said Luke, "and while you're over there, there's another small thing you can do for us. You've heard of that computer whiz-kid Rodney Gates, haven't you?"

"You mean the Welsh boyo who hacked into the Pentagon database and fouled up their systems?"

"That's the one. He was handed over to the United States two years ago and is serving life in a high-level correction center in Syracuse, New York State."

"And we want him back?"

"ASAP."

"Will he come willingly?"

"You must be joking. Ninety percent of the prisoners there are black. Also, they won't let him near a computer."

"Okay, I'll give it my best."

"I know you will, Timber, and that goes for the rest of us."

Luke stood up and outlined his proposals for dealing with the broadcasting media, and one by one, the officers around the table chipped in with their own contribution until finally, Wingate stood up and called time.

Chapter 24

Peter Mandelson, the deputy prime minister, settled back in his luxurious pink leather settee and put his arm around his partner Tonto's shoulders. He had brought home his red ministerial box to go over some urgent papers but the box remained unopened on the rug in front of the Jacobean fireplace. Above the fireplace hung a giant flat plasma screen that filled all the wall space to within a centimeter of the ceiling.

Mandelson had better things to do on this particular evening than put his signature on the lines marked out in pencil by his permanent secretary, for tonight's episode of *Big Brother* had been billed for over a month as the occasion when Rupert and Randy would share a bedroom, appear in the altogether, and perform acts that had never been seen before on terrestrial television; or as Tonto crudely put it, "show the meat and serve it up." The fact that the two performers were shiny, coal-black Congolese served to add yet more spice to the entertainment, and to cap it all, Tonto had managed to come all the way from Oxford University to enjoy the excitement with him. And to show his appreciation, Mandelson had prepared a sumptuous meal, topped off with Soforino sherbets, café-au-lait, and two pink martinis that sat invitingly on the coffee table in front of them.

The titles came up, and he squeezed Tonto in anticipation as the last of the commercials disappeared and the camera cut to the huge lounge where most of the activities were taking place. All eight of the remaining contestants were present, either lounging on the leopard-skin settees, preening themselves in front of the full-length mirrors, or helping themselves to refreshments from the bar. Only two of them were engaged in conversation: Rupert and Randy, both of them clad in brilliant white silk dressing gowns sporting motifs of their native jungle flora and fauna. The microphone moved closer to pick up the exchange, and Mandelson leaned forward, straining to take in what they were saying, only to sit back, disappointed. They were speaking in Congolese, and despite his intellectual prowess, he failed to understand a single word they said. He made a mental note to write to the producer and urge him to include subtitles in any future episode. After all, like all his friends, he was most interested in hearing what they had to say in the privacy of their bedroom.

Rupert and Randy carried on with their conversation for a good ten minutes, and Mandelson waited impatiently for them to finish. Then without warning, they both jumped up and made their way into the bedroom, flicking at imaginary flies with their whisks as they went. The camera in the bedroom caught their gleaming faces as they came through the door and took up positions on either side of the monster bed, preparing to cast off their dressing gowns. Mandelson sat forward again, shivering with excitement, but then his jaw dropped, for at that very crucial, intimate moment, the screen went blank.

He grabbed the remote and jabbed repeatedly at the Channel 4 button, but to no avail. Frantic now, he selected various other commercial stations and found them all to be transmitting normally. However, all BBC channels were blacked out. He went back to Channel 4 and tried again, but the screen stayed blank.

"Bloody hell!" he shouted at the top of his voice. "All the rest of the crap is showing except for the one program I've been waiting weeks to see. I could murder those bloody idiots on Channel 4. Look, they haven't even bothered to put out an apology. They just couldn't care less about the feelings of their paying customers. Tonto, go get the phone book and look up the number for Channel 4. Hurry now, there's a good boy."

He picked up his mobile and tapped his fingers rapidly against it as he waited for the number.

"Heer tis!" Tonto shouted in his fractured English, and Mandelson keyed it in as fast as his fingers would allow.

"Damn," he swore as the busy signal came up, "what a bloody shambles. If I get an Indian outreach operator, I'll sue the beggars for all they've got."

He keyed in the number again and met with the same result. Again and again he tried, and again and again he swore as he failed to get through, until at last he threw the phone onto the floor and gulped down his martini in one go.

The drink seemed to calm his nerves somewhat, and he retrieved the phone and called his private secretary. "Tracy, who's in charge at Channel 4?"

"I don't know off-hand, Minister. Do you want me to look it up?"

"I want you to get him on the phone this minute. No messing about with the staff. The top man himself, whoever he is, and put the call through to me here. It's bloody urgent, got that?"

"Yes, Minister, right away, sir."

Mandelson went to the bar and mixed himself another drink. His hands were shaking, and he clenched them together to steady them before picking up the glass and walking over to the settee. He sat down beside Tonto and frowned as he saw that the boy had switched channels and was watching a football match.

"No, no, Tonto," he said crossly, "put it back on Channel 4, the picture might be okay now."

Tonto pouted as he reluctantly did as he was told and came up with the same blank screen.

"Damn, damn, damn," Mandelson exclaimed, "the bastards still haven't got the decency to put out an apology. You wait, I'm going to make them suffer for this. Indeed I am."

He was about to ring his secretary again when the phone in the study rang. "Don't switch over," he said to Tonto as he hurried over to the study. "I want it like that when I'm talking on the phone." He picked up the phone. "Mandelson here," he said curtly.

"Ah yes, Minister," a plumy voice replied, "Charles Charlton, CEO Channel Four. I understand you want a word with me. How can I help?"

"Do you know your bloody company has deprived the public of an evening's entertainment, for which they pay you an enormous amount of money?" he fumed.

"Are you referring to the loss of picture at 9:00 PM, Minister?"

"You're damn right I am, and what's more, you haven't got the decency to broadcast an apology for your rank incompetence."

"Where are you calling from, Minister?"

"My cottage in Cirencester; what has that got to do with it?"

"I'm sorry, old chap, we've lost control of our Bristol transmitter and are unable to broadcast *Big Brother* or put out an apology for the loss of picture."

"Lost control! What on earth are you trying to tell me? Have you had a power cut, a breakdown, or something? And don't bloody well call me 'old chap.'"

"No, Minister, a lot worse than that. Some extraneous force has broken into our system and blanked out the program. Every engineer we've got is working flat out to try and regain control, but so far we have had no success. Our chief engineer tells me that the force output is double what our normal transmission utilizes, and we would have to install a lot more equipment to counteract it."

Mandelson was flabbergasted. "What do you mean by extraneous force, exactly? Are you actually trying to tell me aliens have taken over your network?"

"No, Minister, the force is most definitely terrestrial."

"Well, can't you track it, find out where it's coming from?"

"That's the problem. As soon as we get a fix, the source switches to another location in milliseconds and maintains the block on our transmitter."

"Bloody hell, this is all science fiction stuff to me. Have you been in touch with the Americans, asked them to help out?"

"Of course we have, they own most of the networks, as you know. They're in the dark, same as we are."

"What? You mean there's more than one force?"

"It looks like it. They've got interference on all of the BBC channels but the only commercial channel affected is Channel 4, sometimes on the program itself but mostly on the advertising slots. All that the viewers who lap up commercials get now is fuzz, pure unadulterated fuzz."

"Piss on the other channels. When are we going to be able to see the *Big Brother* episode we were all looking forward to so much?"

The voice took on a weary tone. "I really couldn't say at the moment. We must wait and see when our transmission is restored before we can decide our scheduling."

"Can you promise me that you will reschedule tonight's episode to follow immediately after restoration? There must be millions of viewers hanging on, for God's sake. You can't possibly disappoint your most loyal viewers in this way."

There was a pause as Charles Charlton took in the implied threat. "I'll make sure that your request gets top priority, Minister. Please leave your set on so that you don't miss anything on start-up. However, there is something you can do to help us combat this unprecedented attack on our transmission, if you would be so kind."

"Yes, yes, what is that?"

"The BBC has hundreds of detector vans all over the country, checking out license dodgers. We would like a hundred of them, complete with crews, placed at our disposal immediately."

Mandelson thought for a moment. "It seems like a reasonable request to me. Do you think they will do the job for you?"

"I can't be sure but our engineers have mapped out a grid system whereby we could track any number of interference beams down to a single source, but we don't have that kind of capability. The BBC does."

"I'll get onto it right away and make sure the BBC gets in touch with you immediately. What area shall I say the detector vans are to be sent to?"

"The southwest, centered on Credenhill."

"Credenhill! Did you say Credenhill?" Mandelson felt the color drain away from his cheeks. He felt physically sick and could feel the martini turning sour and fighting to reverse its natural flow through his digestive system.

A worried voice came over the phone. "Yes, I did say Credenhill. Is there something wrong, Minister?"

"No, no, carry on with your search. I'll contact the home office in the morning and tell them to give you all the help they can."

He put the phone down and looked up at the picture of himself in graduation gown, smiling self-consciously in the quad at Oxford. *What happy days*, he thought. What a blissful and trouble-free experience that was, never to be repeated. Not an enemy in sight. Now they were everywhere, threatening his very existence. It had to be the SAS, the bloody cruel, sadistic, hard-nosed bastards who had persuaded many in the country that they were supermen and were ready and willing to remove the democratically elected government, by force, if necessary. The very thought of the murderous bastards filled him with dread. Even with eight burly policemen from Scotland Yard guarding his house twenty-four hours a day, and a limousine that was built like a Sherman tank, he never felt entirely safe. The picture of the three pigs with their throats cut hanging in the entrance of the Northern Ireland office when he was secretary there still haunted him. He wished now that he had never left his cushy number in Europe, where he only ever needed one guard. It had to be the SAS. They had destroyed all newspapers sympathetic to the government, now they were out to control the broadcasting media as well. It must be them. Anyone else would have been demanding huge amounts of money by now. But was it feasible? The Russians had used countermeasures to blank out the West's transmissions during the cold war, but ways and means had always been found to frustrate them. The government must pull out all the stops and fund the networks, irrespective of cost. And if they couldn't sort it out, then they must search the world for the best scientific brains available. The SAS must not be allowed to succeed. He had heard that anyone in the cabinet who had voted for the wars in Afghanistan and Iraq were for the chop, and he had been one of the most enthusiastic supporters of military action. He shivered uncontrollably. He had also been warned that the guilty ones would be sentenced to death by a military tribunal and hung by the neck until dead.

He left the study and wandered into the lounge in a daze. Tonto had left a note saying that he had gone to bed early, as he had to be back in Oxford by ten in the morning. He smiled sadly at the barely legible scrawl and sat down on the settee. He was not angry with the boy. The golden night was ruined anyway, and he could not concentrate on anything other than the dreadful happenings of the evening. He stared at the blank screen and switched channels again and again to check if they were working. Some were, and his hand shook as he switched back to Channel Four and sunk back into the settee, seething with anger and vowing vengeance on the SAS and all it stood for.

At first, the viewers thought it was a glitch. Older viewers were reminded of the early days of television when the picture would sometimes disappear altogether and wavy lines would take its place. Now and then an apology would appear, but more often than not, the mesmerizing blackness would continue for many minutes, causing people to fall asleep or disappear into the kitchen to brew a cup of tea. But this modern glitch was different. Instead of wavy lines, the screen was full of fuzz, and the high-pitched whine that accompanied it became an irritant that slowly but surely set the nerves on edge and prompted most viewers to reach for the remote or switch their set off.

The nuisance was haphazard at first, similar to the testing of new electronic devices in research and development establishments, where a new product would be tested to destruction. Then the picture would reappear for a few minutes, and often, most annoyingly, just a few seconds. Bristol was the second area to experience the phenomenon; a whole episode of *Coronation Street* failed to appear, and later the same night, the final ten minutes of *Newsnight* suffered the same fate. The next day, thirty minutes of *The Big Breakfast* and all of *Eastenders* and *Emmerdale* went missing. A day later, viewers of *Channel Four News* were denied the appearance of presenter John Snow and his ethnic babes, two children's cartoons, and the last round of a boxing match. Then a film called *Full Frontal Nudity amid Oxford's Dreamy Spires* failed to appear. Reality shows bore the brunt of the interference. *Big Brother, I'm famous Get Me Out of Here* and *The Under twelve X Factor* were lost completely, as was *Africa Calling* and *Little Britain for Sale*. Surprisingly, it was not just the terrestrial channels that were affected. Sky TV suffered huge disruption, particularly in its monopolized sporting presentations, but cable TV remained unaffected. Within a week of its emergence in the Bristol area, the phenomenon quickly spread to Birmingham and London, and then Cardiff, Manchester, Newcastle, Glasgow, and Belfast, until eventually it affected the whole of the UK.

Chapter 25

The deputy prime minister eased himself into Tony Blair's red leather executive chair, and stared at the desk in front of him. It was a glorious summer's day, and the brilliant sunshine pouring through the window seemed to magnify the desk's untidiness. Piles of manila files and papers were scattered upon it, most of them unread and looking all the more distasteful for that same reason. He wrinkled his nose as he picked up a coffee-stained mug bearing the name Tony with thumb and forefinger and dropped it into an overfl owing wastebasket. *How like Tony,* he thought. He couldn't care less about his surroundings or his appearance any more, and if his secretary, or anyone else attempted to tidy up he would fly into a rage and accuse them of interfering with a top secret project he was working on.

No matter. He had been looking forward to the summer recess for, by a stroke of good luck, Alastair Campbell and Tony Blair had gotten their wires crossed and ended up booking a four-week-long vacation on the same date. Tony had flown to Silvio Berlusconi's fortress in Sardinia, while the Campbells had embarked on a hiking vacation in Bhutan. Campbell had been reluctant to go, but he had become increasingly jaded recently, and his wife had insisted on it. That meant he was in full charge of the country and, since Parliament was in recess, he could devote almost all of his time to matters concerning the embellishment of his business affairs in London, as well as entertaining Elton John and his many friends from Brussels in the magnificent setting of Chequers. What a relief it was to be free of the suspicious, hectoring Alastair, who kept him away from Downing Street and his old friend Tony, as well as sending him on useless assignments up and down the country, far away from the London scene.

Then, the very next day, the roof fell in. He was over the disappointment of the *Big Brother* fiasco, and as he had not bothered to watch TV at all while entertaining at Chequers over the weekend, he was totally unprepared for the reception that awaited him on his arrival in Downing Street. A horde of journalists, TV cameramen, and photographers milled around the gates, shouting, screaming, and pounding on the windows of his car as the driver attempted to force his way through.

Three days later and still the mob was besieging the gates from six in the morning until past midnight. Not only that, the phones never stopped ringing, nor did the printer cease churning out hundreds of e-mails day and night. It was not as if all the fuss was about some world-shaking event like the looming war with Iran or the suicide of the Russian president or even the England soccer team losing three–nil to little Andora in the European Championship qualifiers. Nor was it something he could get his teeth into and rise above the occasion with his customary aplomb and sleight of hand. This was dirty business, plumbing depths of trickery and deception that exceeded any he had experienced in his days with the diplomatic service. Television! How he now hated the name, how he wished it had never been invented, and even more, how he wished he had never left the sheltered security of Brussels for the merciless bear-pit of British politics. Why on earth had he let Tony persuade him to take on the post and give up a cultured position where the media referred to him as "Monsieur Mandelson," whereas the riff raff in Britain preferred "Mandy" or worse still, "Kaa"? He looked at his watch and shuddered. A few more hours, and he would have to go downstairs and face the TV bosses and listen to their bloody bitching and whining and use every trick in his agile brain to enable him to weather the storm until Campbell and Tony were back in town.

With a deep sigh, he got to his feet, went into the bathroom, and washed his face and hands. He spread a moisturizer on his sallow cheeks and rubbed it gently over the whole of his face until the grease was completely absorbed. He inspected his clean-shaven face, bared his teeth, and slicked down his long, silken hair, leaving a shank that settled over the arch of his left eyebrow. Finally, he put on his jacket, adjusted the red handkerchief in his top pocket, and straightened his red polka-dot tie. Satisfied with his appearance, he walked into office, sat down, and flipped the intercom switch.

His secretary answered the call. "Yes, Minister," she trilled.

"Get hold of Humphrey Golding immediately and tell him to bring up the TV report I asked him to draw up right away, Tracy," he ordered.

There was a long pause before Tracy answered. "I'm sorry, Minister, but Mr. Golding isn't in the office. He went on leave on Friday night."

Mandelson saw red. "Went on leave? Why, the damned sneaky little sod! He never said anything to me about leave. He accepted my instructions and told me he would have it on my desk first thing this morning without fail. Good grief, that puts me right in the mire. Has the swine got an assistant?"

"Yes, he has, his name is Barney Ilfracombe."

"Did you say Barmy or Barney? Very well, put me through to him right away."

A cheerful voice answered the phone, "Barney here!"

"This is the deputy prime minister, Ilfracombe. Did Mr. Golding talk to you about a survey I asked him to draw up concerning the problems we are having with TV transmissions?"

"Too right, 'ee did."

Mandelson shuddered. The accent was broad East Anglian, most likely Suffolk. He absolutely loathed rural denizens, especially the ones who smiled at him when he approached and put up two fingers as soon as his back was turned. He could imagine the oaf now, wearing a flat cap, smock, corduroys, and green gumboots with a straw dangling from his mouth.

"Well, where is it then?" he said sharply.

"It's on my desk."

"On your desk! Why the devil didn't he bring it up here to me like I told him to?"

"Because 'ee didn't do it, yussee."

"Didn't do it! For God's sake, man, how can it be on your desk if he didn't do it?"

"Cause I did it."

"You did it?

"That's what I said. Humphrey told me to do it. Said he was off on vacation. He didn't tell me what to do with it when I'd finished it, so it's still sitting on my desk."

"I don't believe this. Are you an authority on visual imaging then?"

"Visual imaging? You means TV?"

"Of course I mean TV."

"Yes, I'm an expert at it, I watch it eight hours every day and fifteen hours on Saturday and Sunday, except when there's a skittle match on down the pub. Humphrey says I'm the best there is."

Mandelson was puzzled. "Yes, but you can only watch one channel continuously. While you are doing that, you are missing out on the interference on all the other stations, for heaven's sake."

"Tis true, but Humphrey rang up all the channels and told them to tape every glitz together with the time and date and send them through. I watched BBC1. It's all in this file. Clever lad is Humphrey, you'd do well to look arter him."

"Indeed. Perhaps you'll let me be the judge of that. Bring what you have up to my office right away."

"Sorry, but I'm on my tea break at the minute. I'll be up in fifteen minutes, all being well."

"You'll bring them up now or I'll bloody well have you fired. Do you know who you're talking to?"

"Tracy tells me you're the new deputy, is that right?"

"The new deputy prime minister, I'll have you know. Now enough of this nonsense, bring them up now, right away."

Mandelson slammed the phone down and discovered his hand was shaking. He rubbed it vigorously and swore to himself. He was not used to having his orders questioned, especially by a lowly clerk, and it made him feel uneasy. He checked his watch and drummed his fingers on the desk impatiently, as the minutes went by and his anger grew. It was exactly fifteen minute later when he heard voices in his secretary's office and Tracy ushered Ilfracombe into the room.

Mandelson gasped. The man was huge, at least two meters tall and 120 kilos or more. He didn't quite look like a yokel but he was rustic, all right. Harris tweed jacket, open-neck shirt, check pullover, grey corduroy trousers, and brown brogues. His chubby cheeks were florid, and his sparse reddish hair was plastered down to his crown.

"'Ere's the evidence, DPM," Ilfracombe said casually as he laid a manila folder on the desk. "It's as near as I can get to being right. Monday, Tuesday, Wednesday, Thursday, and Friday is actual but what I put down about Saturday and Sunday is mostly what I remembered."

Mandelson opened the folder and took out a sheaf of papers covered in writing. His color rose as he studied them, and he looked up at Ilfracombe in disbelief. "What the devil do you call this?" he snapped. "I asked for a definitive assessment of all TV interference, and all I get is a load of scribbled mumbo jumbo."

"Beg pardon, DPM, it's not mumbo jumbo, it's all done in shorthand, yussee. I had to write it down quickly as the funny things happened on the box, and the only way was to use shorthand."

"Well, why didn't you get the bloody stuff typed up?" groaned Mandelson.

"Nobody told me to. Any case, it wouldn't do any good."

"Why ever not?"

"Cause it's my own invented shorthand. They would never understand it."

"I don't believe this, I've got a meeting in an hour, and it's imperative I have the information with me."

"Well, I can read it to you if you like. You can make notes as we go along. That's what I used to do with John before he left, and it worked out fine."

"John who?" asked the exasperated Mandelson.

"Why, my old mate, John Prescott, of course."

"Your old mate? Is that how you address your superiors in this building, for heaven's sake?"

"Well, he used to call me mate when I was his superior, and it didn't bother me none."

Mandelson was intrigued and could not resist asking the obvious question. "You were Mr. Prescott's superior? Were you together in the Seaman's Union, then?"

"Not likely, he was a steward on the *Rangitata* when I was first mate. Bit of lad, was John. I helped him out of plenty of scrapes, especially ones with the lady passengers. It was John got me the job in the ministry when I got too old for seafaring. Cushy job too, just like his on the *Rangitata*."

Mandelson shook his head in disbelief and looked again at the sheaf of papers in his hand. "Enough talking, pull up a chair and read out these notes. I'm turning on this tape recorder. Talk to it, and speak slowly and clearly."

Ilfracombe pulled up a chair, made himself comfortable, cleared his throat noisily, and read from his notes.

"Saturday, twelfth July.

BBC-One: *Football Focus*: Fuzz. *When Will I be Famous?*: Fuzz *Weakest Link*: All questions garbled. *Casualty*: Fuzz. *Match of the Day*: All commentary garbled. *News 24*: Fuzz from midnight to 7:00 AM. Repeat Soap: Fuzz.

BBC-Two: *Batfink*, *Astro Boy*, and *Scooby-Doo*: Fuzz. Repeated film: Fuzz. *Never Mind the Buzzcocks*: Fuzz. *Have I Got News for You*: Fuzz. Repeated Film: Fuzz. Repeat of *Prime Minister's Fireside Chat*. Fuzz.

ITV-One: *Horrid Henry and Gruesome Kids*: Fuzz. *Sex Advice for Under Fives*: Fuzz. Repeat Film: Fuzz. *You've Been Framed*. Fuzz. *Karl Marx Diaries*, *Poker Face*: Fuzz. Repeat Film: Fuzz. Football Repeat: Fuzz. All advertisements. Fuzz. *Asia Calling*: Fuzz.

Channel Four: *The Boobs*: Fuzz. *Popworld*: Fuzz. *Horseracing*: Fuzz. Repeat Film: Fuzz. Repeat Film: Fuzz. *Desirable Dream Girls*: Fuzz. *Channel Four Asian Local News*. Fuzz. *Celebrity Big Brother*: Fuzz. *Lesbian Masturbation*: Fuzz.

Africa Calling, Sex Life of Bantu Warriors: Fuzz.

All Sky channels: Fuzz.

ITV2, ITV3, ITV4, BBC3, BBC4, E4. All channels: Fuzz.

Ilfracombe paused for breath and looked closely at the deputy prime minister. The man had gone a deathly shade of grey. He had his elbows on the desk and his head in his hands, staring at the recorder as if it was a cobra preparing to strike. He didn't seem to hear his words, and Ilfracombe had to shake his papers in order to get his attention. "That's it for Saturday, DPM," he repeated. "It's bloody thirsty work, is this. Any chance of a beer? John keeps them in the second drawer of that grey filing cabinet over there."

Mandelson looked daggers. "Certainly not. Not when I'm here anyway. Get on with it, man."

Ilfracombe frowned angrily. "Well, a drink of water then. You don't mind if I help myself, do you?"

He didn't wait for an answer as he got up, walked over to the dispenser, and drained three cups of water in quick succession. "That's better," he said as he wiped his mouth with his sleeve. "Now let's see what we've got for Sunday."

And so Barney Ilfracombe proceeded to rattle off page after page of notes dealing with the TV transmissions, or lack of them, on Sunday, until only two pages remained in his hands. "That's it up to date," he said cheerfully, relishing the pain every word he spoke seemed to be causing the DPM.

"What's on those pages you have left?" Mandelson asked wearily.

"They're a summary of what I think is going on and what will happen as time goes by."

Mandelson sat up quickly. "Do you really think it's going to get worse?" he gasped.

"No doubt about it. The saboteurs are cranking it up gradually. This time next week, we'll be lucky if *The BBC 6 O'clock News* gets on the air. Do you want me to read out my summary?"

"Your summary? How are you qualified to disseminate such technical material?"

"I had to have some kind of a degree to qualify for this job, so I took a Mickey Mouse degree in media studies. Passed it easy and learned a lot more besides. I can tell you this much, the bloke behind the electronics in this caper is a bloody genius, right up there with Einstein, I'd say. To build an interference machine like he's done would be a great achievement even if it was sited in a bloody great big laboratory, but he's gone one better and invented a machine that can be installed in a truck. If that's the case, it's only a matter of time before they will be able to interfere with or shut down every national turnaround channel and local channel in the country."

Mandelson went deathly pale again. "Are you sure about that?" he gulped. "They are roaming around the country like BBC license detector vans?"

"That's a good analogy, DPM," chortled Ilfracombe. "The BBC's been using their machines to spy on the poor buggers who can't afford a bloody license, and now they are screaming blue murder because someone is returning the compliment. Good luck to them, I say. They could shut down all the nation's TV output and that would still leave too much unadulterated crap for any civilized country to put up with."

Mandelson couldn't believe his ears. "You mean to tell me you agree with what these criminals are doing to our country?" he shouted. "Why, they are trying to destroy the very essence of our democratic government: free speech and the independent right to broadcast it. The networks are a credit to the nation, let me tell you."

"That's a laugh, the BBC is virtually a government organ like *Pravda* in Russia, and most of the independents slavishly toe the government line as long as they are allowed to churn out abysmal programs saturated with degradation, violence, and pornography as cover for their moronic commercials. I don't know who is doing this. It might be the Pope, for all I know. But I've analyzed every glitch over five days, and I can see what they are trying to do. They are after cleaning up the mucky stables, restoring the rights of British people to a civilized broadcasting medium as proposed by Lord Reith fifty years ago. They are aiming to eliminate the trash flooding in from abroad; roll back the dominance of gays and ethnic minorities; silence the ultra-liberal chattering classes; and blot out all programs that are distorting the minds of young children, denigrating our heritage and our historic roots. Not to mention denying us our inalienable rights to free speech, as well as restoring the English language to its rightful place in our society. The pattern tells me that they are concentrating most of their fire on the BBC and Sky, for obvious reasons."

"What obvious reasons?" interrupted a flabbergasted DPM.

"Well, the BBC is supposed to represent the aspirations of the British public without fear or favor, but it has now become politicized, and its output now largely represents the views of blacks, Asians, Republicans, queers, drug addicts, pop stars, anarchists, luvvies, and foreigners who bang on about our so-called leading role in slavery."

"And what about Sky?" breathed Mandelson, now red faced and biting his lip.

"Oh, that's easy. Murdoch has supported this bloody awful government of ours for eleven years and for no other reason than to bleed us dry over his virtual monopoly of films and national sporting fixtures that used to be free to BBC license payers. His is an empire built on greed, and I can see they mean to destroy it as completely as he has destroyed the viewing pleasure of millions of Britons, aided and abetted by New Labor."

"Good God, I cannot believe my ears. You are a civil servant employed by the government, and yet you go ranting on like a maniac from the BNP. How you got your job I shall never know, but I can tell you this. You won't be employed here this time next week. You're a disgrace to the service, and a racist and bloody bigot to boot."

"Sure, I am. That's the price of telling it straight to a socialist," laughed Ilfracombe. "But don't worry about giving me the sack. I'm due for retirement at the end of the month, and that will give me the chance of putting in for a job with these saboteurs who are giving you so much grief."

"You would actually do a thing like that?" gasped Mandelson.

"Too right, brother. And if I were you, I'd run away sooner rather than later. I can smell a revolution coming, and if I was a lousy MP I'd black up and catch a plane to darkest Africa tout suite."

Mandelson watched Ilfracombe saunter over to the door and exit the room. He felt very uncomfortable and not a little scared. The man might look like a hayseed but he had a remarkable command of current affairs and knew far more about the present situation than he himself did. A sudden thought entered his mind, and a shiver ran down his spine. *Was it possible the man was actually ... one of them?*

He put the thought out of his mind and quickly rewound the recorder. Switching it on, he reached for pen and paper and started taking notes of the particulars Ilfracombe had put on tape with his ear-grating rustic voice.

Chapter 26

Mandelson had barely reached his seat in the conference room before a rasping American voice pierced the air. It belonged to Rupert Murdoch. The mogul had obviously elected himself to speak for the chairmen of the UK broadcasting media seated around the table, and not one of them had the nerve to raise an objection.

"Nice of you to join us, Peter," the voice grated. "Over a week gone and not a word from the government on the devastating attacks that are threatening to put us all out of business and deprive the British public of the finest entertainment and cultural enlightenment money can buy. Why have you and your underlings ignored all our calls for help? Tony would never have treated us like this, and neither would you before you got yourself brainwashed by the bloody frogs."

Mandelson ignored the insult. "For your information, Rupert, I haven't had more than twelve hours sleep since I took over. I've been working night and day with the experts from the ministry of culture, the ministry of defense, and the home office. What we are facing is an unprecedented attack on our very existence. Dark forces are at work, with the intent of closing down the country's TV networks and, we fear, taking them over by force of arms. But we are fighting back. At this very moment, Section Three Paramilitaries are scouring every centimeter of the country with hundreds of detector vans and countermeasure equipment, seeking to locate and destroy the saboteurs. We've also got the best IT brains from America and Japan working with us. I'm expecting to hear news of their success at any moment, and I will communicate it to you as soon as it is available."

"Does that mean you haven't caught anybody at it yet?" growled Murdoch.

"Well, um yes, Rupert. Vivian Richards at the home office told me last evening that they have got some very good leads, and they are closing in on their target by the hour."

"Who the hell is Vivian Richards?" demanded Murdoch. "Why isn't Moses Mandella handling this personally?"

"Richards is a junior minister, he's looking after things while Moses is away."

"Jesus Christ, you couldn't make it up. Here we are, with the biggest crisis to hit this country since World War II, and the home secretary is away!" shouted Murdoch. "And where in the hell is away?"

"We don't know exactly," Mandelson purred, sensing an opportunity to deflect some of Murdoch's anger away from himself. "He flew to Bogata last Friday, and we've lost all contact with him. Richards tells me he's there to tidy up a deal with the Colombian president whereby he will step up the war on the drug cartels in return for financial assistance from our government."

Murdoch turned to face his fellow businessmen and threw his hands into the air. "Here we all are, getting fucked by the SAS, and our chief protector is somewhere in the jungle greasing the palms of the Goddamn Colombians while we are facing ruin with every day that goes by. Can any of you beat that for sheer bloody lunacy?"

Hilary Bramble, chairman of the BBC Trust, looked at Mandelson suspiciously. "You mentioned hundreds of detector vans, Peter. Where did they get these vans, if you don't mind me asking?"

"Well, from the BBC, of course," replied Mandelson. "Where else?"

"Somebody is telling lies. After the chancellor cut down our subsidy, we scrapped most of our detector fleet. I doubt if there are more than twenty in service today. Anyway, I would have been informed if any were requisitioned."

Mandelson went red in the face. "I'm sorry, Hilary, but that's the information I got from General Kruger only last evening. He actually told me they were close to eliminating most of the wreckers."

"Good God!" shouted Murdoch. "You don't believe anything that bloody Boer says, do you? He's been telling us for months that he's got the SAS bottled up in their base and nothing can get in or out. Tighter than the siege of Mafeking, he boasts. If that's the case, who the devil is it that's causing all this trouble? Don't tell me it's Al Qaeda or the IRA! Or I'll scream blue murder. Now you listen to me, these bastards are able to interfere with all our national turnaround channels and local channels at any time of day or night, though they don't seem to do much between midnight and 6:00 AM, except on my network, which cannot now broadcast so much as a screen saver. My technical people tell me that in order to carry out the volume of interference that we are experiencing at the moment, there has got to be around a hundred bloody great trucks loaded with electronic equipment, charging around the country as if they were taking part in a monster motor rally, but so far no one has ever seen one, although they have been heard at certain times. Goddamn it man, these Goddamn wreckers can't be invisible. Mandella told us he's got two satellite cameras fixed on the Credenhill base twenty-four hours a day, but they haven't yet picked up a suspicious vehicle leaving it. That means they must be parked up and down the country. We figure they must be using all these TA training camps that have suddenly sprung up everywhere. The ministry of defense knows where they are, so why aren't Section Three taking them out? That's what we want to know. Jesus Christ, man, it's imperative we capture at least one of the bloody things so that our nerds can take it apart and find out what we're up against."

"I sympathize with you entirely, Rupert, but what more can I do?" Mandelson replied in his most ingratiating manner. "Coward is on vacation, and there is no one left at the ministry of defense who has the guts to face Kruger down. I've ordered him to report to me on three occasions now, and he's just ignored me."

"Piss on Kruger!" shrieked Michael Brady of ITV. "If he was half a soldier, he would have cleaned up that nest of vipers in Credenhill a year ago. Get hold of the air force man and order them to obliterate the bloody camp. We just cannot allow this to go on any longer. It's intensifying all the time. They seem to be capable of identifying a commercial almost before it appears and zap it, just like the Japs are doing with their DVD players. Two more weeks of lost advertising, and ITV will be bankrupt. It's all right for the BBC, they are protected by the license fee, and Murdoch can't be hurting too much at the moment. He's cushioned by billions of pounds of up-front sporting contracts and Fox TV in the States but that can't last forever."

"That's not true, Brady," protested Bramble. "They are targeting some of our best cultural programs, and we are losing viewers by the thousand. I believe it is ITV and Channel Four that is responsible for all this mayhem, broadcasting trash like *Big Brother*, *Sex in Suburbia*, *Mary Whitehouse's Wet Dreams*, *Fantastic Foreplay*, and all the rest of their pornographic filth."

"Don't give me that," sneered Brady. "You call *All Night Bingo*, *The Black and Brown Minstrel Show*, and *Strictly Lesbian Dancing* cultural? They are doing the nation a good turn zapping them, if you ask me."

"Now now gentlemen, recriminations are not going to help at all," pleaded Mandelson. "I'm sorry, Michael, but laying waste to Credenhill is not going to accomplish anything. These infernal machines are scattered all over the country. What we need to do is spot them and record their movements. As each one is identified, a squad of local Paramilitaries will be alerted and they will move in with anti-tank guns and destroy them. If only we could get some cooperation from the RAF, we could eliminate them in days. But their pilots won't fly, and Air Chief Marshall Watling-Street can't do a thing about it."

"Sounds good on paper, but who's going to do the detective work?" snorted Murdoch. "MI5 and MI6 are so fucked up they couldn't find pussy in a whorehouse, and you know those bastards in Army Intelligence will lay false trails to fool us if we approached them."

"I've thought of that already," Mandelson said patiently. "What I suggest is that you chaps do all the detective work. After all, you can call on the world's best investigative journalists, most of them now laid off. I imagine Rupert's staff from the *News of the World* and the

Sun could just about do the job on their own. Tell them there is some sex involved, and they'll sniff them out like bloodhounds."

Mandelson's weak joke raised a subdued laugh around the table, and even the press baron permitted himself half a smile.

"Who is going to pay for all this, Peter?" he asked. "We're all broke. You'll have to help us out; keeping the peace is the government's responsibility, not ours. For my part, I'm going to hire some electronic experts from the FBI. I know the director well. He will see we get the best."

"I'll refund all reasonable expenditures," replied Mandelson. "I'll take it out of Kruger's budget. Perhaps that might get the man moving."

"You will have to bail us out a lot better than you have with the newspaper plants we're still rebuilding," protested Murdoch. "Despite all Campbell's grandiose promises, we've received less than a quarter of the compensation we applied for. We are nowhere near ready to start production again, and all the while, the Goddamn *Mail* and *Express* are increasing their circulation day by day."

"I had no idea you weren't getting what was agreed, Rupert," lied Mandelson. "Leave it with me, I'll get on to the Treasury immediately and order them to release funding right away."

"Be sure you do," snapped Murdoch. "Now listen, you've got to do something about that Boer bastard, Kruger, and quick. Surely you've got the authority to replace him and then deport him. I can think of a dozen retired army types who could do the job better. I can get one to come to your office tomorrow if you say so."

"Sorry, Rupert, that's something I cannot do. You know what a murderous devil Moses is. Kruger is his pet general. He would have me put away and do the same to all of you if he thought you were treading on his patch. Anybody here ready to challenge his authority?"

The chairmen looked at each other fearfully and shook their heads. Even Murdoch blanched and said nothing.

"I think the way to get rid of Kruger is to expose him publicly," Mandelson continued. "You all know what a checkered career he's had. There must be plenty of dirt to uncover, and if it includes murder, racism, and drugs, as I believe it does, then Tony will have no alternative but tell Moses to sack him. Anybody here willing to take the job on?"

"Our South African correspondent is ex-ANC," said Michael Brady. "He goes back a long way, and I'm sure he'll come up with something. Failing that, we can always ask him to find a couple of assassins. He tells me the going rate for a murder in Cape Town today is less than fifty pounds."

"Good, thank you, Michael. Spare no expense, we want him out as quickly as possible, certainly before Moses gets back," smiled Mandelson.

"Just a minute, Peter," squeaked Cedric Twilly of Channel Five. "Unlike Moneybags Murdoch, we're flat broke. It sounds like what you're asking my boys to do is highly dangerous considering they are messing with the SAS. I think a big bonus is in order for every target they identify, like say £2 million per, and that's cheap."

Mandelson swallowed hard. "Are you crazy, Cedric?" he bleated. "Why, if fifty of the infernal machines are identified, that will cost £100 million. Where on earth do you think I'm going to find that kind of money?"

"Look in Mandella's war chest. What we're asking is peanuts. The cabinet voted him £3 billion for twenty Apache gunships, and not a single one has been delivered to date. You remember that, don't you, Peter? You voted for the funding."

"Oh! I thought they had been delivered," lied Mandelson. "Very well, I'll meet your demand but not in that amount; Moses will have me shot when he finds out what I've done in his absence."

"Then it won't make any difference how high you go, will it?" said Twilly sarcastically. "Okay, we'll split the difference, £1.5 million per vehicle, and that's cheap."

"Damn right," came a chorus from the others, "£1.5 million and not a penny less."

Captain Antonio (Rozzer) Carmichael of Banjo Company, 1st Battalion, Fourth Infantry Division, Section Three Paramilitaries, heaved a sigh of relief when the message came through instructing him to abort his present mission and proceed without delay to a small village on the outskirts of Leeds in Yorkshire. His company was involved in enforcing a curfew that had been imposed on the Eccleshill area of Bradford, following three nights of rioting between the BNP and Pakistanis. It was a dirty, dangerous, thankless task, much more demanding than his previous position of chief inspector in the Shoreditch Police Force. How he wished he'd never got involved with the Yardies; he had been betrayed by one of them in return for a lighter sentence. Still, he was fortunate that Moses Mandella had stepped in at the last moment and saved him from time in jail. Not only that, he had offered him the well-paid post he now held in return for a five-year contract and a 10 percent cut of his salary.

In the beginning, he had anticipated a fairly easy life. Moses had told him that Section Three was not a true military force. Its primary purpose was to provide back-up for the Section One Police Force, a purpose similar to the SWAT squads operating in America. It was also to be the sole provider of protection to Parliament, the ministries, airports, seaports, railways, hospitals, and all major public buildings. But as the economy and the political situation worsened, so did the demand for protection increase. One week they would be in Bristol, escorting busloads of dockworkers, braving the anger of the pickets and howling strikers. Next it would be filling in for striking firemen in Manchester, a hazardous job at the best of times, since none of his men had been properly trained for the work and casualties became a fact of life. Then there was another dangerous job, when the gas tanker drivers went on strike and they were called in to protect volunteer strike-breakers. He had lost four men killed and dozens injured as the strikers turned nasty and bombed at least a dozen tankers before the strike was broken. After that, it was providing escorts for ambulances, garbage trucks, milk trucks, coal wagons, and school buses. At one time, it seemed as though the whole country was on strike and that his Banjo Company was at the center of all the action. At the request of General Kruger, Moses Mandella had shown his appreciation by doubling the pay of every man in it. Section Three was now an army boasting over a one hundred and twenty thousand volunteers, every one of them armed to the teeth and provided with the best body armor and riot gear money could buy. Banjo Company's strength was one hundred and fifteen officers and men, equipped with twenty Warrior fighting vehicles and his own personal staff car, a heavily armored Humvee.

Rozzer hated his assignment in Bradford. He had experienced plenty of rioting in Shoreditch, but it was a picnic compared with the Yorkshire city. All factions showed a great contempt for law and order, and would sometimes combine to fight the security forces, armed with thousands of gasoline bombs, stun grenades, Uzis, and AK47s. Even a curfew failed to deter the worst offenders, who took advantage of the narrow alleyways to ambush the night patrols. After he had lost four men when a Warrior was set on fire, he ordered his men to shoot anything that moved after sunset and anyone who was armed with a deadly weapon in the daytime. A semblance of order was restored, and the body count was approaching thirty-five when he received the new orders from London.

The duty sergeant at the village police station shook Rozzer's hand and showed him into a small, cluttered office where a middle-aged man wearing tan slacks and a short-sleeve shirt stood up and offered his hand. "Captain Rozzer?" he asked.

"That's me."

"I'm Sidney Bishop from Channel Five, I'm to show you to your objective."

"What objective?"

Bishop looked surprised. "You mean to tell me you aren't aware of the purpose of your mission?"

Rozzer shrugged his shoulders. "My orders are to report to this village in full battle order and meet you in the station. You tell me what's going on."

"You've heard about all the problems the TV networks are experiencing with their transmissions?"

"Too right. It's about time they got their fingers out and fixed them. I missed both big Premier League games on Sky at the weekend."

"Well, we have discovered that the interference is being caused by the SAS. They have fitted up dozens of trucks equipped with high-tech equipment that can interfere with any transmissions from a UK channel. How they do it, I don't know, but I myself have tracked down one of these vehicles—the first I might add—and I reported it to my boss, who in turn informed your General Kruger. My orders are to take you to the position occupied by the enemy, and you are then to survey the situation and contact General Kruger for further orders."

"Is the truck out in the open?"

"No, it's in a sort of small wood, and it's very well camouflaged. I waited till it was dark and got near enough to it to hear its generator. Then I climbed a tree, and with my night glasses, I could see some movement as two men climbed up on the roof and fitted a dish and pointed it due north. That's where the Yorkshire TV transmitter is located, about three kilometers ahead on top of Landsbury Hill. After a while, I heard the generator groan like an engine does when it takes a big load. I had my wrist TV with me and turned it on. I went through all five channels and found that ITV1 was all fuzz. I checked my watch and saw it was just gone 10:00 PM. Then I went back to my hotel and checked the *TV Times*. They were blanking out *Desperate Housewives*, and as soon as that ended and the commercials had finished, the picture was restored."

"When did all this happen?" asked Rozzer.

"Last night."

"So how do you know they're still there today?"

"Because I've had my TV on all day, and they blanked out *Emmerdale* and *Coronation Street*."

Rozzer looked at his watch. "It's just gone 8:00 PM, check your TV now."

Bishop turned on his wrist TV and tuned into ITV1. "It's *The Bill*," he said. "They won't blank that out but they will at 11:00 PM."

"Why, what's on then?"

"*Harlem Harlots*."

"So?"

"It's real dirty, makes you want to puke."

"But you watch it just the same," laughed Rozzer.

Bishop went red. "Yes, but only once. I've been checking dozens of programs since I started searching."

"Okay, I get the drift. I'll get in touch with the general and find out how I'm to play this. What about you? Are you going to dog off when we get there, or are you going to hang around while we sort the bastards out?"

"Oh, I'm going to hang around, if that's okay with you. Section Three versus the SAS! Now that's a scoop well worth risking my life for."

Chapter 27

C aptain Rozzer felt his scalp twinge under his helmet as the Humvee drew near to the target with Bishop in the seat between himself and the driver. He hunched forward, his eyes glued on the unlit road ahead. It was not as if he was a coward; he had been involved in many undercover operations with the police and had citations to prove it. It was this thing about the SAS that gave him the creeps, the aura of invincibility and the proven clinical deadliness of their methods.

He considered himself lucky on the day they came to Shoreditch. He was on the other side of London when he got the call to return to the Pathmead substation as soon as possible. The duty officer sounded frightened and garbled his words as he told him that three Section Four Stasis had pulled in with a man they said was an SAS squaddie and were interrogating him in one of the punishment cells. An hour later, he pulled up behind a fire engine parked at the top of Pathmead Street and turned off his engine. He saw that the station was on fire, and as he got out of the car and hurried down the street, he found his way blocked by a crowd of onlookers who were being held back by four masked men in camouflaged uniforms and another four doing the same at the bottom end of the street. The stand-off lasted for a full thirty minutes until the building had burned to the ground. Then the soldiers piled into two army Range Rovers and drove off at speed, shooting up a police car that was attempting to block their exit in the process.

The duty officer told him that the captive had been beaten to death by the Stasis, and twenty minutes later, the SAS soldiers drew up outside and ordered everyone out except for the Stasis, who they locked in a cell. They carried out the dead captive and put him in one of the Range Rovers before returning to smash in the windows on two sides and throw in a number of grenades. A report issued to the press by the SAS recorded that the captive was a fifty-seven-year-old SAS veteran of the Falklands War and was at his home when the Section Four Stasis burst in. His wife was held back by the Stasis as they dragged him away, but as soon as they were gone, she rang a special SAS help number and reported the kidnapping. The veteran was wearing a tiny transponder implant issued to all ex-SAS officers and men, which he had managed to activate during the struggle at the house. Section Four categorically denied that any of their officers were involved and the bodies of the three Stasis found in the ashes were never formally identified.

"Because they were bloody foreigners, that's why," Rozzer had remarked. But he could not help thinking that if he had been at the station at the time, the SAS would most certainly have topped him, no questions asked, for allowing the killing to take place.

The other occasion that scared the hell out of him was when a squad of Section Three Paramilitaries captured two SAS men returning to their base. On the instructions of Section Four, they were taken to Wellington police station to await collection by a Section Four unit. The Paramilitaries were beating up the two captives when an SAS troop arrived on the scene, freed the captives, and burned the station to the ground with the Paramilitaries locked up inside.

Rozzer knew what was going on. The SAS chief was sending out a message: mess with any of my men and you forfeit your life.

Yet here he was, on the brink of messing with God knows how many of the savage bastards and meeting them on the sort of terrain they sharpened their teeth on. If he had known he was going up against them, he would have flatly refused to leave Bradford. Even the hordes of white ruffians and hundreds of screaming jihadis were a soft option compared with the SAS. He felt in his top pocket and took out a slim silver inhaler, which he stuck up his left nostril.

Stiffening his chest, he inhaled the white powder it contained with a single sharp intake and then held his head back and savored the moment as the drug slowly filtered to his brain. "Have some?" he asked Bishop, holding out the inhaler.

Bishop shook his head vigorously. "No thanks," he said weakly, "never use the stuff." He was now a very frightened man. Going up against the SAS was bad enough but with a dope addict in command, it was plain suicide.

Rozzer said, "Suit yourself," and passed the inhaler to the driver.

"I'll snort it next stop," the driver said as he put the inhaler in the map compartment.

"How far now?" Rozzer asked Bishop.

"Just over a mile. If you keep your eyes left, you'll soon see a staging with some milk churns on it. Next to it is a cart track that goes down to the left of the wood, about half a mile farther on, I'd say."

"How did you get down there?"

"I parked my car a hundred meters past the cart track and broke through a hedge and walked it. It's all plowed field and bloody hard going, I can tell you."

Rozzer was silent for a moment or two, deep in thought. "Okay," he said, "the Warriors make too much noise to get that far unnoticed. We'll lay up here and go down on foot like you did. Signal the others and pull in here, Joe."

They were about a hundred meters from the wood when one of his men shouted out and fired a burst into the trees. Within seconds, two flares appeared over their heads and exploded into light. Rozzer went to ground, as did all the troops in front of him. He raised his head just high enough to see two Range Rovers breaking out of the wood, split up, and speeding in opposite directions along the front of his grounded troops. He heard the deadly chatter of their machine guns as they sprayed lead among them, raising screams of agony as they found their targets, one after the other. As Rozzer tried to dig further into a plowed furrow, he heard another sound that made him cringe with fear. They were firing mortars at them from the edge of the wood, and he held his hands over his head as shells landed among them, throwing up mountains of soil as they exploded in a hellish cocktail of fire, smoke, and shrapnel. The air was full of shouting and screams of the wounded as Rozzer got to his feet and shouted to his men to fall back to the road. They obeyed his order with alacrity, but Rozzer was saddened by how few men rushed past him. There could not have been more than fifteen or twenty of them. He turned to join them and was within fifty meters of the road when a bullet caught him in the middle of the back. The force threw him forward and turned his body over into a furrow. As he lay there fighting for breath, he tried to undo the pocket of his jacket and reach for his spare inhaler. *Just one great big snort*, he thought, *just enough to take the awful pain away.* But there was no feeling in his hands or any other part of his body below his neck. The shooting and shelling had stopped now, and as he listened to the cries of his wounded comrades around him, he heard voices and a flashlight shine into his face.

"Looks like he's the boss man," one voice said as a pair of cold hands felt his neck. "He's hurt bad. Doubt if he'll make it to the road."

A masked face appeared and looked closely into his eyes, which were now rapidly clouding over. "Aye laddie," the mask said, "yee have no one but yeeself to blame for yeer misery. Next time you take orders on your mobile, make sure no one else is listening in tuh yee."

Cedric Twilly, CEO of Channel Five, wrinkled his nose as he was ushered into the office of the deputy prime minister, along with his investigative reporter, Sidney Bishop. The air was heavy with the scent of gardenias, and it emanated from the well-groomed person of the DPM himself.

"Have a seat, gentlemen," purred Mandelson. "I'm sure you both know General Kruger, head of Section Three."

Kruger nodded stiffly in their direction, and they both nodded back. It was the first time Bishop had seen the general close up. He was a lot bigger than he had imagined. He reminded him of the right wing Afrikaner, Eugene Terreblanche. He was wearing a pink beret, which bore a badge of a leaping springbok. The red-faced general was staring at him with gimlet eyes, and he shuddered inwardly. It was a look that suggested he was sizing him up for a human sacrifice.

"General Kruger would like a firsthand account of the events of August 11," said Mandelson "You don't mind if I record the meeting, do you?"

Twilly looked puzzled. "I've already submitted Bishop's detailed report to your office, Peter; we have nothing further to add to it, have we, Sidney?"

Bishop shook his head as Mandelson ignored the remark, switched on the recorder, nodded his head at Kruger, and sank back in his chair.

Kruger looked briefly at a paper in his hand and fixed his gaze on Bishop. "It says here that you saw enemy insurgents giving first aid to some of our wounded lying on the ground. How can that be so, when you also said the night was pitch black?"

The voice was thick and interrogatory, a dead ringer for Arnold Schwarzenegger. Bishop could well imagine the man in his native land, beating the shit out of an ANC prisoner with his bare hands.

"Yes, it was dark," replied Bishop, "but I was wearing night vision glasses, and in any case, they were holding big lamps; I could plainly see them applying first aid and giving them injections."

"You did not see them giving first aid, because you did not possess any NVGs."

Bishop was incredulous and looked at his boss enquiringly. But Twilly did not return his gaze. Again, he studied his fingernails instead.

"Of course, I bloody well saw them," he said angrily. "Captain Rozzer gave them to me and told me to stay well back of the action. I'm a top investigative journalist. I tell things as I see them always, without fear or favor. The SAS patched them up as best they could and stretchered them to the road. Then they rang Leeds General Hospital and helped load the badly wounded into the ambulances when they arrived. The walking wounded they allowed to climb into two Warriors and follow the ambulances. Those who were unharmed were put into two other Warriors and waved away. The remaining Warriors they drove away behind the interference truck and four Range Rovers heading south on the Dewsbury Road. For Christ's sake, your own men will confirm everything I've reported. I've spoken to most of the wounded, and they're all full of praise for the way they were treated. Surely you've done the same, haven't you?"

The bloated face was impassive. "You did not see them giving first aid, you did not see them helping the wounded or helping put them in ambulances. There were only four men in the Section Three patrol that went to investigate your tip-off, and they were ambushed by the insurgents. Two of them were killed outright and the other two were wounded and then butchered where they lay."

Bishop stared open-mouthed at the general and then looked appealingly at his boss, who again refused to meet his gaze. "What the hell are you trying to pull, Kruger?" he shouted. "Every word in that report is the gospel truth, and every word you have spoken is a bloody great lie. My report is in the works right now, and I'll be broadcasting it on the main news tonight. How are you going to square your bloody rotten version with that?"

Kruger gave him a thin smile. "Not so, my friend. The insurgents are targeting all Channel Five news bulletins for some reason or other, and until we track them down, it will remain in limbo. Am I not right, Mr. Twilly?"

Cedric Twilly looked straight ahead and nodded briefly.

Bishop looked at him in horror. "For Christ's sake, Cedric," he cried, "it's the biggest story of the year, you said that yourself. What have these creeps got on you that's made you turn chicken? Say something, for God's sake."

There was still no answer from Twilly. Mandelson looked uncomfortable and shifted in his chair but also remained silent.

Kruger put down his paper and looked at Bishop contemptuously. "Be very careful what you say, Bishop. I am considering whether to hand you over to my colleagues in Section Four or not. I can assure you that they would not permit you to use that kind of language on their premises."

Section Four! The mention of the name brought Bishop down to earth with a bump. "Why on earth would you want to get me involved with that bunch of psychos?" he pleaded.

"Because, Bishop, we have reason to believe you deliberately led my men into a trap. They caught you snooping around and spared your life only if you did as you were told."

"You're crazy, the only person I spoke to was my boss and Captain Rozzer. The SAS never got a peep at me, let alone speak to me. You're making it up. Either that or you're trying to screw me out of my bonus."

Kruger looked surprised. "Bonus? What bonus is that?"

"Cut the crap, you must know we're on a £100,000 reward for every interference truck we locate."

"Oh, really? I thought it was the patriotic duty of every citizen to report any treasonable activities to the authorities without any expectation of monetary reward. This is first I've heard of such a mercenary offer. What about you, Mr. Mandelson?"

The DPM squirmed and shook his head firmly.

"And you, Mr. Twilly?"

Twilly's face went white, and he remained silent.

"I don't believe this," protested Bishop, "it's common knowledge in the media, for Christ's sake. There are dozens of people at it, and not too many of them are journalists. I'm being set up, and by God I'll find out who's behind this charade, as surely as I found the SAS truck."

"No, you won't, Bishop. Before he died, Captain Rozzer whispered to a medic that he heard you talking to one of the saboteurs, and the duty officer at the police station said that you had been seen in the company of two strangers at the local pub an hour before you met Captain Rozzer. What have you got to say to that?"

"It's a pack of dirty, rotten lies. There's no court in the land would believe a cheap frame-up like that."

"Who said anything about a court?" snarled Kruger. "If you don't agree to my terms, the only judge you will appear before will be my friend in Section Four, Colonel Hans Hoffman."

The mention of the notorious name made Bishop's knees tremble. How in God's name had a simple journalistic assignment come to such a deadly pass? He shivered again. He knew of four newsmen who had fallen into the hands of Section Four, one of them from Channel Five. Their only crime was to file stories criticizing Campbell and New Labor, and not one of them had been seen since.

"What terms are you offering?" he asked weakly.

"You will leave the country within twenty-four hours. You will travel to Bloemfonteine in South Africa and remain there until we grant you permission to return. I will arrange for you to get a job with the *Bloemfonteine Herald,* but you must never mention your role in the SAS massacre of my men under any circumstances. Do you understand?"

Bishop licked his dry lips. He was going to challenge the Boer bastard but thought better of it. "Yes," he whispered. "I understand."

"Good, you have made a wise choice for your health, my friend. Your boss will make the necessary arrangements for your departure. Now, leave us and wait in reception. I have some other matters to discuss with Mr. Tilly before he goes."

Much to Mandelson's distaste, Kruger lit up a cigar and blew the smoke carelessly across the desk.

"I thought I handled that very well, considering I'm the antecedent of some ignorant *Voortrekkers,* don't you think?" joked the Boer.

He laughed at the expression on Twilly's face. "Are you absolutely sure you are the only one other than Bishop who knows about this?" he asked him.

"One hundred percent sure," replied Twilly, nervously, "and that's the way it's going to stay."

"I hope so, Mr. Twilly, indeed I hope so. It would very embarrassing for the government if this report ever saw the light of day. You are sure that this is the only copy in existence?"

"Absolutely. This was typed up by Bishop on the computer in my office. I saved it to a CD, which I have here in my pocket."

"What in Jehovah's name is it doing in your pocket?" asked an exasperated Kruger.

"It's insurance. Until I get my money."

"Money? What money?"

"Why, the reward money, of course," replied a puzzled Twilly. He was under the impression that Kruger knew all about the deal with Mandelson.

"You mean the £100,000 mentioned by Bishop? That's a lot of money. Do I get a share as well as the disk? After all, it was my men got killed, not yours."

Twilly looked at Mandelson anxiously. Should he keep quiet or disclose the real amount? After all, the other newsmen were aware of it, and Kruger was bound to hear about it sooner or later. He was surprised he did not know about it already. Mandelson had a guilty expression on his face, like a small boy who had been caught stealing pennies from his mother's purse.

"It's a bit more than that, General. It's more like seven figures."

"Seven figures!" There was a pause as Kruger worked it out. "You mean £1 million? My God, who is going to give you that kind of money?"

"Peter is. That's the price all the networks agreed with him. And it's not £1 million, it's £1.5 million."

Kruger looked at Mandelson and grinned like the proverbial Cheshire cat. "What is your end of this caper, Peter? You are surely not going to give it all to Mr. Twilly without taking a piece for yourself, are you?"

"I'm not taking a penny," snapped a red-faced Mandelson. "I promised him £1.5 million and that's exactly what he'll get. I never go back on my word."

Kruger grinned again. "Very well, you won't mind then if I negotiate myself a small slice of the payment with Mr. Twilly, will you? After all, it's too big an award for such a little effort on his part. It's my boys who do all the dirty work and risk their lives. The money will come in handy for compensating the relatives of the ones who get killed. I'll settle for half the reward. That's £750,000."

Twilly was furious. "Not on your life. This is a cast-iron agreement made between Peter and several other members of the broadcasting industry. You have a duty to apprehend the insurgents who are ruining our business. If you want additional payments, then it's up to you to negotiate with Peter or the Treasury."

Kruger looked enquiringly at Mandelson. "How about that, Peter? Are you prepared to sweeten the pot for me? Say a round million, same as you're making?"

Mandelson was now seething with anger. "Certainly not," he snapped. "You don't need extra money. Section Three has got a bigger budget than the regular army even. Take it out of that. You don't deserve a penny for the disgraceful performance your men put up against the SAS. One hundred and fifteen against twelve, and they ran like rabbits. No wonder you're taking your time moving against Credenhill. What are you waiting for, Zulu reinforcements?"

Kruger stood up to his full height, and sent his chair crashing. The remark had stung, as Mandelson knew it would. "You had better be very careful what you say about Section Three!" he roared. "They are fine body of men, and all we are waiting for are the Apache gunships your penny-pinching chancellor promised us months ago. Once we have them, we will eliminate those SAS bastards in double-quick time. As for the Leeds massacre, we were betrayed. The SAS knew we were coming and set a trap. There must have been two hundred of them at least, supported by tanks."

Mandelson and Twilly looked at each other in amazement. Neither of them were prepared for such an outburst or the insinuation. There were many rumors going around about the flamboyant Boer, and the label that came up more often than not was "psycho."

"Betrayed! Who on earth do you think was in a position to betray you?" Twilly asked bravely.

"I've already told you. It's your man Bishop. He looks very crafty to me. I think the SAS caught him snooping around and threatened to kill him if he did not help them with the ambush. If I get proof that he did this, the *Bloemfonteine Herald* will be printing a murder on its own doorstep, that I promise you."

Twilly was about to say, "You're crazy," then thought the better of it as Kruger got to his feet.

"I'll take the disk now," said Kruger, holding out his hand.

Twilly quickly opened his briefcase and handed it over.

Kruger grinned as he picked up his cane and made for the door. He had his hand on the handle when he turned and looked sternly at them both. "Let me tell you this. You and your broadcasting friends can discover a hundred interference trucks for all I care, but when you ask me for help, the answer will be no unless I receive the payment I just negotiated. Understood? Oh, yes, and make sure you destroy that computer. I will hold both of you responsible if a single word of that report is leaked to the media."

Chapter 28

Alastair Campbell had delayed his return as long as he possibly could, but the sheer volume of reports of mayhem in his absence had persuaded him to cut short his vacation and find out what the hell was going on. His ill-temper was hardly improved when, because of a strike affecting all Britain's airports, his flight was diverted to Brussels and he was obliged to catch a ferry from Ostend. His official car was waiting for him on arrival, but because of extensive roadwork, it took another four hours before he reached London, making a total of sixty-four hours since he boarded the plane in Bhutan. And to cap it all, he had picked up an enteritis bug on vacation, which had left him weak and denied him the foaming glass of Thwaites bitter he had been thirsting for since the day he left England.

He had been expecting trouble. Nothing ever went smoothly when Mandelson was at the helm, even for a single day. John Prescott was bad enough but Kaa was something else. The chaos confronting him on his first morning at the office was overwhelming. It seemed as if the entire country was on strike, every city plagued with race riots, and the transport system at a complete standstill. The *Daily Mail* and *Express* were full of horror stories concerning new epidemics out of control in the National Health Service, gridlock on the roads, pandemonium at the airports, and the catastrophic effects of a nationwide strike by power station workers. All at a time when the country was enduring the hottest summer on record, from the

South Coast as far as the Scottish Highlands. But, unsurprisingly, the main gripe was the interference on the TV channels that was playing havoc with programming and depriving viewers of soaps, pornography, cartoons, children's fare, reality shows, football, and horseracing.

His first personal experience of what was in store was the gruesome temperature in the windowless cabinet room. He had called a meeting for 10:00 AM, and within five minutes he had shed his jacket and tie and unbuttoned his shirt. But to no avail. The air-conditioning was out of action, and he had no alternative but to continue with the meeting. To add insult to injury, only three ministers bothered to turn up: Mandella, Coward, and Angus MacTavish.

"Where the fuck is everybody?" he asked the cabinet secretary. "I give up a week of my vacation and only three of the idiots turn up?"

"No one was expecting you back so soon, Alastair," came the reply. "They are either still on vacation or unavailable. And Bronson and Green have called in sick."

"Bloody faggots, no prizes for guessing what they're up to. Where's the DPM?"

"He went on vacation last night. Said he booked it six months ago and couldn't cancel."

"What! He knew I was coming. I sent a message to his office two days ago. The rotten bastard has made a balls-up again and sneaked out of the back door. By Christ, this is the last straw, I'll have him out of the cabinet this time if it's the last thing I do. Where's Tony?"

"Still with Berlusconi, as far as we know. He's due back on Saturday, according to my diary."

"Thank God for that, we've got enough problems without him screwing things up as well.

Okay, you first, Moses. Let's have it." Campbell sat uneasily in the prime minister's chair, his belly on fire and his chest full of bile.

Across the table, looking just as jaded as he felt, sat Moses Mandella with Dudley Coward, the defense secretary, on one side, and Angus MacTavish, the chancellor, on the other.

"Have what?" scowled the home secretary. "I only got back at eight o'clock last night. Thanks to British Airways, I spent the previous two days hanging around airports trying to get back."

"Join the club. Surely you've been kept up to date by your department while you were abroad. My phone never stopped ringing, and always in the middle of the night because of the time difference."

"I had my bloody phone stolen twice," snorted Mandella. "Anyway, what's the good of having a vacation if you can't get away from it all?"

"That's beside the point. You are still responsible for the safety of the country, wherever you are. It was inexcusable for you to leave your office without seeing to it that a minister was left in charge. I rang up eight times from Bhutan, and the only person who answered me was a nutter called Ilfracombe who kept banging on about this TV interference problem."

"Hell, you must have got your communications all screwed up. Harold Shipman was in charge all the time I was away. Anyway, you can't talk. Only a complete idiot would leave a freak like Mandelson in charge of the country for four weeks."

"Three weeks. I came back a week early, I'll remind you. Mandelson is the deputy prime minister, after all, and if I remember rightly, you were among those who voted for him. Enough of this bickering, what are you doing about all these strikes and race riots? The whole country seems to have come to a stop. The roads are jammed with cars, there's no gasoline to be had anywhere, the hospitals are turning away patients by the thousand up north, and now there is no football anywhere because the police have refused to provide protection unless they get triple time. Plus the jails are overflowing and there's more convicts stalking the streets than there are inside. And to top it all, the government cannot get a good word anywhere because our friends in the media are all but choked off. Jesus Christ, man, we're close to the tipping point of James Ramsay MacDonald's government in 1931."

"That's right, blame the home office like always. Let me tell you, most of our problems are caused by your over-mighty unions. It was you caved into them last year and handed them inflation-busting pay rises. Like the greedy bastards they are, they're back for more of the same for less work. It's lucky for us that half the country is on vacation and the schools are closed. You've made Sally Onions the most powerful man in the country with your bloody appeasement policy, and now the chickens have come home to roost. This time, the cupboard is bare and you've lost your best bargaining chip forever. Am I not right, Mac?"

"Aye, that yee are," agreed the chancellor, "the cupboard is bare. Nay a ha'penny to spare."

"If that's the case, then you can put the blame on Moses," retorted Campbell. "Take out health and education, and the home office is responsible for more spending than the rest of the government departments put together."

"And worth every penny," shot back Mandella. "If it wasn't for Section Three, the anarchists would have taken over long ago. For every soldier killed in Iraq, there's ten of my boys killed fighting the bloody SAS or the mobs. They don't go on strike at the drop of a hat. They're proud of their uniform and the job they're doing."

Campbell leaned forward. "I heard rumors about a massacre involving the SAS up at Leeds. Some of them say sixty Paramilitaries were killed, and others say nearer eighty. There's nothing official about it, and it seems the CEO of Channel Five and his reporter, who discovered SAS operation there, have both disappeared. What can you tell us about it?"

"It wasn't a massacre," Moses said, "it was cold-blooded murder. A Section Three patrol came up against over a hundred SAS in a wood, and all four of them were captured and then executed. I'm informed that the reporter deliberately led the patrol into a trap and has now fled the country."

Campbell whistled. "A hundred SAS? My God, who told you this fairy tale, for Christ's sake?"

"General Kruger."

"And you believe him?"

"Of course, he's got my fullest confidence."

"Then why is he so shit-scared of the SAS when just four of his men will take on a hundred of them?"

"You know the reason. His plans call for twenty Apache gunships, and he won't move without them. We've been waiting months for them. They are essential to the success of the operation."

Campbell turned to the defense secretary. "What's going on, Dudley? Something smells fishy to me."

"Moses is right, he asked for the choppers three months ago at least. We've lined up eighteen ready for service at Middle Wallop, with another two being made available at the end of the month."

"So that answers Moses's question then. Why hasn't he been informed?"

Coward looked sheepish. "Well, you see, Alastair, we fought tooth and nail for the choppers and finally got the chiefs to agree to loaning them to Section Three for six months maximum. We've got the choppers but there's a bit of a snag."

Campbell groaned. Whenever Coward confessed to a snag, it invariably turned out to be a major disaster. "All right, what's the foul-up this time?" he asked wearily.

"The crews of the Army Air Corps have flatly refused to fly any chopper placed under the command of Section Three."

"What?" Campbell choked as the knife in his gut dug deeper. "Has everyone around me gone stark staring mad? First the SAS refuses to obey our orders, and then half of the services give them their moral support, and now the Air Corps go on strike. Have our chinless wonders in the ministry of defense completely lost it? What excuse did the useless bastards give you this time?"

"Sir Launcelot Bullington-Barraclough told me that if he disciplines the Air Corps crews, their fellow crews serving in Iraq and Afghanistan will refuse to fly any missions, and that would be an outright disaster."

"Holy shit, Dudley, how many times have I told you not to address anyone by that crappy title in my presence? I absolutely abhor knighthoods and everything that goes with them, more especially by anyone in the armed forces. How can it possibly be respected when titles are showered on financial crooks, failed politicians, footballers, queers, pop singers, cooks, TV presenters, and bloody daft comedians? It's blackmail, sheer blackmail. Whatever happened to discipline in our armed forces? It's about time they took some of these toffee-nosed Sandhurst schoolboys and put them digging trenches. We spend millions training them, and as soon as we ask them to do their patriotic duty, they go on strike. What's with this prick Barraclough? It seems to me the only army he's got left is the Household Division, and I'm not too sure about them. Who appointed him chief in the first place?"

"Tony did. He sacked the last chief because he wanted out of Iraq, if you remember. It was Dick Cheney that put him on to Barraclough. Don't ask me why but there's a story going around that Cheney was on a shoot at Barraclough's estate in Northumberland, and one of the beaters got shot. It was all hushed up and the two have been friends ever since."

"Yes, I remember. Jesus, his moniker alone should have told Tony he was completely useless."

Coward raised a smile. "It's not all doom and gloom, thank goodness, Alastair. The colonel in charge has offered to train Section Three personnel to fly the machines for a small sum per bod."

"How many bods is that?"

"Forty."

"And how much per?"

"Two million."

Campbell's jaw dropped. "Two million per? Why, that's £80 million. Jesus Christ, you didn't agree to that, did you, Dudley?"

"I tried to get them down, really I did. The bastards wouldn't budge. They actually told Barraclough to shove it when he offered them a million per."

"It's blackmail. I hate blackmail. I won't pay the greedy, unpatriotic swine a plugged nickel. God, I loathe the military, always have. They set themselves apart from elected government and shout blue murder if they have to take cuts like other ministries. They are the most class-conscious, racist bastards you can imagine. Always braying about the sacrifices they make, but in reality they love war. It gives them a sense of superiority they don't deserve, especially the top brass. Look at this clown Barraclough. Nobody ever heard of him two years ago, yet he boasts enough salad on his chest to feed a family of eight. He's a bloody disgrace. What we should do is sack the goose-stepping prick and put someone else in charge who will do what he's told or resign."

"Tony already did that twice, Alastair," Coward pointed out. "He sacked Richie for opposing the war in Iraq, and then he sacked

Blackwell for refusing to serve up Colonel Mendonca as a scapegoat to appease the Islamists. Perhaps if you offered Barroclough a peerage, he would try a little harder."

Campbell avoided Mandella's gaze as he answered. "No can do, at least not while this fucking cash-for-honors inquisition is still going on."

"Well, you can at least kid him on. After all, the way things are panning out, there won't be a House of Lords much longer."

"No, by God, not a chance. I wouldn't give the man the time of day." Campbell hoped that Mandella had not caught the drift of Coward's remark but the cold, hard look in the home secretary's cruel eyes told him otherwise.

"You paid the unions what they asked, and that cost billions. You set a precedent and now you're hooked by it," sneered Mandella. "Eighty million is peanuts compared with that."

"All right then, you take care of it. After all, it's your bloody show. Your budget dwarfs the ministry of defense. You can easily afford it."

"No, no, no. My budget does not allow for the cost of policing millions of fucking strikers, millions of race rioters, and fuck knows how many foreign rapists, murderers, thieves, and druggies. We're scraping the bottom of the barrel, and my budget next year will be double what it is now, I can promise you that."

Coward put up his hand. "Excuse me, Moses, when do you anticipate you will be wanting to use the Apaches?" he said in a hesitant voice.

"Hell, I don't know. A month, two months, three even. Why?"

"Well, the Air Corps commander told me that it takes three months to train a flier, even if they've had previous flying experience with fixed wing aircraft."

Mandella shrugged his shoulders. "So it takes three months. Who cares?"

"I do!" shouted Campbell. "For Christ's sake, what do I have to do to impress on you people the danger of allowing the SAS to function as a rallying point for every right-wing, fascist storm trooper who would love to see New Labor smashed to smithereens? The SAS is a monster that is extending its tentacles further and further from its cave in Credenhill. It's no good cutting off these tentacles, as Section Three has been trying to do. There is only one way of dealing with it. Cut off its bloody head, and that means a full-scale attack on its lair in Credenhill."

Mandella was unimpressed. "So we'll mount a full-scale attack in three months. I'm not going to let a bunch of shitty TV moguls and newspaper bosses dictate policy to me. If you ask me, the SAS is doing us a favor shutting down the news coverage, especially on TV. All those bleeding-heart producers do is exaggerate the grievances of the strikers and the deprivations of the vicious bloody rioters. Never a good word for the brave lads of law enforcement. No news is good news as far as I'm concerned. The less vandalism and killing that appears on the home TVs, the better it is for us. There is nothing the British public fear more than pictures of buildings on fire and howling mobs in the streets baying for blood."

"No, Moses, that is not acceptable!" shouted Campbell. "Three months takes us into November. The G8 meeting takes place on the tenth of November for three days, and we cannot have fighting taking place on or anywhere near that date. This meeting is of the greatest importance to us. It could mean the ending of hostilities in Iraq and Afghanistan, as well as giving the city a badly needed boost. The middle of October is the absolute limit."

"In that case, give the job to the Household Division. All they do is change the guard at Buckingham Palace these days."

Campbell looked annoyed. "We've been over that before, you know that the division will not move against the SAS but they are committed to defending the government of the day. In any case, we've got other plans for them."

"What plans?"

"They are to provide security for the G8 summit."

"What! The whole bloody division? Jesus Christ, Kruger could do that with just a company."

"No way. I did suggest that but Obama's security chief wouldn't hear of it."

"Why not?"

"Because he's checked it out. Says there are too many Arabs in Section Three. There has been one attempt on Obama's life already, and he won't take any chances."

Moses swore. "The bloody racist bastard. What if I was to weed out the wogs, chinks, and niggers and provide a pure Aryan escort with blonde hair and big tits. Would he settle for that?"

"I doubt it. You would have to prove they were straight as well, and even I could not imagine you could honor that."

Campbell and the others laughed. The sight of Moses Mandella striking a moralistic attitude was something to behold.

Mandella failed to see the joke. "Piss on the Yanks. Postpone the meeting for a month or two. We're not going in without the Apaches, Kruger won't hear of it."

"So get rid of bloody, arrogant, cowardly bastard," Campbell shouted. I can't understand why you appointed him in the first place."

"I went on his record. He cleaned up the riots in Johannesburg in double-quick time."

"But the rioters were black, for Christ's sake. How could you of all people countenance hiring an enemy of your own race?"

Mandella shrugged his shoulders. "Ninety percent of the population here are white. What did you want me to do, hire a nigger?"

For a moment, Campbell was lost for words, as the knife dug into his stomach again. "All right!" he screamed. "I give up. Keep your bloody racist Afrikaner but order him to do what he's paid for and attack Credenhill without delay."

Mandella was about to shout back when Coward put up his hand again. "I forgot to say that the commander said he could complete the training in less than three months but that would entail a lot of overtime and weekend duties. It would also cost more because of that."

"Go on, tell us how much more," groaned Campbell.

Coward looked at his notes. "Half a million per, approximately."

"Jesus Christ," swore Campbell, "this is like the bloody Olympic Games, it keeps going up and up, with no end in sight."

"Well, that makes it a round 100 mil," said Mandella. "Cheap at twice the price, if you ask me. Don't you agree, Angus?"

"Aye, that I do. But where am I going to get the money, laddie?"

"It's the army is screwing us. Screw them back. Take it out of contingencies for their bloody wars. Christ, they waste that kind of money throwing garden parties every year. Am I right, Dudley?"

Coward made no reply, as all eyes turned to Campbell. "Can you do that right quick, Angus?" he asked the chancellor.

"If you authorize it and sign the chitty, I will see to it," replied the canny Scotsman.

Campbell gave a big sigh. "Very well, go ahead and do it. Now listen to me carefully, Moses, and you other people take note. I want Credenhill cleaned out by the end of October at the very latest. I don't care how you do it or how many casualties you take. I want the bloody SAS completely eliminated, squashed, unable to mount a raid on a chicken farm, let alone an attack on Leeds Castle during the G8 meeting, which intelligence has told me is a distinct possibility. It's high time your bloody expensive army showed its mettle and earned its corn. If they can't do that, then I'm going to sack the bloody lot of them and save enough money to pay the unions double what they're getting. Have I made myself clear, Home Secretary?"

Moses fell silent. Campbell had never talked to him like that before. The man was under pressure, suffering from jet lag, or going round the bend. He was boiling inside. The last man who had dared to talk to him like that in front of other people was Chief Inspector Harrison of the Yard, who was found floating face down in the Dartford canal two days later. His first thought was to face him down, give him two fingers, even signal evil tidings, but he thought better of it. Campbell was the unchallenged boss man now, head of the country, a ruthless bastard who would stop at nothing to get his way. And then there was Arabella. She would never forgive him if he screwed up with the peerage now. Better to bide his time. Campbell had overreached himself once before; people like him always did. And he'd do it again one day. That was a certainty.

"Okay, if I agree with your order, what are you going to do about the unions?"

"What about the unions? They've got nothing to do with this."

"Oh yes, they have. They're tying up thousands of my men battling strikes and riots from Land's End to John o'Groat's. Are you telling me I'm to pull them all out and leave the country at the mercy of the mobs?"

"Goddamn it, man, you've got over a hundred and twenty thousand Paramilitaries, at least that's what the Treasury says it is paying for. Twenty thousand should be plenty to deal with five hundred in Credenhill. That's odds of forty to one or more."

"How do you know how many SAS there are at the base? It could be five, even ten thousand. What you don't understand is that only half of Section Three is combat ready, the rest are support staff, medics, paper pushers, cooks, and bottle washers. We're stretched to the limit. We can't do both."

"I think you had better settle with the unions, Ali," said MacTavish. "Sally Onions is an unreconstructed communist of the old school. He'll bring down the government before he'll give a centimeter, that he will."

"And where is the bloody money coming from to do that? You said yourself we're broke."

"We'll print some."

"Jesus Christ, Angus, are you crazy?" protested Campbell. "Interest rates are at 14 percent already. You'll send them sky high with a trick like that. The housing market will collapse and ruin millions of people."

"I've thought of that. Inflation rates went up to 20 percent under Margaret Thatcher but they soon fell back after a while. I reckon they could reach 15 percent in October, but I'm sure we could do some horse trading at the G8 summit and bring them back down again. Then we can find a way to deal with Onions and his gang to prevent this situation from ever happening again."

"And how do you suggest we go about that?"

MacTavish looked at Mandella and said, "I think Moses is the one to answer that question, Ali, don't you?"

Chapter 29

The Kitcheners action group was in the middle of its weekly planning program when Jock Wingate answered a call on his cell phone. All eyes focused on the boss when he uttered the words, "Good God, not John Gibbons, surely not!" The officers listened intently as he carried on with the conversation, and the grim look on his face as he switched off the phone filled them all with apprehension. "Gentlemen," he said in a sorrowful voice, "bad news, I'm afraid. That was Apollo; he's just learned that John Gibbons of the *Daily Mail* and his deputy have been kidnapped, and they are being taken to East Midlands Airport at this very moment. He estimates they will be at the airport in approximately forty-five minutes." Wingate looked at his watch. "I make it 1608, so they will be there around 1653." He looked at Captain Farnsworth. "Jim, who have we got in that vicinity?"

"I don't know off-hand, but I'll soon find out," Farnsworth replied, as he picked up the phone in front of him.

"Luke, you know Gibbons personally, don't you?" asked Wingate. "How do think he'll react to the situation he's in?"

"He's a tough nut, they won't get any change out of him. I can't vouch for his deputy, but if John's chosen him personally, I imagine he'll be made of the same stuff. Did Apollo say why they're taking him to the airport?"

Wingate's voice was angry. "They intend to put him on an American charter plane, an extraordinary rendition flight that is waiting on the edge of the airfield right now."

There was a roar of disapproval from the officers present and not a few choice curses. "Any chance of getting a chopper airborne and taking the bastards out?" asked one of them.

Wingate looked at Sam Duffell.

"Sorry, no chance for at least two hours."

"Okay, sort one out as soon as possible. Anybody know what type of plane the Americans use for their evil practice?"

"They use Con-Air, Boeing 737 charter planes," replied the intelligence officer. "At least all the ones that land in the UK have been."

"Are they armed?"

"Not outwardly but I imagine they have plenty of automatic weapons on board. Apart from the crew, there are usually four or five guards, and I can't see them carrying bamboo canes when they are looking after a bunch of alleged terrorists."

"How many alleged terrorists are there usually on board?"

"Depends which way they are going, Karachi or Guantanamo. Sometimes it can be as many as forty or fifty poor devils."

"Okay, Jim," said Wingate. "Google the airfield and print out a dozen copies. Then try and find out what kind of manifest they produced and which way they are headed."

"What if they won't divulge the information, sir?" asked Luke Dryden. "These flights are supposed to be top secret. Even the boobies in the government don't know anything about them, or so they say."

"Tell the airport flight controller that if he refuses, we'll make sure he's on the next rendition flight that comes in. Get all his particulars, his home address, his car registration, and his local pub. Give him the works. Then tell him he never had a conversation with you."

"Very good, sir, will do."

"Right, Jim," Wingate said, as he saw Farnsworth put the phone down, "what's the score?"

"Frank Gearson is the nearest we've got. He's at the TA HQ, Ashby de la Zouche, less than twenty kilometers away from the airport. I caught him in a Pinkie on a training exercise. He's got Tim Talbot with him and two trainees."

"Is the Pinkie fully armed?"

"I imagine so; I'll find out."

"Good. Feed Frank all the information you can and tell him to put enough PE on board to blow up an airliner. Oh yes, and tell him to make room for two extra passengers. Jim, I'm putting you in charge of the operation. Be sure you keep in contact at all times. I read the *Mail* every morning, so please don't let me see its editor's obituary on the front page tomorrow."

Tim Talbot found an entrance into a field and drove the Pinkie behind a clump of trees.

"Either of you two know the airport well?" he asked the two trainees. "Take a look at this map on my laptop; HQ have located the target on that spot there, you see it?"

"Yes," answered Trooper Eric Filmore, "I've been there a few times but I know the land around it better than I do the airfield. Can you zoom in and show some roads and by-roads?"

"Sure. How's that?"

"Great, there's Hyams Lane, it runs down this side of the airfield. Get us back on the Ashby Road and move on for about two kilometers and you'll see it on the left."

Tim followed his instructions and turned into Hyams Lane just as a big jet landed on the main runway with an ear-splitting roar and squealing brakes. Frank Gearson stood up and trained his glasses on the airfield as they proceeded down the road. "Whoa, steady as you go!" he shouted. "I can see a tail fin sticking up right down the bottom end. There's no markings on it, so I reckon that could be it. Get ready to pull in when I say so, Tim."

Moments later, Frank gave the signal and Tim pulled in and parked on the grass verge. "Right, out you go and find us an opening, you two," he ordered the trainees, "but not too close to the aircraft if you can help it. I'll wait here for your signal."

He lit a cigarette and followed the pair down the hedgerow with his glasses. "Nice youngsters, Tim," he remarked. "Are both of them farmers?"

"Yes, Eric's dad owns a farm and Vinny works on it," replied Tim. "Big strong lads, aren't they?"

"You can say that again. Looks like they eat half of what they grow. Right, there's the signal now, let's see what they've found."

"This is the best we can find, Sarge," said Vinny. "It will take some time to clear a way through for the Pinkie, though. It's thick hedging, mostly hawthorn and blackthorn."

"Do it then; you're farmers, aren't you? You'll find an axe and spade in the tool box. At the double and keep the noise down."

Frank walked further down the road until he could see the plane's tail fin sticking up over the hedge in front of him. Peering through the hedge, he got a good side-on view of the giant, silver aircraft standing alone in the corner of the airfield, A good two kilometers from the airport buildings in the distance. It had no markings whatsoever, at least on his side. *It had to be the target* he figured. He looked up at the cockpit. It was empty. However, he could hear voices and activity on the other side. He got down and looked beneath the plane's belly and was rewarded with the sight of mobile steps and four or five bodies gathered around them. *Jesus, had the steps just been brought up for uploading, or were they in the process of taking them away and making ready for take-off?* he wondered. Worried now, he hurried down to the Pinkie and surveyed the work in progress.

He was impressed; there was a huge pile of hedging strewn all over the verge and a large opening, easily big enough to drive the Pinkie through. Only they had hit a snag.

"It's a maple, Sarge; we didn't see it until we were halfway through. It's deep rooted and is going to take some digging out."

"Shit!" Frank scratched his nose. "Okay," he said, "break out the tow rope and loop it a meter up the trunk, and then hook it up to the Pinkie. Fasten a rope as far up the trunk as you can and both of you pull forward as the Pinkie pulls it out. I don't want a centimeter of that tree falling backward into the airfield, and don't let it fall onto the Pinkie either. Understood? Tim, take it nice and easy. Keep the engine noise as low as you possibly can."

Tim nodded and waited impatiently as the trainees set about their task and finally gave him the thumbs-up. The engine groaned as the Pinkie took the strain, and then slowly but surely the roots gave up the fight until finally the tree was pulled back enough for it to be laid down on the verge.

"Good work!" exclaimed Frank. "Eric, fill in the hole with some hedging while I speak with Tim and Vinny."

"Tim, we're going down to the plane. When Vinny gives the signal, move in fast as you can and park in front of the plane with a clear view of the cockpit. Get behind the guns and, if you hear any sound of the engines being started up, give the cockpit the full treatment. We're going in under the plane's belly and up the other side. I'll signal you from there. Vinny, tell Eric to follow you and when I say go, move under to the other side and take up positions where you've got a good field of fire on the steps, one bottom and one top. If you see anyone with a gun, take him out. If the exit door is open, it must stay that way, even if we have to prop it open with dead bodies. Finally, Vinny, do you know how to get back to Ashby without using the main road?"

"Sure I do, Sarge. Do you want me to take the wheel?"

"No, Tim will drive. You tell him the way."

The action went without a hitch. The guard at the top of the steps made as if to aim his rifle at Frank when he appeared at the bottom but dropped his gun as he saw Vinny and Eric training their rifles on him. There were two more guards near the steps talking to some civilians and members of the crew, but they were both unarmed. Frank ordered the guard at the top to come down, and as he complied, he signaled for Eric to cover the group and climbed the steps, followed by Vinny.

"Go left but don't enter the cabin," he whispered to Vinny as he went in and turned right. "Christ!" he swore as he glanced down the aisle. "This many?" For one brief moment, he recalled a picture of a cargo of African slaves crammed below deck. He estimated there must have been over forty people on board, every one of them clad in an orange jumpsuit and with their hands and feet chained to the legs of their seats. He pointed his rifle at two guards sitting in jump seats at the far end and ordered them to come up fast with their hands on their head. They both obeyed with alacrity, looking back fearfully at his rifle as they hurried down the steps.

Vinny stood facing the cockpit as Frank looked down the rear aisle. "Anybody here by the name of John Gibbons?" he called out.

"Here!" came a call from a man in an end seat, two thirds of the way down the aisle.

"Thank God for that!" exclaimed Frank. "Mr. Gibbons!" he shouted. "Are there any more guards about that you know of?"

"No, not down here, but I'm not sure about the toilet up that end."

"Check out the toilet, Vinny," Frank ordered.

Vinny stood at the side of the toilet door and tried the handle. It was locked. "You in there, drop your trousers and come out backwards with your hands over your head!" he shouted. "I'll give you three seconds to come out before I empty a full magazine up your ass."

A split-second later, the door burst open and a frightened guard came out backward with his trousers around his ankles and his hands on top of his head.

Vinny burst out laughing. "Where's your underpants, dickhead?" he shouted. "Did you mess them up in there?"

Frank laughed briefly and then turned serious. "Take him down and put him with the others. Signal Tim to come around and take up his position. Then get the keys to these chains and bring them up to me."

"Jesus Christ," he said out loud as he took a closer look at the prisoners. The great majority of them were Asian, Arab, or African. Many of them had their heads shaven and bore deep gashes and ugly bruises on their faces. Others had black spots on their heads that looked suspiciously like cigarette burns, while one man even had a series of holes around his temple with a larger one in the center. Their faces and eyes were heavily bruised, and some had broken noses and torn earlobes. Every face except that of John Gibbons and his companion looked gaunt, with sunken eyes expressing the pain and suffering they had been subjected to. They reminded Frank of the prisoners in the Nazi death camps. The only difference was the clothes they were wearing.

There was a great hubbub among the prisoners as he walked down to Gibbons and knelt down beside him. "Good God, you look as if you've been in a car wreck," he said in a shocked voice.

"It's Robert you should worry about," came the reply, "he's got a broken arm, and they won't do a thing for him."

Frank looked at Robert. He was bent forward, supporting one manacled arm in the other. He looked in great pain.

"Listen, Mr. Gibbons," Frank said in a kindly voice, "my name is Frank. We've come to get you out of here. Now this is very important. How did you get captured?"

"We were coming back from Manchester when we were run off the road by a Section Three Humvee. Robert broke his arm but I didn't get hurt too badly. They pulled us out of our car and put us in a Jeep with three Section Four thugs in it that had pulled up behind us. We were blindfolded and told not to speak or we would be shot. About an hour later, we arrived here, were stripped of all our clothing, and forced to put on these jumpsuits. Then we were put on the plane."

"You said there were three thugs; what happened to them?"

"One went off in the Jeep. I don't know where the other two went."

"The Humvee, did it follow you here?"

"No."

"You're sure of that?"

"I'm pretty sure."

"Good, do you know much about the rest of the captives?"

Gibbons shook his head. "No, Frank, we haven't been on the plane long. We haven't had time to get acquainted. God, are we glad to see you. I do know there's a Brit further back. I heard him swearing at one of the guards in cockney."

The captives had come alive, and many of them were shouting out in languages Frank did not understand. "Are there any Brits down there?" he called out, trying to make himself heard.

"Here, here," replied a voice four seats toward the back.

Frank moved toward him and was appalled at what he saw.

"Jesus, who did that to you?"

"Fucking Yanks, CIA. I was lucky; they cut my brother up and dumped him in a river."

"You sound cockney."

A half-smile appeared on the bloodied face. "I'm from Hackney."

"Nice place. Now listen, we haven't got much time. Do you speak the language of any of the other prisoners?"

"Some of them, Arabic and a bit of Pashto. My name is Asif Sami."

"Mine's Frank. Listen up. I'm getting off the plane. While I'm gone, one of my men will bring up the keys to your chains. Unlock them all and make it clear that they are to remain in their seats until I give the order for you to disembark. When you get my signal, tell them not to rush but walk down in an orderly manner and assemble at the bottom of the steps, where I'll give you further instructions. Keep them quiet; it's important we don't attract any attention from the airport buildings, or we all might find ourselves chained up again. Understood?"

"Yes, sir," Asif Sami replied excitedly. "Are you SAS?"

"See you down below, Asif."

Frank stopped by John Gibbons's seat on his way out. "You'll be disembarking soon, Mr. Gibbons. When you're on the ground, both of you walk over to our Range Rover and get in and stay there. Then we'll get Robert to a doctor."

Vinny met him halfway down the steps with a ring of keys in his hand. "Sorry, Sarge," he said. "I had a bloody awful job finding the keys. I think the bastards are stalling for time."

"We'll see about that. How many hostiles are there in total?"

"Nine."

"Okay. Free Mr. Gibbons and his deputy first and send them down. Free nine captives yourself and collect their chains. Then give the keys to a Brit called Asif Sami, who is sitting four rows farther back, and let him and his pals free the rest. Come back down with the chains and put them on the Yanks. Link them up in a row and fix one end to the steps. And make sure the captain is the last one on the free end. Get Eric to help you. Got that?"

"Yes, Sarge."

Chapter 30

Frank Gearson ignored the Yanks sitting in a huddle at the side of the steps with their hands on their heads. He grinned as he saw Eric standing over them with his rifle at the ready. *Acts like he's rounding up sheep*, he thought.

Tim had parked the Pinkie twenty meters away and was training his glasses on the airport building.

"See anything?" Frank asked.

"Plenty of movement but nothing unusual. Those guys in the tower must have glasses. It's a big wonder they haven't cottoned on to us by now. I don't like it, Frank."

"Neither do I. We've got to get out of here fast. Is the firework ready?"

"It is." Tim picked up a demolition charge and handed it to him.

"Where's the remote?" asked Frank.

"It's my turn to zap."

"Are you sure?"

"Absolutely sure."

"Okay, if you say so, but if you catch a bullet, make sure you press the button before you croak it. What say we ready up a Javelin just in case?"

"Sounds good. Leave it to me, I'll see to it."

"Here come Gibbons and his deputy now. The deputy's in bad shape, been carrying a broken arm all day. Make them as comfortable as you can while I go plant the charge."

Frank strode over to the plane with the charge in his hand and held it up to the nose of the prisoner nearest the steps. "Smell that," he said. "It's FARS–PE, the same stuff you supplied to the fucking IRA. Just pray it doesn't set your asses on fire."

Before the prisoner had a chance to reply, Frank bounded up the steps and pushed his way through the captives gathering inside the door. Once in the cockpit, he peeled off the adhesive protection strips and pushed the charge firmly against the floor under the instrument panel. Finally he flipped the toggle switch and checked to see that the "armed" indicator showed red. He was halfway through the door when he noticed two bulky attaché cases lying in the corner. He hesitated and then decided to take them with him, heavy though they were.

"Gangway please!" he shouted as he squeezed his way through the crowd of orange-clad captives who cried out in foreign languages and tried to clap him on the back or shake his hand. Asif was holding them back, cursing and shouting for them to keep quiet, but he had his work cut out.

Frank put his arm around his shoulder. "Asif, there isn't any more we can do for you, except to wish you the best of luck. Lead your people out of here and turn right at the bottom of the steps. Keep close to the hedge and go about sixty meters, where you'll see an opening in the hedge. Turn left and that will put you on the road to Ashby de la Zouche." He felt in his pocket and pulled out some notes and loose change. "This is all I have on me, but it might help some. And here's my mobile in case you need it. There may be a mosque in Ashby so try that first. By the way, when you get home, telephone the *Daily Mail* and ask for John Gibbons. He will want to talk to you real bad. Must go. Be sure and wait for my signal before you get moving."

Before Asif could say a word of thanks, Frank lurched down the steps, unable to use the hand rail because of the two cases he was carrying. He reached the bottom and looked in amusement at the chain gang standing in a line. Every prisoner was minus his trousers, underpants, and footwear. He choked back his laughter and went to the end of the line, where Vinny and Eric were standing.

"Is this guy the captain?" he asked, staring up at the shaven-headed giant.

They both nodded.

"Okay, free him from the others, we're taking him with us."

"No, you ain't!" the captain screamed as he was parted from his companions. "I'm going with them. I've heard about you fucking murdering SAS bastards. I figure you're going to slit my throat where there ain't no witnesses." He continued to scream and curse as Vinny and Eric wrestled him to the ground and pushed his face into the earth.

Frank knelt down beside him and hissed in his ear, "Listen to me, you noisy, fat bastard, we've got a Black&Decker in the Pinkie. If you don't do exactly as you're told, I'll dig it out and drill ten holes in that fucking thick head of yours and let some air in. Now get moving."

"Cuff his legs and arms as well," he ordered Vinny. "The last thing I want is this fucking gorilla running amok in the Pinkie. Got your mobile with you, Eric?"

"I have."

"Good. Take a few pictures of our horny friends. I'm sure their CIA boss will be real proud when he sees his cowboys showing off their big guns on CNN."

Frank waited until the two trainees had reached the Pinkie with their prisoner and then looked up at the steps and raised his thumb to Asif.

Smiling with delight, Asif led his fellow captives down the steps and turned right. They all hurried along behind him, keeping close to the hedge until they reached the break. Asif stopped, gave a final wave, and then disappeared from view. Frank waited until the last man was gone before turning to the prisoners.

"You look like a Mississippi chain gang," he joked, "only I imagine they'd be better hung than you lot. Enjoy your trip to England."

His remarks sparked off a round of whining and cursing. "You're not leaving us here tied up like this. That's murder, it's plain cold-blooded fucking murder!" shouted one who was wearing red and green striped socks.

Frank turned around and stared at them. "What's the matter with you supermen?" he demanded. "The steps aren't welded to the fuselage, for Christ's sake. Bend your bloody backs and move it."

They stared back at him in silence until finally, they got the message. The prisoner nearest the steps grabbed hold of a rail and started tugging it for all he was worth. The next man also clasped a stanchion and pulled so hard he slipped on the soft ground and fell on his back, pulling down some of his cursing companions. "No, no, no!" one of them shouted. "You're pulling the wrong way. Get all the way round the steps and pull like fuck. Pull straight so the wheels don't jam. All together now, heave!"

Frank grinned and turned to leave as he saw the steps part company with the plane. The only time he had seen men working so hard was when his troop was caught out in the open in Afghanistan and the mortars came homing in like hornets. He was within a yard of the Pinkie when he heard the unmistakable sound of machine-gun fire. "Christ, it's a Warrior!" Tim shouted. "Get down low and stay there. Vinny, grab the guns and stick it to them."

Frank ran forward and nearly collided with Tim as he came round the back of the vehicle and picked up the Javelin missile launcher. Tim carried it round to the side of the Pinkie and set it up on its tripod as Frank knelt beside him, ready to load another round if necessary. "On target, one-eighty meters, steady as she goes … fire!" shouted Tim as he pulled the trigger. The missile had barely left the launcher before Frank leaned over and inserted another round. He grabbed his glasses and trained them on the Warrior.

"Good shooting, Tim!" he cried as he saw the Warrior burst into flames. "Hold fire while I check behind it." He swept the ground as far back as the control tower and then clapped Tim on the back. "All clear. Back in the Pinkie, we're out of here. And tell Vinny to stop wasting ammo or I'll take it out of his bloody wages."

Tim drew up near the exit and stood up, the remote controller in his hand. "They're about thirty meters clear; is that enough?" he asked Frank.

Frank looked out and saw the chain gang heaving desperately and cursing as the steps rocked perilously from side to side over the uneven ground. He was tempted to give the order immediately, but he checked himself.

"Another ten, then go," he replied.

He looked at the blazing Warrior, hoping to see bodies running away from it, but there were none. A split-second after his eyes returned to the plane, Tim pressed the button, and he saw the familiar explosion and fireball envelop the aircraft, sending out a shock wave that swept the members of the chain gang off their feet.

"Okay Tim, let's go!" he shouted. "I think we've had enough training exercises for one day, don't you, lads?"

They had driven about three kilometers before Frank spoke to the Con-Air captain. "You saw how we let your buddies live another day, didn't you, Beefy?"

The captain refused to answer.

"Right, I'm going to ask you some questions, and I want some honest answers, otherwise you are not going to see their ugly faces ever again. Do I make myself clear?"

Again, the captain refused to answer.

"You're CIA, right?"

"I am, and proud of it."

"What's your name?"

"Homer Simpson."

"Very funny. Where did you pick up all those prisoners?"

There was a brief hesitation. "Kabul, Karachi, Baghdad, Cairo, Tunis, you name it."

"And where were you taking them?"

"Guantanamo, of course, where else?"

"The two Brits who were put aboard here, was there any paperwork with them?"

"No idea. Me and my crew just fly the plane, the other guys handle the documentation."

"That's the stuff in the hold alls in the cabin, right?"

"One is my stuff, maps and things. The other belongs to Broderick. He's the boss man. He always sits up front with us.

"So you would have seen if he put some papers in his case after the Brits were put on board?"

"Sure I would, but I didn't see any documents for them. They were put on board at the last minute. They were for the drop."

"What do you mean, the drop?"

"Shit, man, don't you guys know anything? I mean they were tagged for a swim in the Atlantic."

Frank turned and looked at Gibbons. His face was pale but expressionless.

"So you drop people in the ocean as well as torture them. Nice people, the CIA."

"Shit, we don't torture them none, that's all done by the Arabs before we pick them up. We might rough them up a bit in flight, but only if they cause us trouble and try to escape. Anyway, I'm only the captain, Broderick makes all the decisions. And it was your Section Four people who handed the pair over to us and told us to drop them in the drink. Why didn't you pick on them? Both of them were in the line."

Frank cursed to himself. He'd fouled up. He'd forgotten to interrogate the men in the chain gang and missed a golden opportunity to eliminate two of Section Four's murdering bastards. He turned his anger onto the captain. "Pretty shitty business you're in. Makes you proud to be an American, does it? I've had a quick look in the other hold all. There must be hundreds of thousand dollars in it," said Frank, grimly

The captain straightened his shoulders and looked defiant. "I told you, that's Broderick's hold all, and the money was handed to him by the guys who brought the prisoners to the plane. I get paid by the government. These people are enemies of my country. They killed thousands of us on 9/11. There's only one way of preventing them from killing thousands of us again, and that is for us to kill the ragheads first."

Frank turned around and looked at Gibbons.

"Do you want to ask this Neanderthal any questions, Mr. Gibbons?"

Gibbons look disgusted. "No, thanks, Frank, I've got better things to do. I'll let your intelligence section examine his bird brain, then I'll print every Q&A on the front page of both the *Daily Mail* and the *Mail* on Sunday."

Frank laughed. "That might be sooner than you think. You'll be on a chopper heading south later on tonight. Our boss is dying to meet you. By the way, Eric has got some great pictures of your kidnappers caught with their trousers down. Your cartoonist, Mac, will think it's his birthday when he gets them, I'm sure of that."

Chapter 31

"**N**ow then, can you tell me what's so bloody important that you have to get me out of bed in the middle of the night?"

It was past ten in the morning, but Alastair Campbell felt as if he hadn't slept for a week as a result of a riotous evening with the celebrities after the BAFTA wards.

It was a hastily convened cabinet meeting, and every member was present except the prime minister. Campbell stood at the end of the table and stared with bloodshot eyes at the empty chair next to his. "Where's Tony?" he grunted. "Skiving again?"

"I can't locate him anywhere, Alastair," said the cabinet secretary. "I think he must be on the open road somewhere, probably on his way back from a meeting."

"A likely story. Who's guesting at Chequers this week?"

"Silvio Berlusconi, I believe."

"Good God, no wonder you can't get hold of him. When those two get together, they're as thick as thieves planning a bank robbery. You can say good-bye to him for a week, at least."

"He might be on a duck shoot with Dick Cheney," joked the foreign secretary. "Then you can say good-bye for good."

There was a titter around the table before the cabinet secretary called them to order. "Will you please chair the meeting, Alastair? It really is very important, and a matter of great urgency, as you will see."

"Very well, if you insist," croaked Campbell. "I hope to Christ someone around this table hasn't gone and made another almighty cock-up, I don't feel up to any aggravation today."

He made his way to his chair and sat down between the home secretary on his left and the chancellor on his right. "Who's in trouble this time?" he asked.

"We all are, Ali," replied the chancellor. "We're right in the middle of a crisis like no other I can remember."

Campbell's heart sank. As far as he was concerned, things were starting to come together. The unions had accepted his increased wages offer and called off the strikes that had paralyzed the country. A glorious summer had taken the edge off the anti-government hostility harbored by the electorate, and the opposition was taking a beating in the polls as they over-reached themselves with wild promises and unachievable targets that had seasoned political observers rolling in the aisles. True, the economy was balanced on a knife edge, as a worldwide depression gathered pace and the clamor for something to be done to restore the soaps on TV had intensified. But set against that was the good news that some of the friendly newspaper presses were rolling again and putting out pro-government spin and propaganda once more.

"It's scandalous," protested the chancellor. "Someone or something is hacking into governmental databases, both here and abroad. Millions of pounds of taxpayers' money is being withdrawn from Treasury accounts and distributed to thousands of false accounts across the world, and we are powerless to prevent it. We are being overwhelmed by the demand for restitution from intended recipients, and our best efforts to repair the damage are being thwarted at every turn."

The doom-laden pronouncement by the dour Scotsman cast a shadow over those assembled, most of whom had already heard the appalling news or had even personally been affected by it. Campbell took a deep breath and felt every eye fixed upon him, some fearful, some hopeful, and some even accusatory. His foggy mind went through the gears and suddenly a name slotted in and set his alarm bells ringing. Rodney Gates, the Welsh computer wizard! Kidnapped by persons unknown, spirited out of the United States, and now being held in Russia, according to CIA sources. But British Intelligence had told him the kidnapping bore all the hallmarks of a Special Forces operation. Relations between Russia and the United States were at an all-time low but instead of creating a storm, the U.S. response was mute, almost nonexistent. Special Forces! The U.S. Delta Force or the British SAS? Surely not Delta Force. His blood ran cold. The SAS in control of the nation's finances? It just didn't bear thinking about. He shook his sore head and mustered a show of bravado he didn't feel.

"For Christ's sake, Angus. Give us one bona fide example of what you are talking about."

"I'll give you one, Alastair," wailed a voice. "We wired an interim loan to President Mugabe of Zimbabwe yesterday, and it has found its way into the account of Help the Aged in Britain. Mugabe is foaming at the mouth, but we haven't found a way of recovering the money as yet." The voice belonged to Harry Bent, Africa's munificent benefactor at the ministry of international development.

"Fuck Mugabe!" shouted Ed Fowler, the foreign secretary. "What about me? My bank manager rang me at eight o'clock this morning and asked me if I wanted to close my account. My entire balance plus a ten thousand pound overdraft facility has been withdrawn and electronically deposited in the accounts of sixteen E. W. Fowlers scattered all over Britain and abroad. He told me that the bank will attempt to recover the money but it could take months, and there's no guarantee the recipients will pay up."

"It's the same with me!" shrieked Sandra Jewel, the new cultural secretary. "I have an account with Barclays, and they have warned me that I am overdrawn by £18,500, and when I asked why, they said electronic payments had been made to thirteen accounts under my name. They have no idea when my account will be in balance again."

"And me too!" shouted Thomas T. Abaduwallah Swaziwarria, the secretary for deprived communities and local government. "Every penny I have, including my £75,000 overdraft, has been taken out and paid to some twenty-four people with my name. I am now bankrupt, and the bank is chasing me for their money, the greedy, merciless bastards. It's all right for you, Sandra, you're worth millions and can stand it."

The chancellor was astounded. "I can't believe it, T.T. Do you mean to tell me there are twenty-four others bearing your exact name?"

"It's a tribal name. My father has many wives and many children. If the bank tries to get them to pay the money back, they are wasting their bloody time, I can tell you."

"Well, I don't think the Treasury will be in a position to help you out for some time yet, T.T. It's absolute chaos there," complained the chancellor. "This month's Treasury allocation for the salaries and expenses of members of both houses has been mysteriously added to the account dealing with payments to the armed forces, past and present. Salaries have been increased by 200 percent for those based at home and 400 percent for those serving overseas, as have pensions and other allowances. I have also been informed that top judges and civil servants will not been paid this month, and the Treasury has been overwhelmed with complaints. But it doesn't end there. I'm getting reports that council tax credits now exceed debits in some parts of the West Country."

A white-faced Campbell held his head in his hands. "It is the SAS," he muttered to himself. "The bastards are screwing up government finances, just like they are doing with the broadcasting media. Jesus Christ, my own salary would be the number one target." If they cleaned that out, how was he going to pay the mortgage on the grand house he had just bought in Runcorn?

"Go on," he groaned, "what other bad tidings are there in that bloody doomsday book of yours?"

The chancellor turned the pages of his loose-leaf notebook. "Here is a partial list of ministerial ex gratia payments earmarked for certain bodies that have been stopped and redirected to other parties."

Gobi Desert Snowboarding Association: £7,000,000 to Alzheimer Research Fund.

Save Jamaica's Steel Bands Fund: £4,000,000 to The Homeless Children's Trust.

Sub-Sahara Outreach Fund: £8,000,000 to Guide Dogs for the Blind.

Illegal Immigrants Charter Fund: £16,000,000 to Poppy Day Appeal.

Aid for Ex-murderers Poverty Fund: £5,000,000 to Aged in Crisis.

South Armagh Comeragh River Bridge Fund: £25,000,000 to MENCAP.

"Good God!" shouted Adrian Realways, the transport secretary. "Who on earth sanctioned these outlandish payments in the first place, and what's this Comeragh River thing in South Armagh? I know South Armagh like the back of my hand and I can tell you there's not even a brook or stream of that name in the county. Sounds like bloody Gerry Adams has been screwing us again. What say you, Peter?"

Peter Plum, the Northern Ireland minister, blushed a deep red color that eclipsed his trademark suntan. "For heaven's sake, Adrian," he blustered, "how do you expect me to know about every penny that goes into Northern Ireland? We spend billions there. It looks like the Treasury has made yet another of its famous cock-ups. I'll look into it later on and find out where they have gone wrong."

"And so will I," replied the chancellor in an aggrieved voice. "And the first thing I'll look for will be the signature on the chitty. Now then, I haven't finished my report yet. Unfortunately, there is worse to come."

There were groans all around, and Campbell buried his head deeper into his hands.

"The Treasury database that controls parliamentary and civil service expenditure has been interfered with. The records of all MPs, their Lordships, and MEPs together with all senior civil servants and judges have been wiped out and rendered unrecoverable."

Pandemonium broke out as the words sunk in. "Jesus Christ, do you mean I won't be getting my paycheck and expenses?" screamed Peter Plum. "How the hell am I going to manage, I've got barely £15,000 under the mattress."

Alastair Campbell broke in abruptly. "Look, we're wasting time dealing with individual complaints. What we need to do first is find out who is hacking into our databases, how they are doing it, and where they are located. Now then, which one of you is responsible for IT systems and all this database crap?"

"Andew Buchan is," said the chancellor. "So far this year, he's spent well over £18 billion with EDS alone, so he should know what he's talking about."

"Well, Andy," Campbell said sharply, "let's have it straight."

The diminutive minister sat up quickly and peered around the table through his horn-rimmed glasses. "Don't think we have been asleep on this," he said reproachfully. "Everyone at the ministry has been working night and day trying to repair the damage. We have flown in teams of experts from EDS, IBM, Intel, Microsoft, Oracle, and Google, at tremendous expense, but they are all baffled. Most of the software is encrypted and self-restructuring, but the hackers seem to be able to bypass all firewalls and attack and rewrite from within. It's uncanny. As soon as the experts repair one glitch, another replaces it. They are tearing their hair out and blaming each other for failing to pinpoint the problems. The latest development is that the CIA and the Pentagon are sending their experts over. They are shit-scared that a foreign power has made a quantum leap in counter-IT and are testing it out on us."

"Bullshit," said Campbell. "According to Angus, they haven't touched our military databases except to enhance wages. It is a singular attack on this government, and if it is allowed to continue, it will destroy us. Have these greedy so-called experts been able to discover the source of any of the attacks? After all, if the United States is so concerned about it, they could shut down the whole of the Internet and smoke them out if they wanted to."

"Good God, the Yanks would never do that; it would cost them billions. If it was their IT that was under attack, yes, they probably would, but poor little Britain? No chance," moaned Angus."

"But the hackers must be using local phone lines," Campbell persisted. "Surely BT and the others can trace the calls."

"Oh, they can do that, all right, and they are doing it all the time, but the hackers always stay one step ahead of them," said Buchan. "If BT interdict a call, it is immediately switched to another caller in another part of the country or to the address of another server without the knowledge of the user. It's as if they've established robots here and abroad that do their bidding—electronically, of course."

"Well, surely there must be some commonality that can point us to a certain address or server or whatever. A phone number, postal address, code word, anagram, something that people like those at Bletchley Park picked up during the war. We've still got code breakers, haven't we?"

The chancellor pricked up his ears. "Just a minute, there is a remark that alludes to a recurring item." He shuffled through his papers two or three times, much to the annoyance of the other ministers. "Ah, here it is!" he proclaimed at last. "Out of one batch of some thirty-odd embedded instructions, the words 'Union Jack' appeared six times, and we can only suspect that ..."

"What?" shouted Campbell. "Union Jack? Why, that's the name intelligence informs me is the code name for the SAS military coup in the UK. Yes, by God, the SAS is behind it all. The bastards have kidnapped Rodney Gates and are using him to foul up the databases just like they are using that Russian guy to screw up the airwaves."

A shocked silence pervaded the room. "Military coup! Is that really on, Alastair?" Dudley Coward asked, in a tremulous voice. "I thought the General Staff had stymied that idea once and for all. You don't really think the SAS would attempt such a mad attempt on their own, do you? Why, the Household Division alone would make mincemeat out of them. They have hardly any armor and no aircraft to speak of. Even Section Three could keep them penned in their bloody base for a hundred years."

"Don't be so sure, Dudley. They are recruiting like mad all over the country, and there are rumors of Russian transports delivering arms in the most unlikely places. You know very well we are unable to keep the base under satellite surveillance any more. They might have a well-equipped army ready to move at a moment's notice, for all we know. Even if they don't, we must take precautions. Their motto is 'Who Dares Wins,' and that ethos has served them well in many engagements. I don't propose to give them the slightest chance of mounting a lightning attack." He turned to the home secretary, who was toying with a pile of tiny ivory bones. "Moses, it's time to take the fight to the enemy. I insist that you instruct General Kruger to attack the base and wipe out the bastards completely before the end of the month."

"No can do," Mandella retorted contemptuously. "You know as well as I do that Kruger's Apaches won't be ready for action for months yet. He won't move without them. Even then, if there are as many as nineteen ready, he still won't move until there are twenty. He says he needs that number, and twenty it must be."

"It's about time somebody told that overbearing Boer bastard that what he wants is a right good kick up the ass!" shouted Campbell. "We've spent more money on his bloody private army than we have on the regular army, navy, and air force put together. I'm up to here with the insufferable arrogance of the cowardly bastard. Now, you listen to me. You tell him in no uncertain terms that if he does not reduce the base to rubble and capture it within the next three weeks, he will become the ex-commander of Section Three. Not only that, his passport will be confiscated and he will be charged with dereliction of duty and cowardice in the face of the enemy. That means a spell of interrogation by our friends in Section Four, for sure. I move that the home secretary is hereby required to convey these instructions to his Section Three commander without further delay. All in favor of my resolution, raise their hands now."

A pregnant hush descended on the proceedings, as slowly and hesitantly the members of the cabinet raised their hands in approval. All except Moses Mandella, who sat motionless, his coal-black face two shades darker than usual. He remained silent and showed no emotion, bar the movement of his stubby fingers as they snapped in half every single one of the miniature ivory bones in front of him.

Chapter 32

"It's October first!" Luke Dryden shouted excitedly as he burst into the war room and waved a piece of paper. "The Boer is on the warpath, and it's every man for himself."

His fellow Kitcheners laughed and cheered at the announcement, expressing the excitement they felt at the news they had been expecting for months. There was a lot of emotion too, a feeling of relief that at long last they would no longer be cooped up in the base and forced to use clandestine methods to visit their families and loved ones for fear of reprisals against them. Some expressed relief at the end of the cold war as they saw it, a period of stagnation where, except for those fighting in Iraq and Afghanistan, every waking day was devoted to defensive measures and planning for the big push that lay ahead. Inaction! For men of the SAS, it was the very antithesis of everything they had been trained for, and the longer it went on, the greater the debilitating effect it was having on morale, something not seen since the dark days following the end of the Second World War when the Regiment was virtually disbanded. There was relief, too, in the knowledge that they would be fighting the rogue elements of Section Three rather than their comrades in arms in the Home Division.

"All present, attention!" Luke's command brought the team to its feet as Colonel Wingate entered the room and took his customary place at the head of the table.

"At ease, gentlemen," he exclaimed as he dumped a thick pile of papers and his laptop on the table. "Give your brains a rest, for they are going to be overworked for the next week or so, I can assure you of that."

Luke stared at his boss. He looked ten years younger. The color had returned to his cheeks and the heavy lines that had made his face look gaunt had practically disappeared. As for the eyes, there was a sparkle he had not seen before, even when the success of their TV interference program had been celebrated.

Wingate looked around the table and smiled. "I can see you have sampled the starter, now you lucky people can tuck into the main dish Apollo has provided us with. I have here the top secret documents for Operation Rentokil, General Kruger's plans for the complete destruction of the SAS and its base in Credenhill. Luke, please pass them around, one copy per person."

There was a buzz as each officer grabbed his copy and pored over the details. Wingate lit a panatela and sat back, waiting patiently for the first observation from one of those present.

"It's a Rommel trademark, no doubt about it," commented Major Donald Bradman, the Australian commander of G Squadron. It was Bradman who had traced the career of General Kruger and had determined that practically every tactic he employed while fighting for Unita was based on Rommel's desert campaigns, adapted to suit the jungles of Angola. "It looks remarkably like Rommel's offensive against Auchinleck at Bier Hacheim, where he feinted a frontal attack and rolled up both British flanks," he declared.

"Well, he couldn't have picked a better exponent, if you ask me, Donald," said Wingate. "It's obvious the man's no fool. Any general who can fight his way through two hundred kilometers of jungle in less than three months and defeat the Cuban-trained Angolan army, as he did, must be taken seriously. Let's see, he's getting on for sixty and hasn't seen any serious action for twenty-odd years. Must be a bit rusty by now, don't you think?"

"I agree," said Bradman, "and on top of that, he's got a reputation for partying and indulgence with the ladies. On the other hand, Apollo warns that he's licked a good part of Section Three into shape, and that's remarkable, considering that it was only fully formed just over two years ago."

"Yes, I think it will pay for us to treat the man like the old Desert Fox himself," Wingate remarked soberly. "An army of a hundred and twenty thousand soldiers, no matter how well or badly trained it is, cannot be trifled with. Who can see any loopholes in his strategy?" he asked. "Offhand, I'd say he was asking for trouble, splitting his force in two in order to execute a pincer movement where the enemy is well entrenched and protected by armor on both flanks. But then, we are not well entrenched, and we have not got enough armor to protect both flanks."

"Don's right," agreed Major Norman O'Connor, the D Squadron commander, "but how much does Kruger know about our dispositions? If you ask me ..."

Jock Wingate nodded his head and began entering notes on his pad as the comments and observations flew thick and fast around the table. He felt good. As the commanding officer, with at least fifteen years more service than his nearest ranking officer, he had already made up his mind. But he would never force that decision upon his staff until he had gathered in their opinions and modified his own plans to suit. Normally, it was their lives that were on the line rather than his own, and they had every right to safeguard them. But this time, it would be different. He would be bang in the front line with them, sharing their excitement, their fears, and God willing, their triumphs.

By the end of the Q&A session, it was close on lunch hour, and he told them to break up and return in two hours' time. As soon as they were gone, he logged on with his computer and laboriously collated all the information he had gathered into his master plan. Once this was done, he cut to the projector and beamed it onto the screen on the wall behind him. Then he turned his chair around and sat down, extracting another panatela and lighting it before leaning back and staring up at the screen and the map it presented.

For a moment, Luke thought the colonel was asleep when he led the others back into the war room. He was about to tap him on the shoulder when the familiar voice said, "Take your seats, gentlemen, and have a good look at the screen before I begin my presentation."

The officers gathered round the stage and studied the map, passing comments and making mental notes. Then one by one, they took to their seats and buried their heads in Kruger's battle plan. When they were finally all seated, Wingate picked up a pointer and stepped up onto the stage.

"You can see how Kruger has split his army," he said, pointing to two red splotches on the map. "Oddly enough, he has chosen to mass both wings on the two golf courses that straddle Kings Acre Road and put his center bang on Stretton Sugwas. Hands up, those who have *never* played a round at either golf course."

Not one hand was raised.

"Hands up those who have played at least ten matches on either course."

Every hand except Sam Duffell's was raised in affirmation.

"Well, there you are! That's half the battle won. We know the terrain like the back of our hands, while the enemy would probably be bunkered searching for the eighteenth green. However, the initial disposition of Kruger's army on the golf courses or on Stretton Sugwas does not concern us one iota. We are not going to defend the base. We are going to pull out and let them flatten every building on the site, if their gunners are up to the job."

There were gasps of incredulity around the table, some officers even shouting, "Oh no!"

Captain Mike Cadbury even stood up to protest. "But sir, the whole country will be expecting us to make a stand. If we pull out, it will remove the last vestige of hope from every decent citizen who prays that this terrible government of ours will be thrown out before they can complete their aim of creating a totalitarian state. It will make a mockery of all that the SAS stands for."

Wingate held up his hand. "I agree with what you say, Mike, but this is not Thermopylae. The three hundred Spartans who fought there died in vain, and the Persian army conquered Sparta just the same. I do not intend for that to happen to us or our country. No, we are not going to run, we are going to withdraw and fight them on ground of our own choosing. A battlefield that is well known to every man in the Regiment, past or present."

"You mean the Brecon Beacons, don't you, sir?" commented Luke Dryden.

"I do." Wingate pointed to the Brecon Beacons on the map. "I intend to lure the enemy into the hills and bury them there. We will establish ourselves at the western end with vantage points on every hilltop and wooded area along the northern and southern flanks, here, here, and here. Then we will draw them in right up to our guns. The odds will be against us but we will have two very important advantages that will even them out. The first is that they will have no air cover now that the air force and navy have agreed to postpone any hostile action against us. Anyone like to tell me what the other advantage is?"

"They will be unable to deploy their tanks and artillery effectively, whereas we will be able to preposition our armor and guns and dig them in," volunteered Major Tom Bradshaw, the chief gunnery officer.

"Correct, Tom. Kruger's plan calls for a two-hour bombardment by some two hundred guns commencing at 0500. Now I reckon that his stocks of ammo on hand will be severely depleted after such an intense barrage, so I think we can dispense with their artillery as being a threat to us once we are in the Beacons. Finally, once the enemy is engaged, we will launch our own attack from the southern edge of Coed Taf and drive a wedge through to Crychan, effectively splitting their army in two. With this accomplished and with our own guns dominating the heights around, I cannot envisage Kruger's infantry resisting for more than a few hours before they realize the game is up. The one thing I must impress on you all is that we are not in the business of spilling blood indiscriminately. Most of the Paramilitaries are the pawns of the evil politicians in Parliament. If they were MPs and their hangers-on, my orders would be to dispatch every single one of them without mercy. But their pawns are different. They are mostly unemployed youths, ex-soldiers trying to make a living, and layabouts who have been offered the choice of either joining up or having their social security benefits slashed to the bone. They must be given every chance to surrender their weapons and vehicles and then sent packing. If Kruger and any of his senior officers are captured, they must be held for questioning by our own intelligence. That is all, gentlemen, and thank you for your patience. Now I will take questions."

Captain Jim Farnsworth was the first to speak. "Withdrawing from the base is a great idea, sir, but how are we going to evacuate the base and occupy the Beacons without the enemy catching on? It's thirty kilometers to the Beacons. If they catch us in retreat, their guns will still be in range and they will massacre us just as easily as they would if we had stayed put. We could evacuate at night but that would leave an uninhabited base with kilometers of empty fields and roads behind it. They would assume that we had thrown in the towel and dispersed into the countryside. Kruger would surely claim that as a victory."

"Good question, Jim," replied Wingate. "We most certainly will evacuate the base the night before, but we will make our disappearance seem like a disorderly retreat. As we fall back, we will leave in our wake all the paraphernalia of a retreating army: tanks, artillery, trucks, Pinkies, anything unwanted on wheels that can be made to appear broken down and abandoned. We have lots of damaged or unserviceable vehicles on-site that we can use for the purpose, and I want the team to scour the neighborhood and beg, borrow, or steal more from friendly army camps and ministry of defense dumps. While you are at it, collect plenty of timers. We can use them to set off explosives in some of the vehicles and fool the enemy still further. Also we will set mines and booby traps that will delay them give us valuable time to prepare our new positions."

"What about reconnaissance?" asked Major Bradman. "I know we've spooked their satellite but they will surely put spy planes over to see what we're up to before they attack."

"I've thought of that, Don. Two things. Our RAF friends at Shobdon have agreed to provide air cover for the period, November 5 to November 13. Any hostile aircraft or drone flying within forty kilometers radius radius of our base will be shot down, no questions asked. On the off chance that one will get through, I want an experienced AA crew armed with Stingers set up in the Beacons prior to our evacuation."

"But what if Kruger decides he's done enough, destroyed our base, and driven us out? Where does that leave us?" asked Sam Duffell. "We can't set up a new base in the Beacons, it just isn't practical."

"No, I agree the Beacons aren't suitable, but Eastnor Camp is. It's only twelve kilometers away, and the OC has indicated he will be willing to surrender it to us if need be. Anyway, the problem won't arise. Apollo states that Kruger has strict instructions to eliminate us as a fighting unit altogether or face the sack. He's also been offered a bonus of a million pounds if he's successful, and I don't think he's the sort of man who would turn down that kind of money."

It fell to Major O'Connor to ask the final question: "Assuming we destroy the Pinkoes and eliminate them as a fighting force, what do we do next? March on London?"

"No, Norman, that would be premature. Union Jack is set for November 12. We will move into Eastnor Camp and make our preparations there. This little difficulty with Kruger will complicate things somewhat, but if we succeed in defeating Section Three, the capture of their arms and equipment will more than compensate. Any more questions?"

No one answered, and Wingate returned to the table and picked up his laptop and papers. "Right, gentlemen," he said. "We have a lot of work to do in the next two weeks, most of which I will leave in your good hands. Oh, just a couple of things before I go. Army Air Corps at Pershore have officially joined our movement. Their OC has told me that the twenty Apache gunships commandeered by Kruger will support our action in the Beacons if need be. They will arrive in theatre within twenty minutes of our signal for their help. Also, Colonel Stansforth of the Ghurkha Rifles has offered his help. The regiment will be setting up camp in the Beacons within the next two weeks." He looked around at the excited officers. "I thought that would bring a sparkle to your eyes," he smiled. "Let's hope we won't need the Apaches. The less blood shed in the Beacons, the better for all concerned."

Chapter 33

T he huge anteroom adjoining the hall at the home office had been set up for a grand reception to witness the final destruction of the hated SAS and their base in Credenhill. Moses Mandella had seized on the chance to compensate for the many cock-ups the home office had been responsible for in the past year, and he had spared no expense in order to impress upon his guests the military prowess of Section Three and the fighting spirit they were about to show as they attacked the enemy. Although it was barely four in the morning, all the notables he had invited were there, except for the environmental secretary, who had never been known to show his face anywhere before one in the afternoon. There was a good feeling in the room. The guests, all male, had been plied with ample food and liquor, served by skimpily clad waitresses since ten in the evening, and their expectations were high. Mandella had even installed six gaming tables to keep them occupied plus two TV screens placed in opposite corners, each one tuned in to a pornography channel. On the main wall hung a huge panel TV, while a door at one end bearing a "Private" sign opened into a small room that contained a table and six chairs plus four sofas, each piled up with pillows. On the table was an array of silver platters bearing individual portions of powder drugs, tablets, or weed, plus all the complementary equipment required for the preparation of a pleasurable journey to another world.

Most of the cabinet were there, including the PM, Alastair Campbell, and Dudley Coward, the defense secretary. Also present was the chief of the general staff, four members of the BBC Trust, Rupert Murdoch and the editors of the *Guardian* and *Times*, the current president of the EU, the American ambassador and his son, Robert Crippen of Section One, Harold Shipman of Section Two, and Hans Hoffman of Section Four. The rest were junior ministers and their deputies, most of whom Mandella had never seen before.

His watch showed 4:35 AM. *Time to get the herd away from the troughs,* he thought, as he looked with disgust at the shenanigans going on. Supposedly respectable public figures behaving as if they were at a bisexual stag party: fondling the waitresses, singing dirty songs, some even stripping down to their underwear. He hadn't had a drink or a bite to eat since lunch the previous day, but he was past caring. He was totally immersed in the show that was coming up, utterly stressed out and so nervous that he jumped every time a champagne cork popped or one of the bloody fools threw a glass into the open fireplace. It was now or never. Success and he would make Campbell eat every hurtful word he had thrown at him. Failure and he was finished in politics, and with Arabella too.

"Come on, fellas!" he shouted. "Make your way into the conference room right now, or you'll miss the show of your lives. You can bring your drinks in with you, but no food, if you don't mind."

He stood by the door as the guests made their way in, and suddenly he remembered the powder room. The door was closed, and when he opened it, the cloud of pungent smoke that greeted him set his head reeling. *Jesus Christ,* he thought, *the bloody fools didn't even have the brains to turn the exhaust fan on.* He put his handkerchief to his face and ventured in. There were four bodies stretched out, one on each sofa. He recognized Hans Hoffman and Harold Shipman and also Rufus, the American ambassador's son. The other one, he had never seen before. He shook Hoffman violently by the shoulder, but his only reward was a grunt and a sickly grin. He was tempted to punch him in the face but thought better of it. It was no use, they were out cold. He was really angry with himself, he should never have made the room public until after the show was over. Cursing himself, he switched on the exhaust fan, closed the door, and made for the stage.

The big screen was showing a war movie that disappeared as he stepped onto the stage and addressed the audience. "Gentlemen," he called out, "you are about to witness a once-in-a-lifetime event you will be telling your children and grandchildren about for years to come. In exactly ten minutes time, this film you are watching will disappear and you will witness the real time destruction of a fascist organization that is threatening to overthrow our democratic government and establish rule by a military junta in our beloved country. At this very moment, the heroic Paramilitaries of Section Three are preparing to assault the Credenhill base of the SAS and eliminate it and all its occupants. In order to afford the best possible presentation of the operation, we have embedded four BBC camera crews with the troops, three on the ground and one in a helicopter slightly to the rear of the gun emplacements. At precisely 5:00 AM, two hundred of pieces of artillery will concentrate their fire for one hour on the main base and destroy it completely. As soon as the barrage is completed, one hundred and eighty Challenger tanks, followed by fifty thousand infantry, will move forward and occupy the base and, if necessary, pursue any survivors until they are either killed or captured. An edited film will be made of the operation and screened universally as a warning to those in the military who dare to challenge the supremacy of Parliament ever again. Let the world take note. This Labor government of ours bows to no man. Those who seek to destroy it will themselves be destroyed."

The speech electrified the audience. Guests who had nodded off awoke as if by magic, and those who were too drunk to pay attention were shaken up or had champagne splashed in their faces. Cheers rang out, and even Alastair Campbell was seen to be clapping his hands. Mandella stood for a full three minutes, soaking up the unaccustomed adulation, and then left the stage and took his seat in the front row, in between Tony Blair and Dudley Coward. He signaled an usher to turn off the lights, and a hush descended on the room. A picture of huge circular clock appeared with the hands pointing to 4:55 and a red minute hand moving with an extra-loud ticking noise as it made its way around the circumference. The motion of the minute hand seemed to mesmerize the audience as they waited with bated breath for it to reach its final destination. Finally, the waiting reached a climax and the clock vanished, making way for a hellish cocktail of death and destruction as the guns opened up, filling the screen with continuous flashes of red, yellow, and white, accompanied by the thunderous sound of shells exiting the guns by the hundred, amplified by the sound system that Mandella had ordered be turned up above normal for maximum effect.

"Bloody hell!" shouted someone. "This easily tops the barrage at Alamein, and it's in color too."

The stunned audience sat motionless for thirty minutes as the guns blazed away, until the hellish noise started to affect those with weak bladders, who hurried off to the toilets at the end of the room. Another half hour and people started to leave their seats and slink off to the buffet room for a refill until they were enticed back by a sudden roar from the audience. The helicopter that was beaming back the pictures from low altitude climbed higher and brought into view the target of the guns some ten kilometers away, which was now ablaze from one end to the other, throwing off cascades of red sparks and columns of black and orange smoke.

The noise, now exacerbated by the shouts of the camera crew, became too much for some of the more faint-hearted, and a dozen or so left their seats and made for the exit. As the helicopter rose higher still, the camera crew became even more excited but suddenly their babble turned into screams of fear. "We've been hit, we've been hit," screamed the presenter, Baghdad Johnny Simpson. "Oh my God, we've been hit and we're going down. We're going to die. Someone please help us, I don't want to die." The picture on the screen started to roll at a dizzying pace amid a surround of terrified screams, until there was the sound of an almighty crash and the picture and sound disappeared altogether.

"Jesus Christ!" shouted one of the BBC bigwigs. "The murderous bastards have shot down our crew and killed Baghdad Johnny. They'll pay for this. For God's sake, somebody switch to either of the ground cameras and get a shot before it's too late to see the wreck."

But the screen remained blank, and the audience remained seated, transfixed by the empty screen and the minute hand of the clock above it, which showed twenty minutes past six. As the minutes ticked by, the silence became unbearable, broken only by some choice words from Rupert Murdoch as he was seen upbraiding the BBC contingent. One of them got to his feet and was about to reply when the minute hand reached the half hour and the screen came alive again. This time, the sound of the artillery was replaced by the roar of diesel engines, and the split screens from the ground cameras showed a pall of black smoke as the tracks of the mighty tanks dug into the lush green fairways of the two golf courses and lurched forward, followed by hundreds of Warrior IFVs, Saxon APCs, Land Rovers, and Bedford transports, all heading toward the gigantic blaze in the distance. The two wings reached the base unopposed, skirted it on either side, and joined up a mile farther on, where they came to an abrupt halt. One of the camera crews managed to force its way to the front line and aimed its camera on the road leading to the Brecon Beacons.

"Holy shit!" Moses shouted, as he saw the burning wreckage of abandoned vehicles and equipment leading into the distance, with explosions throwing up dirt and debris every few meters. "The bastards are on the run. They're beaten, and they are making to hole up in the Beacons, just as I said they would do. What the fuck is Kruger playing at, calling a halt at a time like this? Has he stopped for tea and crumpets or something? Jesus Christ, I don't believe he lost a man unless some awkward sod has shot himself in the foot. Where's my Goddamn mobile?"

He fumbled in his jacket and pulled out his phone, muttering to himself as he tapped in a number. "This is Mandella here. Give me the general and make it snappy!" he shouted.

"What is it, Moses?" came a languid voice. "I'm in conference with my staff, and I really don't have the time for idle chatter. Can I call you back later?"

"No, you fucking well can't. I'm watching your progress on TV, and I want to know why you have called a halt when you could be halfway to the Beacons by now. Once they get in there and establish themselves, it will take days to drive them out, not to mention casualties."

"I fear they have set a trap for us, Moses. Our advanced parties tell me they have nearly reached the Beacons."

"How far is that from where you are now?"

"About thirty kilometers."

"So your tanks could be there in less than an hour. Are you telling me that Wingate can set up a solid, defensive position in that kind of time?"

"We think the old fox has fallen back to positions they have prepared many days ago. My tank commanders say it's the worst country there is for tank warfare. We fear for the worst, and that is what we are discussing at this very moment."

Moses felt his head bursting with anger. "Discussions, my ass. Now you listen to me. The whole world is hooked up to this transmission, and I'm damned if you are going to make my army look like a bunch of patsies. I've told you before, I want the SAS wiped out for good, and if you're too chicken to do it, I'll get your second in command or even your bloody valet to do the job if I have to. Now then, either get the show on the road or get yourself arrested. Do I make myself clear?"

There was a long pause. "Very well, Moses, if you insist, but don't blame me if things don't go as planned."

Moses sat down on his seat and put his mobile in his pocket with trembling fingers. "Fucking asshole," he said to Dudley Coward. "Fifty thousand against five hundred, and he's talking of holding back. He's for the chop when this is over, believe you me."

"Did he give a reason for calling a halt?" asked Coward.

"He said he thinks the SAS are leading him into a trap. That they have prepared for it over the past two or three weeks."

Coward was silent for a few moments, and then he whispered, "You know, Moses, I think the general may be right. Haven't you noticed something unusual going on?"

Mandella looked worried. "No, what? Tell me, for Christ's sake."

"Well, for one thing, I haven't seen one single body lying on the ground or in any of the wrecked trucks and Land Rovers. Secondly, the SAS can zap any BBC program they want to. Why are they letting us film them, if they are taking a beating?"

"They shot down the helicopter, didn't they? They must have known that it was filming them."

"Yes, but the helicopter crew could see for kilometers. They didn't want it filming their dispositions, if they could help it."

Before Mandella could reply, there was a great roar of engines as the tanks revved up and got on the move again and headed flat out for the Beacons. He watched with fascination at the unique spectacle of two armies fighting each other on English soil for the first time in three hundred years, and he forgot all about Coward's warnings as he clenched his fists and urged them on to victory.

Coward kept silent. Far from joining in with Mandella's exhortations, he was secretly hoping the SAS had set a trap and would give Kruger's troops a bloody nose. As secretary of state for the regular army, he hated Section Three. He had no control over it, and it was siphoning off funds that were badly needed for the wars in Iraq and Afghanistan and giving him a hard time as a result.

"Come on, lads, up and at 'em!" shouted a standing Campbell, now as excited as any fan in his local football club. "Kill 'em dead, slaughter them, put the fear of God into them." The rest of the audience followed his example and got to their feet, shouting and screaming encouragement, baying for blood as their counterparts once did in a Roman arena when their favorite gladiator had gained the upper hand and was posturing for the kill.

Two of the camera crews remained stationary as the advance guard swept past them and raced forward, eager to engage with the retreating enemy. The cameras recorded a seemingly endless procession of armored vehicles as they came from behind and roared past, with their exhausts smoking and goggled tank commanders giving the V sign from their open turrets. After ten minutes, the split screen merged into one, without explanation. It transpired later that a Warrior APC had lost a track and had careered into the left-flank camera crew's Land Rover, turning it over and smashing the camera. The last vehicles were at least a mile ahead before the right-flank camera crew started their vehicle and proceeded to follow up and, for some reason, hesitated to make up the leeway on the army ahead.

"For Christ's sake, put your bloody foot down, you lily-livered pansies!" shouted Rupert Murdoch. "What are you frightened of? A crew of mine would be up front with the first wave, not dogging behind sniffing their asses."

"Shut your bloody mouth, Murdoch," screamed one of the BBC trustees. "Can't you see they've got engine trouble or a flat tire or something?"

"Rubbish, they're shit-scared," came the reply. "You bribed Kruger to give you sole TV rights because you knew my crews would show up your nancy boys for the cowardly custards they really are."

"You lying, bastard ..." There was pandemonium as two BBC trustees tore down the aisle and made for the burly TV mogul, but they stopped dead in their tracks as a thunderous rumble of gunfire filled the room and the picture on the screen brought in the foothills of the Brecon Beacons, bathed in fire and smoke. An hour went by, and the captivated audience sat on the edge of their chairs, watching anxiously, praying that their champions were gaining the upper hand and blasting the enemy out of their foxholes. Another hour went by, and those who could bear the tension no longer rushed for the exit and made for the bar. Mandella and all those in the front row except Tony Blair held grimly to their seats, sweating profusely, hypnotized by the events unfolding before them.

"Christ, they're taking a hell of a long time to flush them out," croaked Alastair Campbell. "There must be hundreds of poor buggers lying there dead or wounded. How much longer are the bastards going to hold out? I can't stand the bloody tension much longer, I can tell you; I've pissed myself twice already."

"Good God, Alastair, this is the SAS they've taken on!" shouted Coward. "It could go on for days, even weeks. They will fight to the last man, I can promise you that," he added proudly.

"Hang on a minute, something's happening down by those woods," whispered Mandella. "I can see people moving around; I think they're coming this way."

His words were repeated by the TV presenter. "Hello, I think something is happening right now. There are people and vehicles coming out of the woods, dozens of them, no, hundreds of them. They are running this way, straight toward us. I can't tell exactly who they are; I think they're SAS. Wait a minute while I pick up my glasses. Yes, they are SAS but they don't appear to be carrying any weapons. They are running like mad. Wait a minute, I don't think they are SAS after all. They are wearing pink helmets. Oh my God, they are Section Three fighters. Now there are thousands of them, running as if their lives depend on it. They are retreating. They have lost the battle and are in full flight, with the SAS in pursuit. Holy mother of God, the SAS! I'm sorry but we shall have to leave now, as we've been ordered to report back. We will leave the camera running and hope to rejoin you later on. Signing off from Credenhill, Trevor MacDonald, *BBC News Extra.*"

The stunned audience watched in horror as the trickle of fleeing Paramilitaries became a flood, a panoramic jumble of men and machines seeking to escape the cauldron of death they had encountered in the beautiful Brecon Beacons. For what seemed an eternity, the wave of fleeing soldiers parted as it came upon the TV Land Rover until at last three black soldiers, all minus their pink helmets and shirts, paused for breath near it. One of them crawled on the hood to look through the windshield and rolled his eyes as his face filled the screen. Another grunted something and they all piled into the vehicle, throwing out the camera to make more room for themselves.

All was silence as the audience stared at the blank screen, until it was broken by the raucous voice of the *Times* editor: "Looks like you fouled up again, Moses. Who's going to pull you out of the mire this time?"

Mandella kept his seat as the audience passed in front of him on the way to the exit. Not one sympathetic glance was cast in his direction. The members of the cabinet filed past one by one, without a word, until he found himself all alone in the smoke-filled room. He looked mournfully at the screen. It was as blank and empty of promise as he knew his own future would be. Gone were his dreams of an earldom and a grand pile in rural England. His marriage was destined for the rocks, and his drug empire would be busted by the SAS just as surely as they had sunk his ship, the MV *Maracaibo*, when they came calling in what seemed ages ago. It was back to Jamaica, the country of his birth. Perhaps he would find peace and happiness there among his own happy-go-lucky kind, unspoiled by the white trash who had sullied his life: Campbell and Blair, Mandelson and Murdoch, et al. He felt in his pocket for his mobile and put it to his mouth. *Oh what the hell,* he thought as he put it away again, *the arrogant Boer bastard might have been captured or even killed, for that matter. Serves him right, he should never have messed with the SAS in the first place.*

But what if he should stand and fight, just as the SAS had? He was still in control of Homeland Security and Section Three Paramilitaries. The SAS were bound to have suffered casualties themselves, and they were without a base to which they could return and reorganize themselves. It would be a year at least before they were in a position to lead an insurrection, and by that time, Section Three would be rearmed and provided with the Apaches that could have made the difference between victory and defeat. Only this time, he would make sure they had not a paltry twenty but at least one hundred of the deadly machines. Yes, by God, he would not give up the fight. He would call a meeting of the full cabinet and lay the blame for the fiasco at Campbell's door. Everyone in Britain knew about his reluctance to attack without the gunships. The *Mail* and *Express* had been taunting him for months about it. Bloody hell, this could mean the end of the road for Campbell. The autocratic bastard was disliked by every member of the cabinet, and if he could get Tony straightened out, he could get him to fire him and let him take over as chief of staff. Yes, that's what he would do. Arabella would be proud of him. And not only would he get to ensure his earldom, he would make sure his two sons got a title each, as well.

He went over to the private room, walked in, and closed the door behind him. The four sofas were still occupied by prostrate bodies, and he turned off the fan and drew a chair up to the table. He picked up a card and expertly cut out two lines of heroin and trimmed them at each end. His hand trembled slightly as he picked up the inhaler and snorted first one and then, after a slight hesitation, the other line. It was the first time in his life that Britain's premier drug dealer had succumbed to the evil product he trafficked but he seemed well pleased with the effect and sat back in the chair, arms folded, eyes closed, and a wistful smile on his pudgy face.

Chapter 34

It was a hastily called cabinet meeting the day after the rout of Kruger's Paramilitaries. Alastair Campbell had spent the rest of the night watching TV repeats of the disaster in the Brecon Beacons, as well as reports from around the world that had turned the BBC film version into a blockbuster movie. He was mortified by the derision aimed at the government from far and wide, and from friend and foe alike; at the ineptitude of the Homeland Security forces and the crazy decision to take on the famed SAS. Even more galling were the plaudits heaped upon the SAS for their incredible victory by the *Express* and *Daily Mail*. "Greater than Thermopylae" ran one headline, and "Wingate's five hundred Spartans rout one hundred thousand Section Three rabble" ran another. Instead of a rebellious army clique bent on toppling a democratically elected government, the Regiment was now elevated to the status of an army of liberation. The name "Wingate" was on the lips of every person in the land, even on BBC announcers who were forced by public outrage to glorify the victory, although in the most grudging terms. Campbell's first instincts were to blame Moses Mandella for the fiasco, rub his nose in the dirt, hang him out to dry. But it was a high-risk strategy. It was he who had pressured Moses into attacking the SAS in the first place, and the man had witnesses to prove it. Maybe if he had waited until Kruger had gotten his Apaches, the outcome might have been entirely different.

Only six people had been invited to the meeting: Ed Fowler, the foreign secretary; Jack Wheatly, the leader of the house; Peter Plum, the Northern Ireland secretary; Dudley Coward; Sir Launcelot Bullington-Barraclough, Chief of the Gemeral Staff; David Cameron, the Conservative party leader; and Nick Klagg, the Lib-Dem leader. The last two had been smuggled in via the back entrance.

Campbell was the first to speak. "The way I see it, the only way to resolve the predicament we're in is to call a general election and let the electorate choose who is running the country, Parliament or Moses Mandella."

There was a stunned silence as the dreaded words sunk in. "Good grief, Alastair," protested Cameron, "you can't be serious. Why, we have backed you to the hilt over Iraq, Afghanistan, and action against the SAS. You just can't pull the plug on us. The way the grass roots are acting at the moment, the only members who would get re-elected are Freedom First, UKIP, BNP, the bloody DUP, and God knows how many Independents. I can't go back to my MPs and tell them that, they would crucify me."

David Cameron was beside himself with anxiety. He knew that if he was chucked out of Parliament, his ignoble, brief career as a politician was over. The same thoughts were passing through Nick Klagg's mind. He was in his sixties. What would he do if people like Jack Churchill and his Freedom First party grabbed power and scrapped all MP pensions, as he was threatening to do? He would be on his uppers. He'd never had a real job in his life and would probably starve to death.

Campbell looked at Cameron in disgust. Sometimes, he thought it would be worth the risk just to get rid of the two-faced, double-dealing fancy Dan, or "Meetoo," as he liked to call him.

"All right then, so you think it's a bad idea. Let's be having your opinion on the subject, Meetoo."

Cameron licked his lips and looked at Klagg for support. Campbell was a devious bastard, as crafty as they came. He had never been able to fathom the depth of his political nous. He knew everything about everybody who was anybody. Every time that Blair made a fool of him in Parliament, he knew instinctively that it was Campbell—his master—who had put the damaging words in his mouth. He looked down at the notes his colleague, Oliver (Two Brains) Benson, had prepared for him.

"Well, something has to be done," he said carefully, "and it's all the fault of your government. Giving all that power to Mandella was asking for trouble. The man was already a ruthless drug baron; did you expect him to play second fiddle to anyone when he was given carte blanche to run the home office? His is a government within a government, accountable to no one, not even you, Alastair, if you don't mind me saying."

"I bloody well do mind you saying," swore Campbell. "I asked you to give me constructive advice, not a load of party political hogwash. We're all in this together, for Christ's sake; the enemy's at the gate, and all you can do is babble. As for Mandella, I never heard you complain when he came asking for exceptional powers to deal with terrorism. You voted for every measure and never raised one single objection. How about you, Nick? Surely you can do better than Meetoo, can't you?"

Klagg nodded sagely, as befitted his advanced years. "You won't like it, Alastair, but I'm going to say it anyway. As Mee—I mean David says, the problem is Mandella. His authoritarian treatment of the decent sections of our society has done untold damage to our national spirit of fair play and the rule of just laws. He has turned class against class and pitted race against race, until we have all become brutalized and self-seeking, willing to shop our neighbors and friends in a vain attempt to enjoy a quiet life. We have averted our eyes as the liberties of others have been flouted and when they have been arrested, sent to detention camps, or in some cases, disposed of. How could a great nation like ours have allowed one man to subdue and subjugate our ancient freedoms to such an extent that we are afraid to speak out for fear of punishment without trial? How is it possible that Mandella can achieve in less than two years what it took Hitler five years to accomplish in Germany? And we in Parliament are the guiltiest party of all. We created this Frankenstein monster and allowed him to roam free."

"Nice speech, Nick, just like most others you make in Parliament. But like everything that's said in that bloody awful talking shop, it doesn't amount to a hill of beans. Now, for God's sake, make a suggestion; that's what I asked you here for."

"Very well, if that's what you want, I'll say it. We have got to destroy our Frankenstein monster, but how we do that, I haven't a clue."

"Thank you, Nick," Campbell said sarcastically, "that's the first time I've heard a fucking MP say something positive in a long time. How about it, Meetoo, can Two Brains improve on that?"

Cameron looked at his notes self-consciously. "I agree with Nick, but how on earth can we get rid of the man? He controls everything from the lord chief justice down to the lowliest bobby on the beat. Why, only last week a friend of mine was talking in the club and opined that he thought the most beautiful women were Asian, and the ugliest were blacks. The moment he left the club, four leatherjackets were there waiting for him, and we haven't seen him since. It was the black barman, you see."

Campbell laughed. "And what's your opinion, Meetoo? Who are the most beautiful, chinks or niggers?"

Cameron scowled at Campbell's crudity. "It's not a fair question. We are all equal in the eyes of God."

"Like rich and poor, healthy and crippled. Try telling that to some of the ex-miners in my working-man's club."

"It's a racist question," Cameron replied evasively. "It's an affront to black women."

"What if the black woman had been a white woman, would that have been racist too? Would they have carted your mate away to the pokey if he'd said that? Would the white barman have canted on him?"

"How the devil should I know? It's all semantics, whichever way you look at it."

"No, it isn't. If it's an affront to black women, it's the same to white women. Do you actually think white women are uglier than black women, Meetoo?"

"Of course not, as I keep telling you, we are all equal in the eyes of God."

Campbell looked pityingly at the leader of the opposition. If the answer to his question wasn't written down for him, he would never get a straight answer from Cameron in a month of Sundays. How he despised the man. He was all things to all men: a toff in top hat and tails in Tory club-land, a doting father, a champion of the middle classes, and a Wellington-booted, open-collared man of the soil to the few members of the working class he happened to meet when he ventured out of London. He never seemed to miss an opportunity to appear on TV with members of the ethnic minorities, mainly black Londoners, and profess his gratitude for their contributions to our multicultural society, yet not one member of his immediate following was black, and only one black man on his famous A list made it to Parliament. There was hardly a bandwagon rolling that he would not jump on and just as quickly jump off, if the polls showed he was backing the wrong horse. His front bench was a joke, crammed as it was with bone-headed old Etonians, none of whom had ever held a worthwhile job in real life. They were a bunch of not very bright public schoolboys, led by a head boy who would tolerate no dissent from any of them but was their equal when it came to asinine behavior and disdain for parliamentary ethics and the welfare of the nation as a whole. Nothing illustrated their juvenility more than their first inquiry at "Ask a Question" time. It did not concern Iraq, Afghanistan, Europe, or the economy, not even inflation. It was, "When in heaven's name are Parliament's bombed-out bars and restaurants going to be available to us once more?"

Again, they were forever presenting their green credentials by cycling to Parliament five abreast, pretending that the five limos following behind at a discreet distance carrying their belongings did not belong to them. But what he hated most about Cameron was his headline-grabbing tirades against legislation introduced by New Labor, which fizzled out when it came to the crunch. On any motion that seemed likely to bring down the government, he would either abstain or make sure enough of his troops were abroad on urgent business to make an opposition victory impossible. The man was an impostor, similar in many ways to Tony, desperately holding onto power by any devious means possible in the knowledge that his head was on the block if he failed.

He turned to Bullington-Barraclough in disgust. "Klagg thinks we should take Moses out, Lance. Your boys are the only ones who can do that. What's your opinion?"

Barraclough drummed his fingers on the table and cleared his throat. "Sorry, Alastair, but you're asking the impossible, old boy. The army can only deploy two formations at the present moment, the Household Division and the Home Division. As you know, the Household Division is preparing to move down to Leeds Castle to protect the G8 meeting, and the Home Division is on standby for Northern Ireland."

"I know that," Campbell said testily. "I asked you if the army could take on and destroy Homeland Security. Give me an answer, yes or no?"

Barraclough cleared his throat again. "Do you mean Section Three as well as all the others?" he asked.

"Of course I bloody well do, Section Three is part of Homeland Security, isn't it?"

"Yes, yes, of course it is, old boy. Well, let me see, those blighters received a jolly good hiding from the SAS. Lost half their armor, so I'm told. I wouldn't be surprised if they're all back in barracks, licking their wounds, right now. By gad, that was a truly remarkable victory by the SAS, as much a part of our army as Section Three is of Homeland Security, you know."

"You don't say," sneered Campbell. "Well, maybe you had better order your bloody Colonel Wingate to stop blowing up our newspapers then. And while you're at it, tell him to stop fucking up TV transmissions, I'm sick and tired of my missus playing tapes of *Coronation Street* and all that crap over and over again."

"You know I don't condone his behavior, Alastair. If I could catch him, I'd have him court-martialled and shot. I was talking about the Regiment as an elite part of the army. He doesn't own it, you know."

"No, and you don't own the Household Division either. I asked you a simple question, are you prepared to take on Homeland Security or do I have to go down the line and ask the division's OC for an answer?"

"No, no, Alastair, no need for that," spluttered Barraclough. "Let me see, Section Three isn't finished as a fighting force by any means but it will take them some time to regroup and rearm themselves. Most of their reserves are scattered around the country supporting Section One and Section Four, keeping the peace, as they call it, and they will have the devil of a job of finding new recruits after the beating they took in the Beacons. Yes, I believe we could take them on and squash them. The Household Division could clean up the south and the Home Division the north."

"No, the Home Division stays where it is."

"But Alastair, they are the only other recognized fighting force left in the country. We can't have them standing idly by while we are heavily engaged in the south."

"You'll have to do without them. The division is on standby for trouble in the north now that Section Three is out of action. You've got bases scattered all over the country; check them out and stir things up. There's no reason at all why you cannot form a new division. Get the navy and air force to help you out. The navy's got the marines, and the air force has got a regiment, if I'm not mistaken."

"I don't think the navy will be able to help us much, old boy. After all that trouble over the Iranian hostages, Admiral Breakwater is not in the mood to contemplate any action he can avoid. As for Air Chief Marshall Plantagenet, he tells me that all flying crews have vowed to resign their commissions if they are ordered to fire on any SAS targets."

"Bastards!" shouted Campbell. "You military types give me the creeps. We spent billions giving the air force the Eurofighter, yet not one of them has fired a shot in anger. Why in God's name aren't they helping out in Iraq? I swear to God you're all in cahoots with this scam. Anything for the quiet life, big parades, and bloody oompah bands. They're screaming out for reinforcements in Iraq, and that's where the lot of you would be if I had my way. You've had it too soft for too long. You all want a good kick up the ass and half-rations for six months, if you ask me."

Dudley Coward was quick to break in. "There are always the twenty Apache gunships that are being prepared for Section Three, Alastair. They haven't been delivered yet, so they still belong to the army, don't they, Launcelot? Wingate doesn't have any either, so they would be a tremendous advantage to us."

The CGS smiled expansively. "Yes, of course, the Apaches. I had them in the back of my mind all the time. They would come in useful, wouldn't they? I will have to check with Logistics. Depending on what they tell me, I will come back to you with a definite answer to your question, Alastair."

"Bloody hell, I can't believe what I'm hearing. Now you listen to me, Barraclough, and this applies to every person in this room. It's now an open secret that Wingate has promised to hang every member of the cabinet who voted for the invasion of Iraq. His list includes every person in this room, so if you don't fancy dangling from a rope in the middle of Trafalgar Square, you had better listen up now or forever hold your peace."

He paused for a moment to let the gasps of horror subside. "Let me tell you something else. I have studied this man's life and times, and believe me, when he orders something, he carries on through hell and high water. He is a mean, ruthless, gung-ho bastard, and the only people he hates worse than us politicians is military people who cravenly follow our orders. That means the only way we can survive is to squash him before he's in a position to do the same to us. We know he's preparing for a coup right now; what we don't know is how long it will take him to build up a big enough force to achieve it. We must beat him to the punch, and that means getting the Household Division into shape and out of its bloody barracks. That's Barraclough's problem. Our problem is to get rid of Mandella, and quick. The first thing we do is get a motion through Parliament condemning the man and all his works and authorizing Barraclough to use any means necessary to wind up Sections Two, Three, Four, and Five. Mandella and his lieutenants are to be thrown in jail and held without trial until we decide what to do about them. By this means, we can gain a good deal of favor with the populace and promise them immediate elections for a new Parliament. This will blunt Wingate's appeal. It is my opinion that as anti-government as the voters may be at the moment, when they have the opportunity to give vent to their feelings, they will opt for democratic government rather than a military junta. Now, an election will take at least two months to organize, so we must take out Wingate well before that time. How long will it take for you to get your troops ready for battle,

Barraclough? Don't forget, you'll be one of the first climbing the scaffold steps if you don't get it right."

Barraclough turned pale. *Lord,* he thought, *what an uncouth fellow Campbell is, not a bit like Tony. If only he was still in charge, he would never have been so blunt or even mention the horrible hangman.*

He looked at his companions. They all looked a trifle under the weather, just as he did. "Well, let's see," he said carefully. "First we have to get the division mobilized around Leeds Castle for the G8 summit. Since its task is merely to prevent any hostiles from assembling within a two-kilometer radius of the castle, the troops will be lightly armed with rifles, stun grenades, and possibly tear gas RPGs. That means the division will have to return to barracks after the dignitaries have left on November 14, reassemble, and then form up with their armor, artillery, and heavy offensive weaponry. A week later they will surround Wingate's new base, demand his surrender, and destroy it if the answer is no. Let me see." He counted his fingers one by one, muttered something in annoyance, and started all over. Finally, he clapped his hands and pronounced his verdict. "Two weeks from today, give or take a day either way. Of course, if the weather is very bad, we may have to adjust for it."

Campbell made a mental calculation and frowned. "I make that November 18. Are you sure you can't do better than that, say November 14?"

"No, Alastair, I don't think you understand what a time-consuming performance it is deploying a force of twenty thousand troops in the field. The communication systems alone would take a week."

"Okay, okay," Campbell said in an exasperated voice. "If that's the best you can do. Just make sure there aren't any more cock-ups, or you're for the high jump, make no mistake about that." He turned to the Leader of the House."Jack, get your goons to round up the zombies. I want a full house a week today and a resounding yes for Mandella's scalp. One hour after that, Tony will go on TV and explain our actions to the nation.

The door had barely closed on the last person to leave before there was a knock and David Cameron entered the room. "Just one thing, Alastair," he said. "Does Tony know about all this?"

"He will when I tell him," Campbell replied curtly.

"Where is Tony?"

"He's in a rest home. Said he needed a break. He'll back in two or three days."

"Can you tell me where he is? I'd like a word with him in private."

"No. If you want a word, tell me and I'll pass it on."

"I said, in private, Alastair. Don't forget, I'm the leader of the opposition. I have the right to be consulted on all matters of national importance."

"I'll still be privy to whatever you say to Tony, so you might as well come out with it now."

Cameron hesitated. "It's about dissolving Parliament," he said finally. "I believe it's your own idea, and I think you're crazy to even contemplate such an extraordinary thing. Why, we will all be wiped out. Jack Churchill and his bloody Freedom First party have won the last eight by-elections in a row with huge majorities and by working underground, at that. What they will accomplish when they are free to campaign openly does not bear thinking about."

"So what do you propose?" Campbell said coldly.

"Get rid of Mandella and leave it at that."

"No, the country is in turmoil thanks to you greedy, devious bastards in Parliament!" shouted Campbell. "While you lot have been free-loading and feathering your own nests, the rest of the world has passed us by. We're flat broke. Our national debt is now greater than at any time since 1918. There are over six million unemployed and another eight million on short time. There isn't a week goes by without a major strike in one of the public services. The hospitals are a national disgrace, with at least a hundred thousand patients dying every year needlessly. Another eighty thousand old-age pensioners are going to die this winter because they can't afford their heating bills. And what do you lot do about it? Why, you hike up your salaries, double your expense accounts, and inflate your gold-plated pensions. You public school infants ought to be ashamed of yourselves. Your greedy, sleazy generation has failed the nation. What we want is a new start and a clean slate, and if that means Jack Churchill and his party, then it can't come soon enough for me. To tell you the truth, I would even prefer Jock Wingate and his men to you and your gang of scumbags. Now piss off, I've got work to do. And don't even think about voting against my proposal if you want to make a *live* appearance at the Notting Hill carnival this coming Saturday."

Chapter 35

S AS Trooper Frank Gearson had no idea why he was dogging the Provo but it was common knowledge in the Regiment that Sean Docherty was a member of the newly re-formed IRA Council, maybe even the second in command. For a man in his position, to venture out into the open and travel down into the Republic alone was highly unusual. Either the man was a complete idiot, or he'd gotten the nod from the police on both sides of the border.

Trailing him was kid stuff. There was no stopping round a bend or double-tracking, nor did Docherty seem to be in any great hurry, keeping to a steady sixty mph most of the time. *Probably listening to some rock and roll or Irish folk music*, Frank mused.

It was just getting dark when his quarry left the main road and entered a side road ten kilometers short of Rosslare. Two kilometers farther on, he turned into a medium-sized industrial estate and parked in front one of the larger warehouses, which identified itself with a faded white sign bearing the name "Kilkenny Auto Spares Ltd."

Tim Talbot, Frank's number two, had parked a good hundred meters past the entrance, and Frank needed to use his NVGs to get a good view of Docherty as he got out of his car. The floodlights lit up the forecourt, and he only got a fleeting glance of the Provo as he walked a couple of meters to his right, opened a door, and went in. They both knew it was too risky to stay where they were, so Frank decided that he would stay on watch while Tim took the car back to the main road and parked on the shoulder, where he would wait for further instructions.

Frank dragged his Bergen and surveillance gear from the car and carted them to the other side of the road. Eventually, he found an opening in the hedge, and he walked up on the inside until he was opposite the entrance gate with a direct view of the main door of the warehouse. He scooped out a squat, made an opening in the hedge, and settled down for a long wait, his NVGs and tape recorder close at hand. Seconds later, he heard Tim come back down the road and watched him turn left and go down the main road to Rosslare.

Lucky bugger, he thought, *he'll have the heater on full blast and the coffee percolator plugged in.* The air was full of the cold Irish damp, which seemed to penetrate even his top-of-the-line thermals. He swore he would swap this lousy climate for the crisp, deep snows of Norway any day.

It was a good hour later when he saw the lights of a car turn in off the main road and drive straight up to the warehouse. Then came another and yet another, until there were eight of them parked on the forecourt; two Mercs, three Range Rovers, two BMWs, and a Renault. There was no attempt at silence as the occupants climbed out. They seemed boisterous and excited, as if they were going to a boxing match or a Gaelic football game. They were jabbering in broad Irish, and try as he might, Frank could understand little of what they were saying to each other.

One by one, they trooped into the warehouse, pushing and shoving each other and laughing as they did so. Every one of them went inside, leaving no one outside to guard the cars.

There seemed to be nothing suspicious or subversive about the gathering, and he began to wonder if he was on some kind of a wild goose chase. He put on his headphones and pointed his probe at the building wall. Although he could hear bouts of laughter and some cheering, he could not pick up any conversation, although it was obvious that some sort of meeting was going on. The building was in range but something behind the brick wall stymied his instrument, and he switched it off in disgust.

He was almost on the point of dozing off when he heard a great cheer go up as the main corrugated steel door of the warehouse shuddered and began to open vertically, powered by an electric motor.

Frank rubbed his eyes as a bus emerged and negotiated its way past the parked cars until it stopped a few meters short of the entrance gate. It looked brand new, an ultra-modern streamlined luxury bus painted in bright orange with lateral green and white stripes. Both sides bore the name "Kilkenny Rovers" in large black lettering, and the notice board above the windshield sported a row of green shamrocks. Frank was more than impressed. In his time, he had travelled around on buses in Rugby Union tours that he thought were pretty comfortable, but they couldn't hold a candle to this beauty. *The chairman of Kilkenny Rovers must be well and truly loaded*, he thought.

He closely studied the people who were standing around. They were all males and mostly young, in their twenties and thirties, he reckoned. Many of them looked a bit seedy, even paunchy, and the air was filled with cigarette or cigar smoke. The more he studied them, the more positive he was they weren't footballers, more like supporters or relatives of team members.

Was it possible that Sean Docherty owned the club? he wondered. If he did, where did he get the money from? Maybe the Lisbon bank heist. The police had never recovered the bulk of the money from that caper.

Speak of the devil! Sean Docherty came barrelling out of the warehouse, shouting orders left, right, and center. Most of the men jumped to it in a sloppy military style, while others climbed into the cars and drove them into the warehouse, one by one. Then they all lined up beside the bus and boarded it, calling out their names as the driver ticked them off on a clipboard and shouted out a seat number.

Jesus Christ, thought Frank as he quickly switched on his listening device, extended the probe, and pressed the record button, *if these buggers are all Provos, our spooks are going work overtime tracking them down.*

Docherty stood by the door until the last man had left the building, and he quickly brought the huge door down with a handset. He hurried to the bus, and Frank picked up his conversation with the driver.

"All present and correct, Fergus?"

"All present and correct, sir. Are we on our way now?"

"Near enough. We've over an hour before the boat sails. Got your seasick pills with you, laddie?" he joked.

Frank switched off his recorder as he watched Docherty climb the steps and take the seat beside the driver. The big bus started up and turned left as it exited the industrial estate. He spoke into his headset and then picked up his gear and stepped out on to the road. He walked about a hundred meters before Tim Talbot came roaring up the road, did a quick U-turn, and welcomed him into the car.

Frank Gearson cupped his hands around the aluminum cup and sipped the hot black coffee gratefully. It was warm in the car, and he felt a great sense of comfort as his face thawed out and his aching limbs gradually reverted to normal. He relaxed and lit up a cigarette before speaking to his number two.

"We've got to put a transponder on the bus, Tim. It won't be easy, as I doubt it will be completely empty while it's on the ferry. Some of them will probably stay on and sleep in their seats 'till they get to London."

"Yeah, it's a shame buses have their own parking section, otherwise I could get right up its ass and make it easy," replied Tim. "It just depends how it's parked, tight up against a bulkhead or spaced out. Kilkenny Rovers, you say. What sort of football do they play, soccer or Gaelic?"

"No idea. Anyway, it doesn't matter a shit. These bastards aren't going to a match. Not with Sean Docherty, they're not."

"You think they've got weapons and PE on board?"

"Not sure. Maybe we'll find out when the customs give it the once-over."

"You're joking, Frank. The Garda won't even climb aboard. Docherty will give them some spiel and a bundle, and they'll be on their way. I wouldn't be surprised if he hasn't got some kind of permit from the Irish government clearing the way. The bastards are the new untouchables of the Irish Republic. You know that."

Frank laughed bitterly. "Too right, mate. Mind you, it will be the same thing when we get to Fishguard. One look at the green and orange colors, and they'll wave them through like they was royalty. That fucking Blair would give them the crown jewels and the keys to Buckingham Palace if he thought it would make them happy. Anyway, there's no need for them to risk anything, there's a dozen places along the way they can pick up weapons, and plenty more when they get to London."

"So it's definitely the smoke they're making for."

"No doubt about it. I heard them talking about it. Trafalgar Square and the big protest march. I'd like to get more info, though, before I call in."

"But why the bug, Frank? There's no chance we are going to lose a big bus like that, even in the dark."

"I'm taking no chances. You remember the White City bomb alert?"

"Sort of. That's the one that didn't go off, isn't it?"

"Correct, and no thanks to our lot either. Charlie Woodward tailed the bombers all the way from Belfast. He was up its ass in traffic in Lambeth when a four-wheeler touched his rear and hooked up on his bumper. It took him half an hour to get loose, and by that time, the bombers were long gone and out of range of his transponder."

Tim looked at his watch. "Christ, I thought my stomach was griping. I don't know about you, but the first thing I'm going to do when we get to Rosslare is to treat myself to two triple hamburgers. How many do you want, you greedy bastard?"

Frank was pleased with the way things were going. The ferry was on time, and the sea was remarkably calm, considering it was November. Now they were back in England, and the transponder was working a treat. As Tim had prophesized, the customs inspections at both ends were a joke. If they had brought a ton of cocaine with them, they would have gotten away with it. It was just as well. In the old days, the hawk-eyes in Fishguard would have found the transponder wedged up behind the fuel tank without even getting their hands dirty. Tim said that when he was fixing the transponder, he had fantasized about wiring it up to a kilo of PE and fitting a reverse signal switch to their own receiver and then pressing it as the bus was going at speed around a bend. Frank had nodded in agreement. If they had carried any PE with them, he would have been sorely tempted himself. There was no love lost between the Regiment and the Provisional IRA.

The only hold-ups were the piss stops, when it seemed that every man on the bus got out to stretch his legs and relieve himself. *They must have downed more than their fair share of porter on the boat over,* Frank thought. Now they were less than sixty kilometers from London.

They were just under a mile behind the bus when Tim put his foot on the brake, pulled into the hard shoulder, and shut off the engine. Frank looked at the transponder display and saw that the bus had turned off the motorway and was heading north along a side road to High Wycombe. As he watched, it carried on for a mile, turned right, and then stopped.

Tim looked at Frank. "We can't stop here. Do we go in or pull over?"

"Go in, then park a hundred meters past. No lights. I'll reconnoiter while you wait."

It was still an hour to daybreak but there was just enough starlight for Frank to find his way down the side of a hedge to the turn-in. He put on his NVGs and found himself staring at a large black notice board with the name "Saint Patrick's Catholic Church" inscribed at the top. A tarmac drive ran uphill, and he could just see the bus at the top, parked close to the church wall. Both sides of the drive were studded with gravestones as far as he could see, and he chuckled with delight. A graveyard was his favorite cover at night. If he got bored with keeping watch, he could move behind one headstone to the next, reading the inscriptions and marvelling at some of the ancient writings. He'd seen plenty of service in Ulster and the Republic and had even picked up a smattering of Gaelic from the epitaphs carved on the stones.

He moved to the left corner and crept up, headstone by headstone, until he had a clear view of a somber churchyard, lit up by an orange halogen light over an arched doorway set beneath a huge stained-glass window. The bus lights were switched off now but he could see a number of cigarettes glowing through the windows and the obscure faces of some of the smokers as they gazed out on the scene outside.

A dozen or more of the party were busy bringing cases and bags from inside the doorway and laying them down by the open luggage compartments built into the side of the coach. They didn't seem in any particular hurry, and now and again, one of them would break off, walk over to one of the headstones, and relieve himself, while another would take a swig from a bottle taken out of one of a dozen or so crates stacked at the side of the doorway.

After half an hour, the last item was loaded up and the luggage doors banged shut and locked. As the loaders climbed back on board, two of them picked up the crates of beer and passed them up to willing hands inside the bus.

The driver started the engine, and as he did so, Sean Docherty and another man came through the doorway and stood outside, engaged in conversation. Frank looked closely at Docherty's companion. He was dressed in a black coat, buttoned up to the throat and long enough to cover whatever he was wearing on his feet. Frank could just about make out his face. It was an old face, heavily wrinkled and drawn. On his head was a floppy black hat that Frank knew identified him as one of the lesser ranks of the Catholic clergy. He put his headset on, switched on the recorder, and gave the probe plenty of air as he pointed it directly at Docherty's head. He was gratified to hear the voices come over loud and clear.

"We're much obliged for your help with handling our supplies, Father. You can be sure the army will be making a sizable contribution to your diocese inside a day or so. Did anyone have any reason to go down into the crypt? You don't seem to have bothered much hiding the stuff down there."

"Don't you worry your head about it, Sean, my son. Nobody around here is a bit interested in our dusty little crypt. It has a bit of a ghostly reputation, and in any case, I keep the only key to it hidden away."

The voice was that of an original son of Erin, as thick as its fabled porter.

Frank heard the priest sigh. "I'm glad to be rid of it, though. I couldn't help but think of Saint Mary's in Castleblaney. That was a terrible thing, Sean. Eight dead and half the church blown away. The good Lord was far away from Ireland on that day, so he was."

Sean Docherty cursed loudly. "It was boys playing at men, Father, and brainless boys at that. None of them was to be trusted with explosives. But that's what we have to put up with these days. Most of the specialists are either dead or retired, and the young volunteers don't want to spend weeks and months learning the business. All they want to do is shoot up the Prots, rob banks, gamble, and snort cocaine. Well, I can assure you they'll have plenty of time to practice shooting tomorrow. Be sure and tune in to the Whitehall service. We are going to show the world that the IRA is still a force to be reckoned with, I can promise you that."

"Tomorrow? I thought the big protest was planned for Monday outside Parliament."

"No, Father. Before that, we are going to wreck the Armistice Day service in Whitehall."

"You scumbags," Frank muttered under his breath.

The priest threw his arms up in the air. "The saints preserve us, Sean. Violence on a Sunday, and at a Christian service to boot. Are you mad? Have you forgotten the anger you caused throughout the world when you bombed Enniskillin on Armistice Day? You will never be forgiven for such sacrilege. The church will have to excommunicate any of you taking part, mark my words. Is that what you want with all those guns and bombs, then?"

Docherty laughed and put his hand over his heart. "Not at all, holy Father. Those are for Parliament on Monday. On Sunday, we are going to prevent the British army from honoring soldiers who have killed thousands of Irishmen in their colonial wars on humanity. This is a heaven-sent opportunity for us. We have agreed with the leaders of the G8 protest that if we give them armed protection on Monday, they will lead fifty thousand marchers down Whitehall and disperse all those gathered around the Cenotaph. We have been assured by the British Northern Ireland office that there will be no military units on parade, and neither will there be a police presence. If there is any fighting, it will be nothing more than fisticuffs and a bit of wrestling. The spectators will be swept away in minutes, and then we will camp in Whitehall overnight until we gather in Trafalgar Square for the march on Parliament."

You lying Fenian bastard, thought Frank. *Is that what you're going to tell another priest at confession?* The hypocrisy of Irish Catholics never ceased to disgust him.

The expression on the priest's face told Frank that he had heard enough. Without another word, he crossed himself, gathered up his coat, and hurried into the doorway and out of sight, leaving Docherty bemused and out of sorts.

Frank had also heard enough. He retraced his steps to the bottom of the drive, and as he did so, he could not resist a look at a military-looking headstone that seemed somehow to stand out from the others, even though it was far more weathered and neglected. The inscription read:

IN MEMORY OF A FINE IRISH BOY
KILLED IN ACTION FLANDERS 1916

He shook his head at the wonder of it all and hurried on to the road and down toward the car, mulling over the message he would send to the OC and the instructions he would get in return.

Chapter 36

Luke Dryden was watching the gathering in Whitehall on his portable TV when his phone rang. "Dryden," he said.

"Luke, we're in big trouble; how long will it take you to get up to Whitehall?"

It was the boss himself, Colonel Wingate. Luke had never heard him sound so agitated.

"How far to Whitehall, Ginger?" he asked his driver.

"About five kilometers," came the reply.

"How long?"

"On a Sunday? Ten minutes or so, I reckon."

Luke spoke into the phone. "Ten minutes, sir. Is there a problem?"

"It's a lot more than that. You've heard about the bloody stupid G8 summit and the demonstration there yesterday?"

"Yes, on Al Jazeera. Bit of a damp squib, wasn't it?"

"It appears that way. Frank Gearson is with the mob and he says the fireworks start today."

"Today? I thought it was Monday."

"No, it's today. Frank has got it from the horse's mouth. It's solid."

"Who's the horse?"

"An old friend of yours, Sean Docherty."

"Docherty? I thought he was breaking rocks."

Luke was surprised. It was over eight years since he put a bullet in Docherty's shoulder when his team had trapped him planting a bomb on the roof of the Cookstown police station. He had cursed himself ever since for failing to put the bullet in the murderous Provo's heart.

Colonel Wingate swore. "He was, but he's out now. The bastard and his Belfast gang are going to infiltrate the mob. Frank says there's at least sixty of them, all armed with AKs and explosives. They are going to mass in Trafalgar Square and mix with the mob as they charge down Whitehall"

Luke whistled. "Sixty! Christ, that many? What's their target?"

"The remembrance service at the Cenotaph. They intend to wreck it."

"How can they do that? The Household Division will stop them, surely."

"The division has been ordered to remain at Leeds Castle."

"What! All of them?"

"Yes. Guards, gunners, tankers, cavalry, bandsmen, the lot."

Luke was shocked. "Jesus Christ, what the hell's going on? Can't the RAF or navy provide the honor guard?"

"No. I've talked to the chiefs, and they're under orders from the ministry of defense not to provide one under any circumstances. The home office has also banned the ceremony."

"But it's still going ahead?"

"What do you think? The veterans are mad as hell. There'll be more there now than there were last year, by the sound of it."

"What about the police?"

"No one knows. Frank reckons they'll pull out when the trouble starts. It's a setup, of course."

"The cowardly bastards. The lousy bunch of shitheads."

Wingate sensed Luke's agitation and softened his voice. "Will the General be there this year, Luke?"

"I'm sure he will. If the Legion is, there's no doubt about it." Luke had a mental picture of his grandfather with his red beret and silver-topped cane leading the detachment of ex-Paras past the Cenotaph.

"Let's hope he doesn't get involved, Luke. Now then, I want you to get up to Whitehall immediately and form a guard around the

Cenotaph. If the mob attacks it, protect it at all costs. Any threatening action, shoot low or above the head. Any hostile action with guns, shoot to kill. As a last resort, use grenades. I'll take full responsibility for your actions whatever you decide. They are not to get near the Cenotaph or damage it in any way. Is that clear?"

"Yes, sir. How many men can you let me have?"

"Your team plus Frank and his number two, Tim Talbot. I'll signal them to join up with you at the Cenotaph."

Luke was dumbfounded. "Twelve of us, sir? Why, from what I heard the mob is at least sixty thousand strong. They'll bury us."

"I'm sorry, Luke, there isn't anyone else. Every man I've got is committed to Union Jack. The service starts in half an hour, and your team is the only one anywhere near Whitehall. I'll try and scramble a chopper for you, but I can't guarantee it. I know this will blow your cover but it can't be avoided. It's important you keep in contact with me at all times. Got that, Luke?"

"Yes, sir, understood." Luke was bursting to ask a hundred questions but he could only think of one.

"Do we return to this OP when it's over?"

"Of course. Any hitch, report directly to me. If I don't hear from you by 1800, I'll dispatch a relief team to your position. And Luke?"

"Yes, sir?"

"Give my regards to the General if you see him."

"I certainly will, sir."

Luke closed his cell phone and shook his head vigorously. Something was going on, he was sure of it. The colonel was trying too hard to make it sound matter of fact. Blowing the cover of twelve operatives? It was unheard of, sacrilegious. And no chopper? Normally old Ironsides would likely have gone and hijacked one from somewhere personally rather than send out a team ill-equipped for a job. But then again, that was life in the Regiment, and he was used to it. When the shit hit the fan, there was only one thing they were expected to do and do it quick—get stuck in.

"What was that all about?" asked Corporal Ginger Hammond. "Is there a change of plan then?"

"Yes, and you won't like it when I tell you," Luke replied.

Neither would the others, he thought as he pondered the gravity of the new situation. The team had been planning its specific role in operation Union Jack for weeks, and a lot of sweat had gone into it. Every man knew exactly what he had to do, and every man was confident they could pull it off. This was their last dummy run before the big bang: the sortie into London in the big grey furniture van, the search for a parking spot in Bayswater, and then surveillance of the locality, traffic, and inhabitants. This was followed by a reconnaissance by each individual up to Marble Arch, across to Portland Place, and then more surveillance, this time on the target: BBC Broadcasting House in Portland Square. The run was the last piece of the jigsaw, the piece that could determine the difference between the success or failure of their operation and perhaps even that of Union Jack itself.

Yet, here he was, sitting in the front seat of one of the two Pinkies concealed inside the van, both of them crammed full of armaments and trained soldiers who knew how to use them with deadly effect. He rubbed his chin. Perhaps it wouldn't be so bad after all. The Provos would most likely be armed with grenades, and maybe even a couple of heavy machine guns and RPGs besides their AKs. His troop could trump that. The unknown factor was the tactics the Provos would use as the mob charged down Whitehall. Would they be in the lead and easy meat for the twin 50mm machine guns on the Pinkies, or would they mingle with the mob and make it difficult to identify them from the anarchists? If they had made a deal with the police, they would probably be confident and dress up in their black uniforms for the benefit of the TV cameras. But what if they had armed some of the mob as well? That would make it very difficult.

"The boss has given us another task, Ginger. Do you know the way to Whitehall?"

"Sure do, I used to live in Lambeth."

"Good man, you'll be lead Pinkie." Luke spoke into his headset. "Listen up, everybody, change of plan. We're going to Whitehall with Ginger leading. Exit the van with all equipment, and last man out, secure the doors. I'll explain the situation to you on the way."

Chapter 37

D enied a bloody victory over the G8 summit meeting at Leeds
Castle in Kent by the presence of soldiers of the Household
Division, the anti-globalization protesters laid waste to a
large swathe of rural England as they marched north into London,
their ranks bolstered by thousands of late arrivals from abroad,
together with local recruits picked up along the way. Unopposed by
a frightened police force, they camped out in London's parks and
public squares and along the Thames Embankment, staking out their
next objective, which, they let it be known, would be the Houses of
Parliament on Monday, November 12.

The protest had been hijacked by the hard men who loathed and
despised everything that Britain stood for and who would stop at
nothing to do her harm. It was composed of people of every race,
color, and creed, men and women, even children in arms. Many of
them wore olive drabs or faded jeans and bomber jackets; others
wore hooded anoraks covering T-shirts emblazoned with obscene
words and portraits of Carl Marx, Fidel Castro, Malcolm X, Pol Pot,
and Che Guevara. They showed none of the good-natured tolerance
exhibited by their forebears in the sixties and seventies. Rather, their
faces were suffused with anger and a hatred of the civilization they
were born into. And their intolerance was broadcast by the weapons
they carried. Not baseball bats and bricks and bottles alone but lethal
small arms, Molotov cocktails, AK47 rifles, bombs, knives, pangas,
and Mace aerosols.

There was no shortage of food, clothing, or accommodation for the rioters. The inner London area teemed with an immigrant population that outnumbered British-born citizens two to one. Many of them were unemployed, and along with disaffected minorities, they welcomed the anarchists with open arms and helped them to prepare for the big demonstration outside Parliament. They gave them street maps, showing the location of strategic public buildings, police stations, and filling stations. They made gasoline bombs for them, marked up every CCTV camera location, and advised them where to take any casualties in an emergency. The BBC and their local TV and radio stations elevated their status to that of revolutionary heroes, and they willingly broadcast every single one of their hate-filled diatribes repeatedly, adding their own anti-establishment bile for good measure. The organization was uncharacteristic, too. Nearly every rioter had a cell phone programmed to connect with a specific section leader or central command unit. These commanders were allotted green, white, and orange-striped vans equipped with state-of-the-art communications equipment and satellite guidance units linked up to a central control room housed in a secret location near Trafalgar Square.

It had been decided that the protesters would assemble in St. James's Park at 7:00 AM, and the march on Parliament would commence at noon on Monday. But first there would be an additional demonstration on the Sunday before, consisting of a mass assembly in Trafalgar Square and a march down Whitehall to Charing Cross.

This decision mystified the foreign elements among the demonstrators, for they could see no possible gain in marching on a Sunday, when Parliament was not in session. In any case, most of the offices and shops would be closed, and residents would be in bed or having breakfast. They protested loudly but the decision stood. It would go ahead with or without them.

Those in the know nodded their heads wisely and placated their comrades with their own explanation of the change of plan. The IRA had a score to settle with the British army, who had fought them to a standstill and forced them to the negotiating table. The spirit of that army was exemplified by the Cenotaph, and no sweeter revenge could be asked for than the total destruction of the monument. This humiliation, together with the sacking of Parliament, would make headlines around the world and would more than compensate for the failure to disrupt the G8 meeting at Leeds Castle.

A cold, crisp November 11 dawned on Whitehall, and already people were taking their places along the ceremonial route, sporting single poppies, and wreaths of the sacred flower.

The government had banned the annual day of homage, citing the danger of a confrontation with the thousands of demonstrators gathering in London on the same day for a protest against the G8 summit meeting at Leeds Castle in Kent. Signaling their determination to enforce the ban, the police surrounded Buckingham Palace to prevent the queen and her party from attending the ceremony and posted armed units to dissuade any unauthorized person from entering Whitehall. The ministry of defense had also issued orders banning any military personnel from taking part.

However, they had completely misjudged the resolve of those in the nation who, ever since its inception in 1922, had come from far and wide to stand silently in wind and rain to pay homage to the men and women who had sacrificed their lives in order that the British way of life should be maintained and never devalued. Many of the ideals that inspired the dead were long gone now, but the imposition of this obscene ban upon one of the nation's last remaining public ceremonies while an armed protest by a motley gang of anarchists was permitted to go ahead ignited a latent flame of indignation that blazed throughout the land. Determined, angry citizens cast aside their subservience, donned their best clothes, pinned on their poppies, and as dawn broke on a cold Armistice Sunday, made their way in their millions to the proud monuments all over Britain that honored the fallen. And as the determined crowd in Whitehall grew in numbers, so did the police presence shrink, until not one officer of the law remained on duty there.

The main homage at the Cenotaph was, for the first time, not covered by the British broadcasting media, which was now almost entirely controlled by the government. The press was under orders to give the occasion as little coverage as possible, while the churches, schools, local government bodies, and publicly funded organizations were also warned against participating, with thinly veiled threats of imprisonment or worse. Only foreign broadcasters had the courage to defy the edicts, which were the reaction of a rotting government, out of touch with its citizens, obsessed with control, paranoid with fear, and desperately seeking to postpone its own demise by every totalitarian means possible.

The Cenotaph stood proud and gleaming white as the respectful crowd gathered around it and stood for a moment's silent prayer, paying homage with a wistful smile or a gentle tear, eyes fixed on the immortal inscriptions and the message they conveyed. With the enforced absence of the queen and Westminster clergy, there was none of the usual somber pageantry or religious ceremony. Instead, its place was taken up by a body of clergy from Northern Ireland, accompanied by their own choir, impeccably dressed in purple cassocks and crimson surplices edged in gold.

The choir gave voice, and the gathering joined in until Whitehall echoed throughout its length to the sacred music that had always been a feature of the service, hymns of grief that expressed the homage of a grateful nation. Not so majestic now with the absence of the massed bands and the queen, but poignant for all that.

Further up Whitehall, the participants had assembled in their groupings for the march past, led as usual by the surviving servicemen and servicewomen of both world wars. Most of this group were British, but among the ranks could be seen the distinctive headgear of the Australians, New Zealanders, Canadians, Sikhs, Ghurkhas, and South Africans, and many other commonwealth nations.

They were fewer now, all of them in their eighties and nineties, many of them infirm, some in wheelchairs, and others blind. Soldiers, sailors, airmen, marines, and the auxiliary services, they wore their medals and their insignia, caps, and berets with unashamed pride. They waited patiently, longing for the moment when it would be their turn to march past the sacred monument and give the "Eyes left" to the memory of their fallen comrades, as they had done many times before and would continue to do until they joined them in the grave.

Behind them were the ranks of veterans of subsequent wars: Korea, Suez, and the Falklands plus the wars in Iraq and Afghanistan, the insurgency wars in Palestine, Malaya, and Kenya, and the terrorist war in Northern Ireland; all of standing them proud and upright like the older soldiers who headed the parade.

Following up on Horse Guards Parade were gathered the massed ranks of the British Legion, carrying the brightly colored banners of their individual branches, the true representatives of the veterans and a beacon in their hour of need. Behind them stood thousands and thousands of the old voluntary services and reservists: medics and nurses, firemen, ambulance drivers, coast guards, merchant navy, and many other services, all waiting for their turn to pay their respects.

The eleventh hour was fast approaching, and the gathering grew silent. People near the Cenotaph looked up in vain at the foreign office balcony, where members of the royal family normally gathered, dressed in black and reflecting the sadness of a nation. Nor were they rewarded with the sight of a respectful queen making her way down the steps to take her place by the memorial just two minutes before Big Ben struck the hour.

At last, the time had come, and with less than a minute to go, thousands of poppies pinned to coat and tunics, berets, and hats merged with those that beautified the Cenotaph and others entwined in wreathes yet to be laid: glowing blood red as the sun broke through at last, suffusing the ceremony with patriotic memories, love, and hope and glory.

"Good Lord, Ali, where on earth have you been? We've been looking everywhere for you. I really thought you'd done a runner and left me in the lurch."

Alistair Campbell didn't answer. He closed the door, walked swiftly to the window, and stood looking out over the grounds of Leeds castle for what seemed an age. "Who's we," he grunted, as he finally turned away and collapsed on the double bed.

"Why, your friends of course. We thought you were in a car crash or something like that. You were supposed to be here yesterday. You could have phoned at the very least. All our guests have arrived and every one of them has been asking after you, even Dick Cheney."

"What!" Campbell sat up with a jerk and nearly slid off the bed. "Don't tell me that fascist bastard is actually here in this building. Jesus Christ, what's Obama thinking about consorting with likes of him? I thought he was dead."

"Unfortunately he's very much alive, and he's causing us trouble already."

"What sort of trouble?"

"Oh, I don't know. Something about his bedroom. It doesn't suit him."

"That's a big surprise. They should have put the creep in the dungeons. Anyway, what's he doing here except causing trouble?"

"Joe Biden took poorly from the swine flu epidemic sweeping Washington and Obama couldn't find a well person to take his place so he called on Cheney and made him temporary vice president."

"Jesus, God help America. So why is he over here? Can't Obama handle things on his own for Christ's sake."

"No, no, Obama's not here, he's in Washington. Said it was imperative that he remains on call until this Iranian crisis blows over."

"A likely story," snorted Campbell, "I thought this G8 meeting was the place to discuss that. If it's left to Cheney the first thing on the agenda will be a motion to bomb the shit out of Teheran."

He got to his feet and went over to the window again, staring out as if he was hypnotized.

"What on earth's the matter, Alastair?" said Blair. "I've never seen you so agitated. Is it something to do with the vote last Thursday? I told you it was a crazy thing to do putting a motion down like that. Cameron and Klagg were bound to bring the government down after the hammering Section Three took at Credenhill. It was a gift and they accepted it like any politician would do."

"Like hell they did. It was Mandella who won the day. I know for a fact that his goons visited Cameron and Klagg's families beforehand and put the wind up them. They hadn't the guts to see him off. Now he's more powerful than ever. Cameron will do exactly what Mandella tells him, and the first thing Mandella will do is come looking for us. All he's waiting for is the end of this bloody talking shop and the departure of all the big shots. Section Four goons have been following me since Friday. I think it's to make sure I don't leave the country. And you couldn't find me because I was making arrangements for Mary and the kids to go somewhere safe."

"My God." Blair's face was as white as a sheet. He jumped to his feet and peered out of window, keeping his head well below the sill. "There's nothing out there," he shouted. "Just guards from the Household Division, as far as I can see."

"They're out there all right, son. I came in with Lance in a Warrior and there were two of the bastards on our tail. You can't miss them. They might as well have a bloody great sign with Section Four on their limos if they kid themselves they're invisible."

Blair came back to his seat, keeping as low as he could. "Damn you, Alastair," he screamed. "You've put me in great danger with your bloody gambling. You don't give a shit about anybody else as long as it comes out right for you. It's a good job Cherie and the kids are with Silvio, but that's no thanks to you. Why didn't you leave well alone, for God's sake? We could have done a deal with Moses. All he wanted was a title and a place in the country."

"If you believe that you'll believe anything," said Campbell, scornfully. "The man's obsessed with power, just like Mugabe, Idi Amin, and that butcher from Liberia. It's in their genes, especially when it comes to lording it over white men. It started when they began boiling missionaries in their cooking pots for Christ's sake. One way or another I reckon Moses has caused more deaths in England than the bloody swine flu has. Another thing, he didn't take kindly to that beating he got from the SAS. He's after scalps, and we're wearing two of them."

"Don't talk like that, Alastair. I can just about put up with the nightmares I had abroad but I never dreamed I would be in danger in my own country."

"Well, you're in it deep now so you might just as well shape up and take it like a man. We're safe enough here until Wednesday when Lance takes the Household Division back to London. That means your uncle Alastair has got to find a way to deliver you to your loved ones in Italy, and make myself scarce at the same time. While you are hob-knobbing with the big shots I'm going to busy myself with the small fry. I'm on good terms with some of the German and Spanish delegations and also some of the Canadians. You concentrate on Angelo Merkel, Stephen Harper, and your buddy-boy Sarkozy. You might try your luck with Cheney, even. After all, the Yanks owe you after the Boston bomb plot."

Blair looked at Campbell with new respect. *Maybe he did screw up with Mandella but he could not recall any other occasion when Ali had got him into serious trouble. More often than not it had been the other way round, Ali getting him out of trouble with his incredible knowledge of the political scene and his down to earth methods of putting it into practice*

"Sorry, Ali," he said. "I didn't mean what I said. It's just that I'm right up to here with the upsets in my life lately, and you know how I hate violence of any kind. I'll do what you say. After all, there is bound to be one member of the G8 who will help us out after all the favors we've dished out to them over the years."

Chapter 38

L uke Dryden looked anxiously at his watch as his Pinkie reached Parliament Square and hit traffic. "Bloody hell, Ginger!" he shouted. "I thought you said ten minutes to Whitehall. Half an hour to go, and we're stuck fast."

"Sorry, Luke, I wasn't thinking, I forgot about the remembrance service. Look, I'll lean on the horn if you'll use the bullhorn. It would help if Randy and Baldy went ahead on foot and did some swearing too."

Ginger's plan worked. Luke shouted himself hoarse as he set the bullhorn to maximum and begged the drivers in front to give way and let his team through. Gradually, they forced their way through until they came up to Parliament Street and found the entrance blocked by a series of steel barriers. Behind the barriers was a solid mass of people stretching up to the Cenotaph and beyond.

Luke raised his bullhorn again and shouted into it. "Please, will everyone clear Whitehall? You are in great danger from the mob in Trafalgar Square. Get as far away from here as you can, immediately. We will let you know when it's safe to come back. Clear Whitehall. I repeat, clear Whitehall." He was worried now as he gazed at the huge crowd gathered in Whitehall. He knew that Carol, her sister, and the General were on Horse Guards Parade with the British Legion, and probably were safer there than in Whitehall. But he knew how dangerous conditions could be when bullets and RPGs and mortars were fired indiscriminately. *Please, God,* he prayed, *don't let them have RPGs and mortars, or grenades either.*

At first the crowd was hesitant, unwilling to be ordered away from their vantage points, but as they took in the two Pinkies and the uniformed soldiers begging them to make way, the word was passed around and they fell back slowly, dispersing down Derby Gate and King Charles Street.

Four of the team jumped out and made short work of tearing a gap in the barricades. The two Pinkies lined up abreast, and with two men on foot on either side of them, the team advanced slowly toward the Cenotaph as the crowd melted away in front of them. Luke continued to address them urgently until they were a good twenty meters past the monument and within sight of Downing Street. He looked up at the Foreign Office and the Department of Health building on the opposite side. They both looked deserted, without even an outside light or an inside light showing. The crowd was still retreating in front of them but more slowly, as those at the back stood firm. He stood up on the hood of the Pinkie and looked over their heads with his glasses. "Good God, he shouted, "they're jam packed right through to Trafalgar Square." It was a solid mass of humanity streaked with red splashes of poppies and multicolored headgear. "Clear Whitehall!" he shouted again and again through the bullhorn. "Your lives are in great danger. Leave Whitehall now."

Luke dropped the bullhorn and looked at his watch. Twelve minutes to the hour. He jumped down and saw Frank Gearson who, along with Tim Talbot, had emerged from the main doorway of the foreign office. Frank had no time for small talk. "Luke!" he said through his head phone, "you're in trouble parking here. There's Provos in the foreign office and the DOH both. They're waiting for the signal, the first chime of Big Ben."

"How many?" asked Luke.

"I'm not sure, around a dozen in each building, I'd say."

"How many in the square?"

"About seventy or eighty. They're fixing to blow Nelson's statue."

"Are they wearing their fucking balaclavas?"

"Yes, they've got 'em on in the square. I'm sure these here will have too."

Luke thought for a few seconds. "Okay, Frank, you, Tim, Ginger, and Williams take out those in the foreign office. Arm yourselves with whatever you need from my Pinkie and line up on the wall clear of the main entrance. We'll blow the doors, and then you move inside. Wait there until we've gunned every window and I give the order to move in for the kill. I want a man in each of the second-floor windows. If anything moves on the ground floor and first-floor windows and the windows above the second floor, we'll take care of them. Concentrate on the mob and top any person you see carrying guns or grenades. Be sure and keep to the second floor until I give the all clear. Grab a headset and keep in touch."

Gearson's face looked grim. "You'd stand a better chance if we all took over both buildings, Luke. You'll be sitting ducks out here in the open."

Luke didn't reply. He turned to Sergeant Pat Gray, who was standing by. "Take three men and target the Department of Health building, Pat. Same instructions I gave to Frank. Kiwi will cover you from his Pinkie."

"Jesus, Luke," protested the sergeant, "that leaves you with Kiwi and two others. How the hell are four of you going to stop the mob? They'll bury you."

"Easy," Luke said, pointing to the machine guns on the Pinkies. "With those, if we have to. Now get going, time's getting short."

Luke settled down behind his guns, aiming them at the far-end balcony on the second floor of the foreign office. Beside him sat Ben Miller, the quiet Australian, chewing gum as usual, aiming his RPG launcher at the main door. Luke raised his hand to Kiwi Bowman in the other Pinkie and received his acknowledgment. An eerie silence had descended on Whitehall, broken only by the distant sound of drums and bugles in Trafalgar Square. Then came a series of cracks that Luke recognized as gunfire, followed by a two huge explosions. In spite of the noise, there was hardly any movement from the onlookers massed just beyond Downing Street and Richmond Terrace opposite, making it hard to believe that they were still unaware of the danger they were in. It was almost as though they were witnessing the actual ceremony and waiting patiently for the first quarter chime from the famous clock. Even when the chimes rang out, the sound made him jump, and he looked across at Kiwi, who had his guns trained on the upper floor of the DOH building. It seemed to take an age as the other three quarter chimes rang out and even longer as he waited for the first chime of the hour.

The boom finally came, and before the second chime struck, all hell broke loose.

It was only a fleeting glance but Luke caught movement and opened up with his guns. The window collapsed and he swung the guns to the next, blew it out, and again the next, until he had traversed the second floor completely. He brought his gun to bear on the first-floor windows this time, from right to left, and blazed away until each one had been destroyed. "Third, third second left!" shouted Miller. Luke raised the guns, caught the movement, and gave it a burst, checked for a moment, and then switched to the ground-floor windows. In the brief moment of stoppage, he heard what sounded like an echo from his own guns and was comforted by the knowledge that Kiwi was doing the business. Good old Kiwi, the best machine-gunner in the Regiment.

"Roof, Luke!" Miller shouted as he grabbed his rifle and gave it a burst. They got their first direct sight of the enemy as the sniper fell from the roof and lay spread-eagled on the pavement below, his rifle landing within a yard of his lifeless hands. Luke traversed the length of the parapet and lowered the guns when he saw it was clear of hostiles. He waited for five seconds and spoke into his headset. "All clear, Frank, make ready and go in as soon as the door is blown. Now, Ben, take it out."

Miller took aim with his RPG and shouted "Bingo!" as the huge door disappeared in a cloud of smoke.

"Roger. Going in now," came the call from Gearson.

Almost immediately, there was the sound of gunfire followed by the explosion of hand grenades. Luke watched anxiously for what seemed an age before Frank appeared in the second-floor window over the main entrance, and then he saw Williams in the window next door.

"First floor and second floor secured," came the message from Frank, "ground floor partial."

Luke breathed a sigh of relief and turned his attention to the Department of Health building. The whole front was a clinical mess. The broken brickwork showed the pattern Kiwi had chosen, horizontal then vertical, a zigzag, and back to the horizontal again. He stopped firing, and the deafening noise of the machine-gun fire was replaced by the loud screams coming from the spectators in front of them. Shots were ringing out behind them, and panic set in. They were trapped, and the only exit from Whitehall was Downing Street and Richmond Terrace. Like a torrent of brown water, the crowd turned into Richmond Terrace and flowed down to the safety of the Victoria Embankment, dropping their wreaths, poppies, and other accoutrements. Some of the younger ones attempted to scale the gates at the head of Downing Street but they were shot down by the security guards behind it.

"Bastards!" shouted Ben Miller. Like lightning, he jumped out of his seat, grabbed three hand grenades, and ran toward the gates. "Stand clear!" he screamed at the climbers. "Go down Richmond Terrace." He waited until they were clear and then edged along the wall and lobbed in two grenades, one after the other. As soon as they exploded, he placed his remaining grenade at the base of the gate, ran back to the Pinkie, and climbed in.

"Hope that fucking Blair poked his nose outside to see what all the noise was about," he said laconically. "I'd love to see what his reaction would be to be on the receiving end of a bomb for a change."

"Good man, Ben," said Luke. "Get ready, I think the uglies are nearly upon us. Take over the guns, I might want to parley with them if I feel it's right." He glanced up at the windows of the Department of Health building and breathed a sigh of relief as he saw Pat Gray signal that the building was clean. Then he stood in between the two Pinkies and waited with his bullhorn ready in his hand.

"Listen up," he said, talking into his headset. "When I give the order, top any hostile you see carrying a weapon, especially those wearing a black beret. Concentrate your fire on targets ten meters back and beyond; we'll take care of the front section. If it gets rough, use RPGs. The boss has promised he'll get a chopper to us, so for Christ's sake, don't get excited and shoot it down. Can you spot any blackheads from up there, Frank?"

"Sure can," came the reply. "Scattered all over. There must be thirty all in one bunch a hundred meters back. And there's plenty hiding behind the front and second rows. Easy pickings, I'd say. There's also plenty of AK47s about. They're waving them about like they was Arabs in Baghdad."

"Good, use RPGs on them and save on ammo."

The onlookers were melting away quickly now as the crowd thinned out, running as quickly as they could to escape the mob behind them. Three or four fell over in their haste and others picked them up and helped them turn into Richmond Terrace. Finally, the last one moved away, and Luke got his first sight of the enemy moving toward them.

"Hold it right there!" he shouted through his bullhorn. "Another yard and everyone in the front five rows is a dead man, like your comrades in the buildings on either side."

There was some confusion as the front row put the brakes on and struggled to avoid being pushed forward by the crush from behind. "Give them an air burst, Ben!" he shouted, and Miller obliged almost before the words were out of his mouth. The effect was immediate. The front row took root and even managed to retreat a yard as some of the faint-hearted turned around and pushed back.

Luke walked forward toward them and stopped about twenty meters short. *Jesus Christ, the dregs of humanity*, he thought as he stared at the rioters in the front row. *If any one of them has washed or shaved for a week, I'm a Dutch uncle.* There was a hush now, no shouting or banter, cursing, or violent gestures such as he'd seen on TV accounts of past demonstrations. They were mute, looking neither right nor left, just staring at him as if he was some kind of apparition.

He raised his bullhorn again. "Okay, you've had your fun, now turn around and go back to the square. I want Whitehall cleared completely in ten minutes. Understand?"

Not a single word came back in reply, and neither was there any movement. It was as if they were all deaf and dumb, staring blankly at him. He spoke again, repeating the warning, but with more menace in his voice this time. Still they stood and stared back, as if daring him to repeat the instruction again.

Something was wrong, and for a moment, he felt a shiver run through his body. "What do you think, Kiwi?" he muttered. "They're acting like a bunch of bloody zombies."

"It can only be because they're scared shitless, Luke. Too scared to attack and too scared to retreat, like there's something bad behind them."

"I dunno, I've got this feeling I got sometimes when we were on patrol in West Belfast. Everybody in a doorway or peeping through a curtain. They were waiting for something to happen, something bad. And one time it did happen, and we lost four men that day."

"Can't see it," said Miller. "Not one of the bastards in the front row is carrying a gun, and those I can see in the second row aren't either. You know, I think the buggers are waiting for us to fire the first shot. There's TV cameras focused on us. They want to make us look like the baddies."

"Well, I'm not going to fall for that. Nobody fires a shot until I give the order, understood? I'll give it one more try, and if that doesn't work, we'll wait them out and pray the chopper gets here soon. If that doesn't shift them, nothing will."

Luke was just about to speak into the bullhorn again when he heard the roar of an engine coming from behind. He swung round and stared in disbelief as he saw the front tracks of a tank emerging from King Charles Street, and seconds later the main body came into view as it swung left in a crashing of gears and headed in his direction. Luke's stomach hit the floor. It was a Challenger 1, the army's main battle tank until it was replaced by the Challenger 2.

"Luke, it's trailing its gun!" shouted Kiwi. "Looks like it's heading for the Cenotaph. Get back, I'll try a sixty-six but I don't think it will stop it."

No, thought Luke, *there was no way an RPG would stop a Challenger with its Chobham armor; it would be a miracle if it did.* He thought of the Javelin launcher in the back of the Pinkie and then abandoned the idea. It wasn't loaded and there was no time for that. He looked at the tank again. It was swerving and stuttering, struggling to get into top gear. And not one bullet had been fired from its machine gun. Frightened of hitting the mob, more than likely. It moved left and then straightened up dead in line with the Cenotaph, jerking as the driver crashed the gears and still failed to get into top, leaving a cloud of thick, black smoke behind him.

Luke had an idea. "Cover me, Kiwi!" he shouted. "I'm going in."

He quickly ran back, jumped into the Pinkie, and grabbed three hand grenades and a smoke bomb. He put the grenades in his shirt and ran toward the tank with the smoke bomb in his hand. Oblivious to the threat of its machine gun, he closed in on the tank, which was now about thirty meters from the Cenotaph and laboring heavily. He threw the smoke bomb directly in the path of the tank and then raced through the billowing smoke to its rear and climbed up onto its back section. The cloud of yellow smoke came billowing over the turret and he took a deep breath, leaned over the right-hand side, and tossed a grenade into the track enclosure before scrambling back behind the turret. The explosion hurt his ears and very nearly shook him off the tank, but it carried on unharmed, rapidly closing the gap on the Cenotaph. Cursing and coughing amid the pungent smoke, Luke pulled out another grenade and crawled back to the side of the tank again. This time, he stuck his head well over the side skirt so that he could actually see the huge track and wheels, whirring away with a hellish metallic noise. He aimed for the gap between two wheels and tossed in the grenade. He only had time to drag himself back, fall face down on the deck, and put his hands over his ears before it exploded. The force of the explosion swept him off the tank and deposited him painfully on the tarmac. But he was oblivious to the pain, for the tank suddenly veered right and crashed into the wall of the foreign office building, less than twenty meters from the Cenotaph, trailing its broken track behind it. There was a nerve-jangling crashing of gears as the driver attempted to reverse backward on the good track, but he only succeeded in forcing it further forward into the wall.

Whooping with joy, Luke picked himself up and was about to run up and throw another grenade into the undamaged track when he heard gunfire from up front. He began to run back to his Pinkie and saw the mob had started to push forward, led by a dozen men armed with automatic weapons. "Shoot, men!" he screamed. "Give them everything you've got!"

The machine guns on the Pinkies responded immediately, as did the rifles from the windows of the buildings, but as he pulled out his revolver and ran forward, he saw his own Pinkie explode and keel over on its side. "Jesus!" he shouted. "Hold on, Ben, I'm on my way."

Frank Gearson's voice on his headset stopped him dead in his tracks. "Luke, Luke, look behind you right now."

He looked over his shoulder and cringed. The tank was still buried in the wall with its engine running, but its gun was no longer trailing. The turret was slowly rotating and bringing the gun to bear on target. *Holy shit, what target? Was it Pat Gray in the DOH building, Kiwi's Pinkie, or the Cenotaph? Jesus, he had to forget about Ben and do something quick.* There were bullets ricocheting off the ground, and he made up his mind in a flash. Confident now that the tank's machine gun was out of action, he ran back through the smoke, climbed up on the hull, and heaved himself onto the deck just as the gun was approaching the side-on position. Sweating profusely, he hauled himself up onto the turret and clambered onto the base of the traversing gun. *It's like in training on a suspended rope,* he thought, *only this time he was on top and the bloody rope was moving.* Slowly, he dragged his body up to the muzzle and just as he reached it a terrific pain shot up his thigh as his artificial leg was torn from its socket. Cursing mightily, he gave up every ounce of strength he had left in him to hang on and prevent his body from sliding downward.

Pressing his cheek tightly against the barrel, he felt in his shirt and took out his last grenade and pulled the pin. Grasping the safety lever tightly, he put his hands forward of the muzzle, dropped the grenade into the barrel, and let go. He heard the explosion and then felt another as his body hit the ground. There came a blinding light inside his brain that set off flashes of indescribable sounds and visions, all merging into one final crescendo.

He saw Richard the Lionheart in his armor and shield bearing the cross of Saint George, followed by a mounted Henry the Fifth with his sword held on high, Nelson with a glass to his good eye, and Wellington on his white charger. Then came the stern face of Kitchener pointing with his finger, and Tommies charging through the mud with their rifles at high port, and another line of blind Tommies, all with their eyes bandaged, one hand resting on the shoulder of the comrade in front for guidance. Then, the flashes of the guns at Alemain, the parade through Tripoli, the VE Day parades, Churchill on the balcony at the palace, and finally, the charge of the Paras at Goose Green in the Falklands. The visions were accompanied by the sounds of martial music that complemented the triumphs and tragedies of a warrior race. He heard the bagpipes playing "Flowers of the Forest" and the massed bands playing "Men of Harlech," "Lillibullero," and "Tipperary." Then came Wagner's funeral march, the last post, Reveille, and in the very last moment before he lost consciousness, the glorious clatter of a Lynx gunship directly overhead.

Chapter 39

I
t was Tex Hightower's second G8 summit at Leeds Castle in Kent,
England. The first had been with Dubya, and it took place over a
glorious weekend when the sun shone forever and temperatures
approached those he was accustomed to in the big country along
the Rio Grande. But on this occasion, it was autumn, and a damp,
cold, and dreary English autumn at that. On his customary pre-
summit security examination of the premises, Tex was delighted to
see nothing had changed. It was a security chief's dream: a castle
in the middle of a lake, with access limited to a solitary, narrow
causeway and with just one easily protected access point. A far cry
from the city-based G8 meetings, where he was presented with the
nightmare operation of safeguarding the president and his entourage
as his convoy sped daily between meeting place and hotel, tying up
traffic and incurring the enmity of the populace. Moreover, this
time around, it was even better, for the prime minister had ordered
the British Household Division to surround the castle and stop the
anarchists from getting anywhere near it for the duration of the
summit. That meant that instead of the five hundred-plus security
force he had been obliged to provide at the previous summit, he
would only need in the region of two hundred, most of them air
defense Special Forces and a detachment of frogmen. But, as was so
often the case, there happened to be at least one annoying snag, and
this time it concerned the security of a lousy, dumb-ass bedroom.

Acting Vice President Cheney was asthmatic and was unable to sleep at night unless he had copious amounts of fresh air entering his bedroom from outside. Even if there was a gale blowing, he would still insist on this requirement. Professing himself a great admirer of King Henry VIII, he had chosen to sleep in the famous king's bedroom, which was situated on the third floor beneath one of the famous turrets overlooking the lake. The bedroom was huge, but the only source of natural light was a glazed double door that opened out onto a stone balcony. To call it a balcony was a joke, for it was barely wide enough to allow the doors to open three-quarters of the way, and the only purpose it could possibly serve was to allow a person to open out the doors and prevent him from falling accidentally into the lake below. This was confirmed by Tex's read of the castle's history, which stated that on at least six occasions, a person had fallen from the room and drowned in the lake below. Whether the accident was deemed voluntary or involuntary was not disclosed.

Tex condemned the doors immediately and ordered that they be removed and replaced with six-inch-thick steel plates fitted with motorized louvers and wired up to a variable controller at the side of the president's bed. And that was when he fell foul of the curator of the castle, Sir Archibald Ponsonby-Summers, the head of Kent County Historical Monuments Commission.

Leeds Castle was a Grade One-listed building, and as such, permission was required from the commission for the slightest alteration to its structure, even replacing a broken window pane or adding a coat of paint to a frame. Sir Archibald's reply to Tex's request was short and to the point: the application was returned with the word "Refused" stamped upon it in large red letters. His second request received the same treatment, as did the third, only this time the letter was accompanied with a twelve-page document warning him that any such transgression could lead to a lengthy stretch in jail. Tex asked the American ambassador to intercede on his behalf. This he did and ended up appealing to the prime minister himself after six government departments, the cultural secretary, and the Lord Protector refused to get involved.

Tony Blair hated Dick Cheney, and the ill-feeling was mutual. He asked Alastair Campbell for advice and received the answer, "tell him to get stuffed." Blair was half-inclined to take Alistair's advice, but after being told that Ponsonby-Summers was the type of Englishman who would have himself nailed to the doors in question rather than have any part of his beloved castle despoiled—more especially if the barbarian happened to be an American—he suggested that a compromise was in order: Let the president sleep in Queen Isabella's bedroom instead.

Dick Cheney went through the roof when Tex put the offer to him. "I am the most powerful man in the world!" he screamed. "And there is no way I am going to have a Limey creep like Ponsonby dictating to me where I sleep. If this guy ain't careful, I'll get Haliburton to buy the Goddamn pile and let them tear it down stone by stone in front of his bloody eyes and ship it to Alaska. I'm sleeping in Henry's Goddamn bedroom. End of story."

Accepting defeat, Tex repaired to the balcony with his deputy, Slim Jakes, and began to plan an alternative method that would prevent an expert climber from entering the bedroom through the open door. He jotted down the width, length, and height and stared at them for what seemed an age. "Okay, Slim," he said finally, "we'll keep one door permanently open and the other one closed. That should give him plenty of air. It will also give the guard just about enough room to stretch his legs and keep his eye on the Veep, which he couldn't do if they were both open."

Slim's jaw dropped. He was holding onto the door for dear life to prevent himself from toppling over the balcony parapet, which was a mere twelve inches high and barely eighteen inches from the main wall. "Jesus Christ, Tex," he wailed, "there ain't enough room for a pigeon to crap up here, let alone for a man to stand guard for four hours with his rifle at the ready. What if a guy drops off for even a minute? It happens all the time. It would be curtains, that's for sure. Who have you got in mind for the job, Spiderman?"

Tex frowned. "Slim, the watch is from the time the Veep retires until the time he goes down for breakfast. I'm not having guards changing shifts through the bedroom when he's asleep. If he woke up and saw any movement, he'd have his twelve gauge out in a flash and blast away. You know he always keeps a gun by the side of the bed, don't you now?"

Slim gulped and stared down at the waters below. "Aw, come on, Tex, why pick on me? I'm your number two. There's plenty others can do the job. They'll be younger and not so ready to drop off as me."

"And they're all at least twenty pounds heavier," replied Tex. "They wouldn't fit, and they would be more concerned with their comfort than looking out for hostiles. It's only for three nights, for Christ's sake, and you can have the rest of the day off and go into town."

"Thanks for nothing. How about sinking an anchor in the wall and fixing it to a safety harness? That would give me peace of mind."

"Sorry, Slim, Ponsonby would have a couple of those grenadiers down there shove their bayonets up my ass. And don't even think about pissing on the wall either. If you have to, direct it onto the water down below."

"Oh sure, and how am I going to do that, with no hands free? It's either piss my pants or fall overboard."

Tex laughed and thought for a moment. "Tell you what, Slim, I'll make it easy for you. Pick up one of those foam rubber bedding rolls from supply. You can fold it over and squeeze it into the space there. Then you can sit down on it with one arm on the parapet and the other holding your rifle, like you're in a bathtub. I'll okay it, provided you don't fall asleep. Fair enough?"

Slim nodded his head sadly. "If I must. Now, just tell me how I'm going to aim my rifle if someone takes a potshot at me?"

The first night of the meeting went well. Dick Cheney let it be known he'd had the best night's sleep in a long while in King Henry's bed, and although Slim complained about a sore back, he didn't raise any objections to another night on watch.

The next night, however, the weather changed for the worse, and a heavy rain set in at 0200. Tex sat up in bed and went through his checklist, calling up each duty guard in turn for a situation report. There was no answer from Slim. He called again five minutes later, and still there was no reply. He looked at his watch and swore. It was possible his cell phone was on the blink or he had dozed off. Jesus, it could be he had fallen into the lake and no one had noticed. Cursing, he put on his boots and overcoat and walked down the corridor to Cheney's room.

"Heard anything from inside?" he asked the guard by the door.

"No, sir," the guard replied, "not a thing."

"I'm going in. Close the door quietly after me."

The room was dark, and Tex crept silently in the direction of the cold breeze coming from the open door. He was nearly there when his foot caught something on the floor, and he went sprawling. "Goddamn it," he swore to himself, as he felt around, "it's Slim. What the fuck are you doing inside?" he whispered savagely as the body sat up. "Why didn't you answer my call?"

"Sorry, Tex," Slim whispered back. "It pissed down with rain, and I got soaked. I turned my phone off so Cheney couldn't hear it."

"You'll hear plenty from me when you come down later. Now get back to your post and stay there, even if it blows a blizzard and freezes your balls off."

Sunday was the most exciting day of Tex Hightower's life since he went to watch the Yankees win the World Series when he was eleven years old.

Cheney had attended a service in the small chapel and was settling down in the conference room with the other G8 members to watch the Al Jazeera presentation of the Armistice Day ceremony on television. Tex sat at the back of the room and started a conversation with Bob Harding, a burly ex-paratrooper who was his British opposite number. All of a sudden, the sombre background music was interrupted by a great roar coming from Trafalgar Square. The TV camera in the square focused on three vehicles that had entered the square. One was a large luxury bus painted orange with green stripes, bearing the name "Kilkenny Rovers" down each side. The other vehicles were huge moving vans, and they had hardly come to a stop before twenty or thirty men jumped from each one and began to unload dozens of crates and boxes and stack them on the ground. Every man was dressed in black fatigues with matching leather gloves and balaclava: the official uniform of the Provisional Irish Republican Army. They were joined by another fifty or so from the bus, all dressed exactly the same and headed by a portly figure waving a pistol and shouting instructions to a man following behind bearing the flag of the Irish Republic. His voice was drowned out by the roar of the crowd, which increased in volume as the word was passed around to demonstrators unable to see what was going on. A work party set to and began to open up the goods, carefully laying them out on the ground and, in some cases, assembling them on the spot.

"Christ almighty," whispered Harding, "they've got enough weaponry there to start World War III. AKs, mortars, HMGs, RPGs, ammunition, and what looks like a load of PE. Next thing you know, there'll be armor be coming in."

Tex nodded in agreement. "What are they doing with those boxes they're taking up to Nelson's column?" he asked.

"Not sure. Wish to God the camera would give us a close-up of the boxes. Do you know, I do believe they are going to blow old Nelson up. Good God, have you ever seen such a dirty, filthy bunch of freaks in all your life? Look, the Provos have armed themselves and are handing out guns to supporters in the crowd. That spells plenty of trouble. I figured they'd do something like this tomorrow. Why the hell are they exposing themselves today?"

"If you ask me, it's because there's no law around to stop them," said Tex. "You know, I can't see a cop or a soldier anywhere in the square. That's crazy. Maybe the government want them to blow themselves out today and come down hard on them tomorrow."

Harding shook his head. "If that's the case, why is no one protecting the Cenotaph? And why does Al Jazeera have the only camera crews broadcasting? It looks to me like the others have been warned off. They always make a big thing of the service every year, even the BBC. I wish they would cut to the camera covering Whitehall and show us what's going on by the Cenotaph."

Tex looked at his watch. "10:32," he said. "Surely they'll be there any time now." He felt uneasy. The Canada meeting had been bad enough, but this was something else. The thugs there were mean all right but none of them had guns; just baseball bats and iron bars. There was lot of concerned talk going around the room now, and he saw Cheney turn round and look at him at him enquiringly. Tex got the message. "Back in a sec," he said to Harding and left the room.

"Anything I should know?" he enquired as he entered the surveillance room and glanced at the rows of TV screens."

"Not a thing so far, Chief," replied the head observer, who was watching the main screen showing Trafalgar Square. He leaned back in his chair and put his hands behind his head. "The Guards are forming up across the water and are giving a parade shortly. They're also going to give a fourteen-gun salute to break the two-minute silence, so I'm told. You'll see the guns on the main screen in a minute or two. There's plenty going on out there," he commented, nodding at the Al Jazeera main picture. "There they are now."

Tex looked closely at the row of cannons and the smartly uniformed soldiers manning them. Then he studied all twenty-four of the CCTV screens, one by one. He sat down and scratched his head. "Do me a favor, John. Concentrate on the crowds. Look for anything out of the ordinary, like you always do. Check faces, especially if Al Jazeera show any close-ups. There's something weird going on out there, and I'm hoping it's not related to our little get-together here."

"Will do, Chief. It's a shame about the balaclavas, though. Take them off and I'm sure I'd name at least twenty wanted by Scotland Yard."

Chapter 40

The scene had shifted to the Cenotaph as Tex returned to his seat in the boardroom. He was just in time to see the arrival of two Range Rovers and their crews, wearing scarves over their faces. He turned to Bob Harding. "SAS?" he asked.

"Yes, but there's barely a dozen of them. Where in God's name are the police and the honor guard? And where is the queen and the royal family?"

"Looks bad. What the hell are your government doing? This could never happen in Washington. Why aren't most of the Household Division on guard there, for Christ's sake?"

"Beats me," replied a worried Harding. "The last time there was trouble in Whitehall, the mob broke a lot of windows and damaged some statues, but the police brought in the heavy gang and soon cleared them out."

"It's a setup, Bob, I can feel it in my bones. Those people gathering in Whitehall are going to be in real trouble if they don't evacuate. The SAS know it, and that's what they're trying to tell them. Goddamn it, if the IRA use their guns on them, it will be a massacre."

Tex's nerves tightened as he saw the SAS squad split up and take up positions against the walls of the buildings opposite, leaving two men in each vehicle crouching behind their twin machine guns. Just then, a camera cut to a picture of Big Ben and showed the giant hands pointing at exactly one minute to eleven. He leaned forward expectantly, as did the rest of the audience. A hush had descended on Whitehall as the crowd looked in the direction of the clock, for all the world acting as if they were waiting for a messiah to appear from behind it or even a spaceship, like in the film, *Close Encounters of the Third Kind*. The tension became unbearable as the seconds ticked by and the hour hand refused to budge, until at last, it gave a reluctant jerk and triggered off the first quarter chime and then the other three. The boom of the first hour chime had barely sounded before the SAS machine guns opened up with a hellish noise and pounded the two buildings on either side. The cameras were positioned perfectly, and as they panned from one side to the other, Tex saw the windows shatter and two masked bodies tumble from the roof and lie crumpled on the pavement below. There came a commotion further up Whitehall in the direction of Trafalgar Square and then a number of explosions and rifle fire. The onlookers left on the street came surging forward like a tidal wave, and as they sought to escape down a side street, they were attacked by an angry mob of anarchists, many of them armed with automatic weapons.

"What was that," Tex asked Harding, "fighting in the square?"

"No, it was below that. I think it came from Horse Guards Parade. That's where the British Legion forms up for their march past the Cenotaph. Look out! They're shooting up the onlookers as they try to get away!"

"Swine, bloody swine. Murderers, murderers," came the protests from the audience in the room as those climbing the Downing Street gates were shot down without mercy and then a great roar of approval as an SAS soldier ran forward and lobbed grenades over the gates.

Tex looked on in admiration as the soldier with the bullhorn moved forward and calmly ordered the mob to retire. He got to his feet as the same soldier looked over his shoulder at the tank roaring up from behind and ran back to confront it. This time, the whole audience, except Blair and Campbell, got to its feet and cheered as the smoke cleared and they saw he had crippled it and then clawed his way up the gun barrel and put it out of action. They groaned as he fell and groaned again as a comrade ran back to help him and was shot down from behind within a meter of the tank. The front rows of the mob melted away to reveal the armed Provos behind them. Firing as they ran, they rushed the remaining Range Rover and were cut down by its machine guns and rifle fire from the windows in the building. An RPG hit the other vehicle, setting it on fire, and they were nearly through to the monument when a thunderous clatter was heard and the rioters in front starting falling down as if blown over by a sudden gust of wind.

Tex recognized the sound immediately, even before the helicopter came into view. The audience cheered it on as it swept the mob before it like a gigantic garden blower, firing short, deadly bursts from its chain gun. The Al Jazeera camera followed it as the panic-stricken mob fought to escape from the confines of Whitehall, leaving dozens of lifeless bodies in their wake, the majority of them wearing Provo uniforms. The chopper reached the square and concentrated its fire on the bus and two trucks, rocketing them until their gas tanks exploded and threw burning wreckage skyward. One group of Provos managed to aim a rocket launcher at the chopper, but it missed and they perished in a hail of bullets before they could reload. The pilot gained height and a bullhorn bellowed out a message: "Put your weapons on the ground and clear the square. Any person bearing arms will be terminated instantly. Clear the square immediately." The message was repeated again and again as the chopper circled the square until at last it was cleared, whereupon it sped back down Whitehall and set down near the Cenotaph.

The rotors had hardly come to rest when a shattering explosion was heard and a huge column of smoke was seen rising from the vicinity of the square. "Jesus, what was that?" shouted Harding. The camera zoomed in on the square again and they saw that Nelson's column had been totally destroyed, and only the famous admiral's head was now recognizable, having come to rest near the King Charles statue.

"They must have triggered it by remote control," Harding muttered angrily. "These bastards don't give a shit for anything. They would destroy the whole world and reduce us to living in caves if they had their way, with them wielding the big clubs."

The camera cut back to the Cenotaph again and caught the SAS soldiers loading their dead and wounded into the chopper.

"What are they waiting for?" Tex asked Harding as one of them clambered into the chopper and slid the door shut, leaving the others standing easy.

"Search me," replied Harding, "I expect they're waiting for orders from HQ." The answer came seconds later as another Lynx came into view and landed nearby. A troop of SAS soldiers quickly disembarked and formed a ring around the Cenotaph, along with their comrades on the ground. They stood to attention and saluted as both choppers took to the air and headed west at full speed. They had barely disappeared when one of the soldiers produced a bugle and faced the inscription on the front face of the monument. His comrades came to attention, and the melancholy sound of "Last Post" echoed around the now-deserted streets and buildings around Whitehall. He was saluting the fallen heroes of the past and those of their own who, only minutes earlier, had made the ultimate sacrifice. There was a pause as the final note rang out, and then the bugler broke out with the stirring strains of "Reveille."

The silence in the boardroom was electric. Tex looked sideways at Harding and saw tears streaming downs his cheeks as he watched the scene. "Goddamn," he whispered as he felt his own eyes moisten and his whole body shivered. It was a long, long time since he had experienced such emotion. He felt humble and very, very angry. The lousy politicians in the room would have forgotten the event even before they returned to their pampered existence in their own lands. To them, it was just another World Series or Cup Final, but what he had witnessed this day would remain engraved in his memory to the end of his days.

Tex Hightower woke up suddenly and cursed mightily as his head connected with the edge of the stone parapet on the balcony. He had done the same thing earlier on and bore a painful lump to prove it. Now he had two, Goddamn it. As he nursed his head, he wondered again what in Sam Houston's name he was doing sleeping on the cramped balcony of a nine-hundred-year-old castle, thousands of miles from his comfortable ranch house in Brownsville, Texas. Damn Slim Jakes. The bastard had taken the hump and flatly refused to return to his watch on the balcony. That left him with the choice of a dozen heavyweight guards or himself, with his own not inconsiderable bulk. To hell with it, he decided, he would do the job himself and shame the lot of them. After all, it would only be for two nights.

The first time he had moved was to adjust his right leg, which had become locked up against the balcony wall and was causing some considerable pain. The second time, it was nothing to do with his body, it was a dull sound, far off and regular, like a pulsating big jet approaching on an airless night, but far more expansive. He heaved himself out of his stone roost and sat on the edge of the parapet, holding tightly to the edge of the closed half-door with one hand. The sound was coming from the south, and he craned his neck to focus in its direction. It gradually got louder, and suddenly lights appeared in the sky, colored lights, red, green, and yellow, lots of them, some of them blinking, extending east and west as far as the eye could see. The pulsations gradually gave way to clatter as the lights came closer and revealed formation after formation of helicopters no more than a mile high with similar formations of big transports above them but much higher. It was an impressive sight. It reminded Tex of films of the D Day invasion and the hundreds of troop transports and gliders heading for France. It was not so large, of course, but what it lacked in numbers it made up for in the collective noise of the choppers' engines and rotors. They were almost overhead now, and the voice of the rooftop watch came in, querying the situation.

"No, no offensive action whatsoever!" Tex shouted. "There's no sign they're after us, and even if they were, it would be curtains. Any fire from us would be sure to invite retaliation."

Lights were being switched on all over the castle now, and the guards below were shouting and pointing up at the sky. Tex shifted his position, and as he did so, he inadvertently closed the open half-door. Cursing himself, he reached for its handle and was still groping when it was flung open, knocking him off-balance, and a voice shouted, "What in God's name is going on out there?" Tex fell backwards and landed in the coldest water he had ever experienced in his life. He shot to the surface and looked up in time to see the vice president disappear into the room and emerge seconds later with a twelve gauge in his hands. "We're under attack!" he screamed. "What are you waiting for? Give the terrorists everything you've got."

"No, no, Mr. Vice!" Tex spluttered. "Don't shoot, please, please don't shoot."

But he was too late. Cheney aimed his gun skyward and blasted away as fast as he could pump, until the shotgun was empty. Cursing loudly, he made to go back in for more cartridges, but as he did so, he lost his footing and fell into the lake a few meters from where Tex was treading water. He disappeared from view, and Tex went under, desperately searching for him but unable to see anything in the murk. He came up for air and went down again and stayed down until his lungs were bursting, but to no avail.

He came up once more and was about to dive again when a voice shouted, "Leave it to us, Tex! We saw where he fell. We'll get him."

Tex scrambled up on the bank near the keep and sat there, gasping for breath, as he saw three frogmen circling in the water. Two of them dived and seconds later came up holding Cheney's head clear of the water.

"Is he okay?" Tex gasped.

"I think so," came the reply. "I'll get him up on the bank and pump him. Call for the medics just in case."

Tex lay on his back, shivering. It was all over in a flash, but in that time, the air armada had passed over, undisturbed. He could just see the lights of a transport winking in the distance. It was heading northeast. To London, of course.

For a brief moment, Tex forgot about his discomfort as goose pimples replaced the shivers. He was reminded again of the Allied air armada that flew in the opposite direction on D Day and the brave men heading into the unknown, ready and willing to give up their lives in the cause of freedom. He also remembered the tear-stained face of Bob Harding as he got up and planted himself in front of the TV, urging his compatriots on with passionate oratory. Suddenly, a long-forgotten quotation from Shakespeare came to mind and he recalled the dog days of the first Gulf War. He was just about going round the bend, staring at the desert sands, when he picked up a book of Shakespeare's works and read every one of them. One quotation that had impressed him now came to mind, and he struggled to put the musings into context. It was from Shakespeare's *Henry V* on the eve of the battle of Agincourt, and from his jumbled memory he was able to piece together the lines:

And gentlemen in England now a'bed,
Shall think themselves accursed they were not here
And hold their manhood cheap whiles any speaks
That fought with us upon Saint Crispin's day.

Deeply moved, he picked himself up and hurried up the path leading to the keep. A quick shower, and he would be back in the boardroom, expecting more excitement that he would proudly relate to the folks back home.

Chapter 41

"Please, Michael, I'll only be a few minutes, it's most important that I see the vice president. My very life could depend on it." Tony Blair was panting from his exertions and could barely get the words out.

"Sorry, but he's under sedation. There's a danger he might contract pneumonia, and the doc says no visitors," replied Michael Pinkerton, the chief of staff.

"But Michael, you don't understand, those SAS bastards have threatened to hang me and most of my cabinet. It looks very much as though they might depose my government and take control. If they do that, my life won't be worth a damn."

"From what I saw on TV, there's no 'might' about it. They have taken control of all the airports and TV stations, occupied Parliament, and declared martial law. If I were you, I'd pack my bags and leave the country pretty damn quick."

"But Michael, that's what I want to see Dick about. I want him to grant me asylum, take me back with him when he leaves."

"That's impossible. We've had instructions to the effect that departure from any UK airport is dependent on screening for any person holding a British passport. All defaulters will be denied passage and taken off the aircraft."

Blair's face went pale. "You mean that you've been in contact with the bloody fascists? You've actually been talking to them?"

"Of course. We've got a hospital plane coming in from Germany this afternoon. It should be at Gatwick around 4:00 PM. They'll get an ambulance to us right away, and take-off is scheduled for 6:00 PM, provided we're in the clear."

"My God, you mean to tell me you've actually cut a deal with the bastards? Why, that's tantamount to recognition of their bloody coup. I must see Dick right away, I'm sure he can't be aware of the seriousness of the situation. Good God, man, he can't possibly leave us in the lurch like this. He's got to help us re-establish control at once. You've got plenty of troops in Germany, you could fly them over in no time at all."

"Sorry, Blair, we're not doing regime changes this year. Why don't you ask your friends in the EU? You've been a lot closer to them than us this past year. You know, the ones who don't want to know about Afghanistan and Iraq and have persuaded you to pull some of your troops out, against our wishes."

The voice was decidedly unfriendly and disrespectful. Blair looked puzzled. "Good grief, Michael, you can't treat your best friends like this. I was the first to back George W. in both wars. It could so easily have cost me my job, but I stuck by him through thick and thin. If he was here, he would be the first to acknowledge that."

"Maybe so, but that was then. You've been saying some mighty unkind things about Dubya just lately, and Dick doesn't like it, and neither do I, for that matter. Now, if you don't mind, I've got work to do."

Blair looked at the chief of staff in amazement. How dare he speak him like that? Not long ago, he would have been honored to take his bags up to the finest bedroom in the White House. It must be Cheney. He had never gotten on with the man. He was hard-nosed and ruthless, just like the crooks who had brought down Enron. And he had taken umbrage when he complained to George W. about the obscene profits Haliburton and the others were making out of the reconstruction contracts in Iraq.

A terrible panic came over him. Things were moving too fast and getting out of control. He must make haste and try his luck with the members of the EU. Surely they would not refuse to help, after all he had done on their behalf, especially his rescue of the Lisbon treaty.

Alastair Campbell was sitting alone at a small table in the center of the huge dining room when Blair finally found him. There was a bottle of Famous Grouse on the table, alongside three glasses, two of which were full to the brim.

"Good God, Ali, I've been looking for you all over. I thought you'd done a runner on me."

"Not me, old son. When I do, I'll tell you first. Any luck with Cheney?"

"None at all," Blair said bitterly. "He's given me the brush-off, at least that's what the chief of staff told me. He's sick and they're all leaving at six tonight, the cowardly bastards."

"I'm not surprised. It's like rats leaving a sinking ship. Funny how politicians always crap themselves at the first smell of grapeshot. How about the others?"

"Berlusconi's left already, so have Harper, Merkel, Taro Aso, and I can't find Putin or Sarkozy."

Campbell whistled. "Christ, that was quick. Forget about Sarkozy. The only help you'll get from that weasel is a gun to blow out your brains."

"Not true, Ali, he's a friend of mine. We hit it off right away."

"Bullshit, that's what he wants you to think. He wants us out of Europe. Jesus Christ, man, where do you think those planes came from, Heathrow? They came from Normandy, every last one of them. Now that our Rapid Reaction Force is back here, it won't be going back, thereby leaving the French the kingpins in the European army. So that leaves Putin. Do you really fancy setting up home with mad Russians? Putin will insist on you living well out of sight, in Siberia, for instance. What will Cherie and the kids think of that, going to the outside toilet when it's forty below? Forget about the big boys, I can get us out of here pretty damn quick."

Blair's eyes lit up. "Golly, Ali, do you really mean that?"

"I do, but it's going to cost you."

The alarm bells rang in Blair's brain, and he looked at Campbell suspiciously. He had obviously had plenty to drink, but he was still the same old rough-tongued rascal he had become dependent on for more than twenty years. There were times when Ali didn't give a damn about anybody or anything, and this seemed to be one of them.

"How do you mean, Ali?" he asked warily.

"What kind of value do you put on your life, son?"

"Do you mean in money?"

"What else?"

"I dunno. Everything I've got, I suppose, but I'm not sure Cherie would agree with that."

"Like ten mil?"

Blair was incredulous. "Ten million pounds? Good God, Ali, you know damn well I haven't got anything like that kind of money."

"No, but Cherie's loaded, and there's your house in Berkeley Square and your old home, plus the flats in Bath and that stately home in Buckinghamshire."

"Ali, they're mortgaged up to the hilt, I doubt if our equity on the lot is worth two million."

"Okay, so Cherie must be worth two mil with all the loot she's made on the lecture circuit, plus your take. That's four mil. How much are you getting for your memoirs?"

Blair looked uncomfortable. "Four million, I think."

"That's as is. What do you think they'll be worth if you're in hiding and every bastard in Britain and the Middle East wants to see you hanging from a tree or a lamp post?"

"Good God, Ali, don't talk like that. How could I possibly know that?" replied Blair, a frightened look on his face.

"I reckon another two mil on top, making your assets ten mil in all. Now listen to this. There's a big yacht anchored just off Folkestone, ready and willing to carry us off to a safe haven where the sun shines all day and there ain't no extradition treaty with Britain, or any other European country, for that matter. You can send for Cherie and the kids within weeks, and the safety of us all will be guaranteed absolutely. All you have to do is sign over the deeds to your property, your assets, the full rights to your memoirs, and a note for two mil, and we're home free. What do you say to that, you lucky bugger?"

Blair was flabbergasted. "I can't believe what I'm hearing. How could you have possibly made all these arrangements in less than forty-eight hours? You've been confined to the castle, the same as I have. Is our savior one of the G8 members, then?"

"Of course not. You forget what a wizard I am with communications. Good old Vittorio Berlusconi been a big help, and so has Bill Clinton. Between us, we've moved mountains. Now all we need is your signature on some documents, and it's anchors aweigh. Vittorio will witness and countersign for Cherie, and the captain of the yacht will do the same for you. But time's all important now, we've got to be out of here and in Folkestone no later than eight tonight."

"You actually talked to Vittorio?" gasped Blair. "Don't tell me you spoke to Cherie as well."

"I did. She agrees with everything as planned. As soon as it is safe, Vittorio will fly them out to your new home."

"God, Ali, you're going too fast for me, I just can't take it all in, it's too fantastic for words. In the first place, where on earth is this new home of ours?"

"Can't tell you that, son, it's hush-hush. If I disclose it to anyone, all bets are off."

"Do you honestly believe I would take my wife and kids to some place I've never heard of?"

"You've heard of it, and you'd approve of it if you knew. I can't wait to get there, believe me."

"You're going there too?"

"Of course. I value my life too, you know. It's as secure as Fort Knox."

"You mentioned a note for two million pounds. What on earth is that for?"

"That's for me, son. Once we're safe and sound, the two mil I'm getting for my memoirs will be worthless. They'll be published, all right, but if so much as one dollar was channeled to me, my enemies would be sure and pick up on it, and we'd all be dead meat."

Blair's eyes blazed. "You rotten devil, Ali, after all I've done for you. You'd still be peddling gossip on the *Mirror* if it wasn't for me. Or flogging tickets for that crappy football club you support. You deserve to be hanged." A cunning look replaced his anger. "So what happens if I say no? You'll be left high and dry. I can take my chances with the SAS. You know how good I am at persuading people. After all, the chiefs of staff were dead set against invading Iraq, and I turned them in the end."

Campbell tossed off his whisky and pulled a full glass toward himself. "Don't talk like a prick, Tony. You've been mixing with the moneyed classes for too long. Wingate isn't like any of the champagne-swigging armchair warriors you've cultivated, mate; he's a soldier of the old school. If you offered him every title in the New Year's honors list, he would piss on your boots. He hates politicians, and he's a great believer in capital punishment. Gordon Brown told me that a colonel from the Blues and Royals informed him that one of Wingate's first priorities is to try us, find us guilty, and hang us high. His men are probably outside the castle at this moment, but they won't make a move until all of our guests have left."

Blair blanched at the terrifying words and looked at the bar apprehensively. "My God," he whispered, "what if they are? How are we going to get out of here?"

"I've bribed one of the staff. There's a secret tunnel that takes us clear of the Household Division. He'll arrange a car and drive us down to Folkestone." Campbell pushed the other full glass forward. "Here, have a swig, it will steady your nerves. You look like shit, believe me."

Blair took a sip and looked appealingly at Campbell. "Gosh, Ali, do you really think we can save our lives and live to fight another day?"

"Of course I do, son. If only you'd listened to your best mate in the first place instead of dumping me years ago, we wouldn't be in the bloody awful mess we're in right now, would we? Come on, time's getting short. Are you going to sign up with uncle Alastair, or are you going to let that bastard Wingate have the pleasure of dangling your body in front of fifty thousand bloodthirsty peasants in Trafalgar Square?"

"Stop talking like that, for God's sake; I need time to think. The first thing I want to do is have a word with Cherie and then Silvio. I'll go upstairs to my room and call from there."

"You'll be lucky. Every phone in the castle is bugged by the SAS. I hope you haven't bad-mouthed any of our guests. Everything you've said will be on the front page of the morning newspapers."

Blair went pale. "Bugged? I thought our security people swept the whole castle daily. God, what is happening around here? It's become a bloody madhouse."

He looked at Campbell suspiciously. "If that's true, then every word you've spoken to Cherie and the others is common knowledge. They'll know about the yacht and everything."

"Not so. I did all my talking over Tex Hightower's communications system. Even our nerds from Bletchley Park couldn't penetrate that."

"So I'll use it myself. This is our show, for Christ's sake."

"Too late. The Yanks have gotten orders to evacuate immediately. The last thing they want is to get mixed up in a civil war. And by the way, our bodyguards have done a runner, which is why I said we should leave like yesterday."

"What? Our bodyguards?" gasped Blair. "You mean every one of them?"

"Except two. I bribed them. Cost me plenty."

Blair looked around the room and up at the ceiling. "Good God, Ali," he whispered, "if they've bugged the castle, they will have heard every word we've said. They'll grab us both as soon as we're outside."

"No, they won't. Why do you think I'm sitting here and not at the bar? I've checked the table with my personal sweeper and it's clean." Campbell patted his jacket. "I take it everywhere these days. Wouldn't be without it."

He stood up abruptly and looked down impatiently at Blair. "Okay, I'm off. You with me or not?"

Blair looked up at Campbell despairingly. He was about to say something but he choked the words back. He nodded his head, and as Campbell set off, he followed behind him, his head bowed and his shoulders hunched. Like a lamb being led to the slaughter, or a murderer to the gallows.

Asif Sami was halfway through his gap year from Manchester University, and was visiting his family in Alfallujah, Iraq, when three American soldiers burst into the house and arrested his brother, Raji. They tore the house apart until they found an AK-47 rifle stashed inside a mattress. They set about Raji and beat him up, accusing him of belonging to Al'Qaeda. Then they dragged him outside and threw him into a military vehicle. Asif tried to prevent them from leaving but they clubbed him with their rifles until he lost consciousness. He woke up to find himself in a prison, along with around thirty detainees, all of them accused of belonging to Al'Qaeda. He protested his innocence but they ignored his pleas and proceeded to torture him along with the others. Unable to take any more punishment, Asif took the advice of one of the prisoners and pleaded guilty, whereupon they cleaned him up and issued him with an orange jump suit. Two days later he was put on board a helicopter and taken, under cover of darkness, to Baghdad airport, and put on a passenger plane, along with forty or fifty other prisoners. It was on the journey that one of the prisoners told him that his brother had died under torture and Iraqi soldiers had thrown his body into the Euphrates river.

When he was released from the aircraft at East Midlands airport, Asif and four other prisoners found their way to a mosque in Ashby, where they were given food and clothing. Two days later they were sent down to London and told to report to the main mosque in Bayswater in London. There, they were taken under the wing of Abdullah Rahal, a fiery cleric. He was well known to British Intelligence, who had sent him for trial on two seperate occasions, but were unable to prove their case. Rahal was a senior member of Al Qaeda's cell in London, and he immediately set about indoctrinating three of the group in the aims and methods of the movement.

The cleric had no trouble converting Asif. The student was boiling with anger over the death of his brother, and the treatment he had received himself. All he thought about was revenge, and his dream was to be sent to Afghanistan to join the Taliban and fight the Americans there.

But Rahal had other plans for Asif and two of his friends. Al' Qaeda had been trying to sabotage a G8 meeting for years, but the massive security measures put in place had always defeated them. This time there was a golden opportunity, for their intelligence had discovered the existence of a secret tunnel leading from the cellars beneath Leeds castle to a disused quarry just over a kilometer away, well inside the cordon thrown around the castle by the British army.

The plan was for the two men to enter the tunnel under the cover of darkness and hide there until the next day. A third man would guard the entrance overnight in case of intruders. Then, at precisely 10:30 AM they were to blow the thick oak door, and run up the steps to a corridor leading to the main meeting room. They were to shoot their way in and detonate their explosive vests in the center of the room. The tunnel and its overgrown entrance had been reconnoitered and measured, and the mission pronounced do-able.

All went well on the day. They entered the tunnel at 8:00 PM, stuck Semtex around the door, trailed a wire from the detonator to a spot fifty meters down the tunnel, and hunkered down for the night. They were both asleep when Asif heard a grating noise coming from the castle end. The noise abated and was replaced by the sound of men cursing, and then the blinding beams of flashlights exposed their presence. Asif grabbed for the plunger and rammed it home, but nothing happened. Shaking with fear he dropped the box, picked up his rifle and charged towards the lights, firing as ran. His companion picked up his rifle and joined him but was unable to shoot past him in the narrow tunnel. Screams came from the interlopers as his bullets hit and flashlights hit the floor. But there was still enough light blazing from them as he made out a large body closing in on him, firing wildly with an automatic. He brought the man down, but not before a bullet tore into his chest. The searing pain caused him to stumble and as fell face down upon the ground a blinding flash threw him sideways, and he screamed as his body was torn apart and the roof came down to bury him.

Chapter 42

L uke Dryden opened his eyes to the blinding whiteness of a hospital room and a pulsating feeling behind both ears. He tried to move his head but nothing happened, and his eyes remained fixated on a ceiling spotlight directly above him. His brain began to whirr, and for a moment, panic set in as a picture of a limbless soldier trapped in his wheelchair flashed before his eyes. He blinked his eyes rapidly and was rewarded with their normal functionality, plus a painful increase in the pounding behind his ears. He put out his tongue slowly and rolled it around his parched lips, drawing comfort from the relief it brought. Still filled with apprehension, he clenched and unclenched his hands and sighed with relief as he brought them up slowly and placed them on his chest. Again, he felt panicky and wiggled his toes, to see if his lower limbs were in order. He smiled as his right leg responded, and he moved his left thigh to confirm that there was no further damage. Much happier now, he put his hands to his head and found it was in some kind of brace that disappeared into a foam collar covering both shoulders. Very gently, he put both hands behind his head and pulled it forward in order to stare at the foot of the bed.

"Jesus!" he shouted as a blinding light flashed before his eyes. He let go immediately and, at the same time, noticed that a red light was now blinking from an instrument panel on the table at the side of the bed.

Within seconds, the door opened and a blue-uniformed nurse rushed into the room. "My goodness!" a beaming face cried. "I cannot believe this has happened on my shift. Just wait until I tell the others."

She quickly switched off the warning light and looked down at him anxiously. "Goodness, you look as if you're in a lot of pain, my dear; I'll get the doctor to you right away."

Luke managed a weak smile in spite of his pain. The lilting Welsh accent was a bonus in itself, but the ruddy cheeks and matronly figure reminded him of Sergeant Owen Parry from Signals, and he was greatly comforted.

"No, please nurse, stay a minute and fill me in on where I am please."

"You're in Hillingdon Grange Hospital, room twelve, second floor, Major Dryden, and I'm staff nurse Bronwyn Richards."

"How long have I been here, Bronwyn?"

The nurse went to the foot of the bed and studied the medical chart. "You were admitted on November 11, and today is the thirtieth. Nineteen days."

Luke was astounded. "Nineteen days! How can that possibly be? I was in London yesterday, Armistice Day."

"You've been here nineteen days and in a coma all that time. My goodness, won't the staff be pleased? Nobody expected you to last the day, let alone this long."

"This long? Am I on the mend, then?"

"I should say. How do you feel? Are you in any pain at all?"

"Only if I try to move my head. Then I wish I hadn't."

"Of course you will, my dear. You fell bang onto the top of your head. Serves you right for not wearing your helmet. Oh! I'm so sorry, I really didn't mean that. Please forgive me." Bronwyn blushed deep red and put her hand on his shoulder.

Luke managed a short laugh. "If I was daft enough to fall without a hard hat, then I deserve all I got," he reassured her. "Tell you the truth, I haven't got a clue how I've ended up like this. I must have been in a car crash."

It was Bronwyn's turn to laugh. "My goodness, you mean a tank crash. You saved the Cenotaph single-handed, surely you remember that."

"Afraid not," Luke replied, searching deep in his memory.

"Well, I've seen the film at least ten times, just like millions of other viewers, and I can assure you that you did. You're a national hero, same as all those brave lads who were with you that day." Bronwyn took a tissue from her pocket and dabbed her eyes. "God bless every one of you for what you did that day."

Luke was moved by the passion in the voice, as the memories started to flow. "That day at the Cenotaph? Tell me, Bronwyn, did we win?"

"I should say. Not just you, the whole country won that day, thank God."

Luke changed the subject. "What's my condition, Bronwyn? I can't feel too much. Is the rest of me okay?"

"A few bruises on your back, that's all. The doctor has checked your body but he's worried about your eyes and hearing. He will be right pleased to find there's nothing wrong there. Now then, I'm being very unprofessional. It's the doctor who should be talking to you about your wounds, not me. I'll go and get him right away. I'll only be a minute or two."

Luke was deep in thought when a tall figure with grey hair and gold-rimmed glasses, and wearing a long white coat, entered the room, followed by an excited Bronwyn.

"Well now, this is a pleasant surprise," the doctor beamed, as he took Luke's hand and shook it warmly. "My name is Gerald Franks, and I'm the one responsible for that awful headgear you're wearing. Would you mind if I took a look-see at your eyes and took your blood pressure?" Without waiting for an answer, he took out his ophthalmoscope and carefully examined each eye before wrapping a cuff around his upper arm and pumping the blood pressure instrument up. He checked the readings twice, and took notes of the readings "Now for your chest. Don't worry, I won't ask you to turn over, just the front will do for now."

Luke lay still as the doctor probed with his stethoscope, praying hard that his damaged lung wasn't acting up. He looked apprehensive, as the doctor straightened up and shook his head slowly.

"Remarkable, absolutely remarkable," he said, shaking his head. "What on earth do they feed you SAS bodies on, cast-iron sandwiches?"

"No, Doctor," grinned a relieved Luke, "just hard rations that taste something like that."

"Call me Gerald. It's Luke, isn't it?"

"It is, and thank you for your treatment. I can see I'm in good hands."

"Don't thank me, it's the nursing staff who deserve all the credit. They've been fussing over you like a flock of broody hens. I don't suppose the queen herself gets better treatment. Isn't that right, Staff?"

Bronwyn blushed. "Not a bit of it, we'd do the same for any soldier," she scolded. "Mind you, this one is a bit special. Nothing but the best for him."

"How much longer do I have to put up with this special treatment?" asked Luke.

Dr. Franks drew up a chair and sat down, looking serious. "Luke, you've had one of the worst cases of concussion I've ever treated, and I've been in this business going on thirty years. It was bad enough falling on your head from that height, but the shock waves from the gun explosion compounded the injury. There are hundreds of ex-servicemen alive today who have suffered the same sort of injury, and many have never recovered from it. How much do you remember of the action? Did you know there was a shell in the tank's breech when you inserted the grenade?"

Luke was about to shake his head and thought better of it. "Sorry, I'm beginning to get the drift, but I haven't gotten that far."

"Well, I'm sure you can imagine the effect. You're very lucky to be alive, and I aim to keep it that way. Now that you're conscious, it doesn't mean you are out of the woods. You'll be in that head brace for a good two weeks and confined to your bed for at least another four after we take it off. You'll be taken for a scan tomorrow and every five days thereafter. No visitors whatsoever on these days."

"What about other days?"

"You mean visiting days? Staff has the chart and will fill you in. Let me warn you that as soon as the news is out that you're conscious, the world's media will besiege this hospital, and I mean 'besiege' in every sense of the word. They will try every trick in the book to get inside and take a picture of you. I'd like you to be patient and forget about visitors for the rest of the week. Don't rush your recovery. Take things easy and start by going back five years or so and make notes with a tape recorder we'll give you. Dr. Staples, our resident psychoanalyst, will visit you daily and organize a regime for you to follow. Keep your brain active but don't overload it. First sign of a headache or a dizzy spell, drop what you're doing and call the nurse. There's plenty to keep you occupied: books, newspapers, DVDs, and, of course, TV and radio. I'll be going now but I'll be back later this evening. By the way, the DVDs in the blue sleeves are a recording of your exploits on Armistice Day and the airborne assault on London. They should make happy viewing for you."

"Thank you, Gerald," Luke said, as the doctor turned to leave the room. "Nice chap," he remarked to the nurse, as the door closed behind the doctor.

"The best there is," replied Bronwyn. "He'll be sorely missed here when he leaves, I can tell you."

"Leaves? Where's he going to?"

"He's retiring early in the new year. Going to work for his son in his Devonshire boatyard."

"Lucky me."

"Indeed. Now then, let's make notes of your visiting hours and the names of the people you want to see first."

Luke felt a chill. No people on earth expressed sadness like the Welsh did, and Bronwyn's face was full of it as she sat down on the chair and waited for her to tell him the worst.

Jock Wingate was Luke's first visitor, and his spirits rose as the boss strode into the room and clasped his hand as if greeting a long-lost friend. "I am so glad to see you, Luke," he said warmly. "The nurse says I can have one hour. Are you up to it? Say no when you've had enough."

Luke smiled up at the kindly face. "Not on your life! All day would suit me. I can't wait to hear the news from the horse's mouth. Union Jack was brilliant, absolutely brilliant. Went like clockwork."

"You've seen the DVDs, both of them?"

"Four times over so far. Beats any war documentary I've ever seen."

Wingate pulled up a chair and shook his head sadly. "Luke, I can't tell you how sorry I am about Carol and Kate and the General. I feel personally responsible for their deaths. I should have diverted two choppers to the square and cleaned out those murderous bastards before they had a chance to deploy their armaments. The scale of their assault took us all by surprise. AKs and grenades, yes, but 100mm mortars and RPGs? No. They must have gotten them from the Section Three bastards. Frank Gearson swears they only brought light weapons and explosives in with them."

"No, sir," protested Luke, "there was no way you could have prevented it. The whole operation was balanced on a knife edge, any diversions from the main battle plan could have meant all the difference between success and failure. The General would have understood that, and so too would Carol and Kate. Was it clean? Did they suffer at all?"

"It was clean. The General was escorting them off Horse Guards Parade when the mortar hit. I doubt if they even heard it coming. There were more casualties on the parade ground than there were in Whitehall itself, many of them veterans marching with the Legion. One hundred millimeter mortars, for God's sake. It was an absolute massacre."

"What about the children? Where are Elizabeth and James?"

"They are with Carol's mother. They are being well looked after, I'm sure of that."

"God, what am I going to say to them? I don't even know if I can face them. And the families of Ben Miller, Kiwi, Tim Talbot, and the others. What do I say to them?"

Wingate was silent for a moment. "I think the fact that you're a national hero will help soften the blow, Luke. Having a famous stepfather will be a big advantage as the children grow older. As for the men, they are my responsibility. I went to every funeral and comforted the bereaved."

Luke was indignant. "Famous!" he snorted. "Every man in the Regiment was famous that day. The kudos belong to guys like Kiwi and Ben and Tim, not me. They gave their all and paid the ultimate price. I was only doing my job, like everyone else. I can tell you for a fact that I'd rather do the same thing twice over than have to go round paying my condolences to their wives and parents. Now that did take courage."

Wingate grimaced. "Luke, every army needs a hero, someone whose actions epitomize the very ethos of the military formation he belongs to. You know that the SAS have never been able to exploit the bravery of its members, for security reasons. In this case, your individual action was performed in full view of the entire world and has brought great credit on the Regiment. Never again will we live under the threat of being disbanded by evil politicians. From now on, we will continue to form a vital part of the British army for as long as it exists. You and I know that as far as the Regiment is concerned, the actions of yourself and the other casualties were all in the day's work, but that is not how it appeared to the general public. We live in an age where bravery and disregard for one's own life is for the birds, where a heroic act now consists of a heavily armed and armored policeman gunning down a weirdo waving an imitation revolver.

"The fact that our people are fighting and dying under the most appalling circumstances in Iraq and Afghanistan doesn't even register above three on the TV Richter scale. It's all about image, crudity, and the cult of personality, and once something is seen to catch the imagination of the public, however trite and banal it might be, it is hammered home until even the unbeliever is caught up in the hysterical adulation. This event is something we must capitalize on until we are in a position to rid the airways of such obscene travesties of our national character. Unwittingly, the left-wing media has been hoisted on its own petard. The scenes at the Cenotaph and the airborne assault on London, honestly captured by foreign camera crews, have served to reawaken the pride and reverence the discerning public have always maintained for the armed forces. They cannot get enough of the scenes of battle, especially the professionalism and bravery of the Paras as they forced entire companies of Section Three Paramilitaries to surrender. I'm told that the networks are offering hundreds of thousands of pounds for any movie clips of the action, even those snatched by iPhones and the like."

Luke smiled. "I hope our publicity boys took full advantage. Anything we sent to the networks used to go straight in the trash can."

"Indeed, they did. They're putting the finishing touches to their production right now. It should bring in millions for all the forces' charities. But that's only for starters. One shot of you battling with the tank is right up there with the iconic picture of Kitchener in the First World War. As a result, our recruiting offices are being overwhelmed with volunteers, not just from the UK but from the dominions and other countries overseas. And of course every one of them wants to join the Regiment. As you lost your scarf during the action, your face is now known worldwide, and we must capitalize on this for all it's worth. Like it or not, you are now a national hero. For years now, the decent people of Britain have been yearning for a leader who will deliver them from the evils of our rotten government. Now they've found one, and they'll follow your lead no matter how hard the road ahead."

"Fat lot of good I can do," groaned Luke. "The doc said it will be weeks before they take this bloody cage off my head. He didn't even give me a clue about what would happen after then."

"Relax; he told me that you're making remarkable progress. I wouldn't be a bit surprised if you're not up and about by Christmas. Look how quickly you recovered after your amputation. Another few weeks after that, and you'll be back in business."

"Does it matter that much, sir? From what I've heard and seen, Keith Dawson is doing a great job. The whole effort is a team job, and it's gone like clockwork. Why change horses in midstream, especially with a lame one?"

"Keith is a fine officer, Luke, but he hasn't got your political nous, as he would be the first to admit. Very few military men have. The army can't afford to be in government even a day longer than is necessary, and the faster we can set up a new civil government, the better for all concerned. We've planned for two years of military rule, but we want to shorten that if at all possible. That's where you come in. Jack Churchill of the Freedom First party and Will Palmerston of UKIP have both indicated that they would be willing to be part of the military regime under your leadership, as have many independents. As titular head, you will be able to run the country almost by decree and, at the same time, construct a parallel civil government in waiting. You will also have the luxury of vetting the suitability of each and every candidate without fear or favor, and once we are out of the European Union, we will be able to wipe the slate clean and rebuild our country in the image of those who gave their lives for the freedoms we once took for granted. Furthermore, we will also restore the covenant between a civil government and its armed forces, which was all but destroyed by Blair and his revisionists."

"What about the United States? There hasn't been much talk about their reaction in the media. I can't believe the neo-cons aren't screaming blue murder about our actions. They must know their deal with Blair to invade Iran is shot to pieces."

"Simple, we're not talking to them. Every time their ambassador or Obama himself attempts to get in touch, it's pass the buck. All they get is a promise of a top-level reply, which never materializes. Their defense secretary doesn't know it, but he was once on the phone with a mess corporal in C Squadron, who hung up on him when he started cursing. We're going to keep it that way for a week or two and see what happens."

Luke smiled contentedly. "Good, it's time someone brought them down to earth. Do you think they will dare go it alone?"

"Not a chance. After their experiences with the Viet Cong in Vietnam, they will always want someone to back them up. We've been told by the CIA that Bush would never have invaded Iraq if Blair had refused to support him. That's why the creep used to be so popular over there, as he knew he would be. You've heard the news about Colonel Pickens?"

Luke nodded with a saddened face. "I intend to go over and meet his wife some day. I understand that Brad was due for a furlough but he turned it down because he didn't want to leave his men, as long as Collins was in command. Needless to say, he was right up front when he got killed. What a waste. God help us if the U.S. Army top brass becomes politicized like ours was."

Wingate swore angrily. "Brad was a professional soldier. He could have taken the easy way out but he chose to honor his commitment to the men of Delta Force. I feel for him, as I do for all brave soldiers, but it is the plight of the ones they leave behind that hurts me most. Like all the other wives, his wife lived with the constant knowledge that he might never come home, and when the bad news is broken, their lives are utterly destroyed and can never be the same again. For her, there are no medals for bravery or high-flown tributes from the high command and from the politicians. Hers is a life bereft of the love that brought them to the altar, and without that, she has lost the best part of her courageous life."

Wingate sighed and looked at his watch. "Time to go. Your doc gave me an hour and it's been almost that long already. Alexander and Montgomery want a session with you as soon as possible, so I'll arrange that on my way out. Anything I can do for you before I go?"

"No, thanks, I've never had it so good. There is one thing, though."

"And that is?"

"Is it true about Blair and Campbell? I can't believe the official story is genuine. It's just too fantastic for words, like something Hollywood would cook up. Were we involved? And if so, who did the business? I would like to thank them personally."

Wingate held up his hand, palm outward. "As God is my witness, what you have read is the absolute truth. We had Leeds Castle wired up like a Christmas tree, but at some point, both of them disappeared off our radar. I received a message from intelligence, stating that there had been an explosion just outside the castle and six bodies had been discovered, all of them dead. Two of them were identified as Blair and Campbell, through papers found on their bodies. I immediately contacted the OC of the Household Division and ordered him to personally deliver the bodies to the nearest mortuary and arrange for a coroner to make proper identification through DNA and all that business. Three days later, I received confirmation that two bodies were definitely Blair and Campbell, two others were Blair's bodyguards, and the other two were thought to be Arabs who were too disfigured to be recognizable. The explosion took place inside a tunnel that led from a basement in the castle to a disused quarry half a mile away. According to the investigators, a firefight took place between the bodyguards and the two Arabs before one of them detonated an explosive belt he was wearing. I sent Jim Farnsworth down to check it out, and he confirmed their findings, whereupon I released the story to the press. They are still digging but they don't think they will find any more bodies."

"Unbelievable," Luke said, shaking his head. "So we had nothing whatsoever to do with their deaths?"

"Not a thing. Well, not directly anyway."

"Explain—not directly."

"You remember John Gibbons of the *Mail* and the American rendition incident?"

"I do."

"Well, Gibbons received a postdated letter from Asif Sami, who, as you know, was among those rescued from the plane along with Gibbons. Sami wrote that the Americans had tortured his brother in Iraq and fed his body to the crocodiles. Seeking revenge, he contacted Al'Qaeda, who apparently had been plotting to attack the G8 meeting and had somehow discovered the existence of the secret tunnel leading to the castle. The plan was for the two of them to shoot their way into the conference room and blow themselves up in the center of the room. However, Asif confided that if they gained access, both of them would detonate their explosives as close to the American president as possible and make sure they killed him. He thanked Gibbons for the *Daily Mail's* campaign to expose rendition flights through Britain and asked him to thank Frank Gearson personally for saving his life."

"So it was a freak accident?"

"It certainly appears that way."

Luke tried unsuccessfully to whistle. "Asif Sami, of all people. Poor devil, he's yet another victim of Blair's bloody war in Iraq. I was hoping to see Blair and Campbell hang for their crimes, but I suppose it's poetic justice that their deaths should be at the hands of Muslims even if it was not planned that way. How are the proceedings going for bringing the rest of Blair's gang to justice?"

"The trials start next month. All being well, we should have convictions early in the new year. We've got most of the guilty ones locked up. Mandella and his Section chiefs are on hard rations in the Smithfield jail they created. All except Hoffman. He took poison, just like the Gestapo killers did."

"You were lucky to catch McGuinness and Adams so quickly."

"Very lucky. Another hour and we would have lost them for sure. They were booked on a flight to Dublin and it was only the warning of a bomb aboard that kept them waiting in the departure lounge."

Luke's face hardened. "Good," he said through clenched teeth. "I'll be on my feet by then. There's no way I want to miss being there in person to see the pair of them get their just desserts."
